what she left

ROSIE FIORE

Published in trade paperback in Great Britain in 2017 by Allen & Unwin

Allen & Unwin
c/o Atlantic Books
Ormond House
26–27 Boswell Street
London WC1N 3JZ

Phone: 020 7269 1610
Fax: 020 7430 0916
Email: UK@allenandunwin.com
Web: www.allenandunwin.com/uk

A CIP catalogue record for this book is available from the British Library.

Trade paperback ISBN 978 1 76029 249 2
E-book ISBN 978 1 92557 525 5

Printed and bound in Great Britain by Bell and Bain Ltd, Glasgow

10 9 8 7 6 5 4 3 2 1

For my sons.

PROLOGUE

Helen brushed her hair and smoothed it away from her face, then used a hair tie to secure it. She combed the length of the ponytail until it lay smooth and shiny over her shoulder, split the hair into sections and plaited it neatly. She checked her reflection: light eye make-up and a becoming, pale pink lip-gloss. She went into the bedroom, where she had laid her dress out on the bed, a cotton maxi-dress, covered in big blue flowers. She slipped it over her head and slid her feet into flat white pumps. A spritz of her citrusy perfume and she was ready to go.

She went down to the kitchen. She'd cleaned up after breakfast, before she'd taken the girls to school. To an outsider, the kitchen would have appeared spotless, but Helen picked up a cloth and wiped quickly at a tiny smear on the otherwise pristine worktop. The washing machine hummed quietly, but other than that, the house was silent.

In the living room, her handbag, a large, soft leather one which matched the blue of the flowers of her dress, sat on the coffee table. She'd packed it carefully, as usual, but she checked through its contents one more time. Looking out of the window, she saw their next-door neighbour, Mrs Goode, leaving her house, Sainsbury's Bags for Life in hand.

Helen glanced around the living room, then took a quick tour round the downstairs to check that all the doors and windows were securely fastened before picking up her handbag and stepping out of her own front door. As she locked it, she called a cheery greeting to Mrs Goode, who was standing in her driveway, clearly waiting for a lift. Mrs Goode waved back, and Helen, dropping her key into her bag, headed off up the road on foot.

As was her habit, she set off at a brisk, focused pace. She imagined Mrs Goode watching her. She didn't look back. She walked quickly to the end of their quiet road, turned the corner, and disappeared.

PART ONE

CHAPTER ONE

Lara

Every middle-class London school has a Helen. Perhaps the Helen at your school has shining blonde hair or twinkling dark eyes. Perhaps she's called Sarah, or Rebecca or Shariza. The principle is the same. Our Helen had a clear, bell-like voice, and you had to speak to her for a little while before you picked up the slight twang and upward inflection that told of her Australian origins. She had a smooth, chestnut-brown ponytail, clear, pale skin and wide blue eyes. You would often see the ponytail swinging as she ran briskly through the park, half an hour before pick-up time. But more often than not, you'd see it swinging as she laughed among a bustling group of parents in the playground. She'd be there before school, after school, at every school event, at the school gate collecting for the summer fete that she'd organized. She'd be at the open day, merrily guiding a group of prospective parents from classroom to classroom. She'd wink kindly at the harried mothers rushing in late, as her own demure girls, their smooth ponytails equally perfectly brushed, waited by her side. She produced perfect cakes for the cake sale, perfect costumes for the class assembly and perfect financial records after the astonishingly successful Christmas fayre. She was perfect.

And then she vanished.

It turned out that I was the first person at school to know she'd gone missing. Ella Barker did an interview with the *Daily Mail* and said she was the first 'because Helen was always at the school gates, so I noticed immediately when she wasn't there'. But that wasn't true. Ella was long gone when we realized, and so were all the other Year Three mothers. Ella didn't care if what she said wasn't true. The *Mail* sent a stylist and took a picture of her in her neat front garden, and said how much her house was worth, so she was thrilled.

Ella was gone, and the playground was all but deserted when I ran in, rattling the pushchair ahead of me, sweaty and out of breath. It's a long story, but not a very interesting one – any parent who has a toddler and a child at school knows it well. The toddler runs around like a lunatic, then spends some hours screaming blue murder, resisting their nap. Then they finally fall asleep fifteen minutes before school pick-up time. You end up stuffing them clumsily into the pushchair and running to school with a dozy, wailing, hot and miserable child. And, of course, you're late, and your eight-year-old is the last child left at the classroom door, next to the tight-lipped teacher who has several hours of planning ahead of her, delayed because of your poor time-keeping.

Except, on that muggy day in late May, Frances wasn't alone. Miranda was there too, her socks still spotlessly white and neatly pulled up and her hair tidy. Mrs Sinclair had a sharp crease between her eyebrows. She expected me to be late – it happened at least twice a week. But Helen was never late.

'Did you see Helen on your way in?' she asked as I hung Frances' rucksack on the handles of the pushchair and handed my daughter a brioche as an after-school snack. 'She's very late, it's most unlike her. Perhaps there were problems with parking.'

'The road's clear outside,' I said. 'And anyway, I think Helen walks. Did she leave a message with the office? Maybe Miranda was supposed to go on a play date with someone and forgot.'

Miranda regarded me with all the contempt an eight-year-old girl can summon.

'I didn't forget,' she said coldly. 'And anyway, my dad was supposed to pick us up today. He's supposed to come to my ballet class to see us perform, and now I'm going to be late.'

Mrs Sinclair looked at her, surprised. 'Your dad? Your dad never picks you up.'

'I know,' said Miranda. 'But he was supposed to do it today.'

At that moment, Marguerite's class teacher walked up, holding Marguerite's hand. Marguerite is six and in Year One, rounder and softer than Miranda, shy, but just as immaculately turned out. She had clearly been crying and her soft cheeks were puffy and wet. The teachers exchanged a glance and a quick word.

'She wants to be with her sister,' said the Year One teacher. 'Can I leave her with you, and I'll go to the office and see if they can't get hold of Helen or her husband?'

'I have Helen's number on my mobile,' I said quickly. Jonah, my two-year-old, had stopped wailing but was grizzling and twisting against the straps in the pushchair. I should just have taken Frances and left, but I wanted to help, if only to show Mrs Sinclair I wasn't a total dead loss as a parent. I pulled my phone from my pocket and dialled. Helen's phone went immediately to voicemail, so I left a message with my number. The two teachers and four children looked at me expectantly.

'Voicemail,' I said unnecessarily. 'Maybe she's stuck on the Tube or something. Or her battery's flat. Or she's lost her phone.'

None of these were likely. Helen's efficiency, forward planning and organization were legendary. Even I could hear how lame it sounded.

'I could take the girls home with me,' I heard myself saying.

Frances and Miranda weren't especially good friends. Helen had had Frances over for a play date, but only because she always conscientiously invited every little girl at least once during the course of each year. I'd meant to return the favour but never had. I'd been intimidated by the prospect of having those spotless little girls in my chaotic house, and I'd have had to clean for a week if Helen were coming to collect them and stay for a cup of tea. But now it was a case of needs must. I couldn't leave them at school.

'We can't release them to you without their guardian's authorization. I'll keep them in my classroom,' said Mrs Sinclair. 'Perhaps, Miss Jones, you could go to the office and get the family contact details? You might be able to get hold of the dad, if he's the one who's supposed to be picking them up.'

Miss Jones, a plump, self-satisfied woman, nodded. 'I'll go and call from the office.'

I would have left then, but as soon as Miss Jones walked away, Marguerite began to cry. My Frances went into full mummy mode and bustled over, taking Marguerite by the hand and leading her to the book corner in the Year Three classroom. Frances settled on a cushion and drew Marguerite on to her lap. She pulled a book out of the stack and began reading in a high, babyish voice, which she clearly thought was the way one spoke to six-year-olds. Miranda stood by coolly and watched as Frances cared for her sister. Jonah let out a roar of frustration. He'd tried to wriggle downwards out of his pushchair straps and had got himself stuck. I unstrapped him and straightened the straps, but when I tried to do them up again, he arched his back and let out a wail of pure fury. He shoved my hands away and climbed out, toddling over to Frances and Marguerite.

'I can't begin to think where she might be,' said Mrs Sinclair.

'Has something bad happened?' Miranda asked flatly.

'Of course not,' Mrs Sinclair and I said in unison.

'Miranda, love,' I said as sweetly as I could, 'are you sure your dad was supposed to pick you up today? Has there been some kind of a mix-up?'

Miranda looked at me coolly. 'Of course there's no mix-up. Dad wanted to come and see my dance show.'

'But wouldn't Helen—' I began, but Miranda cut me off.

'She's doing a course today. She said she would come along later,' she said.

That made sense and explained why Helen's phone was off.

'Do you know what sort of course? Or where?' Mrs Sinclair asked, but Miranda shook her head.

'It's just one of those things,' I said. 'I'm sure Helen or Sam will be along any minute.'

Miranda stared at me like I was some sort of idiot.

'I'll make some calls,' I said. 'Maybe she told one of the other mums where she was going.'

I ran through all the local families in my mind and decided to call Linda. She always asks a lot of questions and generally seems to know everything about everyone. She listened to my garbled account of what had happened. 'She didn't say anything this morning at drop-off,' she said, 'but I'll start a phone chain to see if anyone has heard from her.'

I felt better knowing someone as practical as Linda had taken charge. I glanced over to the children. Marguerite had stopped crying and was sitting happily on Frances' lap, sucking her two middle fingers as Frances read to her from a book of ancient Greek legends. It struck me that Marguerite was quite babyish for a child nearly in Year Two. But perhaps it wasn't fair to judge her in that rather stressful situation. Miranda stayed where she was, close by Mrs Sinclair's side, looking up into our faces. She's one of those wide-eyed, quiet children who listens intently to whatever adults say. 'Little bat ears,' Helen would often say when Miranda was nearby and we were chatting. 'Be careful what you say. She misses nothing.'

Miss Jones came back into the classroom. 'I spoke to Marguerite's dad,' she said. 'He was supposed to pick up the girls, but then he was called away unexpectedly to Manchester on a business trip. He sent a message to his wife and asked her to collect them, but clearly she somehow never got it. He's on his way back now, but it's going to take him some hours to get here. Lara, he asks if you could kindly take the girls with you. He has no idea why Helen isn't receiving his messages, but he says he'll keep trying to get hold of her. I left a message on her mobile saying that the girls would be going home with you. Perhaps you might send them both a text message with your address, if they don't have it?'

I nodded and did so, although I was sure Helen had the address of every child in the class in a perfectly annotated spreadsheet somewhere.

'Girls,' I said brightly, 'it looks like Helen's busy somewhere, and your dad's on his way. I've let him know you're coming home to my house.'

Marguerite managed a watery smile, and Miranda didn't say anything. I gathered their things and piled them into the pushchair. Jonah wouldn't get back into it without a fight anyway, so he'd have to walk, or rather be shepherded, home.

It took us twice as long as usual. Jonah was so excited to be free of the pushchair and to have two extra girls to show off to that he ran amok. Frances and Marguerite dawdled beside me, chatting, and Miranda walked slowly and reluctantly a few paces behind. She didn't say anything for a long time, and then, out of nowhere, she spoke. 'It's our ballet performance for the parents today,' she said. 'I was supposed to be a firefly. I've got a costume and everything. And now I'm going to miss it.'

I know how seriously Miranda takes her dancing – she and Frances were in the same class initially, but Miranda progressed much more quickly and is now in an advanced group. Even as a chubby five-year-old, she used to approach the class with fierce concentration. While the other girls were busy swinging their little pink skirts and giggling together, Miranda was focused on the teacher, pointing her toes and making pretty arms. I felt angry with Sam and Helen for letting her down so badly on this important day. I gave her narrow shoulder a pat. She stiffened slightly, and I took my hand away.

I got the kids back to my house and settled them at the table with cups of squash and a snack. I briefly considered taking Miranda to ballet myself, but her costume was at home, and as I don't drive, there was no way we could get to the ballet school in time, not with me wrangling four children on the bus. Someone had to let them know she wasn't coming though, and I was pretty sure Sam wouldn't think to do it. I managed to find the ballet teacher's number online and went into my bedroom to make the call. She was clipped and rude, as if it were my fault. When I turned round after I had hung up Miranda was standing in the door of my bedroom.

'I just remembered, Helen said she'd be back in time to watch the show,' Miranda said. 'She said she'd meet us at the dance school at four-thirty. It's four-thirty now. So where is she?'

Sam

I'd only just arrived in Manchester to take a short-notice brief from a brand-new client – a massive, multinational health-food company – when the school rang. I phoned the client as soon as I realized I would have to go back to London and told them there was an emergency with one of my children. That seemed serious enough that they might consent to reschedule. I couldn't say, 'My wife didn't get the message to pick the kids up from school and I don't know where she is.' What would they have thought?

I could only get a first-class seat on the train back to London, which was screamingly expensive, but at least it meant I could sit in relative quiet. I wanted to keep my phone free in case Helen rang, so I used email to cancel all my meetings. It didn't even bear thinking about what Chris, my boss, would say.

I know it sounds heartless when I put it like that – worrying about the cost of train tickets, worrying about what people would think. But at that point I honestly wasn't concerned about her. I was a little annoyed, actually. It just wasn't like her to let me down. I know she'd said she was on a course till after school pick-up time, and I had promised to leave work early and collect the kids, but then Chris told me I needed to go and take that brief. The account was worth a fortune and we'd been trying to get in with that company for ages.

I left a voice message, explaining what had happened. I figured Helen would have her phone on silent and would see my call and then listen to the message on her lunch break. She'd have to leave her course early to pick up the girls, but I knew she wouldn't mind.

I'd anticipated arriving in Manchester for the meeting, then calling Helen to say I'd be staying over. She was used to that – I often took the opportunity to spend an evening with clients. There are certain deals that only get done when the sun has gone down, the booze has flowed and the client in question feels he's got all the perks he deserves. I always kept a bag at work with a change of shirt and underwear and a toothbrush for days like that. Helen knew how unpredictable my work could be, and she always took the unexpected meetings and changes of plan in her stride. So this complete collapse of our arrangements really threw me.

This was Helen. Calm, capable Helen. Something had happened, that was for sure, and I didn't give much thought to what – a broken-down car, a lost phone. Something minor. I'd swallow my annoyance, because she was always so amazing, and it was actually slightly my fault for changing the plans at the last minute. By eight o'clock that evening, we'd all be sitting around the dinner table, laughing about it. She'd have sorted out whatever the problem was and smoothed things over. She'd even have dropped off a thank-you gift for Lara, the mum who'd taken Miranda and Marguerite home. I'd do my best to grovel to the man in Manchester and set everything up for another day.

Nevertheless, my phone stayed ominously silent for the whole journey. Shortly before the train pulled into Euston, I rang Lara. It was just after six o'clock. She'd heard nothing. Apparently Jilly, who lives in our road, had popped past our house to have a look. There had been no answer when she rang the doorbell. I knew, as I had dialled it intermittently, that Helen's mobile phone remained switched off. I think that was the moment I began to be concerned. Helen had said she'd be at the dance school by 4.30, and it was over an hour and a half past that now. She had a thing about 6 p.m. 'I like to have the girls home by then,' she'd say. 'Wherever we've been, six o'clock is home time – time to get homework done and baths ready.'

I wracked my brains, trying to remember what Helen had said about the course she was going on. Something about effective social media for small businesses? Had she said where it was? I didn't think so. I tried Helen's phone one more time, to no avail. I began to feel a little anxious then, and started to run. I'd planned to just get on the Tube, but I couldn't bear the idea of being stuck underground, even if it was for only twenty minutes, so I jogged to the taxi rank. Miracle of miracles, there was no queue and within seconds I was in a black cab and we were gliding through Camden on our way north.

Once I was in the taxi, I began to calm down. It had to be a misunderstanding. Maybe the course had gone on late. She did love her courses, I reminded myself. She was always doing them, learning about something new. She'd done several, one about starting a blog, and a few about search engine optimisation and basic computer coding.

Lara's house turned out to be quite near ours – maybe three or four minutes closer to the school. The front fence was unpainted and the little garden was a profusion of wild flowers. I kicked a football out of the way and rang the doorbell. Lara opened the door, a pretty woman with a narrow, freckled face and a tangle of red curls. I vaguely knew who she was and had heard Helen talk about her. She was a single parent, I recalled. She ushered me in and we went through to the back of the house where my girls and her two kids were eating around her big wooden kitchen table. An older woman, I assumed her mum, was sitting at the table, chatting to all the kids. She smiled kindly at me. They'd given the children what we would have called 'tea' when I was little – fish fingers and smiley-face oven chips, which Marguerite was enthusiastically dipping into a massive puddle of ketchup. Miranda was sitting up straight, cutting her fish fingers into neat squares with her knife and fork and eating as she'd been taught. The girls usually ate dinner with us a little later – proper, adult food served in the dining room. On any other day, this would have been considered quite a treat.

'Hey, girls!' I said, and my voice sounded bright and fake, like a children's television presenter. They both looked up.

'Daddy,' said Marguerite, in the babyish voice she uses when she's tired, and she jumped down from her chair and ran to me. I scooped her up and cuddled her. She curved into my arms, her plump arms and legs still soft. She's lovely to hold, and I took a moment to hug her and sniff her hair, which smelled of the strawberry shampoo Helen liked to use on the girls. Whenever I hug Miranda, which she will sometimes reluctantly allow, she's all sharp angles – pointy elbows and narrow, bony limbs. 'Finish up your food,' I said, gently putting Marguerite down, 'and we'll head home.'

The girls continued eating, and Lara drew me out of the kitchen and into the living room.

'Any news of Helen?' she asked.

'Nothing,' I said. 'But I'm sure there's a reasonable explanation. I'm absolutely certain she'll be at home when we get there.' I smiled at her, and she looked at me oddly. I suppose it must have seemed as if I were trying to reassure her. I didn't know what to say. 'Come on, girls,' I called. 'Let's get going!'

It took fifteen minutes of faffing to gather the girls' school bags, jumpers and shoes from the chaos of Lara's living room. We thanked her and her mum again and left the house to walk home. As we turned the corner out of Lara's road, a name came to me. Crystal Spectrum. They were the people who ran the internet courses Helen went on. I stopped in my tracks, ran a quick search on my phone and came up with a number for them. It was late, but there was a chance someone was still there.

Eventually a crisp-voiced woman picked up. I gave my name. 'My wife, Helen, was booked on to a course on social media today—' I began, but the woman cut me off.

'Helen Cooper? I know her well. She's attended a lot of courses here. I'm Diane, the director of Crystal Spectrum. Hang on a minute. . .' I could hear her typing, accessing records on her computer. 'Oh,' she said, and she sounded surprised. 'Yes, she was booked on the course this morning, but she was a no-show. That's not like her.'

'No,' I said. 'Are you sure?'

'Absolutely sure. There's even a note here that the trainer got our receptionist to ring her. There was no reply.'

'What time was she due to get there?'

'We started at eleven,' Diane said, and then she added hesitantly, 'I do hope everything's okay.'

So did I. I thanked her and rang off. So Helen could have gone missing as early as eleven that morning. What could have happened? The girls were looking up at me curiously, so I popped my phone in my pocket and walked us home.

I could see the girls were getting worried, so I tried to look and act cheerful. I chided myself for being a worrier and freaking them out. It was a beautiful, balmy evening, sunny and still, the kind of summer evening where Helen would serve dinner on the patio outside – grilled salmon, new potatoes and a salad with her homemade dressing. I imagined us walking into the house and seeing the patio doors flung wide, with music drifting from the kitchen radio; Helen, wearing her duck-egg blue skirt, feet bare and hair caught up in her trademark ponytail, would turn and smile as she carried the salad bowl outside.

We turned into our road, and I could see Helen's Prius parked in the driveway, just as it always was. I began to believe my own fantasy. I could practically smell the salmon. Helen might be a little annoyed that the girls had already eaten, but Marguerite at least would be up for a second meal.

I put my key in the door, but it refused to budge. Whenever

one of us was at home, we'd only use the Yale lock. We'd only lock the mortice if everyone was out. I took a deep breath and sorted through my keys to find the correct one, unlocked the mortice and then the Yale and the door swung open.

The moment I stepped inside, I knew she wasn't there. The air was dead and silent. There were no dinner smells and no music and the doors out to the patio were locked. There was no Helen to turn and smile, a dish in her hand and her blue skirt swishing round her smooth, tanned legs.

As if someone had forcibly punched me into another time, I was hurled back to that other night, five and a half years ago, when I stepped into an empty house for the first time. I couldn't help myself. My knees just gave way, and I found myself kneeling on the hall carpet in the dark, with my daughters standing beside me. Marguerite came to me and patted my shoulder, but, unexpectedly, it was Miranda who began to cry, in high, quick sobs.

'Daddy, get up!' she said sharply. 'Get up!'

I didn't get up. I fumbled in my pocket and brought out my phone. I dialled 999.

'Which emergency service do you require?' said a tinny voice on the other end. 'Police, ambulance or fire?'

'Police,' I said. 'Police. My wife is missing.' And then I began to cry.

CHAPTER TWO

Sam

They asked me a lot of questions on the phone. When had I last seen Helen? Was this out of character? Had I rung her friends? I know they have to ask the same questions of everyone, to find out if it's a genuine missing person or simply the kind of chaotic household where people come and go and disappear, but I wanted to scream with frustration. In the end they must have believed me because they said they'd send some officers round.

I knew I had to do something with the girls. They were glued to my side, wide eyed and scared, and it was getting late. Marguerite would usually have been in bed by 7.30 and Miranda by 8.30. I certainly didn't want them around when the police arrived.

'Listen, girls,' I said, as calmly as I could manage, 'it's time for baths and bed.'

'We can't go to bed,' Miranda said. 'How will we sleep?'

'You need to try. Tomorrow is another day, and you've got school. I'll go and run the bath,' I said as decisively as I could manage. I broke one of Helen's unbreakable house rules and put on the television to distract the girls while I got things organized.

While I was filling the bath, it occurred to me to call Mrs Goode. She's our next-door neighbour, a softly spoken woman in her early seventies. She adores the girls and always chats to them, and she'd often babysat for us in the past. Perhaps she would come and sit with them, if they were still awake when the police arrived? I turned off the taps, and, calling to the girls, stepped out of the front door and crossed the shared driveway to knock on Mrs Goode's door.

I explained everything as quickly as I could, and she grabbed a cardigan and her handbag and followed me across to our house. She was calm and cheerful, and her presence instantly made me feel better. She bustled the girls upstairs. I stood on the landing and listened to her singing them a silly song, which they'd clearly heard before because Marguerite joined in with the chorus.

I laid out the girls' pyjamas. While they were in the bath, Mrs Goode met me on the landing.

'The police will have questions,' she said. 'They'll want to know what she was wearing, what she had with her. You might want to check.'

'I have no idea what she was wearing,' I said, desperately. 'I left early. . . I had to get to the office. . .'

'A floral dress, the one with the big forget-me-nots on it,' said Mrs Goode. 'I saw her go out. About nine-thirty, maybe? The floral dress, and she was carrying a blue handbag. Do you know the one I mean?'

I thought I did. Helen had a lot of handbags, but there was one, a bright royal blue, which she liked to use when she wore the forget-me-not dress. It was big and squashy, more casual than most of her bags. She usually went for a more rigid, satchel-style bag, better for keeping everything she needed neatly compartmentalized.

'So, the floral dress, the blue bag... did she have anything else with her?'

'Nothing. She was walking. I assumed she was off to the station. Going into town, probably?'

That sounded right, if she was going to the course. But 9.30 would be early to leave if she was only due there at eleven. Maybe she'd had another appointment, one I hadn't known about? I wished I could see her schedule, but, unlike me, she didn't use an electronic diary – she had a black leather Filofax, her constant companion, which I was certain would be in her handbag.

'I don't know if she came back, though,' said Mrs Goode suddenly. 'She might have come home and changed and gone out again. I went to Sainsbury's and then had lunch with a friend.'

I could hear the girls talking in quiet voices in the bath. I walked into our bedroom, which, naturally, was immaculate, the duvet smooth, the pillows plumped. I opened the wardrobe, and all Helen's clothes were neatly hung. I stared at them helplessly. Everything looked as it usually did, but who was to say if something was missing? I couldn't see the forget-me-not dress, but if she had come home and changed, she'd have put it in her laundry basket, wouldn't she? I opened the white wicker basket. It was empty, apart from a few jumpers and silk shirts, items she usually hand-washed. As I leaned over the basket, there was a sudden wave of Helen's scent – the delicate floral perfume she wore, the sweet cocoa-butter aroma of her body lotion and the warm, spicy smell of her skin.

Mrs Goode found me sitting on the edge of the bed, looking into the open laundry basket.

'Any luck?' she asked. I stared at her blankly. 'Can you help me get the girls out of the bath? Teeth and so on?'

I nodded and got up. We went through the motions and got the girls into bed. Marguerite didn't want to sleep in her own room, so I let her snuggle in with Miranda. Miranda would never normally have agreed to this, but she was happy to scoot close to the wall and let her little sister in beside her. I put on the soft nightlight and let the girls choose a bedtime story. Helen had been reading them a chapter of *Anne of Green Gables* each night, but they chose a picture book, an old favourite we'd read to them hundreds of times when they were much smaller. I lay across the bottom of the bed and read to them, keeping my voice soft and low. Marguerite's eyelids grew heavy and she dozed off quickly, but when I looked up I saw Miranda's wide, dark eyes, so like her mother's, watching me closely. I didn't have anything to offer her. No answers at all.

At that moment the doorbell rang. The police. Mrs Goode, who had been watching quietly from the doorway, said, 'You go. I can sit with Miranda.'

I squeezed Miranda's hand and she gripped back tightly. Then I rose and went downstairs to talk to the police.

The officers were so young. I felt like my dad, moaning about how coppers were all still wet behind the ears these days, but in all seriousness, the man looked about twelve. He clearly didn't need to shave more than twice a week, and the woman was a fresh, round-faced girl who looked like she hadn't quite grown out of her adolescent softness.

I brought them into the living room and we went through everything I'd already told the officer over the phone. Helen was a very reliable person, she had no history of drug or alcohol abuse, she had no financial problems, no history of mental illness, she wasn't taking any medication. This was entirely out of character.

They asked to see a photograph of her, and I took down the one we keep on the mantelpiece – Helen and the girls at the bottom of the Eiffel Tower, taken at Christmastime last year. Helen is wearing a green coat, and her cheeks are pink from the cold. She's bending down, her arms around the girls, and they're all laughing at me.

'And these are your daughters?' the female PC asked.

'Yes, Miranda is eight and Marguerite is six.'

'And you were alerted that your wife was missing because she didn't collect them from school?'

'Yes. I was supposed to do it, but I was called out of town. I left her a message. . .'

'But she didn't confirm that she'd received it?'

'No,' I said reluctantly. Both police officers looked disapproving. They clearly thought I was negligent and Helen wasn't much better.

'Has she ever done that before? Failed to collect them?'

'Never,' I said adamantly.

'What do you do for a living, Mr Cooper?'

'I work in advertising. I'm a client relationship manager.'

She didn't ask me anything further, but she wrote down what I'd said.

The male PC looked sceptical. 'And you earn enough doing that that your wife doesn't need to work?'

'We do all right,' I said, aware that I sounded defensive. 'Helen takes care of the girls, and the house. She does some courses. She's very involved at the school. Everyone knows her. She's always organizing things and working for the Parents' Association.'

They asked for a list of family.

'Helen's an only child,' I said, 'and both her parents are dead. I can give you my parents' details – but I've already spoken to them and they haven't heard from her.'

'So no family at all on her side? No cousins? Grandparents? Aunts or uncles?'

'An elderly uncle in Vancouver, but that's it. I've never met him – he wasn't well enough to attend our wedding.'

'What about friends?' the female PC asked. 'You say she was involved at the school.'

'Yes, she's very popular. We have spreadsheets of names and addresses. I can mark the people I'd say Helen is closest to.'

'That would be helpful. What about other friends? Old friends from school or university? Old work colleagues? Anyone spring to mind?'

I wracked my brain. 'No one springs to mind. I mean, no one that she's seen recently. We met at work. She joined the company just after she moved to the UK – she's originally Australian. She left a few years ago, and she hasn't really stayed in touch with those people, but I'll give you any names I can think of.'

'And friends of yours as a couple?'

I jotted down a quick list of our closest friends.

They asked me, as Mrs Goode had predicted, what Helen was wearing and I told them my best guess. They asked if she had any distinguishing marks – scars, tattoos, that sort of thing. I almost smiled at the idea of Helen having a tattoo. 'She does have a scar though,' I said. 'Her left earlobe has a raised ridge on it. When she was a teenager, she accidentally had an earring torn out, dancing at a music festival. It's quite distinctive.'

The female officer nodded and noted it down. She asked me to describe it, and I saw her draw a small, childish sketch of an ear, with a visible scar running vertically through the lobe.

'Do you have any good, recent photographs you could let us have?' asked the male PC. 'One that doesn't have your kids in it?'

I remembered then that I had taken a picture of Helen on my phone at a party some weeks before, wearing the floral dress. They asked me to email it to them. That was the picture they showed on the news and put in the papers – Helen walking towards me, holding two glasses of wine. When she saw I was taking a picture, she wrinkled her nose and smiled at me. Her hair was loose on her shoulders. She looked beautiful.

Then we went over what she would have with her. I could only guess what would be in her bag – her phone, purse and Filofax. Make-up, perhaps? A notebook and pen for her course? I told them that as far as I could see, all her other clothes were there, but it was difficult to tell. Who could give an accurate inventory of all of their partner's clothing? Helen probably could of mine, but as she did the majority of the washing and ironing, that wasn't surprising. All I could say with certainty was that there were no obvious gaps in her wardrobe.

'What about identification? Travel documents?'

'According to our neighbour, she walked to the Tube. She didn't flee the country.' I checked myself. Being sarcastic with the police probably wasn't helpful.

'Your neighbour?'

'Mrs Goode. She's upstairs with the girls right now. She's the one who saw Helen leave the house around nine-thirty this morning.'

Unsurprisingly, they asked to speak to her. 'And while we're chatting to her, perhaps you might have a look for your wife's personal documents? Identification, passport, that sort of thing? Just so we know what she might be carrying with her,' said the male PC.

I went upstairs as quietly as I could. Mrs Goode was sitting in the armchair in the corner of Miranda's room. Marguerite was fast asleep, her hair fanned on the pillow and her cheeks pink. Miranda was lying on her back beside her, arms by her side, staring at the ceiling, eyes wide open.

I motioned to Mrs Goode, and she stood and tiptoed out of the room. Miranda's eyes flew to the doorway and locked with mine. I tried to smile and failed. She turned away and went back to staring at the ceiling.

We returned downstairs. Mrs Goode seated herself opposite the police officers and I went to search through Helen's desk in the conservatory. The filing drawers containing all our bills, correspondence and important documents were locked, but I had a key. I opened the top drawer and went carefully through each section. There were the girls' birth certificates, our driver's licences, our marriage certificate, and our four passports, rubber-banded together. Helen bought matching leather passport holders in different colours to make it quick and easy to identify whose are whose when we travel. Mine's cobalt blue, hers is green, and the girls' are pink and purple. Everything was where I expected it to be.

The male PC came looking for me, and I showed him what I'd found. He nodded. 'Clever idea with the passport holders, that. My wife spends ages sorting through them for the kids every time we travel.'

He didn't look old enough for a wife and kids, but it wasn't the time for small talk.

'So nothing appears to be missing?'

'Not as far as I can tell,' I said, and I opened the lower drawer. Here Helen had all our bills and correspondence neatly filed, each section labelled – bank, insurance, mortgage, utilities.

'Very organized, your wife,' he said.

'Very.'

'She certainly doesn't look like the kind of person who'd just go walkabout, does she?' he said conversationally. There was an awkward moment of silence.

I looked over his shoulder into the kitchen and suddenly

remembered my manners. 'Can I offer you a cup of tea? Coffee? Some water, maybe?'

'I'm fine, thanks,' he said. 'Now tell me, Mr Cooper, where were you today? Out of town, I think you said?'

'Manchester, for a meeting. As soon as I arrived there, I got the call from the school to say Helen hadn't turned up, so I got straight on a train to come back.'

'Were you travelling alone? With a colleague?'

'Alone.'

'Did you talk to anybody? Anyone who could confirm that they saw you in Manchester at that time?'

It took me a moment to work out what he was asking. He wanted to know if I had an alibi.

'I bought a ticket from the ticket office. You can talk to the woman who works there. She might remember me because she sold me a first-class ticket for a train that was just leaving. And I'm sure I'm all over CCTV.'

'What time did you leave for Manchester?'

'Around twelve. I was at my office in Soho before that.'

'Can we check that with your colleagues?'

'Of course.' I kept my voice calm, but I thought back through the day, hoping that someone in the office would remember seeing me and saying goodbye to me and could attach times to their recollections. I couldn't believe I was having this conversation. That morning I had kissed my wife goodbye. Now I was trying to find ways to prove I hadn't murdered her. Wait, *had* I kissed her goodbye? I'd left in a rush. Had she been in the shower? Had I just yelled goodbye as I rushed out of the door? It was entirely possible. If that was the case, had I missed my last chance to kiss her, hold her?

I shook my head. She was missing, that was all. There was no proof something bad had happened to her. I had read somewhere that 90 per cent of missing people returned home within twenty-four hours. I had to believe she was coming back.

I realized the PC was standing watching me.

'I know this must be hard,' he said, 'but we have to ask all these questions. Do our best to work out what happened.'

Together, we walked back to the living room, where I could hear Mrs Goode talking to the other officer. She was sitting with her back to the door and clearly didn't hear us come in.

'. . . lovely couple. . .' she was saying. 'Never a cross word, although he does work away a lot. It must be lonely for her.'

'What kind of hours does he work?' the woman PC said softly. 'Evenings? Weekends?'

'He's away overnight quite often,' Mrs Goode began.

'I thought you were asking her about seeing Helen this morning,' I burst out. 'Not pumping her for information about our family.'

'Mr Cooper. . .' said the PC, in a conciliatory tone.

'Instead of assuming I've murdered my wife and hidden her in the cellar, wouldn't it be more useful if you actually got off your arses and got some officers out looking for her? For God's sake!' I knew I was yelling. I had to stop. I'd wake the girls.

But Miranda was awake anyway She'd come down the stairs and was standing in the doorway that led from the hall, watching me yell at two police officers, hearing the word 'murder'. We all saw her at the same time.

'Randa. . .' I said, reaching for her.

'I'm sorry if we woke you,' said the woman PC in a honeyed voice. 'I'm PC Shah and this is my colleague, PC Stevens. We're here to see what we can do to help find your mummy.'

'She's not my mother,' said Miranda calmly, and the two PCs stared at her in silence.

Miranda

Marguerite doesn't remember our mother, but I do. Her name was Leonora, and she was born in Italy. She came to England when she was eighteen years old to go to university, and that's where she met our dad. He says he liked her the moment he saw her, but she ignored him for two years. Once, I asked him if he had asked her out, and he said no, he just used to see her walking from class to class, but for ages he was too shy to talk to her.

'But if you never spoke to her, how was she ignoring you? If she didn't know you, how was she supposed to notice you?'

He laughed. 'I guess because I noticed her, I thought she might notice me. But she didn't. She'd just walk around alone or with her friends, and she was tall and slim and beautiful and mysterious.'

But then one day they met at a party and he did ask her out, and then they were together. They were sweethearts. I like it when he tells me the story and he says 'sweethearts', because that sounds old-fashioned and romantic and forever, like in a film.

And then they left university and started to work, and our mother was a musician, with a degree in music, and trying to make money playing her violin for concerts while she studied to be a music teacher, and our dad was a designer, trying to get work in advertising, and they lived in a flat in south London that was tiny, just one room and a bathroom, and they were as poor as church mice. I asked him why church mice were poorer than other mice, and he said because there was nothing to eat in the church but hymn books.

Anyway, then our mother got a job being a music teacher and then they had a little bit more money and then they got married. They saved some money and then they went travelling. Backpacking, it's called, when you put everything in a big bag like a tortoise's shell on your back and you go to stay in grotty hostels and sleep on the beach. They went to lots of places, and I've seen pictures of them in India and Japan and riding elephants and in South America too. They were always laughing, and Dad had a big beard then and our mother was dark brown from all the sun.

And then they came back to settle down and start nesting. First they were church mice, and then they were birds building a nest, and whenever Dad tells the story, then he says, 'And then along came you,' as if I was just passing by and I moved in with them, but what he means is I was born. My dad still didn't have a very good job. He was still trying to be a designer, so after a few months my mother went back to work as a teacher and Dad stayed home and looked after me. They got a little house in south London where they had lived before, and my mother worked in a school nearby. I was a baby, so I don't remember that part.

And then two years later, Marguerite was born, and my mother stayed home with her for six months and then she went back to work. Dad says she worked hard, teaching in the school and also teaching violin to other children in the evening and weekends to make money. And one day she was teaching at school and she fell down. They thought she had fainted, but she didn't wake up and they called an ambulance. And when the ambulance took her to the hospital they found she had died. Something broke in her brain, a vein or something.

'Did it hurt?' Marguerite always asks.

'I don't think so,' Dad always says. 'I think it was more like a light going out.'

'Do you think she was scared?' I want to ask. 'Do you think before the lights went out she thought about us and what would happen to us?' But I never do ask, because I don't want to know the answer. I don't want to think of her seeing the darkness coming and not being able to stop it.

Anyway, that was a very hard time for our family, and Dad didn't know what to do, so he had to come back to north London and we moved in with Granny and Grandpa. Dad stopped trying to be a designer and got a job doing client services in the advertising agency, which is different, and you have to wear a suit and go for dinner and drinks and do schmoozing, but you get a lot more money. And after he had been doing that for about a year, he met Helen at work. She had come from Australia to live in England, not too long before Daddy met her. 'Down Under,' she said. She didn't say under what.

The first time they went on a date, Marguerite and I came too. We all went for a picnic in the park. Helen was kind and pretty, and when we walked in the park, she and Dad each held one of my hands and said, 'One, two, three, wheee!' and swung me off my feet, and then Marguerite, who was two, said, 'Me! Me!' and they did it for her too. It was nice. Actually, I'm not sure if I remember it, but there's a picture of us all in the park that day, and Dad has told us the story often. He couldn't believe a lady from work could be so nice to his two little children. Anyway, Helen started spending more time with us all, and as Dad likes to say, the rest is history. They fell in love and got married, and then Dad got a big promotion at work and bought this house. That meant that Granny couldn't look after us and pick us up from school because it was too far, and Helen gave up her job to look after us.

It's not a secret at school that Helen isn't actually my mother – the teachers know and everything – but I don't talk about it to my friends. Marguerite calls her Mummy, but I don't like calling her Helen, and she isn't actually my mother, so I don't call her anything. I like it that everyone at school says she's the best mum – the prettiest and best at organizing and cakes and stuff, and I don't say 'She's not my mum' when they say stuff like that. Some of the other children are late, or their school uniform is dirty or they don't bring their homework on the right day, and that never happens to us. It's not so stressful that way, with Helen making everything okay. I sometimes wonder what my real mother would have been like – would she have done my hair so perfectly for my ballet exam as Helen does, or would she have been one of those messy, late mothers? Would I have minded if she was my mum? I don't know. Life has lots of questions we will never know the answers to.

CHAPTER THREE

Sam

Mrs Goode left shortly after the police did. I think she was embarrassed to have been caught talking to them about Helen and me. I wasn't upset with her. I knew she would have had to answer any questions they asked her, and it's not as if she was badmouthing us.

Miranda was still wide awake. 'Do you want to go back to bed?' I asked her.

'Marguerite is all star-fished across my bed now,' she said. 'There's no room for me.'

'Let's watch some TV,' I said, and she looked at me cautiously. Still up at ten o'clock, an offer of TV on a school night – the rules really had gone out of the window.

On Miranda's instructions, I found an animated series on Netflix about a school for vampires, featuring improbably wide-eyed, emaciated girl characters in tiny skirts, who, despite being undead, were worried about boys and being popular.

Miranda sprawled across my lap, her long, skinny legs dangling over the arm of the sofa. We both stared at the screen in silence. I let episode after episode roll over us. It took longer than I expected – until nearly midnight – for her to fall asleep. When I finally felt her head go heavy against me, I sat for another half an hour or so, comforted by the heat of her and the tangle of her hair on my arm. Then I slid out gingerly and settled her head on a cushion. When I went upstairs to check, Marguerite had indeed taken over the bed. Rather than risk waking either of them, I fetched a blanket from the linen cupboard and covered Miranda where she slept on the sofa.

The house was so quiet. I wasn't used to being up that late – I need my sleep, and I'm often in bed by ten. Helen could manage quite happily on four or five hours a night and she'd frequently be downstairs long after I went to bed. She'd use the time to read or catch up on emails for whichever school event she was currently involved in. The quiet, night-time house was her domain. I wandered from room to room, then went back upstairs and looked at our bedroom. The novel Helen had been reading was resting on her bedside table, with a bookmark between the pages about halfway in.

I went into our en-suite bathroom, and there was her toothbrush and the neat white box in which she kept her make-up. There was her face-wash, her moisturizer, body lotion and deodorant. I opened the medicine cabinet, and there were her contraceptive pills. Every outward vestige of Helen was exactly where it should be. It was absurd that she wasn't downstairs, her fingers flying over her computer keyboard.

I wandered back downstairs and stood by her desk again. How was it possible that she was just gone? My head pounded and my stomach twisted in knots. What was I doing there at home? I should be out, running from street to street, looking for her, calling her name, saving her. When I met Helen, after Leonora died, I was a basket case, shuffling along, barely living, just surviving. She saved me then – gave me a reason to live, gave structure and purpose to my life. And now, when she needed me most, where was I? At home, failing her.

I sank into her desk chair and felt the tears begin to come. 'For heaven's sake, pull yourself together,' I said aloud.

I picked up the card PC Shah had given me, her direct line and mobile numbers handwritten in neat figures, and called her. She answered after a single ring.

'Mr Cooper?' she said. She must have recognized my number. 'Any news?'

'I was ringing to ask you the same thing.'

'We're working as fast as we can, Mr Cooper.' Her voice was kind, but there was a hint of impatience. 'We've rung all the local hospitals, and the photos you gave us have been shared with police all over the country. We've contacted the Missing People organization and they'll be publicizing your wife's details too.'

'Thank you,' I said lamely. 'I'm sorry. This is so hard. I want to be doing more, but I don't know what I can do.'

'Sit tight,' said PC Shah, and her voice was gentler now. 'Keep your phone on, and keep ringing anyone you can think of that might have seen your wife.'

'I will,' I said, conscious that I was tying up both her line and mine with the call. 'And thanks again.'

'If we haven't heard anything by the morning,' she said, 'we'll be handing this over to the missing person's team and we've agreed we'll issue a media appeal.'

We hung up and I sat at Helen's desk for a while, scrolling through my phone trying to think of anyone else I could ring. There was no one. And besides, it was midnight.

It suddenly occurred to me that though she kept her appointments in her Filofax, there might also be something on her computer – if it was a hair appointment or something, there might be a record of the booking, or if it was a social thing, there might be an email from a friend. There might be a web search for an address, or some notes with a date on. I turned on her PC and waited for it to boot up.

I never used Helen's PC, but I had the security passwords and her email password. She had made me record them in a note on my phone in case I ever needed anything off her machine. I opened her email. There were a few new messages – mainly marketing emails and some from the school. I scrolled back through the last few days but couldn't find any emails that suggested someone had asked her to meet them. I opened her documents folder and looked at the most recent files – again, nothing that gave me any clues. There were spreadsheets of costs for the event she was planning at school, and a series of photos of Miranda practising her dance moves, plus a recipe for a Danish cake, which, I recalled, she'd baked the weekend before. I opened the web browser and looked at the history. She had last performed a search some days ago – Monday. The items in the list were innocuous and predictable: reviews for a film we'd talked about seeing, news sites, Facebook. Nothing out of the ordinary. She clearly hadn't done anything on her PC for a few days. I opened Facebook, but she was never much of a social media person: she'd not posted anything for some weeks, nor had she said yes to any events. Her feed was a never-ending parade of posts by other people – inspirational quotes and pictures of cats and children. Another dead end.

I went back into her email and opened her contacts list. I selected all the names – there were a lot, three hundred or so – and opened my own email account. Then I sorted through the list, removing all the companies and leaving some two hundred people, some of whom I knew, some of whom I didn't.

I composed a short message with the subject line 'Have you seen Helen Cooper?'

Dear all,

My wife, Helen Cooper, went missing this afternoon, Wednesday 24 May, from our home in north London. She left the house around 9.30 a.m., wearing a blue floral dress, and has not been seen since. If you have seen her or have any idea where she might have gone, please contact me.

Thank you,

Sam Cooper

I added my own mobile number and email address, attached the photo of Helen in the dress and hit 'Send'. I got four or five bounce-backs immediately. I knew it was a mad, scattergun approach, and Helen, if she was fine and well somewhere, would hate the public nature of it, but I had to do something. I went on to Facebook, logged out of Helen's account and into my own. Using similar words to my email, I posted the same thing, asking people to share it. It looked just like those dodgy, widely shared missing-person posts that show up in my feed all the time. I'd often said to Helen that they always seemed like hoaxes, but I found myself praying that mine at least looked genuine.

I sat staring at the screen for a long time, hoping that replies would begin to pop up, but it was 1.30 a.m. and everyone who might know something was probably asleep. She'd been gone for sixteen hours. I got up and wandered restlessly around the sleeping house. I checked both girls, straightening Marguerite's limbs, flung wide in sleep, and tucking Miranda's foot back under the blanket.

I stood for a while in the dark hallway and then opened the front door. Helen's car was still in the driveway and our road was silent. I imagined her walking briskly away from the house and vanishing into thin air. I sat down on the doorstep, the front door open behind me, and kept watching the end of the road, as if by sheer will I could make her come round the corner, wave to me and walk down the road and into my arms. But the road stayed silent, and no one came round the corner at all.

I sat on the doorstep until about 4 a.m., when light began to creep over the tops of the houses. I was cold and my whole body ached. I got up creakily and went into the house. The girls were as I had left them. I went upstairs and got my warm dressing gown and then sat in the armchair by the front window. If she came home, I'd be able to see her as she turned into the road. I must have dozed off for a while because the next thing I knew, I was being jerked awake by my phone ringing on the arm of the chair beside me.

'Hello?' I sounded fuzzy and gruff.

'Sam!' The voice was female, breathy and light. I didn't recognize it. 'I'm so sorry, did I wake you?'

'No, no.' I struggled to sit upright, ran a hand through my hair. 'Who is this?'

'Ella, Helen's friend from the school. I was just ringing to see if you'd heard anything. Such an awful thing, isn't it?'

'No news,' I said, trying, in my bleary state, to remember which of the women Ella was. I glanced at my watch. It was just after seven.

'Nothing from the Facebook post?' she asked. 'That's gone crazy. I thought you might have got some calls from that.'

I got up from the armchair and, with Ella still talking in my ear, wandered over to Helen's PC and turned it on again. Ella was explaining that she and some of the other mothers had made us some food and would be dropping it off once they'd taken the kids to school.

'We won't stay, of course,' she said. 'We don't want to intrude. . .'
There was a note of wistfulness in her voice, as if she were hoping I might ask her to come in. I found that strange. Did she really want to be in the middle of our family disaster?

The PC had booted up and I opened Facebook. I had four thousand notifications. I didn't know it was possible to have four thousand notifications. My post had been shared hundreds of times, and there were multiple comments attached to each share. I looked through a few of them, but as far as I could see, they were all people 'sending love and prayers', or saying how pretty Helen was and they hoped she would be found safe. I had dozens of private messages and emails too, but these too were all messages of support rather than any concrete thoughts on where Helen might be. There were so many, though, and it had spread so far, that I wondered if I'd be able to find the one comment which held a real clue, even if there was one.

I was still holding the phone to my ear and I could hear Ella twittering anxiously.

'Thank you so much,' I said, although I hadn't heard anything she'd said for the last few minutes. 'I'll be in touch as soon as we hear anything.'

She kept talking, but I said, 'I have to go. Bye, Ella,' as firmly as I could and disconnected the call.

I heard a faint noise behind me and turned to see that Miranda was awake, lying on her side on the sofa, watching me with her big dark eyes.

'Is she back?'

'No, honey.'

'Is she dead, Daddy?'

'No, my love,' I said, going to sit beside her and hug her. 'Of course not. She'll be back, I'm sure of it.'

In all of Miranda's eight years of life, that was the first time I had ever lied to her. Helen had simply vanished. Helen, who was as constant as the sea, who had been my touchstone for the past five years. If she was gone, how could I be sure of anything?

Lara

My phone didn't stop. I had to put it on silent, so the constant ringing and bleeping didn't wake the kids and Mum. Linda's phone chain had not revealed Helen's whereabouts, but it had set in motion a mad flurry of gossip and speculation. Someone had seen a suspicious group of men sitting on a bench in the park. Someone else thought they remembered Helen saying she had a manicure appointment that morning, or maybe she had said that last week. Anyway, did I think she should tell the police? Linda rang at about ten and we chatted for a while, and in the course of the conversation she mentioned something about Helen not being the first wife Sam had lost.

'Well he hasn't *lost* her,' I said. 'She's only been missing for twelve hours or so.'

'You know what I mean.'

I suppose I had been told at some point that Helen was the girls' stepmother rather than their mother, but it hadn't been significant at the time. She was so clearly devoted to them, concerned and involved. She didn't look any different to the rest of us.

'What happened to the mother?'

'Died of a brain haemorrhage, when Miranda was a toddler and Marguerite was just a baby. Tragic.'

'Poor Sam,' I said.

'I wouldn't be in a hurry to "poor Sam" him,' said Linda. 'You know it's almost always the husband—'

I cut her off. I'm not usually that assertive, but I had to say something. 'He was in Manchester. If something has happened to her, God forbid, Sam had nothing to do with it. And anyway, I think you're being ghoulish. She's not dead. At least there's no indication that she is.'

'You're right,' said Linda, and I was glad that her down-to-earth nature meant that she hadn't taken offence at my sharp tone. 'It's probably just one of those things. She'll be back at the school gate tomorrow.'

But she wasn't, and neither was Sam. The girls weren't in school, and there were a couple of officers at the gate, stopping people and asking if they remembered seeing Helen the previous morning.

We all hung about much longer than we usually would, talking, once the kids had gone in. For lots of the mums, Helen's disappearance was the most exciting thing to have happened to them in ages. The speculation about the men in the park had expanded into a full-blown rumour, and a few of the women let rip with some *Daily Mail*-style xenophobic sentiments about illegal immigrants. One mum took particular delight in dredging up every scare story she could think of. I looked at the circle of women around her, hanging on her every word. They were all enjoying it far too much. I thought of Miranda's strained, thin little face and Sam's forced cheer. I turned and pushed Jonah's pushchair up the hill as fast as I could.

I wanted to do something to help, but I didn't know what. I didn't want to ring – I imagined Sam's heart leaping every time his phone rang, thinking it would be news of Helen. I considered offering to take the girls but decided he probably wanted to keep them close. I thought of sending a text, but that seemed too informal, given the gravity of the situation. In the end, I fell back on the old standby of taking food round. In a crisis, no one has time to shop or cook, and people often forget to eat properly. I also had a clear memory of Helen laughing in the playground about how useless Sam was in the kitchen.

'He's a star about laundry and he mows a mean lawn,' she'd said, 'but he can't boil an egg. Without me or his mum, I think he and the girls would live on cereal and stir-fries.'

Mum had gone out, so while Jonah had his morning nap, I roasted some chicken pieces and made some mixed roast veggies. It was basic, but there you are. I'm a competent cook, but nowhere near Helen's standard. I was just trying to prevent them from starving, really. When Jonah woke up, I put the food into a disposable foil tray with a lid so Sam wouldn't have to worry about returning dishes, balanced it on the top of the pushchair and set off.

There was a police car outside Sam and Helen's house and I hesitated, wondering whether to leave it on the doorstep. But then I imagined some big, clodhopping policeman opening the front door and ending up with a shoe full of roasted peppers and courgettes. I rang the doorbell.

I heard quick footsteps in the hall and Sam opened the door. He looked awful, still wearing the shirt he'd had on the night before, now rumpled and stained with sweat. He obviously hadn't slept. His face fell when he saw it was me.

'I'm so sorry,' I said. 'I, er, I thought maybe you could do with some food.' I held out the warm foil tray.

'Thanks,' he said vaguely. His glance slid off me and he looked up the road, as if he expected Helen to come strolling along.

'It's just chicken and veggies. Bung it in the oven for twenty minutes or so to warm it through when you want to eat. . .' I knew he hadn't heard a word I said, but his hands came out automatically and he took the tray.

'Okay, I'll go now,' I said, aware of Jonah twisting and grizzling in his pushchair behind me. 'I know everyone says this, but if there's anything I can do, anything at all. . .'

Suddenly Sam's gaze came to rest fully on me. His eyes were bloodshot, but still mesmerising.

There's an in-joke at the school gates about Sam. He's known to everyone as Handsome Dad. He's tall, about six-two, I'd say, broad in the chest and well built, with curly golden blonde hair and wide blue eyes. He has a Viking look to him. In the past, whenever he dropped off his girls or attended a school function, a whisper would pass through the playground and eyes would swivel. Within minutes, he'd be surrounded by a crowd of chattering, animated mums, flicking their hair and making their wittiest jokes. Helen tended to stand back and smile when that happened.

'Thank you. Really,' he said, and he almost managed a smile. 'If you hadn't taken the girls home with you after school yesterday, I don't know. . . well. . . I want to say I appreciate it. And thanks for the food. That was kind and thoughtful.'

He looked worn out and so vulnerable. The urge to go back and hug him, or at the least touch his arm, was strong. But I reminded myself that I barely knew him, and that he'd probably find it inappropriate if I did, or, worse, it might make him break down and cry. I couldn't begin to imagine what he was going through. And after losing his first wife too.

'It's just one meal,' I said hesitantly. 'I could bring you something tomorrow. . .'

'That's kind,' he said, a little embarrassed, 'but the fridge is absolutely chock-a-block. Everyone from the school has been so nice, and the freezer was already full. Helen seems to have crammed it with cooked meals, like she was expecting a siege.'

I felt like such a fool. Of course my food idea wasn't unique or original. The yummy mummies would have been falling over themselves to take care of Handsome Dad. Handsome, tragic Dad.

'Well. . .' I said awkwardly, realizing he was dying to get away and shut the door again. 'Anything I can do. Anything at all. Just let me know.'

He gave one more nod and another weak smile and the door closed.

'Come on, Jonah,' I said. 'Let's go to the park and kick a football hard.'

'Balls!' Jonah shouted loudly, and I couldn't help but agree.

When we got to the park, I unstrapped Jonah from his pushchair and he went racing off across the grass like a small, chubby greyhound. It was typical, all the yummy mummies wanting to cook for Sam, fluttering around to see if a little of his tragic glamour would brush off on them. I could imagine them hoping that a media outlet would approach them for a 'source close to the family' comment and give them their fifteen minutes in the spotlight. Or maybe they were harbouring a fantasy that Helen was gone for good and they could take her place, 'comforting' Sam. I was sure half of them would ditch their boring, balding husbands for a pop at him.

But as I took off after Jonah, who showed no sign of stopping, I had to laugh at myself. Was I that different? It had been thrilling, being at the cutting edge of the story the day before and looking after his kids. And I'd have been lying if I said I didn't find Sam attractive.

Later on, when I got home and Jonah was down for a nap, I turned on my computer. When I logged on to the BBC website, Helen's face smiled out at me from the front page. I checked a few of the newspaper websites and she was there too. The *Daily*

Mail article was the most comprehensive, with a picture of Sam and Helen's house and a range of shots of Helen that they had gleaned, I assumed, from her Facebook account. It was so odd to see the pictures on a national newspaper website and to read about people I knew, and our neighbourhood. This was the closest I had ever come to being in the public eye, although it didn't mention me by name; the article just said, 'Mrs Cooper failed to collect her children from school,' which wasn't strictly true – it was Sam who'd failed to collect them. It didn't elaborate on what happened after that. At the end of the article there was a quote from Sam. 'If anyone has seen Helen or has any idea what might have happened, please let us know. We love Helen very much and we want her home safe.' I could imagine him saying it, his blue eyes wide and serious. I pictured the way his jaw would have clenched, the set of his shoulders. They should put him on TV, I thought. That would certainly draw attention.

I made the mistake of scrolling to the bottom of the article and reading some of the comments. There were a selection saying how gorgeous Helen was, and one that actually said that it was no wonder someone had stolen her away. Ugly though that was, it was by no means the bottom of the barrel. Others assumed Helen was dead for sure and were quick to arrest, try and convict Sam. 'It's always the husband,' wrote one commenter in an echo of what Linda had said. 'Mark my words. They'll find her beaten to death or strangled, and it'll have been him.'

'A woman like that will have had plenty of admirers,' said another. 'She's probably got herself a richer boyfriend and run away.'

One comment said simply, 'I would.'

People are scum, they really are. I closed the page in disgust.

Horrifying though the comments were, I suppose similar thoughts must have gone through many people's minds. How does a woman just disappear? Especially a woman like Helen, whose life seemed so stable. It would take something big, an act of extreme violence, to knock her from her path, surely?

I mean, there are people who feel solid and secure in their lives – people like Helen. And then there are people whose lives are much more chaotic. Like Marc. I always get angry when I read rants in the right-wing press about single mothers – as if we all made a deliberate choice to raise our kids alone, as if we had no use for a man. But all the single mums I know are like me – women who took a gamble, as we all do when we go into a relationship, and just picked the wrong guy.

I didn't even pick Marc. He picked me. I was working as a restaurant manager in a pub. We'd just got taken over by one of the brewery chains and they wanted us to host karaoke evenings. When Marc came in that first time and set up his machine, he was trailed by a crowd of giggling, overweight, forty-something women – karaoke groupies who were happy to go to any pub where he was working. They ordered wine by the bottle and bar-snack platters and stayed all night. They adored Marc, and I could see why. Lean, tall and tanned, with shaggy, dirty blonde hair, he wore double denim and managed to make it look cool, in a strange post-modern-cowboy way. He moved languidly, and smiled at you like you'd shared a delicious private joke or a great kiss, even if you'd never said a word to him. I took one look at him and knew he was bad, bad news.

I mentally wrote him off, but he had other ideas. He turned up at the pub every day and brought me lunch – beautiful soups and salads, homemade and sealed in Tupperware. If I mentioned I liked a song, he'd buy me the CD. He didn't make any romantic moves at first; he acted like a really sweet, reliable friend, until I let my defences drop. And then he chucked romance at me. He acted like a lovesick teen in an eighties film. He wrote poetry, cupped my face between his hands and sang to me. It was fabulous, and irresistible, and I knew it wasn't real. I allowed myself a glorious six months, believing that when the romance faded, he'd be off. But then I got pregnant.

I considered having an abortion, but I couldn't bring myself to do it. I'd always wanted kids, but I knew even then that Marc wasn't the right guy. He went out of his way to prove me wrong. I knew that doing it on my own would be nigh on impossible, both financially and logistically, so I chose to believe him. It was a gamble. Turned out the long-haired-karaoke-dude act was just that – Marc came from money. A lot of it. His dad was a barrister and the family home was this mansion in Warwickshire. Taking me home to meet them, a quirky, pregnant restaurant manager ('waitress', his mother called me at lunch), went down rather poorly. They did their best to be polite, but I could see they were horrified. Still, they gave us an enormous deposit for this house, and wished us all the best.

Marc gave it a go, I'll give him that. He was at the birth and seemed besotted. He took literally hundreds of pictures of Frances in her first days of life. But he wasn't cut out for domesticity, or Rhyme Time at the local library. He started doing karaoke gigs again when Frances was about three months old and he was coming home later and later. I put up with it. I mean, how could I not? I wasn't earning and I was living for free in the house for which Marc was paying the mortgage.

But then things took a turn for the worse. His behaviour became more erratic. It took me ages to work out that the 'hangovers' that made his temper so foul were comedowns from all the coke he was doing. He got fewer karaoke gigs but stayed out in the evenings just as much, if not more. It was almost a relief the first time he didn't come home at all – it gave me licence to start the shouting row that had been brewing for months.

He left after that, but he continued paying the bills, at least for a while. And then I got a polite call from the bank to say a mortgage payment had been missed. I panicked. I didn't know what to do. I took a deep breath, borrowed money from my mum, put six-month-old Frances into day care and took a job running an upmarket coffee shop, so at least I was working reasonable daytime hours. We got by. I tried my best to keep Marc in Frances' life, making sure he saw her every weekend, but he was so unreliable. By the time she was two, whenever I said, 'Daddy's coming today,' she'd go still and make her face expressionless. She'd already learned to manage her disappointment. When my mum, who'd been a teacher, retired, she moved in with Frances and me, and her pension helped with the mortgage. Having her there also meant I could go back to my old job, managing the pub, which paid better.

Then Marc took off for Florida – 'to get my head straight,' he said – and disappeared from our lives completely. We had four good, peaceful years in our all-female household and our future looked assured and predictable.

He came back one spring day, just turned up on the doorstep, hair cut short, wearing a beautiful bespoke suit. There was a tale of a stint in rehab, a start-up business that had taken off, a fortune made. He wanted to make everything all right with us. At first I did my best to keep him at arm's length. I tried to stop him turning up every day with expensive presents for Frances. I would have stopped him paying off the mortgage if I'd known he was going to do it, but he just went to the bank and wiped out the balance. He felt it gave him the right to be in the house, and, yes, legally, it did.

Gradually, unsurprisingly, he chipped away at my resistance too, making a huge effort with Frances and with my mum (who, by the way, was never fooled, not for an instant). And inevitably eventually I let my guard down, I let him in and before I knew it,

I was up the duff again and Jonah came along. He was a colicky screamer. Ding-ding, round two: late nights, unpredictable behaviour, grumpy Marc. And then he was gone. Eight months ago now. I'm back at the old pub, working four evenings a week, while Mum looks after the kids and Marc is living in Florida. So yes, I know all about mercurial people who continually let you down and never do what they say they'll do.

But that was never Helen. If Helen mentioned in passing that she'd lend you a book, she'd be there at the school gate the next day with the book in a plastic bag. She was the anti-Marc – never late, always predictable in her moods, always where she said she'd be. Until now.

CHAPTER FOUR

Sam

The day after Helen went missing, the girls and I didn't leave the house. We stayed inside and I answered phone calls and watched the social media storm as my post was shared and reshared. None of the messages contained any real clues. I did my best to read them all, but I knew the police were watching them too. PC Shah had been snippy with me about launching my own social media campaign. 'We prefer to partner with one of the recognized missing persons' charities,' she said. But when she saw how many responses there were, she nodded, and said, 'Well, we'll see how this plays out.'

There were a few approaches from news organizations. The police told me to direct all enquiries to them. Nevertheless, at about 10 a.m. I answered the door to a fast-talking reporter who tried to inveigle his way into the house. I said a few polite nothings, gave them PC Shah's name and then retreated before they could ask anything else. I registered the flash of a camera, so I knew they'd have snaps of me looking dishevelled and shocked. After that, I always checked cautiously out of the living-room window first. I did open the door to the succession of ladies from the school bearing meals and managed to get rid of all but the most persistent by saying the kids needed me. After one particularly tenacious mum kept talking, I instructed Miranda to call me loudly if I spent too much time on the doorstep. That worked well.

I wouldn't have answered it at all, but my parents were on their way. They had been away on holiday in Cornwall but had set off back to London as soon as I called them in the morning. My dad never exceeded the speed limit, so I knew it would take them a good seven hours, and I counted the minutes until they arrived.

My mum and dad. There are no words for how grateful I am to them. I was a horrible teenager – sullen, rebellious, stupid and ungrateful. But through those years these two dear people, Alan and Rosamond, held steady, loved me, didn't alienate me, and waited. They waited for me to grow into the man they hoped I'd be. And against all odds, I sort of did, largely though the patience, love and firm hand of Leonora. She'd been raised to have great respect for the older generation and she adored my parents as soon as she met them. If I was ever short-tempered with them, or rude or unreliable, her shock and disappointment in me brought me up short. When I saw myself through her eyes, acting like an immature brat, I was disappointed in myself too. And of course when Miranda and Marguerite came along and it dawned on me that the all-consuming, heart-crushing love I felt for my daughters was the same love Alan and Rosamond had, in their mild way, felt for me, I was doubly chastened. As I reached my thirties, our relationship deepened and improved. Although, to be honest, I think moving away from them and seeing them less often helped keep our relationship cordial and close.

And then Leonora died, and they turned into a pair of bona fide saints and heroes.

'Just come home,' my mum said when I rang her, weeping with pain and fear as I realized the depths of the practical and financial horror I faced.

'Come home,' said Dad. 'We can work it all out together.'

And we did. They got their financial advisor to help me sort out the knotty mess of Leonora's estate (unsurprisingly, she had died without leaving a will), and Mum looked after the girls, allowing me time to search for work and also to fall apart and grieve for my wife.

And here they were, flying in to rescue me again. I was watching out of the window when Dad's Vauxhall Astra pulled slowly into our road. Dad parked with his usual painstaking care, and I watched them get out of the car. I know they were stiff from the long drive from Cornwall, but it was painful to see how slowly they moved, Mum putting her hand in the crook of Dad's arm as they walked up the path. I saw them glance at one another and take a deep breath before they rang the doorbell. How hard it must be for them, I thought. Your kids are supposed to grow up and be independent and ultimately look after you.

By the time I opened the door, they had their kind faces plastered on.

'My poor darling,' said Mum, and gave me a hug, offering me her soft cheek to kiss. Then she slipped past me and called out for the girls. Within seconds I could hear all three of them chattering away happily in the kitchen. Marguerite and Miranda had been creeping around me in silence and I think being able to talk freely to Granny was a big relief.

My dad was all practical. He wanted to know what I knew, what the police knew, what the police had done. 'Are they doing their best to trace her?' he asked. 'Are they really? I mean, there's stuff in the paper, I know, but what about search parties? Dogs? Have they got all the available men out looking for her?'

'They've been good, Dad,' I said. 'I know they're making door-to-door enquiries, they're checking CCTV on the high street and at all the stations, and they're monitoring her mobile phone and banking so if she or... anyone... withdraws money from her account or uses her phone, they'll be able to track them.'

'And so far?'

'So far nothing,' I admitted. 'But they're working on it. They're putting me in contact with Missing People, that's the charity that helps people... people like me. And hopefully they may have other ways of tracking her.'

'It makes no sense,' said Dad. 'Helen. I mean... Helen.' He had nothing further to say. He gave me a pat on the shoulder and together we went out to the car to bring in their bags.

Even though they live only a few miles away, we'd agreed that in the short term it would be a help if they stayed with the girls and me in the house. We were well over twenty-four hours past the last definite sighting of Helen, and while in the beginning I'd been certain, almost cocky, that there would be a simple explanation and a quick and easy resolution, the bubble of dread in me was growing into a cloud of deep blackness. I was sure that the next knock at the door would be the police and the news would be dreadful, final and life-altering.

Dad and I went into the kitchen, where Mum had already done all the washing up and had got a pot of tea brewing. The girls were sitting at the table, doing a jigsaw puzzle I had never seen before. The picture on the box looked like some kind of Cornish fishing village, so I guessed Mum had produced it out of her capacious handbag. I sat down at the table beside Marguerite and absent-mindedly began sifting through the pieces looking for edges. Mum, passing behind me, gave my shoulder a squeeze.

'I'll remake the bed in our room,' I said, looking up, 'and you and Dad can be in there.' I couldn't imagine sleeping in that bed without Helen, so being able to give it up for Mum and Dad was a relief.

'Are you sure, darling?'

'Of course. I can put a futon in one of the girls' rooms, or downstairs, for me.'

'And where are you going to put Tim?'

'Tim?' I said stupidly. But I should have known.

'He's got to work lunchtime, but he's coming up straight after,' said Mum. 'You didn't think he wouldn't come, did you?'

My younger brother Tim is a chef, a single guy with no children. He runs the kitchen in a classy bistro in Bristol. Although we were close as kids, I hadn't seen him much of late. This was partly because he worked such punishing hours, and lived two hours away, but also because he and Helen had never got on. I'd never understood it – it was a chemistry thing. Helen usually got on with everyone, and Tim was irresistible to almost all women. But somehow they rubbed each other up the wrong way.

Tim would come into a room, smiling his roguish smile, dispensing charm and witty comments and winning over men and women alike, and Helen, uncharacteristically, would get thin-lipped and leave. She said he was a hipster and a dilettante. She found his piercings and tattoos and his long curly hair unbearable. I never understood why, because she wasn't judgemental about people usually. Although Tim never said so, I think he probably thought Helen was uptight and humourless. He tried his best with her, but after a while he appeared resigned to the fact that family occasions would always be something of a strain, and he came to see us less and less. The two of them could manage to be perfectly civil for birthdays and Christmas and Easter, but that was about it. If he was in town, he'd come and meet me at my office and we'd go out for drinks and dinner, just the two of us.

Hearing Tim was coming gave me the familiar grip of tension I got whenever he came over, knowing that it would put Helen in a bad mood. But, of course, Helen wasn't there. And having my kid brother, whose sunny nature and easy warmth always made me feel better, would be a wonderful thing.

In the course of the afternoon, PC Shah came by.

'We've made contact with the people in your office,' she said carefully, 'and we've had colleagues look at the CCTV and transaction records in Manchester Piccadilly. It seems you were exactly where you said you were.'

'Yes, well,' I said, 'I know you had to do that. I hope now you can put all your resources into finding Helen.'

She nodded and set about filling me in on what they had discovered, which, essentially, was nothing. There had been no blip from Helen's mobile phone and no transaction on any of her or our bank accounts. That scared me, because Helen used her contactless card for even the smallest purchases.

I reasoned that if Helen was out there, and in control of her own life, she'd leave a trail as clear as a path of light. She usually used her debit card as a travelcard on the Tube too, so there'd be a record of her movements, of food bought and accommodation. She also used her phone constantly – texting, ringing people, searching for stuff on the net. But there was nothing. Not a blip, not a sighting on any CCTV camera between us and the station, nor in the station itself. It was now clear she had not headed for the Tube as we initially assumed.

'Have you been looking for suspicious people? Anyone exhibiting odd behaviour? Strangers in the area?' I asked PC Shah.

'We're pursuing a number of lines of enquiry,' she said carefully.

I wanted to scream. I knew she had to give me the official story. Even though my own alibi was watertight, the jury was still out on whether I was involved in Helen's disappearance. The notion that I might have organized a 'hit', got someone to do her a mischief... it seemed implausible and absurd to me, but a small, rational part of my mind knew that to the police it remained the most likely explanation. Middle-class, stable, married women don't just walk out of their houses and disappear into thin air. And the homicidal stranger is a lot rarer than people might imagine.

After PC Shah left, promising again and again to phone me the moment 'anything changed' (I tried not to think about what that might mean), we all stayed holed up in the house, fielding sympathetic calls – Dad was particularly good at shielding me from those. Mum organized a series of activities for the girls, but I could see they were getting cabin fever, so I suggested she take them out to the park for a run around. It was a relief to wave them goodbye and stop having to smile and make conversation. I felt tired to my bones. It wasn't just the lack of sleep, it was the grinding fear, the impotence, my anger at my own sheer uselessness. I lay down on the sofa and closed my eyes and within seconds fell into a deep and dreamless sleep.

It seemed like minutes later that I was wrenched awake by the front door slamming. I heard feet pounding up the stairs and my mum's voice calling Miranda's name in a rise-and-fall song of despair. I struggled into a sitting position and glanced at the clock. It was indeed just fifteen minutes since they had left. As I rubbed my face blearily, Mum came into the living room, her shoulders slumped, with Marguerite by her side, clutching her hand. Marguerite's eyes were wide and serious.

'What happened?' said Dad, coming into the living room, wiping his hand on a dish towel.

'Oh,' said Mum faintly. 'Well, maybe the park wasn't such a good idea.'

'Why? What was in the park?'

'Dogs,' said Marguerite in an awed whisper. 'Big dogs. And police.'

'Well, yes,' said Mum. 'I somehow didn't expect that.'

The police must have come to the same conclusion that I had, that Helen had to be close to home, and had therefore redoubled their local search.

'And pictures of Mummy,' said Marguerite suddenly, brandishing something crumpled in her fist. It was an A5 leaflet, with the picture of Helen in the blue dress, a description of her disappearance and all the contact details of the Missing People organization.

'Posters on every tree,' said Mum, 'and heaps of these leaflets everywhere.'

'I'm sorry, Mum,' I said. 'I didn't know.'

'Of course you didn't. How could you?'

'What's up with Miranda?'

'She was very upset. She ran practically all the way home. She didn't want to talk to me at all.' Mum looked distressed.

'I'll go up and see her,' I said.

'I'll get dinner on,' said Mum. 'Marguerite, are you any good at washing potatoes? Come on.'

Miranda had gone into my room and got my iPad and was sprawled on her bed, watching something on Netflix. She looked up defiantly, ready to challenge me if I chastised her for this flagrant flouting of the rules. I decided to let it go and sat down on the bed beside her.

'Hey, Randa,' I said quietly. 'Not so good in the park, I believe.'

She didn't say anything. She continued to stare fixedly at the screen.

'I know it must be hard to see,' I said as carefully as I could, 'but the police are doing what they can to find Helen. The posters and things might help to jog someone's memory, if they were in the park. . .'

'I know,' she said dully and turned slightly away from me. She was clearly desperate for me to go.

I persisted. 'I know this is difficult, my love. I know you must be worried and scared. The police are doing everything they can to find Helen and make sure she's safe and well. . .'

'It's embarrassing!' she burst out.

'I. . . what?'

'It's so embarrassing. All this fuss, and Helen's face on every tree. When I go back to school, everyone's going to stare and whisper and feel sorry for me. . .'

It took all my strength not to explode at her. Instead, I said quietly, 'Helen is missing, God knows where, and God knows what has happened to her, and you're worried about being embarrassed?'

Miranda stared at me for a long moment. She didn't drop her gaze. She was unbowed, still defiant.

'I just want things to be normal,' she said and then turned back to her screen.

Downstairs, Mum had begun peeling potatoes to make dinner, and Dad and Marguerite were snuggled together in front of the television. I had nothing to do, and no way to vent my fury, so I began loading the dishwasher, banging in cups and plates and jangling cutlery. Mum winced at the noise but let me get on with it.

'Miranda all right?' she asked quietly once the potatoes were bubbling on the cooker.

'If all right means she's a selfish, self-absorbed little brat, then yes, she's fine.'

'She was upset in the park.'

'She says she's *embarrassed*,' I spat, loading the word with as much sarcasm as I could. 'Helen is. . . I don't know where. . . but wherever it is, it's not good, and Miranda is worried about how she'll look to her friends!'

'I think she's struggling to find a way to express how she feels,' said Mum.

'She's perfectly articulate.' I rinsed a crusty plate under the tap. 'She has always been able to express herself clearly. The word she used was "embarrassed".'

'Well, embarrassment and shame are quite closely related.'

'Ashamed?' I almost yelled. 'What the hell does she have to be ashamed of?'

'I didn't say "ashamed",' said Mum. 'And don't yell at me. I said "shame". As in loss of honour or respect.'

'You've lost me.'

'She's eight. She's not really capable of imagining how Helen feels, or what she's going through or even what you feel. It's not because she's bad, it's just how her brain works. All she knows is that two days ago her life was ordered, and she was popular and Helen was a big shot at her school with all the reflected glory that brings. And now Helen's gone and Miranda's a freak, the centre of attention for all the wrong reasons. I don't expect you to understand it, but try not to hate her for feeling what she's wired to feel at her age.'

My mum is a clinical psychologist and knows more about the human mind than anyone I've met. She's retired now, and while she's calm and warm and grandmotherly, she is not averse to telling you when you're plain wrong.

'None of this is easy,' she said, her voice slightly gentler now, 'but being cross with your children for having the emotions of children isn't going to make it any easier.'

We worked together peacefully in the kitchen after that. She gave me some carrots to peel and chop while she got a chicken into the oven. We were about to go through and join Dad and Marguerite in the living room when the doorbell rang; three short bursts and then a long one. Tim.

He enveloped me in a wiry hug. He smelled of fresh sweat and kitchen – a faint hint of oil and garlic lingered in his hair. He wears it loose when he's not working, but because he'd come straight from the restaurant, it was twisted into a loose bun at the back of his neck. I tugged on it affectionately. 'What the hell is this? Is it one of those man buns I hear the hipsters are wearing these days?'

'Don't know, bro,' said Tim. 'You're much more the hipster than I am, with your Soho offices and your folding bike.'

'Come in,' I said. 'The folks are in residence and working miracles as usual.'

Tim grabbed the rucksack he'd dropped at his feet and came into the house. He brought a gust of energy with him. Mum lit up – he's her favourite, although she'd strenuously deny it. Dad got up and Tim gave him a long hug. He's always been demonstrative. Dad and I might, over the years, have become the kind of stiff English father and son who shake hands, but Tim will have none of it. He hugs everyone, including Dad, whenever he sees them. And because he hugs Dad, I've had to too. I'm secretly glad of that. My dad gives great hugs.

Marguerite rushed over, and Tim got down on his knees to hug her and whisper to her. Even Miranda, hearing Uncle Tim's voice in the hall, came hesitantly downstairs and was drawn into his embrace.

He stood up and sniffed the air.

'Already cooking, Mum? Couldn't wait for me?'

'Well, I'm sure it'll benefit from your special touch,' said Mum, smiling.

Tim went into the kitchen with his entourage of women. He turned on the kitchen radio and tuned it to something cheerful, and began chopping, singing and bashing pots and pans about. It sounded as if life had somehow breezed into the house with him. I left them to it, but then Tim yelled to me that he couldn't find the garlic crusher. When I went into the kitchen, he and the girls were dancing to 'Uptown Funk'. Miranda spun around as I came into the room, and her face was a mask of guilt. I managed a weak smile. If Tim could get them smiling and dancing, who was I to stop them?

It felt wrong to see him in Helen's kitchen; he would certainly not have cooked there had she been around. He'd occasionally brought over dishes he'd made at home or at Mum's, but having full access to Helen's utensils, herbs and ingredients – she'd never have stood for that. Was I being disloyal letting him do it now? Would she ever know? I had no answer to that, nor to any of the thousand other questions that whirred around in my head. I could only answer one question with any certainty. That question was: did I want a drink? The answer was yes. Hell yes, I did. A stiff one, and right away. I opened the fridge and took out a bottle of wine, pouring myself an enormous glass. I raised the bottle and my eyebrows in Tim's direction and he nodded, so I poured him a similar glassful. The wine was crisp and cold, with a sharp apple scent. It was delicious and I had to stop myself downing it in one go and pouring another. I should stay sober enough to drive, I reminded myself. In case. . . In case something happens.

I didn't stay sober. I polished off three quarters of the bottle of wine on my own before Tim got dinner on the table. I reasoned that if we needed to drive somewhere, Dad or Tim could take me. All I knew was that for the first time in twenty-four hours the dark waves of panic weren't crashing mercilessly over my head. Somehow, the wine and Tim's presence were keeping them at bay.

We all sat down round the outside table, and I opened a second bottle of wine. The food smelled good, but I couldn't imagine eating. Mum saw I hadn't put anything on my plate and served me a thin slice of chicken breast and a few vegetables.

'You have to eat,' she said quietly. 'You have to. For all of us.'

I put a forkful of the chicken into my mouth, but it dried up and clung to my palate. I took another big gulp of wine to force it down. One mouthful, one sip. It probably wasn't quite the nutritious meal Mum had in mind, but it was something.

Mum went to the kitchen to serve up a dessert of fruit salad and ice cream. Tim asked a few discreet questions about the police investigation and I filled him in as best I could, constantly aware of Miranda listening in.

'So there's no evidence of. . .' Tim stopped. I knew he wanted to say 'foul play', or 'violence' or something.

'Nothing. No suspicious sightings or at least none that can be verified. No one who shouldn't have been in the neighbourhood. And no sign of a. . . scuffle or anything.'

'What's a scuffle, Dad?' asked Miranda. I knew I'd gone too far, saying that.

'A fight.'

'Do they think she had a fight with someone?'

'They don't think anything yet. Helen is missing, but so far there's nothing to say anything bad has happened to her.'

'But she's disappeared,' Miranda said insistently. 'People don't just disappear. They get seen by witnesses or on CCTV. They don't just vanish.'

Tim raised his eyebrows at this rather sophisticated statement from his eight-year-old niece. I shrugged at him.

'TV,' I said. 'They learn about criminal procedure from TV, like we did.'

'What about money things? Cash withdrawals? Card transactions? Can they access those?' asked Tim.

'They're tracking all her accounts, but so far nothing,' I said. 'Which is odd. I can't imagine how she hasn't used a card. She never carries cash.'

'What's cash, Daddy?' asked Marguerite, snuggling in next to me.

'Money. Real money. Ten-pound notes and such,' I said, hugging her.

'And twenty-pound notes?'

'Exactly.' I smiled down at her.

'Is cash like cashback?' she asked.

'What do you mean?'

'Like when we go to the supermarket and Mummy says, "Can I have thirty pounds cashback?"'

I laughed. 'You funny little thing. The things you remember. You can't have heard Mummy say that often.'

'Every time,' said Marguerite.

'What do you mean?'

'Every time we go shopping, Mummy says it. And she puts the money in the secret inside pocket of her bag.'

Tim and I both laughed at this, and Marguerite got the sharp little crease between her brows that foreshadowed a tantrum. 'It's true!' she shouted. 'Don't laugh at me!'

'I'm sorry, sweetie,' I said. 'We didn't mean to laugh. I'm just imagining Mummy hiding away lots of twenty-pound notes in a secret pocket in her bag.'

I know what kids are like – quick to translate a one-off event into 'always' and 'forever'. No doubt Helen had withdrawn cash once or twice, for the window cleaner or possibly the tooth fairy, and Marguerite had remembered it because it was unusual.

'It is true,' piped up Miranda, unexpectedly. I looked at her, surprised. She's generally more likely to torment Marguerite than come to her defence. 'She does get cash every time we go shopping. I always think it's funny when she says she has no money and you have to pay. She must spend it all when we're at school.'

Tim leaned back in his chair, folded his arms and raised one eyebrow. I wasn't quite sure what he was implying. That I didn't know my wife? That this cash thing was in some way significant? I felt an irrational flash of anger.

'Come on, girls,' I said, standing up abruptly. 'Bedtime.'

Miranda and Marguerite put up a token protest, but they were both tired. Mum and I took them upstairs and got them through their bath and bedtime routine. Mum took them both into Marguerite's room and read them a story. I hovered for a while, but the girls were loving their time with Granny, and I was desperate for another glass of wine.

I went to sit on the patio, looking out over the long shadows stretching over the lawn. I heard Mum come downstairs and tell Tim and Dad that the girls were both asleep. There was a soft, murmured conversation in the kitchen behind me. I couldn't hear what they were saying, and I didn't want to. I was so tired, and I didn't want to talk to anyone. I rested my head against the back of the sun-lounger and watched the last glimmers of sunlight on Helen's lavender bushes.

I must have dozed off because when I opened my eyes again it was cooler and properly dark. My wine glass had tipped over in my hand, and there was a wet, dark puddle of wine on the seat beside me. I sat up, confused, cold and headachey. It took a moment, but then the full crushing horror came rushing back in. Helen.

I swung my legs sideways off the lounger and looked around. In the shadows, under the eaves of the house, I could see a tiny red glow, the tip of a cigarette.

'Tim.'

'Evening,' he said quietly. 'I was wondering whether I should wake you.'

'Where are Mum and Dad?'

'Bed. I said I'd sit up and keep an eye on you.'

'Whassatime?'

'About midnight, I think.'

I stood up unsteadily, looking around me. 'I should. . . I should. . . The police. . .'

'I've had your phone with me the whole time,' he said soothingly. 'There've been no calls or messages. I would have woken you the second there were.'

'I need to. . . I should. . .'

'Go for a pee, wash your face and I'll make you a hot drink,' said Tim, standing and coming towards me. 'Then we'll put you to bed for real.'

I nodded. It was quite a relief having someone tell me exactly what to do, even if it was my pipsqueak younger brother.

When I got back from the bathroom, Tim had made me a mug of the special drink Mum used to make for us when we were kids – warm milk with a teaspoonful each of butter and sugar and a sprinkling of cinnamon. Being Tim, he hadn't been able to leave it alone, so the milk was artfully frothed, there was a hint of nutmeg, and the cinnamon had been sprinkled in a perfect geometric pattern. Nevertheless, it was a perfect taste of childhood, and I smiled as I took a grateful sip.

I knew Tim had hoped it would make me sleepy, but I felt remarkably awake. The few hours' doze on the lounger had refreshed me and sobered me up. Tim came and sat opposite me at the kitchen table. He'd found a bottle of something amber – whisky or bourbon – and had an inch of it in a glass with a few ice cubes. I raised my chin at the glass enquiringly.

'Jack,' he said.

'I didn't know we had any Jack Daniels.'

'You didn't. I brought it.' He reached into the rucksack at his feet and produced the familiar square bottle. 'Want one?'

'Yeah, why not?'

He fetched a glass and poured me a drink. I noticed it was smaller than the one he had poured for himself. I was being managed, but I didn't mind. We sat in silence for a long time, sipping our drinks and looking out into the dark garden. I liked the fact that he didn't try to soothe me with platitudes. He was happy to keep vigil with me. Then, unexpectedly, I heard a buzz, the vibration of an incoming text. I jumped, looking around wildly for my phone, but it was Tim's. He drew it from his pocket, read the message, smiled, typed a quick reply and pocketed his phone again.

'Who's texting you at this time of night?'

He touched the side of his nose with a forefinger but didn't answer.

'How old is this one?'

'Shannon? Twenty. Or twenty-one. I forget.'

'Aren't you a bit old for that now?'

'For what? Sex with a hot young thing? Not that I'm aware. I can still keep up.'

'Not that. I mean for. . . not-serious relationships.'

'How do you know it's not serious?' I looked at him for a long moment, and he laughed. 'Well, I haven't bought a ring or anything. But we have fun.'

'What do you talk about? Her homework? What time her dad wants her home?'

'I may be getting old, but not as old as your jokes. Listen, it's fine. I work such unsociable hours, I couldn't expect anyone to put up with that on a long-term basis. Shannon and I hook up, we have sex, we have a laugh. Ultimately she'll get bored and move on, or I will, and no one's heart will be broken.'

'But don't you want more?'

'More what? A life companion? A suburban house? Kids?

Not yet. That stuff is expensive. Not just financially – spiritually. There's so much to lose. I mean, I know they say it's better to have loved and lost than—' He stopped suddenly, horrified at what he had said. 'Fuck. Sam, I'm sorry. I'm an idiot.'

I nodded. He was an idiot.

'I'm sorry,' he said again. 'Look, I can't imagine what you're going through. I'm babbling. I mean, after Leonora, for this to happen. . .'

'Stop talking, okay?'

He did, and mercifully saw this as an opportunity to top up both of our glasses. He wasn't so stingy with mine this time round.

'I'm sorry,' he said eventually. 'I. . . Look, I know Helen and I have never got along brilliantly, but I know you love her and she loves you. I can't imagine how hard this must be.'

'What do you think of her?' I said suddenly. I didn't mean to say it. It just came out. Tiredness, booze, whatever. I'd said it now, and knowing Tim, he'd answer. He did, but he thought for a long time before he spoke.

'She's. . . polished. Very smooth. Beautiful, accomplished, friendly and lovely – don't get me wrong, she's absolutely lovely – but I've never really got to know her. Never seen beneath the surface.'

I nodded. He was being kind. To someone else, he might have said she was a stuck-up bitch.

'Helen came along. . .' I said, then paused and took a big gulp of my drink. 'Helen came along at absolutely the darkest point in my life. I was living in chaos. From moment to moment. I was a mess.'

'I know, I was there.'

'She was neat and beautiful and capable. She was reliable. If she said she was going to do something, she did it. The first time we went out, she talked to Miranda about a book – *Possum Magic* it was called. She'd read it when she was a little girl in Australia. And the next time she saw Miranda, she'd managed to get hold of a copy. She never made a promise she didn't keep. And somehow, out of the turmoil of our lives, she made order. She made things tidy and predictable. She made us all feel safe.'

'I could see that,' he said. 'And I can't imagine how this must feel. I'm sorry, man.' He reached across the table and put his hand over mine. His hand was warm, and I could feel the calluses he'd got from wielding knives in the kitchen.

I heard an owl hoot, in the distance, a few gardens along. It was very quiet.

'What was the word you used? Polished?'

'Yes,' he said quietly. 'Polished seems about right.'

'It's exactly right. A smooth, unbroken, shiny surface. In five years with her, that's all I've ever seen too.'

'What do you mean? Do you mean she's never cried?'

'Never. I've never seen her cry. Never seen her let rip and really laugh either. I've never seen her properly angry, or sad. I've never seen her lose control.'

'You must have had a fight where she yelled at you.' That was, of course, Tim's experience of women. He got yelled at a lot.

'Never. When we disagree, she turns icy and quiet and goes away, then she'll come back after a while and steadily present her case to me. If I lose my temper or raise my voice, she'll walk away until I calm down.'

'Wow,' said Tim, leaning back in his chair. 'I don't know how I'd handle that. A woman who never loses control? Not even when you. . .?' He saw something in my face and paused. 'You did have sex, didn't you?'

I left a long silence. It was a difficult question to answer. Then I said, 'Not for the last six months. Maybe more.'

'What? Why?'

'I wanted a baby. She didn't,' I said baldly. 'For the first few years of our relationship, she kept saying she didn't want to think about it until the girls were absolutely settled and our family was on an even keel. But when I finally begged her to make a decision, she said no. Non-negotiable. Not now, not ever. She doesn't want one of her own.'

'Wow,' said Tim again.

'I asked her to go to couples counselling, asked her if she'd consider talking to someone on her own even, but she refused, point-blank.'

'Have you told the police any of this?'

'Any of what?'

'That you've been having. . . problems.'

'We've not been having problems,' I said stubbornly. 'We're happy. Things have been fine. We'll resolve the baby thing, one way or the other.'

I could have said more. I could have said that I hadn't had sex for six months – with Helen. And that, deep down, one of my darkest fears was that she might have found out about my occasional out-of-town. . . indiscretions. They meant nothing, of course. They're par for the course in my line of work. But I suspected that if Helen knew, she might not see it that way. I can't see how she could have found out, though. I was always so careful. No full name, no contact details. Just the occasional fumble on a business trip. It's something everybody does. What happens out of town stays out of town.

I was aware that Tim was staring at me and that I'd been quiet for a long time. I spoke briskly. 'But she'll come back soon, and everything will be all right.'

He was kind, my brother. He didn't respond, or tell me I was talking bullshit. He topped up my Jack Daniels, encouraged me to drink the special milk before it got cold, and moved us to the sofa. He found us a mindless film to watch, one that involved men growling at one another and a lot of car chases. I let it wash over me, and Tim sat beside me until we both dozed off.

I woke up at dawn, cold, with a stiff neck and a foul taste in my mouth. Tim had stretched out on the sofa opposite and was snoring softly. I got up quietly, went to the kitchen for a drink of water and watched the light creep over the trees. Another day. Nearly forty-eight hours since Helen had been seen.

Once again, I found myself wandering around the silent house. I returned to Helen's desk and opened the drawer with all her paperwork in it. I drew out a recent bank statement from her current account and ran an eye down the list of debits – new school shoes for the kids, a trip to the hairdresser's, books on Amazon, visits to coffee shops, supermarket shopping. I looked carefully at those transactions. Helen did all the shopping, and we ate well – organic fruit, vegetables and meat. She shopped several times a week and often at different supermarkets. She was fussy about ingredients and had never been happy with getting groceries online. Did the costs seem particularly high? I had no idea. It was quite possible that she'd added on twenty or thirty pounds each time, in cashback transactions; I would never have noticed. But why? She had access to the joint account my salary was paid into, and she had a credit card too. If she'd wanted more money, she only had to ask. It made no sense.

I decided to switch her computer on again. Perhaps an email had come in, or there was a document I'd missed which might contain some clue to her whereabouts. I bent over and hit the power switch.

The tower whirred but the screen remained blank. Was it not plugged in? I looked behind and, sure enough, one of the cables had become disconnected. It had fallen down behind the desk. As I pulled the desk away from the wall, I heard an odd thump. A bulky object which had been wedged between the desk and the wall had slipped down and dropped to the floor. I wriggled my hand in to draw it out. It was one of Helen's satchels – a lemon yellow one of which she was particularly fond. It felt heavy, as if there was something in it. I undid the buckles and opened it.

The satchel had different compartments. Helen liked a bag like that – it allowed her to keep everything she needed to hand. She liked a bag to have a pocket for her phone, a space for a notebook and pen, one for her purse and diary and so on. Every compartment in this satchel was full. I drew out Helen's purse and opened it. It contained a picture of me and the girls, and all her cards – debit and credit cards and loyalty cards for a number of stores – but no cash. In the slot next to the purse was her Filofax. I opened the front pocket, and there was her mobile phone. The screen was dark, and when I pressed the power button, nothing happened. Clearly the battery was flat. Other compartments held her make-up bag, a sheaf of notes about an upcoming quiz night at the school, a few tampons, some change, and her keys. Every object I would have expected her to be carrying in her blue handbag was there, in that satchel wedged behind her desk. Why had she left everything behind? And if all of those things were there, what was she carrying in the bag she'd taken with her? Gym things, maybe? Swimming things? If she were headed for the gym or the pool, it was possible she might have left her purse, phone and make-up behind, but her keys? Had she locked herself out accidentally, and had something unspeakable then happened to her? If she'd had no phone, she couldn't have called me, or anyone else. It made no sense though – she knew everyone in our road, and in the wider neighbourhood. If she had been locked out, she could have gone to a friend's and called me from there.

I knew I had to let the police know. There was no point in them continuing to try to track her phone if it was there, or to track her financial transactions when all her cards were on the desk in front of me.

I felt a wave of terror the like of which I had never experienced. Imagining Helen alone, out there in the night, was bad enough, but Helen with no money, no means of contacting us, nothing – it felt as if she was adrift in a sea of blackness and there was nothing I could do to reach her. I hugged the satchel to my chest and tried to get my rasping breathing under control. I had to calm down, somehow. I had to ring PC Shah and let her know what I had found.

CHAPTER FIVE

Sam

PC Shah came up the path to the house a little after seven in the morning. She looked neat and tidy, her hair drawn back under her hat. She can't have had much sleep over the last two days, but she looked okay on it. I, on the other hand, was in dire need of a shower and a change of clothes. I was conscious that my breath must smell awful, and I hadn't shaved. I let her in and we went into the kitchen. The kids and my dad were still asleep upstairs, and my mum was pottering around, making a pot of tea. I looked into the living room, but Tim was still stretched out on the sofa in there. I hesitated for a moment, and then Mum said, 'I'll take your dad's tea upstairs. You two sit in here. There's plenty in the pot.'

She walked out of the kitchen quickly and I was about to turn to PC Shah and offer her tea, when she gestured to the chairs and nodded that we should sit down. I obeyed, and she glanced behind her at the open doors leading into the hallway and the living room. She walked over and closed them both before coming to sit down opposite me.

I was confused. I had rung her and told her about finding the satchel. 'I was on my way over to see you anyway,' she said. I had imagined she would ask to see the satchel straight away, but so far she hadn't mentioned it. Perhaps she needed to wait for forensic officers? I looked at her enquiringly.

'Mr Cooper,' she said, and her face and voice were so serious, I knew instantly that she hadn't come for the satchel. She'd come with news. And it didn't look like it was going to be good news. Bile rose in my throat and I swallowed with great effort. There was nothing in my stomach but Jack Daniels and curdled milk, and I didn't want to vomit that up. I gripped the edge of the table hard.

'I've come to tell you that Mrs Cooper is safe and well.'

I burst into tears like a child and sobbed loudly and uncontrollably, my mouth open. I couldn't stop. The noise woke Tim, who flung open the door and rushed into the kitchen. He stared from me to PC Shah, his eyes wild.

'What's happened?' he demanded. 'Sam?'

'They've found her,' I managed to say. 'And she's okay.'

'Where?' Tim said to PC Shah. 'Where is she? Why haven't you brought her home? Is she hurt?' He was being forceful, and I wanted to tell him to calm down, to be polite to this woman, my saviour.

But PC Shah didn't seem offended. She held up a hand to Tim to slow his flow of words. 'And you are?' she asked.

'My brother, Tim,' I said, finally managing to get my breathing under control.

'Could you sit down?' she said to Tim, firmly.

He obeyed, pulling out the chair beside mine and leaning forward on his elbows towards her. 'Where did you find her?' he asked insistently.

'We didn't find her,' said PC Shah carefully. 'Mrs Cooper became aware of the media campaign surrounding her disappearance. She attended a police station and supplied them with identification. The officers performed a safe-and-well check.'

'A. . . I'm sorry. . . A what?' said Tim sharply.

'It's standard procedure when someone has been reported as missing. We ascertain that they are safe and well, and that they are not in any danger.'

'What police station? Where?' I asked, standing up. 'Tim, can you drive me?'

'Mr Cooper, can you sit down, please?' said PC Shah.

'Why?' I said. 'I want to go and get her. Can't we talk in the car?'

PC Shah didn't say anything. She continued to sit at the table and look at me. Tim had obviously seen something in her expression because he put a hand on my arm and drew me back down into my seat. When I was sitting down, PC Shah spoke quietly.

'Mrs Cooper doesn't want to return home. She made it clear to the officer she spoke to that she left of her own free will, and she doesn't want her whereabouts to be revealed.'

'What the fuck. . .?' I said. 'What? That's not true. There's something very wrong here. Someone's made her say that. Or the officer got it wrong, or it wasn't her.' I stood up again, knocking my chair down. 'It wasn't her. Of course it wasn't her. How could the person prove it was her? All her ID is here. Look, I'll show you.'

PC Shah started to protest, but I beckoned her and went into the conservatory, where the contents of the satchel were strewn all over the desk. 'See? Look. Her driver's licence, her cards, everything's here.'

'Where's her passport, Mr Cooper?' asked PC Shah quietly.

'I showed it to you guys before,' I said, feverishly yanking open the desk drawer. I pulled out all four of our passports and handed her Helen's green passport holder. She opened it and leafed through it, before taking the passport out of the holder and handing it to me.

The top right-hand corner of the passport had been cut, and every page had the word 'Cancelled' stamped on it. It wasn't even a British passport – it was Helen's original Australian passport, in her maiden name.

'I don't understand,' I said.

'She took her current passport with her,' said PC Shah. 'That was the identification she showed at the police station. I've seen a copy of it. I'm so sorry, Mr Cooper.'

We must have been making an almighty racket because the noise had brought Mum, Dad and the girls downstairs. Tim looked up and saw them all standing in the living room, looking in on us. He stepped past me and began to walk towards them, heading them off before they came in.

'Tim!' I called after him. 'The girls. . . don't. Not yet. I'll talk to them.'

He turned to face me, his back to the others. 'I'm going to say she's alive and that we don't know any more than that. Is that all right? Just so they don't think. . . you know.'

I nodded. He went into the living room, pulling the door closed behind him.

I turned to PC Shah. 'I need to talk to her,' I said. 'Please. You know where she is.'

'I'm sorry,' she said again. 'There is nothing I can do.'

'But this is a police matter,' I said angrily. 'She went missing.'

'And she's been found. No crime has been committed. I'm afraid it's no longer a police matter. We've informed you that she's safe and well, and the case will now be closed.'

'No crime has been committed?'

'It's not illegal to go missing. If a person over eighteen wants to leave their home and move on, they're within their legal rights to do so.'

I stared at her, quite unable to form words.

'Again, I'm so sorry,' said PC Shah. 'This must be very hard.'

There was a blankness to her expression. She'd been kind and sympathetic through the whole process of searching for Helen, but something had shifted. She was there to convey the news and to protect Helen's privacy. All her sympathy for me had evaporated. What had Helen said to the police officers? Or was this merely PC Shah making assumptions? If a well-to-do woman walks away from her home, there must be a reason why. Maybe that nice husband is secretly a violent psychopath? Was that what she was thinking? Was that what everyone would think?

I sat down heavily in the chair at Helen's desk.

'So what happens now?' I said quietly.

'We'll issue a statement to the press saying Mrs Cooper has been found safe and well. That'll run in the papers and on all the media sites.'

'And that's it. My wife has gone.'

On Helen's desk there was a small misshapen clay bowl which Marguerite had made in nursery. Helen had filled it with paper clips. I turned it slowly. 'Just gone. What about us? Our lives? What about everything she's left behind? And what do I tell my kids?'

'Mr Cooper, I'd strongly suggest you seek counselling for you and your daughters,' said PC Shah. 'And I'd contact the Missing People organization if I were you.'

'Why? Will they be able to find her for me?' I grasped at this tiny glimmer of hope.

'No. They'll tell you what I've just told you, that she has a right to go missing, and they'll protect her right to anonymity.

But there are a lot of people there who'll understand what you're going through. There are support groups. . .'

'Support groups?'

'And legal advice. You may have some. . . challenges, if you had joint finances and so on.'

I knew people went missing, but they were people with mental-health problems. Addicts. People who were being abused. Not people like Helen. Not middle-class women with good marriages, homes, busy lives, families and friends. Something somewhere was very wrong and I was going to have to work out what. However, it was clear that PC Shah, and most likely the Metropolitan Police, were going to be no help at all. I stood up.

'Thank you,' I said, offering her my hand. 'I. . . I need time to get my head around this.'

'This is an. . . unusual case.' PC Shah hesitated and then added carefully, 'I do urge you to seek help. I've made a list of useful numbers for you.'

She took out a notebook and tore out a page, which she handed to me. I took it. Her handwriting was neat and rounded, like that of a good child. Not unlike Helen's, as it happens. She shook my hand then, and I saw her out.

Mum and Dad had put a film on the television for the girls, and we met in the kitchen. I told them what PC Shah had said. Dad blustered and asked a lot of questions. Once I'd explained it to him twice over, he stood up and paced up and down the kitchen.

'This is mad,' he said finally. 'It's got to be a mistake. Maybe we could do our own media appeal. Exclude the police. They're clearly useless.'

'Alan. . .' said Mum. 'Helen is a grown woman, of sound mind. The police will have done all the necessary checks. This is what it is.'

'It is what it is?' Tim turned on Mum furiously. 'You can't say that. This is Sam's life.'

'Keep your voice down, Timothy,' Dad said, and the three of them rounded on each other, bickering viciously in muted tones.

I sat down at the table and rested my head on my folded arms. I felt my brain closing down, and the pain and panic of the past two days began to recede. I felt, curiously, nothing. Nothing at all.

It took them all a few minutes to realize I was not participating in the conversation. Mum was the first to catch on, and she broke off what she was saying and came to sit beside me at the table.

'You must be exhausted,' she said, stroking my hair. 'Listen, this is what I suggest. We tell the girls that Helen is safe and unhurt but we aren't sure when she'll be back. But mainly, we reassure them that there's nothing to worry about. Then Alan and I will take them home with us for the weekend. We'll plan lots of fun activities and keep them busy. It's Friday, so they can skip school today and go back on Monday. And Tim will stay here with you.'

I wasn't looking at her, but from the firmness of her tone I was sure she was giving Tim The Look – something we both remembered well from childhood. He wouldn't dare argue with The Look.

'You need time, Sam. Time to think about this, time to sleep and recover. And then we can all get together on Sunday afternoon and make some practical plans. How does that sound?'

'Fine, Mum,' I said. 'That sounds fine.' I had no idea if it was fine. All I knew was that, more than anything in the world, I wanted everyone to stop talking and go away and leave me alone.

Miranda

Helen's gone away. She hasn't been killed by a bad man. She's just gone, and Granny says she probably isn't going to come back. I understand that. It's like when Mummy died, I knew she wasn't coming back. I was only three, but I knew. People used to say, 'Miranda is so little, she won't understand,' and I would say, 'I do understand. Dead is dead.' People didn't know what to say then.

This is different, because Helen definitely isn't dead. Granny promised me that and she doesn't lie. She's just gone. Marguerite is quite confused about it all. She keeps saying, 'When will Mummy be back?' That's annoying, but then she's such a baby, what can you expect? Granny has asked me to try and be patient with her, so I haven't yelled at her or anything, but I wish she'd stop asking. I believe Granny when she says 'probably never'. What scares me the most is that I think soon Marguerite will start asking 'Why?' and then I will have to tell everyone why and they are all going to hate me.

I knew as soon as Dad didn't come to pick us up and they couldn't find Helen, you see. I knew it was my fault.

This is the story. Daddy has an iPad, and sometimes he takes it to work and sometimes he leaves it at home for me and Marguerite to play on. Helen sometimes lets us have a go on it for half an hour while she makes the dinner. The problem is, Marguerite and I don't like the same games. I like Minecraft, and she likes those babyish Disney games. So we always fight about what we're going to play. Helen makes us take turns, but one day she was tense and busy, like she was thinking about something else, and when Marguerite said she wanted to choose the game, Helen said yes. When I said it was my turn to choose, she said all crossly, 'For heaven's sake,' which wasn't an answer, and she walked quickly into the kitchen. I tried to take the iPad away from Marguerite, but she made that whiney noise she does when she's about to scream like mad, and took the iPad through to the kitchen.

Anyway, then I knew I wasn't going to get my turn to play. When I said Helen was cross, I meant she used her 'I'm disappointed' voice and got that line between her eyebrows. Helen never shouted or lost her temper. I've seen other parents do it – yell at their kids, and go all red in the face. I even saw Conor in my class get a smack once for running into the road without looking. Helen never did any of that. I think Marguerite and I are quite good children anyway, so she didn't have to shout and scream, but actually her disappointed face was usually enough to make me feel bad. I didn't need shouting.

So on the day of the iPad, I went to sit on the sofa and I was really cross. It was unfair, and I couldn't wait to tell Daddy. I could have asked to put on the television or I could have read a book or gone to my room to play, but I stayed on the sofa. I wanted to play Minecraft and anyway it was my turn. After a while I got bored, so I started balancing on the arm of the sofa on my stomach, trying to hold my whole body straight like a plank. We're not supposed to do that. Helen says it's dangerous and we'll end up damaging the fabric. But she was in the kitchen with smarmy Marguerite, so I did it anyway. I got the balance wrong and nearly tipped head-first over the arm of the sofa. I managed to catch myself in time, but when I was hanging with my head down, I saw Helen had put her handbag down the side of the sofa (she liked to keep it there 'out of the way'). I heard something inside go 'ping', like a phone does when you get a text message or email or something.

Now, one of the number-one rules in our family was: 'Don't Go Into Helen's Handbag. It is a private space and it's rude to dig in other people's private things.' Still, I wasn't going to open it. I would just take it to her. Helen liked to have her phone with her all the time, so I thought it might make her happy with me and then she'd ask Marguerite to let me have a go on the iPad.

I pulled the bag out from next to the sofa and carried it through to the kitchen. Helen was stirring something on the cooker.

'I heard your phone make a noise in your bag, so I brought it to you,' I said, and I put the bag on the counter next to her.

'You must have been mistaken,' she said, not looking up from the cooker. 'My phone's right here.' And it was – she had it on the counter next to her and she was typing a text with one finger while she stirred.

But right as she said that, there was a ringing sound. Not Helen's phone on the counter. A ringing sound from the bag. I looked at her and she looked at me.

'There's a phone ringing in your bag,' I said.

Her face changed then. It went all pale and funny. She turned off the cooker, and she grabbed her bag and rushed out of the room. And that was when everything went wrong.

If she'd let me pick the game on the iPad, I wouldn't have been in such a bad mood. And if she'd said thank you to me for bringing her the bag, instead of rushing off without saying anything, I might have left it. But I didn't. I followed her as she ran upstairs holding her bag.

'Why do you have another phone?' I said.

She didn't answer, just went into her bedroom and shut the door. I stood outside the door and kept yelling questions.

'Whose phone is it? Why didn't you answer it? Does Daddy know you have two phones?'

When she didn't answer, I didn't stop. Helen was always so calm, and she always answered questions. Because I was angry at her, I liked the fact that she was all freaked out and I couldn't stop.

'Why aren't you answering me?' I said 'Are you not supposed to have that phone?'

Suddenly she pulled the door open, grabbed my arm and dragged me into the room. She held my arm tightly.

'You're hurting me,' I said.

'You never know when to stop, do you?' she said.

I had never seen her face like that – it was blotchy and tense and she looked furious. Helen was never furious.

I don't cry much, and I didn't cry then. I could tell that the phone was what had made her so upset. I stood still, but inside I was terrified. I had never seen Helen like that. It was like a bad spirit had come and taken over her body. I don't know how long we stood and stared at each other. It felt like forever. The she talked, very quietly.

'You are not going to tell your dad about this. You are not going to tell anybody at all. You are going to forget you heard a phone ringing. There is no phone. Do you understand?'

I did understand. I didn't tell anybody. I wanted to, but I didn't. And it was only a week after that that Helen disappeared. Maybe I said something in my sleep, or maybe she thought I was going to say something. But she went away forever and she's never coming back, and it's all my fault.

Sam

I slept. Twelve, solid, dreamless hours. It was like being knocked unconscious. Once Mum and Dad had packed up the girls' things, loaded Miranda and Marguerite into their car and gone, Tim pushed me upstairs and into the bathroom. I showered, shaved and brushed my teeth, and then went to lie down on the bed for a minute. When I woke up, it was dark outside. I didn't jerk awake, as I had every time I'd managed to sleep since Helen disappeared. I gradually came to consciousness, lying on my back on the bed, staring at the dark ceiling. I was cold – I hadn't managed to get under the covers before I passed out. I looked over at the digital clock – 9 p.m. I listened to the silent house.

Slowly, I rolled over and sat on the edge of the bed. I felt numb, but I was experienced enough in emotional pain to know that that state was temporary. I suppose it's like when a shark bites your leg off. You might intellectually know that your leg is gone, but there's a lull before the pain and the bleeding and the realization that you'll be spending the rest of your life without a limb. I was in the lull. It was such a relief to be freed from the crushing fear that Helen had been abducted and murdered that I wasn't able to move on to the new storm of emotions that awaited me – anger, bitterness, heartbreak. My wife had abandoned me and my children, had walked away without a backward glance and had made certain that I had no way to reach her and ask her why. She'd left me with a mess to deal with, and no mistake.

I couldn't think about that just then, however. I had a pressing need to pee, I was thirsty, and, I realized, for the first time in days, hungry. Very, very hungry.

When I got downstairs, Tim was sprawled on the sofa. He'd managed to connect up my old Xbox and was playing some shoot-'em-up videogame I'd forgotten I owned. He looked up as I came in.

'Crikey, you slept,' he said. 'I came up and checked on you a few times, but you were unconscious.'

'That's what forty-eight hours without sleep will do. Now I'm wide awake and I'm bloody starving.'

'That I can fix,' he said, pausing for a moment to save his game and then jumping up and heading for the kitchen.

He went for speed over style and produced a plateful of fluffy scrambled eggs, bacon and multiple slices of toast in a matter of minutes. I sat at the kitchen table and wolfed it down. When I'd finished, he dumped a big mug of tea in front of me and sat down across the table.

'You're not going to sleep for hours now,' he said. 'Shall we go out?'

'I can't,' I said automatically, and simultaneously realized that of course I could. The girls were with my parents, and Helen was. . . Well, who knew where Helen was? 'Scratch that. Of course I can. Where shall we go?'

'I'd say somewhere local, but you probably don't want to run into your neighbours in the pub tonight.'

'Good point.' I thought for a while. 'Well, there's always the Bell and Anchor. It's nearer Mum and Dad's than here, so we're unlikely to bump into anyone we know. And I'm sure they have a late licence.'

'Cool,' said Tim, getting out his phone.

It took him moments to arrange a cab, and I had just a few minutes to change out of my crumpled shirt and comb my hair. Soon we were in the back of a minicab, moving quickly through the dark streets.

It felt unbelievably strange. It wasn't just that my life was in ruins – I was still dazed and the reality of that hadn't hit. It was more the oddness of the moment: Tim and me, off to get pissed late at night, like we used to when I came home from uni. He was already working as a junior chef, so we could only go out when he knocked off work. We had lots of late-night sessions at the Bell, although in the old days we'd have gone there on the bus from Mum and Dad's and come back on the night bus with greasy cones of chips. Or sometimes we'd walk, weaving along slowly, putting the world to rights, singing old Smiths' songs.

Now we were in the back of a Mercedes, gliding swiftly towards our destination. I was wearing a fitted shirt from Hawes & Curtis and I had a crisp wad of twenties and a selection of credit and debit cards in my wallet. I felt as if I were standing in a hall of mirrors, at a weird junction between a life I had known years ago and my life now. Except of course my life now no longer existed. In a funny way, all that existed were the deep leather seats, the cloying odour of artificial pine from the air freshener which dangled from the rear-view mirror, and the intermittent flashes of neon from shop windows as we passed by.

We pulled up outside the Bell and Anchor. It was quiet, although clearly still open. It had always been a raucous local pub, often with a local duo playing live music in the corner, known for its good food and friendly ambience. But in the intervening years, it had obviously changed hands. Tim and I glanced at each other, unsure if we wanted to see the changes, but we were there now, so we went in.

It was unrecognizable. The old floral carpet and leather banquettes were gone, replaced by stone-coloured walls, scrubbed tables and discreet art. It had become an upmarket gastro-pub, but one of the large chain ones that try to look quirky and unusual and somehow fail. Tim picked up a menu from a nearby table and I saw him wrinkle his nose in disgust. He named the brewery that had bought the pub. 'Same menu everywhere you go,' he said, 'and it's all shit. I'm glad we're not planning to eat.'

'I'm sure their beer is fine,' I said, and we took a seat at the bar.

The young barman strolled over, looking bored and supercilious. We were one of only five or six people in the place, and I'm sure our late arrival had ruined his plans for nipping out for a fag, or hitting on the waitress or something. Tim tried to ask about the various ales on tap, but the barman clearly had no idea what he was talking about. In the end, Tim chose a pale ale for himself and a bottled wheat beer for me.

We got our drinks and found a table in the corner. Tim tasted his gingerly. 'Better than I expected,' he said. 'Someone here knows what they're doing.'

We drank in silence for a while, then Tim said, 'Listen, you're going to have to give me a lead here, mate. Talk about it or not talk about it?'

'Not talk about it right now, I think. I haven't got my head around it. At the moment I'm tremendously relieved that she's not dead. I haven't quite grasped the other part yet.'

'It's a fuck-up and no mistake.'

'That's true,' I conceded and gulped down two thirds of my beer in one go. I looked over to the bar, thinking I'd signal the barman to get me another, but he'd vanished.

I could see Tim wracking his brains for a safe topic of conversation. He'd already tried football, although neither of us were huge fans. He'd mentioned films he'd seen recently, but with a hectic job and two small children, I'd not been to the cinema in months. He knew not to try politics – our views had never coincided.

I was starting to feel antsy. My drink was finished now, and I definitely needed another one, but there was no one behind the bar. I stood up abruptly.

'Going to look for that useless barman,' I said. 'I'll get you one too.'

There wasn't a single staff member in the whole bar section, so I walked through into the dining room part of the pub. There was a woman standing behind the reception desk, obviously checking over the reservations for the next day.

'Can we get some service in the bar, please?' I said, and my voice may have sounded louder, ruder, sharper than I meant it to. I really wanted a drink.

She looked up quickly. 'Sam?' she said, and her face registered real shock.

I stared at her. Sometimes, when you see a person out of context, or looking slightly different, even when you know you know them your brain can't make sense of what it's seeing at first. After an endlessly long few seconds, I realized who it was. It was the red-haired mum from Miranda's class, who'd taken the girls back to her house the night Helen disappeared. Whenever I had seen her at school, she'd been wearing jeans, or casual skirts and tops. Here she was wearing a tailored blouse, pencil skirt and heels, and her hair was drawn back in a neat bun. I guessed she must be the manager.

She'd obviously seen my confusion because she pointed to herself slightly awkwardly and said, 'Lara.'

'Lara, of course, I know. I'm so sorry. You caught me off guard,' I said.

'Same here. I was surprised to see you too. Still, nice to see you here. We heard the good news at school.'

'Yes,' I said. This wasn't a conversation I had expected to have tonight.

'Is she here with you?' Lara craned her neck to look past me into the pub.

'No,' I said, but I didn't elaborate.

The silence grew between us, enormous and awkward. I could feel Lara's enquiring eyes examining my face closely. Then she shook her head and said quickly, 'I'm so sorry. I'll get someone to come to the bar and serve you now.'

She walked away quickly, and I went back to Tim in the bar.

'Well, that's a cock-up,' I said as I slid into my seat.

'What is?'

'One of the mums from the girls' school is the manager here.'

'Oh?'

'It's obvious that all they've heard at the school is what they've seen on the news – that Helen is safe and well. No doubt they're all expecting her to turn up on Monday morning as if nothing happened.'

'Ah. That is a cock-up. What are you going to do?'

'I don't even know what drink I'm ordering next. I don't have a clue what to do about the utter wreckage of my life. I mean, how do I tell people? I didn't think I'd have to face it this evening, that's for sure.'

'Do you have to face it this evening?'

'Well, I have to say something. She's clearly already realized that something's not right.'

'And you reckon she'll be at the school gates on Monday spreading gossip and rumour if you don't tell her the truth?'

'I don't think she's like that – she's not like some of them. She's sweet, actually. A single mum, bit of a hippie, I think. But still, if she tells people she saw me out in a bar the night Helen was found. . .'

'I'll talk to her,' Tim said suddenly.

'You? Why?'

'Damage limitation. I'll tell her a carefully managed version of the truth.'

'Like what?'

'That Helen is away for the moment, but she'll be back soon.'

'But that's not true.'

'Isn't it?'

I realized he was genuinely asking me. 'Do you actually think she's coming back?' I asked him incredulously.

'Well. . . I thought it was likely. I mean, people don't just walk away from everything, from their whole lives like that, do they? I figured it was a nervous breakdown or something, a blip. That you guys would work it out somehow. Don't you think so?'

I sat back in my chair and stared at him. 'Do you know, I actually don't. Not for one second, not for even half a second since PC Shah told me she'd gone voluntarily has it crossed my mind that she might come back.'

'Really?'

'Do you know Helen?'

'Not like you, but I have a reasonable idea of who she is.'

'Have you ever known her to be less than certain about something? To do something half-heartedly? Do you remember the level of detail that went into planning our wedding?'

Tim nodded ruefully. As best man, he'd been on the receiving end of endless emails and spreadsheets.

'Helen always does everything to the best of her ability. To the best of anyone's ability. She's the ultimate perfectionist. So I can tell you one thing for sure. If Helen has disappeared, it'll be the best fucking disappearance the world has ever known. Jesus, now I think about it, she even stocked the freezer with food before she went. She knew she was going. She planned for it. And she's definitely not coming back.'

That stunned Tim into silence. He sat back in his seat and had a long drink of his beer. He'd been drinking a lot slower than me and still had some left. Until that moment, I don't think he had grasped exactly what had happened to the girls and me. But Tim is nothing if not adaptable. He rallied, and smiled.

'That might be true, but no one else needs to know that yet, do they? They need an explanation, and as Helen isn't here to give one, you get to choose what you say.'

'So what do I say?'

'Whatever you think will make people ask the fewest questions.'

'I don't know. I don't know what to say.'

'I think saying she's not well is okay. She isn't well.'

'Isn't she? I have no idea.'

'These are not the actions of a sane person.'

'Maybe not,' I conceded.

'I think you should say—' At that moment Lara came over to our table, carrying two beers.

'Sorry to interrupt,' she said, putting them down. 'Tristan seems to have gone AWOL, so I thought I'd bring your drinks over myself.'

She smiled at me and then smiled enquiringly at Tim. He couldn't help himself. He engaged his weapons-grade roguish grin, stood up and offered her his hand.

'Tim Cooper, Sam's younger brother,' he said, leaning lightly on the 'younger'. 'Thanks so much for the drinks. Do you have time to sit down and join us?'

She took his hand lightly, but I saw her smile switch off like a light. She clearly wasn't taken in by bad-boy flirtatiousness. I was surprised, and it made me like her a little more.

'Thanks, but I still have a few things to take care of,' she said. 'Give me a shout if you need anything else.'

'We definitely will,' said Tim, unaware that his charm wasn't working. Lara walked quickly away.

'Jesus,' I said, more impatiently than I meant to, 'do you have to hit on absolutely every woman you meet?'

'I wasn't hitting on her. Much,' he said, sipping his drink and watching the doorway through which Lara had gone. 'But she's very sexy.'

Was she? I genuinely couldn't drum up the energy to think about it.

Suddenly, I was tired. Achingly tired. I was irritated by Tim, deeply uncomfortable at seeing Lara, and the fact that we had come out to a pub on this night of all nights seemed awful, wrong and callous. I could imagine it becoming a story that would come back to haunt me once everyone knew what had happened, that

Helen had left voluntarily. If Lara happened to mention that the very night I heard she was gone, I was out on the lash. . . It didn't bear thinking about. I felt a wave of panic as powerful as nausea. I stood up suddenly and my glass rocked and splashed beer on the table.

'Let's go,' I said.

Tim looked up at me, surprised. He waved a hand as if to indicate our full glasses but then quickly understood and got to his feet too. 'Sure. I'll go and pay,' he said. 'I'll get a cab at the same time.'

He took his drink to the bar with him, and I sat back down, shaking. I kept half an eye on him as he chatted and smiled with Lara, handing her his card while ordering a cab on his phone and gulping down his beer. At one point, as he bent to key in his PIN, Lara glanced over his shoulder at me. She was too far away for me to read the expression in her eyes, but it looked like concern or pity rather than revulsion.

Tim straightened up, gave Lara a last big grin and then swept over to me. He had me out of the door and into a waiting cab before I had time to blink, and then we were gliding through the sleeping streets, back to my empty house.

CHAPTER SIX

Sam

I woke up at five the next morning. That is to say, I found myself sitting bolt upright, wide awake, in the bed, my heart racing and my breath jagged and raw in my throat. The pain that hadn't hit the night before? It was here. Its force was devastating, crushing and extreme. I was in the middle of what must be a panic attack, I realized. Either that or I was having a heart attack and my daughters were about to lose a parent for the third time.

What lunacy was this? The police had told me that my wife of five years had voluntarily walked away and I'd just accepted it? I remembered telling Tim in the restaurant that I knew she wasn't coming back. Well, that was absurd. She was Helen. My wife. Stepmother to my children. My companion and friend. Our lives were inextricably entwined. There was no way she could just have walked away. What the hell had I been thinking?

I got out of bed and leaned on Helen's dressing table, willing my breathing to calm down. There had to be an explanation. At best, if there was a best in this appalling situation, she was ill. Mentally ill. Possibly following a blow to the head, amnesia or an undiagnosed manic episode. I remembered reading somewhere that two thirds of homeless people have mental-health problems. Not that Helen was homeless. Was she? Could she be out on the street? Surely not. But what if my terrors were right? What if, somehow, she'd found out that I'd fooled around a little? What if she'd seen me somewhere, or someone at work had ratted me out? It was very unlikely, but not impossible. If I could only get to her, find out what she knew, explain it all away, we could fix this thing.

I couldn't believe I'd gone a whole night without looking for her, without going to the police and insisting that they let me speak to her. How could I have believed them, or my mum? What did they know? They didn't know Helen like I did.

It was so obvious to me now. I had to go to the police and make them tell me everything. I had to make them understand that she was ill, or had been kidnapped or something. They had to let me talk to her or take me to where she was.

Clothes. I had to get dressed. I was in a T-shirt and pants. I pulled on some jeans and slipped my feet into trainers. No time for socks. I headed for the door. Before I flung it open, I remembered Tim was in the house. I needed to be quiet or I'd wake him and he'd try to talk me out of it. I eased the door open and tiptoed out into the hallway. I could hear Tim's soft snoring and glimpsed him through Miranda's half-open bedroom door, sprawled face down on her bed. He was out for the count. I crept downstairs, grabbed the car keys and let myself out of the front door.

The street was silent, and even though it was only just past five, the sun was already fully up. It was going to be a beautiful day. I slipped into the driver's seat of Helen's Prius. I'd decided to take her car because my Range Rover would have woken the whole street. I sat for a moment in the pristine interior, breathing in the faint scent of her perfume. Other people left litter or personal detritus in their cars – hairpins, a chewing-gum wrapper, a receipt from shopping – but Helen's was as clean and impersonal as the day she brought it home from the showroom.

The engine barely purred as I turned the key. I reversed into the road and drove through the empty streets to the police station. There was one sad, tired-looking male officer on duty behind the desk when I got there. It had obviously been a rough night. Or maybe a rough life. Luckily, he didn't seem to have any pressing demands on his time. He looked up as I walked in, and I saw him take in my rumpled T-shirt and unbrushed hair. He sagged a little lower.

'Hi,' I said, trying to be as brisk, sane and professional as possible. 'I'm Helen Cooper's husband.'

If I'd hoped that this statement would spark comprehension and a rush to help me, I was out of luck.

'She's missing,' I said. 'It's been all over the press.'

He nodded then, still unsure what I was talking about. I looked around and saw a copy of last night's *Evening Standard* lying on a chair in the waiting area. Helen's face smiled up at me from the bottom right-hand corner of the front page. I picked it up and shoved it over the counter at him.

'Here,' I said, jabbing the picture with my forefinger. 'This is my wife.'

He looked down at the picture and the caption below it. 'It says here, sir,' he said slowly, 'that she's been found safe and well.'

'That's what they told me yesterday,' I said. 'But she's not.'

'She's not?'

'You see, she just walked away from the house. With nothing.

And now they tell me she's fine but she doesn't want to come home. It's not possible.'

'Well, sir, people do sometimes just—'

'Not Helen,' I said. 'Not Helen!' And I realized I was shouting.

He took a half-step back from the counter and his face shut down. 'Sir, if you're going to be abusive. . .'

'I'm sorry,' I said quickly. 'I'm not abusive. It's just. . . you don't know her. She's the most, calm, organized and sane person. She wouldn't just. . . walk away. It's not possible. Something terrible must have happened to her.'

He looked unsure, and I saw him glance down at the newspaper article. 'It does say here—'

'I know what it says,' I barked, and dimly realized I was shouting again.

'Sir, the police wouldn't have halted the investigation if they thought there was any possibility—'

'What if there is a possibility? What if they've made a gigantic mistake? What if the woman who walked into the police station wherever it was wasn't Helen? What if she's being held somewhere? Against her will?'

'Sir, we do have appropriate safeguards in place. They would have confirmed her identity. I am sure it was her. There's been so much press around this case. . .'

He didn't finish the sentence, but I knew what he meant. Helen's face had been on every news service. They wouldn't take a chance on this. If they got it wrong and stopped looking for her and she ended up chopped into bits and stuffed into a suitcase – well, the implications wouldn't be good for the police, would they?

I tried to stay calm. 'I am sure you can understand, though, that unless I see her with my own eyes, and talk to her, it's impossible for me to believe that.'

'I can understand that this is difficult, sir—'

'It's not difficult, it's impossible. I need to see her. There must be a central record-keeping system. You must be able to tell me where she is. What police station she reported to. She must have given some contact details to someone?'

He started to look uncomfortable. 'Sir, could I ask you to step back from the desk a little?'

'Why?' I said. 'Can you answer my question? Can you call up the details on that?' I gestured to the computer beside him. I was leaning on the counter, my palms spread wide. I wasn't shouting or being threatening. He just wasn't doing anything. I wanted to shake him.

'I'm afraid I wouldn't be able to gain access to that sort of information, and. . .'

I could have finished that sentence for him too. Even if he could, he wouldn't give it to me. Who knew what kind of crazed, violent lunatic he was dealing with?

The fight went out of me and I stepped back from the counter as requested. I felt wobbly suddenly, as if I might faint, and I backed up until I felt my legs touch the row of plastic bucket chairs which were bolted to the wall opposite the desk. I sat down and rested my head in my hands. When I lifted my eyes, the officer behind the desk was looking at me with less distrust and more. . . well, sympathy was probably pushing it. Benevolent indifference.

'Safe and well,' I said. 'What does that even mean?'

'We ask a series of questions, make some checks.'

'Like what?'

'We try to find out why they went missing. If they've been subjected to violence, abuse or bullying, if there's been drug or alcohol abuse, if they've been a victim of crime or if they've committed a crime, that sort of thing.'

I wanted to object. None of those questions had any bearing on

Helen's life. They sounded like the sort of questions you'd ask of someone who lived in a chaotic environment – the sort of people you saw yelling at each other on terrible documentaries and chat shows, baring their missing teeth and raising threatening, tattooed fists. Not people like us. I knew that thinking like that made me seem a massive snob, but I couldn't reconcile it.

'None of that. . . none of that sounds like Helen,' I said finally. 'She barely drinks, she's never taken drugs. There was no violence in our home. And yes, I know that, as the husband, I would say that, but it's true.'

He didn't say anything, just let me sit there and stare quietly at the mottled linoleum floor between my trainers. 'The police,' I said finally, slowly. 'The police who did the check. Would they know where she is?'

He hesitated for a moment and then said, 'They would have made sure she had a fixed address, and they'd have offered her any help she might need.'

'Could you at least find out for me where she is? Or put me in contact with the officer she spoke to? I'm sure if I could speak to her. . .'

'Sir, all I can do is put you in contact with the Missing People charity. They can offer you support and tell you what you can do. But I do know that if a missing person says clearly that they don't want their whereabouts disclosed, then we have to respect that. It's their right.'

'I beg your pardon?'

'It's their right,' he said. 'People are allowed to go missing. It's not a crime. They have a right to privacy.'

'I see,' I said, and I surprised myself at how calm I sounded. 'PC Shah said that too, when she came to tell me about Helen. She said it was her right. And what about my rights? What about the rights of my children? What are we supposed to do?'

'I know this must be difficult, sir. . .' he began, and I'm sure he would have come out with a wonderful platitude. He never got to finish the sentence though, because I launched myself out of the bucket chair, threw myself half over the counter and punched him squarely in the mouth.

PART TWO

CHAPTER SEVEN

SIX MONTHS LATER

Sam

Writing-icing, my arse. You can't write with it, or draw with it. It gives you blobs and gaps and a massive cramp in your thumb from trying to squeeze it evenly, and a genuinely shitty effect. I stood back from my efforts and flexed my aching hand. I'd spent ages drawing the Harry Potter design on paper. I'd driven out to Costco in rush-hour traffic to buy the pre-baked, plain, iced cake I'd ordered. I'd even managed to copy my design reasonably well with a sharp knife-point on to the pristine icing on the cake. And then I got out the tubes of icing and it all went to shit.

It was Miranda's ninth birthday and the first I'd had to do on my own. She was already furious with me. I had failed in every possible way with the plans for this birthday. I had spent far, far too much money on presents – more than I could afford, and about three times more than she had ever had in previous years – but I knew it still wasn't going to make her birthday okay. It didn't matter what she got, all she would be thinking about was what she wasn't going to get.

She wasn't going to get one of Helen's masterpiece cakes – a miracle of flavour, design and ingenuity. She wasn't going to get gorgeous food, perfect decorations or an impeccably planned disco party on our patio. She was going to get a trip to the cinema with her friends, then dinner at the local pizza place and this cake. That was if I didn't hurl the cake against the wall in frustration.

I went to the fridge and fetched another beer. I stood staring at the cake for a long while. Harry Potter looked as if someone had done a face-melting spell on him. I dug around inside a drawer and found one of Helen's icing knives, similar to a painter's palette knife, and skimmed his face off. I absent-mindedly ate the icing off the knife. It didn't mix too well with the lager, but I was past caring. I picked up a toothpick and drew the face into the icing again. It didn't look much better, and I gouged so deeply that a few cake crumbs came to the surface, marring the whiteness. The number of beers I'd drunk may have had something to do with my general uselessness. I could have rung Mum, or even Tim (he's no baker, but even he would have been able to do better than this). But I couldn't bring myself to ask for more help. It felt like all I did was ring my family up and whine for help. I could do this. I could.

In the end it took a Google search and the simple revelation that resting the tubes of icing in a cup of hot water made them easier to work with. I managed to do a halfway decent job eventually. If you squinted your eyes and concentrated hard, you'd probably guess it was Harry Potter. Or at least Harry Potter as reimagined by Quentin Blake or Salvador Dali. I wrote 'Harry Potter' in wobbly letters below the image, then realized I should probably have written 'Happy Birthday Miranda' instead. Too late.

It was late, actually. I glanced up at the kitchen clock. It was 1 a.m. It was always 1 a.m. I swigged the last of the beer from my bottle and carefully carried the cake over to the fridge. It took some reshuffling to make a space big enough to slide the cake inside. Two beers had to come out to make room. Oh well, it wouldn't do for them to get warm. I carried them through to the living room and slumped on to the sofa.

I turned on the TV, muting the sound and choosing a twenty-four-hour news channel.

I made it to halfway through the second beer before I dozed off – that is, the second beer I'd taken from the over-full fridge. It was possibly my fifth of the evening, if anyone was counting; I know I wasn't. There have been a lot of fifth beers recently – a fact I can see reflected in my bloodshot eyes every morning and in the undeniable softness around my middle. The fact is, without the fifth beer, there is no sleep. With the fifth beer, there are a fitful, dream-ridden few hours, usually on the sofa, before I wake because the dregs of the bottle have spilled in my lap or when the crick in my neck becomes too painful. Without the fifth beer, there are just the long hours of night, sitting trapped in the house with my sleeping girls, staring into the black pit of my bottomless rage.

Fuck me, that sounds melodramatic. It is melodramatic. I'm not falling apart. I'm functional and everything. I work. I look after the girls. I get them up in the morning and get them to school and they're clean and they do their homework. Things are harder financially, of course. We always used to rely on the bonuses I earned from signing big accounts. But now I'm working reduced hours – or normal hours by most people's standards – so I'm not bringing in those big cheques anymore. I'm having to fork out an eye-watering sum for extra childcare too. The ends are still meeting – just – but there's not much overlap.

Yes, things aren't the same as when Helen was here. Marguerite is always tired – with breakfast club and after-school club, she spends ten hours a day at school. Our meals are basic to say the least – a lot of ready-made lasagne, and pasta with pesto (although I always try to make them eat some salad with it). And while I keep up with things like laundry and bills, the housework defeats me. I can't seem to get round to all the hoovering, dusting, bed-changing and bathroom cleaning that happened as if by magic when Helen was here. I do my best, but the house is starting to look dingy. Things pile up on tables, the carpets have a coating of fluff, and the kitchen floor is always slightly sticky. I wish I could afford to get a cleaner in, but there isn't that flexibility in the budget right now.

My parents have been amazing; they looked after the girls through the summer, but then my mum fell over in the garden and broke her leg, and I had to make other childcare plans. We still go to see them most weekends, though, and they never fail to lift our spirits.

Tim has done his bit too, in his own, inimitable Tim way. He turns up some nights, about once a fortnight, usually without warning. If he finishes early in the restaurant or isn't working, he'll sometimes just get in the car and drive over from Bristol. He always brings an expensive bottle of spirits – good vodka or whisky – and we sit together and drink and talk until the early hours. He crashes on the sofa. In the morning he delights the kids with a fancy breakfast and then walks them to school before heading back to Bristol. It's with Tim I feel most able to be myself. I can swear and rage and fall apart. With everyone else, I have to keep playing the part of someone who's keeping it together. Tim is also the person I've talked through my finances with. He may look like a trendy lightweight, but he's surprisingly prudent with money, and good at financial planning. When it became clear that there was a gap between my reduced income and our expenses, and not in a good way, I turned to Tim for advice. At his suggestion, I sold the Range Rover and the Prius and bought a ten-year-old Ford Focus. With depreciation, I got next to nothing for the two cars, beyond being able to pay back what I still owed on them.

So we are limping along, but it's a very different life to what I had before. I used to travel all the time for work, all over the UK and Europe. It was glamorous and jet-setting, with a lot of socializing, pressing the flesh, and winning clients over with bottles of champagne and charm and bullshit. I loved it and I was good at it. It had its perks too – bright, shiny, professional women who hung on my every word, laughed at my jokes and were sometimes keen for a little post-meeting fun. And I never had to worry about what was going on at home, because Helen kept all that humming along seamlessly.

Now I spend my evenings going over lists of spelling words and ironing little pleated skirts. I find myself digging through piles of wet washing in the machine first thing in the morning to locate socks, and 80 per cent of the text messages I get are from the school, reminding me about flu-vaccine forms or homework policy. I feel snarled in domestic detail, like I can't take a step without some banal, ridiculous problem to do with the girls or the house tripping me up. But at the same time, if I ignore that stuff, the whole structure comes tumbling down and we end up living in chaos. To be honest, it makes me want to punch someone, but, as we know, that hasn't worked out too well for me in the past.

I was lucky that I didn't get sent to prison for assaulting a police officer. I was let off with a caution, and they were much kinder to me than I deserved. They put me in contact with Missing People, who have been amazing and have given us boundless support. They suggested that the girls and I might benefit from some family therapy. So I dutifully drive us all to see our counsellor every few weeks.

We sit in a room and Tana, a well-meaning and kind woman, tries to get us all to talk. Marguerite goes over immediately to the toy corner and plays with the family dolls. If Tana tries to engage with her, she reverts to baby talk. Miranda sits in silence, arms folded, and glowers at us all. I can't be upset with Miranda for her anger. Because however angry she is, it's nothing compared to my all-encompassing, crippling rage. In the beginning, I used to babble on, trying to get them to start talking, but it made things worse. Now I answer Tana's questions about how things are going with practical, impersonal responses. Yes, they seem settled in after-school care. No, we haven't planned a holiday this year (I can scarcely pay the gas bill, let alone buy flights to Greece). Yes, Marguerite is sleeping a little better. But as for talking about Helen? About how I feel? No chance. Not in front of the girls, and not to this nice, middle-aged woman, who probably isn't qualified to deal with my detailed fantasies of murder and humiliation.

She suggested to me that it might be helpful to keep a journal.

'Write down what you feel,' she said in that soothing, condescending therapist tone, 'it's valuable to keep a record of how you feel in the moment. You can look back on it then, and see how you've moved on.' She recommended the same thing to Miranda, who nodded, but gave no indication if she planned to do it. I haven't pressed the issue with her. She can write if she wants to.

The next week, Tana asked me how I was getting on with the journal.

'Good,' I said guardedly, 'it's helping, I think.'

She looked delighted. 'You can bring it to our sessions for discussion, if you like.'

I don't like. I see the value of writing down what I'm thinking and feeling, but I'm certain that what is in these pages is not for Tana's genteel eyes.

You see, I want to kill Helen. No. That isn't enough. I want to torture her, and humiliate her, and torture her some more, and then kill her. She took my broken little family and put it back together, and then she smashed it to pieces again. And this time I have not a hope of repairing it. How can I make the world safe for two little girls who have lost a mother not once but twice?

But to kill someone, you have to know where they are, and she is gone. Vanished off the face of the earth. In the days and weeks following her disappearance, I searched her computer with forensic care. I checked every email, every web search. I read every single document. Nothing. I went through everything in her recycle bin. I became convinced that she must have deleted websites off her search history, so I rang a guy I knew from school, Clive, who had his own computer-security consultancy. I paid his astronomically high rate and he came round to the house and ran a file-recovery programme on Helen's PC. Still nothing. However she'd planned her escape, she hadn't done it from that PC, that was for sure.

I logged into her Facebook profile on my phone and set it up to bleep for any kind of notification and alert me if someone logged in from another device. Every time my phone trilled, I jumped, but it was always someone tagging her in a post ('Miss you, **Helen**. Xxxx'). There were no new posts from her at all.

But then I woke up one morning from an alcohol- and tear-sodden sleep to discover that her profile had disappeared. It had been deleted in the night and I hadn't heard the bleeps of the alert. With it I lost five years of posts and memories, pictures of us together, of the girls, of parties we had attended. They weren't images we'd taken ourselves (those, naturally, were filed in strict date order and impeccably labelled, on Helen's PC and in our Cloud storage). The pics that were gone were the chance ones others had taken – the eye-witness snapshots of what I had believed to be our happy family. It felt like another death.

It took a few days for it to dawn on me that I had been using Helen's Facebook profile to spy on her, setting alerts to see if she logged in. She had probably done the same to me. Wherever she was, she'd have known I was obsessively checking it, and she'd deleted it in the middle of the night to snap that last possible thread of connection. It was the first, incontrovertible contact from her, if you could call it contact. Was it the opposite of contact? It was so callous. Yet what did I expect? I rang Tim and told him. He was the only person I had told about my Facebook snooping.

'It's for the best, mate,' he said gently. 'You know it is. There was no way you were going to learn anything that would make you happy.'

'I know. But it was all I had.'

'You didn't really have it though, did you? It's not like you were supposed to be on there. She knows where you are. If she wants to contact you, she will. But she seems to be making it clear she doesn't want to. I know there's no point in saying "move on", but, well. . . move on, Sam. What you were doing was very fucking unhealthy.'

He was right, of course, but that didn't stop my obsessive online searching. I trawled through hundreds of pages of searches for Helen Cooper, Helen Knight (her maiden name), H Cooper, Helen Rosemary Knight, and every possible variation on her name. About 90 per cent of the returns were for other Helen Coopers and Helen Knights. Of the ones that referred to her, I found little to help me. There was some work stuff from when she first joined Superhero Inc., the company where we'd met and where I still worked, the odd fundraising page for a fun run she'd done, and a few mentions in the local press for events she'd organized. She'd left Australia in 2009, and I found almost nothing that pre-dated her move to the UK. All there was was a listing on the alumni page of the university in Brisbane where she gained her degree, and a blurry photo from a school sports day of a long-legged Helen in brief shorts, aged maybe fifteen or sixteen, grinning at the camera and holding up a medal. That photo was on the school's website and had been posted as part of a larger batch from school sports days through the decades. She didn't appear in any others on the site. I set up Google alerts so I got an email every time someone posted online about a Helen Cooper or a Helen Knight, but I got so many emails, all irrelevant, that I deleted the alert after a while. Wherever she was, whatever she was doing, she wasn't making a new digital trail as Helen Cooper or Knight.

In those early days I also tried talking to the women Helen would have considered her close friends – other school-gate mums, a few people from her yoga class she mentioned frequently. These were all women I thought I knew; we had socialized together, visited one another's homes, even in a couple of cases taken holidays together. But every one of them reacted with coolness. They all said the same thing: that Helen had been perfectly normal up until her disappearance. They had had no cause for alarm and had not thought she was stressed or behaving out of character in any way.

The oddest thing about those chats with Helen's friends was that none of them had known her well, or at least they weren't admitting to having known her well. They talked of lunches and play dates, of shopping trips and planning meetings. None of them could offer me any insight into her emotional state. Perhaps they knew more than they were letting on, but I didn't get a sense of that at all. The anecdotes they shared showed a version of Helen I recognized: the public Helen – polite, perky, efficient, but always, somehow, separate. I couldn't imagine her curled up on a sofa having a good cry or a bitch, or admitting a weakness. God knows, she had never done it with me.

It hadn't struck me so forcibly at the time, but she came into my life without any of the usual baggage – no old friends, family or acquaintances, no old boyfriends or favourite local haunts. Of course she hadn't been in the UK long when I met her, but most people coming to London have at least someone they know, and they certainly have people back home that they are in contact with. Helen seemed serenely independent and became so swiftly and seamlessly absorbed into my life with the girls that I didn't give it much thought. It wasn't as if she wasn't sociable – she collected people everywhere she went. We had a full and busy social life, but all the people we were close to were either friends of mine whom Helen had adopted, or friends she'd made through the girls' school.

And I think it was at that point, pondering Helen's lack of a past – on my thousandth-millionth-infinityth go through the facts, as Marguerite would have called it – that I fell asleep, with the ticker tape of the twenty-four hour news, rolling endlessly across the screen. Which meant that when Miranda woke up on the morning of her ninth birthday, she found her father asleep, sitting slumped and fully clothed on the sofa with a beer bottle in his hand. That's how precious and unique memories are made. There's another jewel for you, Miranda, my darling. One to remember forever. My pleasure.

I had, thank God, had my shit together sufficiently to arrange all the wrapped gifts on the coffee table in an impressive pile of guilt and money, so Miranda came in and gave me one look of undisguised loathing before falling to her knees and ripping the paper off the biggest gift in the pile. As I struggled to my feet and headed for the bathroom, I couldn't help remembering Helen's birthday rituals of ceremonial present opening at the breakfast table: cards first, paper opened and folded, not ripped, and each gift savoured, with the giver carefully thanked.

I splashed water on my head and rinsed my mouth out, combing my hair and avoiding my own eyes in the mirror. I grabbed a fresh T-shirt from the bedroom and returned to the living room with my most cheerful grin plastered in place. Miranda was tearing the paper off each present as if she was searching for something. Once she'd opened it, she'd glance at the object and then cast it aside, as if it definitely wasn't what she was looking for, then she'd grasp the next one and the process would begin again.

Marguerite came stumbling down from her bedroom, her curls in abundant disarray. She blindly pushed against my thighs until I sat down in an armchair, and then climbed into my lap. I wrapped my arms around her and rested my cheek on the top of her head. 'Ouch, Daddy,' she said fuzzily. 'Scratchy chin.'

'Sorry, poppet,' I said.

We sat together in silence, watching Miranda lay waste to her presents. At one point Marguerite leaned forward off my lap and reached out a finger towards a Monster High doll and Miranda whipped around and snarled at her.

'Miranda. . .' I said mildly.

'They're not hers,' she said fiercely. 'They're mine. She can open her own stupid presents when it's her birthday.'

With this, she tore the paper off the last gift, a carefully chosen sparkly top, which I had hoped she might want to wear to her party in the afternoon. The look on her face was pure scorn when she held it up, and she flung it behind her on the carpet.

She surveyed the carnage around her of ripped paper and tumbled gifts. 'Where's the DVD of *Into the Woods*?' she said coldly.

I could have said, 'Granny and Grandpa have got it for you. You'll get it at their house at the weekend,' which was true, or

I could have tapped my nose conspiratorially, recalling an old, shared joke. But I was exhausted. I smelled like a sweaty brewery and I found everything about this scene so wrong and so sad that I stood up, tipping Marguerite off my lap, and said, 'As if all these presents weren't enough! You ungrateful little cow. You haven't even managed to say thank you. I don't think you deserve a party.'

The problem is, she acts so grown-up. Helen and I always used to joke that she was eight going on thirty-nine. But of course she isn't. She's a little girl who lost the only mum she really remembers. And now she was being told off on her birthday morning by her old soak of a dad. Miranda looked at me, her face white and her eyes big and afraid. It was in that moment I realized I hadn't so much said those words as bellowed them. I had really shouted at her. She scrambled to her feet and ran to her room, slamming the door, and Marguerite, who had been sitting where she had fallen at my feet, let out a siren wail and began to cry. I had to fix it all, somehow, before the party in the afternoon. I had to rescue this, or it would end up being the worst birthday of Miranda's short life, and she'd already had a couple of awful ones. I was so tired and suddenly also hot and claustrophobic. I went over to the window, ignoring Marguerite's sobs, and opened the curtains, wanting to fling the windows wide and breathe some fresh air. Outside, it might as well still have been the middle of the night. The clouds were low and black, and rain fell in unrelenting grey sheets. I rested my forehead on the clammy windowpane. Fantastic.

Lara

It's all about logistics, isn't it? Frances had to go to Miranda Cooper's party, even though she didn't really want to ('She's not very nice anymore, Mum,' she'd said carefully). It was at the big cinema complex off the ring road, and I couldn't face trekking all the way there on the bus, then home, then back again a few hours later, especially since the heavens had opened and we'd have been better off in an ark rather than a bus. Frances was definitely too old for me to come to the party with her, and even if that hadn't been the case, you don't invade a nine-year-old's party with a boisterous three-year-old in tow. I decided that even though it would be hell on earth, I'd take Jonah to the indoor soft-play place in the same complex. He could tear around and burn off some energy.

I dropped Frances off in the cinema foyer and smiled at Sam, who was looking pasty and puffy around the eyes. Miranda was equally pale, and she was glowering, although she managed half a smile when Frances handed her her present. 'Thank you,' she said carefully and clearly. It made my heart ache.

'Six o'clock at the pizza place?' I asked Sam, who nodded. I hesitated for a second. I felt bad leaving him to the mercies of a herd of small girls and wondered whether I should offer to stay and share the responsibility. But then Jonah went off at top speed across the foyer, heading straight for the exit, roaring like a jet engine as he went.

The soft-play place was every bit as awful as I had thought it might be. Overcrowded with cabin-feverish toddlers, it was like one of those brawling taverns in a Western film. After a few near-misses and one particularly tense stand-off with a nasty older child and his bullish father, Jonah and I escaped out into the fresh air.

The rain had abated and we played happily in the muddy park until the big fat drops began to fall again. I looked at my watch. The film would be coming out shortly and they'd be heading to the pizza restaurant. Perhaps we wouldn't embarrass Frances too much if we ate at another table. It'd keep us out of the rain and I could get the chefs to give Jonah a lump of pizza dough to play with.

'Come on, little bear,' I called. 'Pizza!'

I loaded him into the pushchair and galloped back down the hill. We went so fast and the rain and wind were so dramatic that we were both laughing and pink-faced when we stopped under the awning in front of the pizza restaurant. The owner was standing in the doorway, his face a mask of consternation. I was about to go inside when he held up a hand to stop me.

'We are closed. Sorry,' he said.

I glanced over his shoulder and saw three waiters with brooms and mops, attempting to sweep puddles of rainwater out of the door. The whole restaurant floor was awash. Clearly their location at the bottom of the hill was to blame – it simply couldn't cope with the torrential rain that had continued almost without a break since the early hours of the morning. The owner looked mortified and apologetic. 'I can do takeaways,' he said.

'Not to worry,' I replied. We could do without pizza. But then I thought about Sam, coming out of the cinema with six little girls all expecting a pizza meal and birthday cake. There wasn't another restaurant anywhere nearby, and, anyway, it was pouring with rain. Miranda hadn't looked too happy at the start of her birthday party, and Sam had looked strained, rumpled and possibly hung-over. This was gearing up to be an unmitigated disaster.

At that moment I saw Sam come out of the cinema complex holding Marguerite's hand. The bigger girls trailed behind him in an excited knot, chattering animatedly, probably about the film. Miranda had a little colour in her cheeks and was smiling. I stepped towards him and waved. I could see Frances' lips tighten when she saw me, because I was being 'an embarrassment.' Never mind, I was used to that.

'Little hitch,' I said brightly, and I saw the smile fall from Miranda's face like a shadow. I took Sam's elbow and led him a little way from the girls.

'The restaurant's closed,' I said quietly. 'They've had a flood.'

I don't know what I thought he would do. I suppose I expected him to behave like most people would under the circumstances – maybe swear, then come up with a solution. A bus trip to McDonald's or something like that. But he sort of slumped, and his eyes went red. I genuinely thought he was going to burst into tears.

'Sam?' I said, concerned.

'I don't know what to do,' he whispered. 'I don't know what to do. Today's been such a fuck-up already.' He paused for a long second. 'I can't take them back to the house. It's a tip. When I asked Miranda if she wanted her party at home, she told me she'd be ashamed to have people in our house because it's so messy and dirty. I don't know what to do,' he said again, and his voice cracked. And then he did cry, or at least a tear escaped and rolled down the side of his nose. He brushed it off clumsily, and then he looked up and stared into my eyes, and his whole face was a mask of pleading. 'Please help me,' he said in a hoarse whisper. 'I've got nothing.'

There was no time to think. I spun on my heel and turned to the little knot of girls who had crowded round Jonah's pushchair and were talking to him in exaggerated baby talk.

'Right!' I said briskly. 'We've got a tiny emergency, but we have a solution. The restaurant has had a bit of a Noah's Ark situation, and it's flooded.'

There was a collective wail. 'But. . .' I cut in with my best crowd-management voice, 'we've got a plan. They can still do takeaways, because the kitchen is upstairs from the main part of the restaurant, so we're all going back to my house, and we'll have a rainy-day picnic on the living-room floor!'

The girls started to chatter and squeal all at once and bombarded me with questions. I dealt with each issue one at a time. Sam and I would ring all of their parents and let them know about the change of plan. Sam would take three girls in his car, and the other three would come with me and Jonah in a taxi. Look, I was ringing for one now. I spoke firmly to Sam, as if he too were one of the children, and sent him into the pizzeria to order the takeaways. I even reminded him to collect the birthday cake from the proprietor, with whom he had left it before the film. I took all the girls back into the cinema complex to use the loo, and then managed to load everyone into the various vehicles. En route, I rang my mum, to warn her of the impending invasion.

She's a legend, my mum. By the time we got to our house, she had cleared the living-room carpet of toys and spread picnic blankets. She'd made a couple of jugs of juice and squash and put crisps in bowls (thank heavens I'd done grocery shopping that morning), and she'd even tuned the radio to Radio 1 and cranked up the volume so music blared through the house. The girls all spilled into the living room, chattering and giggling. Miranda still looked pale and miserable, but her friends were so full of bubbling excitement, it was hard for her to stay upset.

I got them all on to the picnic rugs and we opened the pizza boxes. While the girls ate and talked, I put together a quick playlist on my iPod, closed the living-room curtains and turned on the fairy lights we have draped around the fireplace. With Taylor Swift singing and plates full of pizza and crisps, the girls looked happy to hang out. Jonah was delighted at this turn of events and he wandered between the girls, eating off all of their plates and putting up with being hugged and cuddled wherever he went.

'This is so cool, Miranda!' said Florence, biting into a huge, floppy slice of pepperoni pizza, and I saw Miranda allow herself a small, twisted smile. It was kind of cool – a bit hippie and bohemian, not at all the sort of thing Miranda would have chosen, and a million miles from the perfection Helen might have engineered, but in a funny way that was probably better. There was no way this birthday party would remind her of any of the ones that had preceded it.

I realized I had forgotten Sam altogether. I looked around for him and he was standing awkwardly in the doorway, still holding the big, grease-spotted cake box, looking with bewilderment at the scene before him. I went over and took the cake box out of his hands and motioned for him to follow me to the kitchen. Mum was already in there, and she had a pot of tea brewing.

Sam sat down at the kitchen table and my mum plonked a mug of tea in front of him. 'Thank you,' he said weakly. 'I'm not quite sure what happened, but you averted disaster, and somehow Miranda's having the time of her life.'

'I think that depends on us staying in here, out of the way, and not going through to be lame parents in the sitting room,' I said. 'Just let them hang out. It's only for an hour or so, and then their parents will be here to collect them.'

He nodded and sipped his tea. 'Thanks again,' he said, and I could see he had regained his composure. He'd plastered on his usual, charming, slightly distant mask again. I felt a small pang of regret. It had been revealing and interesting to glimpse the real, damaged man behind the smooth facade.

Everyone at school keeps going on about how well he's doing. He drops the girls off every day, on time and neatly dressed, and looks smart and together himself. All of those school-gate mums believe that their husbands are useless morons, so any level of competence from Sam seems to astound them. They can't quite believe he can get the girls into their uniforms and into school punctually. Their own husbands couldn't do that if their lives depended upon it, they maintain.

I know from experience that sometimes making sure everyone's hair is brushed and that you're on time is the only, wafer-thin, barrier between you and total meltdown. It's having to do the little, practical things that keeps you going. In public, Sam appears to be functioning far better than might reasonably be expected. But in that moment outside the pizzeria, I had glimpsed the real Sam. The one who doesn't sleep, who weeps and rages, who possibly drowns his pain in booze, or videogames, or porn or God knows what. I suppose the school gate isn't the place to let that side of him show. I'm sure he has friends and family with whom he could let his guard down. . . people who will support him when it all gets too much. I hope so.

He was chatting to my mum now, easily and charmingly, about books. She was smiling. She tends to regard all men with amused detachment, as if they're a species of large and dangerous animal – nice to look at, but you wouldn't want one in the house.

I heard the music being turned up in the living room – a Justin Bieber song was playing – and lots of whooping and excited chatter followed. Sam looked towards the door enquiringly.

'Dancing, I think,' I said. 'Unless we hear glass breaking, I'd leave them to it.'

'Will the neighbours not complain?' he asked.

'The ones on the left-hand side mow their lawn at seven on a Sunday morning. And the ones on the right have a seventeen-year-old who owns one thrash-metal album and a set of drums, or at least that's what it sounds like. No one complains about noise in our road.'

I managed to make him laugh. He looked handsome when he smiled. But sitting that close to him, I could see the damage. He'd gained weight and he was in need of a haircut. His nails were chewed and looked terrible. And while the girls were always neat, the T-shirt he was wearing was frayed at the collar and had a bleach stain near the hem. Helen would never have stood for a garment like that.

Helen. She hovered like a ghost in the room, ever present, never mentioned. I glanced down and saw Sam was still wearing his wedding ring. Of course he was. He was still married. When would that change? Could it change? Can you divorce someone who has simply chosen to disappear? I had no idea. Marc and I never married (thank God). And what had Sam done with all of Helen's stuff? I knew she had left everything behind when she disappeared. If someone dies, you would dispose of their things, wouldn't you? But Helen wasn't dead. Was Sam living in a house that was still full of Helen's clothes and toiletries? Or had he had a giant bonfire at the bottom of the garden?

I realized Sam had asked me a question. I'd been so busy speculating about where Helen's Clinique had gone, I'd tuned out.

'Sorry,' I said. 'Miles away.'

'What time is it?' he asked. 'Only the mums are coming at six, so I thought we should probably do the cake if it's getting close to that.'

I glanced at my watch. 'Five-forty, you're right.' I jumped up and fetched plates and napkins and a knife, and dug a lighter out of the kitchen drawer (one of the few relics left from Marc's last whirlwind visit to our lives).

Sam carefully lifted the cake out of the box. It was a generic Costco cake, but on the top he'd iced a detailed picture of Harry Potter flying on his broomstick.

'That looks amazing,' I said, looking over his shoulder. 'I didn't know you could draw like that. And especially not with that writing-icing. It's a bastard.'

'Thanks.' He smiled at me as he studded candles in a crescent shape above Harry's head. 'All those years as a graphic designer had to be worth something. It wasn't easy, though. You're right, that icing is a bastard. Many Anglo-Saxon expletives were uttered during the icing of this cake.'

'Well, excellent job. I bet Miranda will be totally thrilled with it.'

'I doubt it,' he said, and there was real sadness in his voice. 'I mean, nothing about this birthday is right and if Helen. . .' He ran out of words as soon as he said her name. He clearly wasn't up to dropping her casually into conversation yet.

'So what's the plan of attack then?' I interrupted cheerfully. 'Shall we put the cake on the table and then orchestrate the Happy Birthday singing, or enter in procession, already singing?'

'Oh, orchestrate,' he said, recovering quickly. 'A procession of singing parents with cake. . . it is actually possible for nine-year-old girls to die of embarrassment, you know. We don't want to be responsible for their early demise, do we?'

I picked up the plates and led him into the living room.

The impromptu disco was in full swing. A few of the girls, Frances included, were doing self-conscious jiggling from leg to leg, but Miranda and one or two others who do ballet or tap or jazz dancing were giving it their all and showing off their moves. Jonah was bouncing up and down on the spot like a tiny, enthusiastic pogo dancer. Dodging a high kick from Florence and a flamboyant pirouette from Lily, I got the plates to the table and waved my arms to get their attention. 'Cake time!' I called, and turned down the music. They gathered round expectantly and Sam brought in the cake and placed it in front of Miranda. There was a moment of silence and then Jonah let out a long, husky, appreciative 'Wow.' No one else said anything.

I should have known, of course. They're nine-year-old girls, not three-year-old boys. They attend a nice, middle-class school and have mummies who either bake as a kind of competitive sport or buy in designer cakes because they can afford to. Those girls could spot a bought, supermarket cake and bit of homemade icing at a hundred paces. And they weren't impressed. They were well-brought-up and polite though, so after a silence which was far too long, Lily piped up in a bright, stagey voice, 'That's a brilliant cake, Mr Cooper! So cool! Blow out your candles, Miranda!'

Miranda managed a desultory puff and the girls all cheered. They stepped away from the table immediately, and Frances started the music up again. I turned to Sam. 'Let's cut it up in the kitchen and wrap slices in napkins. They can take them home.'

The mums all came promptly, and the girls left happy and enthusiastic, chattering about Miranda's cool picnic party. Even if the cake hadn't been a winner, I thought we could declare the party a success overall.

I said goodbye to the last of the mums and daughters and turned back into the house. Sam was in the kitchen washing up, and Mum had gone to sit in the living room, where Marguerite and Jonah were flopped on the sofa side by side, watching a Disney film. When I glanced in, they both had that glassy stare which suggested they'd be asleep within fifteen minutes or so. Frances and Miranda were nowhere to be seen. I assumed they'd gone upstairs to play in Frances' room.

But when I stepped out into the corridor, I saw a shadowy figure standing in the darkness at the bottom of the stairs. Miranda was staring up at a framed photograph on the wall. She jumped when she saw me coming towards her.

'You all right?' I asked.

'Is this you?' She pointed at the picture.

It's a black-and-white image from years ago – years and years ago. I must have been about nineteen. I was dancing in an avant-garde piece at the Edinburgh Festival. In the picture, I'm wearing a sheer white leotard and I'm in a pose one could only describe as 'crane about to take flight', poised on the toes of one bare foot, the other leg high and bent in front, arms raised like wings. There's a diaphanous scarf twisted around my body. I look improbably thin, lean and muscular, and my hair is flying around my head like an electric cloud. Marc discovered the image in a box of old pictures and dug around until he found the negative. He had it blown up and framed. I don't look at it often. It reminds me how earthbound I have become.

'Yes,' I said shortly.

'I didn't know you danced.'

'Not any more. I did, when I was younger. Even professionally for a while.'

There was a long silence, and she said in a small, quiet voice, 'I'm a dancer too, you know.'

There was something in the way she said 'dancer', with a hint of reverence in her voice, that let me know how serious she was.

'I do know,' I said. 'I remember seeing you in the babies' class, when you were little. Even then you were very good.'

She nodded, acknowledging the compliment. 'Why did you stop?'

Why had I stopped? There was no money in dance, obviously. So I'd started working in bars and restaurants to make ends meet between gigs. And gradually the gigs had got further apart and the bills had got bigger, so I did more and more restaurant work. I was very close to being a restaurant manager who danced a bit, rather than a dancer who worked in restaurants, when Frances came along, and then I'd put my dancing shoes away forever.

I looked again at the girl in the picture. She was so strong and fiery and certain. Even though the image was in black and white, she crackled with colour and energy. I didn't recognize her at all.

'It was a long time ago,' I said lamely. I knew this wasn't an answer to Miranda's question, but I didn't have one that wouldn't do damage to her dreams.

There was a noise behind me, and Sam came out of the kitchen, drying his hands on a tea towel. Miranda turned and saw him, and her face tightened.

'Almost time to go, sweetie,' he said. She turned back to the picture and ignored him. He came up behind us to see what we were looking at.

'Who's that?' he asked.

'It's Lara, *obviously*,' said Miranda, her voice dripping with weary sarcasm, even though she'd asked the same question not two minutes beforehand.

'Really?' Sam leaned in. I felt suddenly self-conscious – I was all but naked in the photo and you could, if you looked closely, see the faint shadow of my nipples through the white leotard. Sam spent a long moment examining at the picture. 'Exquisite,' he said quietly, almost to himself. 'The shadow of the collar bones, and the line. . . beautiful.'

I remembered that he'd said something in the kitchen about being a graphic designer. He was obviously viewing the picture with an artist's sensibility. And anyway, it wasn't a picture of me. It was someone I had once been, for a tiny, fleeting moment when gravity did not apply.

CHAPTER EIGHT

Sam

Debit: We had a row about the presents first thing.

Credit: I apologized and we made up.

Credit: She liked her sparkly top after all and she almost smiled when I said she looked pretty before we left.

Credit: All the girls liked the film.

Debit (massive): The flooded restaurant.

Credit: Lara's amazing rescue and the impromptu pizza picnic.

Debit: My lame cake.

When the girls were in bed and I was on beer number three, I ran through the events of the day in my head. I'd emerged if not unscathed, at least just lightly scratched. I thought I'd probably come out with a positive balance where Miranda was concerned. It had all looked ropey in the morning, but when she had had her bath and climbed into bed, I got a quiet 'Thanks, Dad' as I switched off the light. I didn't turn back to her, or try to begin a conversation. I paused in the doorway and said, 'It was an absolute pleasure, chicken,' and then I went.

The day was something of a milestone, I think. Not just because it was the first major family occasion we'd got through without Helen, but because there were moments when things felt, if not normal, at least not tinged with insanity. There were moments when I smiled, even laughed, when the girls relaxed and had fun. And it was all thanks to Lara. She's a nice woman, and her mum's a darling too.

I should have been tired after all the upheaval of the day and the late night the night before, but somehow my sleep cycle has got reversed. No matter how grindingly exhausted I am during the day, I can't sleep at night. In the early days after Helen went, I spent hours online but also hours roaming the house and obsessively going through her things. I searched her clothes, checking every pocket. I went through every bag and suitcase and every drawer, looking for a clue. I needed to know two things. I needed some hint as to why she had gone. Was there someone else? Where was she? Was she ever coming back? And secondly, I needed to know how she had done it. When I told Tim this, he laughed and said something about stable doors and bolted horses.

'There's no point, mate. The fact that there's no obvious trail says to me that she planned it carefully. And that suggests that she doesn't want to be found.'

He stopped short of saying 'Move on' that time, but he'd made it clear that was what he thought I should do. But I couldn't. Helen had always seemed so open, so transparent and honest, I had never had reason to doubt her or be suspicious. I had access to her PC. I knew the unlock code to her phone. She'd never, to my knowledge, had locked drawers or private hiding places that I was forbidden to see. But I suppose if you're hiding enormous secrets, acting like you have no secrets at all is the best possible defence.

A month or so after she'd gone, I was faced with the awful conundrum of what to do with Helen's stuff. I couldn't bear to live with it in the house. Opening the wardrobe and seeing her clothes hanging beside mine cut deep every single time. Even so, I didn't feel I could take it all to the tip or the charity shop. It wasn't mine to give away, even if she had left it all behind. In the end, I packed all her clothes and personal things into suitcases and boxes and rented a storage unit. It was a surprisingly small one. She didn't have a lot of personal items. She had a lean, well-coordinated wardrobe (she was forever taking clothes she wouldn't wear again to the charity shop), only a few books, and no heirlooms, photograph albums, old teddy bears or keepsakes. I'd always put this lack of hoarding down to her practical nature, and also to the fact that she must have left her childhood possessions in Australia. But maybe it was more sinister and premeditated than that. She didn't want to own anything she wasn't prepared to leave behind.

So when I loaded up all her stuff, it all fitted into a single car load, with her bicycle on the rack. I drove it over to the storage place and piled it on a trolley to take it to the unit. The boxes and suitcases took up next to no room; I'd only taken a slightly bigger unit because I had to fit in the bike. It took me just five minutes to pack it all in. I took one last glance at the small pile of stuff, then swung the door closed and secured it with the new padlock I'd bought from the disinterested, gum-chewing woman at the desk downstairs. The unit was an additional monthly cost I could scarcely afford, but I genuinely didn't know what else to do. How long would I have to keep paying for it? Who knew?

As for the question of how she'd done it, I was equally at a loss. It was likely that Marguerite and Miranda's story of her regularly getting cashback in the supermarket was true, but if so, for how long? How much had she stockpiled? And, of course, I now knew she had taken her passport too. So she had identification, and an unspecified amount of cash. In this era of electronic banking and our ineradicable digital trail, was that enough? How far could she get with that? Was she still in the country or had she bought an air ticket and fled abroad?

But even before that, how had she got away from the house without being seen? Before we found out she was safe and well, the police had scoured CCTV on major roads and at bus stops and train stations for several miles around. They'd spoken to taxi drivers. No one had seen her. It was so unlikely. Helen was a striking woman, beautiful even. People would have noticed a beautiful woman wearing a floral dress. But no one had. She had simply vanished.

It seemed to me, as I went over the facts for the thousandth time, that she could only have done it with help. She must have walked away from the house, as Mrs Goode said, and then been collected in a side road by someone driving a car – a friend, an accomplice, a lover? But who? Who was helping her? Where had she met a man, begun an affair and planned an escape, all the while being the perfect wife and mother, being at the school gate on time, living a busy, productive life? How had she managed it? Was this faceless lover scheduled for sex between 11.45 and 12.30 every Thursday, between yoga and her summer-fair committee meeting? Or what if he wasn't someone she'd met recently? What if he was someone who'd always been there, in the background? It flabbergasted me. Yes, I'd played away a little, but it hadn't meant anything. It was just sex, part of the work game. I could scarcely remember the names of the few women involved. But Helen? Her steadiness was the rock on which our family was built. If she had been having an affair, was our whole marriage a lie?

Even after six months, it's impossible to halt the relentless flow of questions. I can't stop myself from going over every detail of the last few months with Helen. I've dissected every conversation I can remember, thought about moments when she was away from the house or was distracted or distant. With hindsight, everything is significant. But the truth is that at the time there wasn't anything that aroused my suspicions. And that means one of two things. Either Helen was the most brilliant liar in the history of liars, or I was a total mug. Every time I work my way through this particular sequence of thoughts, it leaves me with a mess of anger, misery and self-pity. And so I drink. I think myself sick and then I drink.

I know I can't go on like this. It's not going to help Marguerite and Miranda one little bit if I fall to pieces. I cannot let them down. That isn't an option. I have to pull myself together and go on living. Up until this point, there has been no way off the nightmarish merry-go-round of despair. But, somehow, Miranda's birthday has offered the tiniest chink of light.

Lara's nice. Her mum's nice. They're kind people who helped me out when I needed it. It's embarrassing how I fell apart when Lara told me the restaurant was closed. She was amazing. Calm, practical, not at all judgemental. I said thank you, of course, and washed dishes, made sure their house was left tidy before I took the girls home. But it didn't feel like enough. Maybe I could invite them out for dinner or something. Nothing fancy, just a nice meal with the kids and some friendly chat.

Lara

There was school-gate gossip about the birthday party, of course there was. It had been blown out of all proportion by the time I got there to drop Frances off. I was immediately drawn into a crowd of chattering mums, all of them asking me what had happened, and then, before I had a chance to answer, breathlessly telling me how amazing I was to save poor Sam.

Somehow, the flooded restaurant, which no one could have foreseen, was cited as an example of Sam's helpless maleness. It would never have happened when Helen was around, they said, shaking their heads, or if he had a woman to organize him. Then they all glanced over at me, appraisingly. Sam had clearly sung my praises and told everyone how I'd opened my home to them. I could see into the hive mind and they had me and Sam married off, blending our households and popping out a new baby to seal the deal. It wasn't even 9 a.m. yet.

'It was nothing,' I said shortly. 'Anyone would have done it. I just happened to be there.' Then I waved cheerily over my shoulder and hurried out of the gates.

I was glad of the big hill and the effort it took to push Jonah's pushchair up it. It helped my frustration and general discomfort with the scene I'd just left. Individually, I'm sure they're all lovely women, but collectively they're like a. . . a giant cliché amoeba. They don't have an original thought between them. Most of them are so utterly committed to creating the perfect middle-class illusion, it's impossible to find the real people underneath. With their gym-sleek figures, their beautiful, spotless homes and their smarmy 'No, I don't work, they're only young for such a short time,' as if those of us who do work are deliberately robbing our kids of an idyllic childhood. They all pretend to be such good friends, and have nights out and coffee mornings and play dates, but no real conversations ever take place. No one is allowed to admit to fear, or worry or, God forbid, boredom.

As I got to the top of the hill, it struck me that Helen had been queen of them all – the sleekest, the prettiest, with the most beautiful home and the most perfectly cared-for children. She'd also been the one with the most banal and pleasant conversation. And yet she'd had the biggest secrets. She'd lived a whole other life and planned a devastating escape without anyone having the first hint that she was going to do it. I laughed, a little out of breath, startling Jonah. Maybe I underestimated all the school-gate mums. Who knew what enigmas were lurking under those M&S-clad bosoms?

The energy of my anger got me to the nursery to drop Jonah off and all the way home. Jogging down our road, I glanced at my phone and noticed a text had come in from Sam. 'Hey Lara, thanks again for yesterday evening. You and your mum were lifesavers. Would you four be free for dinner next Fri night to say thank you? We could go to a restaurant with an upstairs section. . . or a lifeboat!'

Dinner with Sam. Well, dinner with Sam, my mum and four children. Even put like that, it sounded good. I wasn't working on Friday night, and Mum would enjoy a night out. As long as I could prevent Jonah from tearing the restaurant to pieces, it'd be great. I fired off a quick 'Thank you and yes!' message, and allowed myself a quick smile. It was exciting to have a weekend evening plan, even if it was just a trip to the local all-you-can-eat buffet and colouring in.

Sam

The Sunday after Miranda's party with her friends, I took the girls to my parents' for a birthday tea. On the drive over there, they bickered incessantly, until I yelled and told them that no one was to speak until we got there. The silence in the back of the car was thunderous, but at least it was silence. My head was pounding and even though I'd brushed my teeth twice and rinsed with mouthwash, there was a foul, rotten taste at the back of my throat that I couldn't get rid of.

We stopped at a traffic light, where the road we were on crossed a main arterial. I knew from experience that we would be there for some time. It was a ridiculously long change. I leaned back against the headrest and glanced in the rear-view mirror. Both girls had forgotten to sulk and were silently playing a game with two plastic figures they'd found in the back, left over from a Happy Meal, or a Kinder Egg or something. I sighed with relief and looked forward through the windscreen. The traffic on the road crossing ours was crawling along, bumper to bumper. I hoped they'd leave the intersection clear when the lights changed or we'd be gridlocked. There was a car broadside to mine, completely blocking my lane. They'd better bloody move, I thought, and tried to catch the eye of the driver.

The shock hit me like a punch to the gut. It was Helen. Her straight nose, her olive skin, her narrow, pretty hands high on the steering wheel.

'Jesus!' I swore, and faintly behind me I heard Marguerite say, 'Daddy! Don't say the J-word!'

Inexorably, the traffic on the main road began to move. In seconds, Helen would drive away and be gone forever. I pounded on my horn as hard as I could, bashing it over and over, and the woman driving the car turned sharply in surprise, so she was looking fully at me.

It wasn't Helen. It was nothing like her. The woman was at least ten years older, with a sharp line between her brows and smaller, narrower eyes. She gave me a filthy look, clearly thinking I was hooting because she was in my way. Helplessly, I raised my hands and mouthed 'Sorry'. For an agonizingly long second, she kept glaring at me, then the car ahead of her moved off and she followed and was gone.

It was a huge relief to be at Mum and Dad's. Miranda was wily enough to know she wouldn't get away with being rude to me in front of Granny, so she was on her best behaviour. She was also grudgingly thrilled to get her *Into the Woods* DVD. However, she was even more delighted with her hilariously inappropriate gift from cool Uncle Tim – a karaoke machine.

The day was bright and fine, but cold. Mum's leg was much better and she was keen to walk and give it some exercise, so we put a leash on their old Labrador, Baxter, and all set off towards the common near their house.

The girls romped ahead, throwing a ball for Baxter, who made a half-hearted attempt to fetch it. Dad and Tim were arguing about something they'd heard on the news before we came out. Mum was walking well, but a little slowly. She had a stick, but I offered her my arm and she took it. I kept an eye on the path, watching out for stones and potholes. She definitely didn't need another tumble. We dropped a little behind the others.

'So how was the birthday really?' she asked quietly. Over lunch we'd had a raucous account of the party, and the 'supercool picnic' Lara had created. Miranda and Marguerite had interrupted and shouted over one another to tell the story. From their version, it all sounded like a hilarious caper.

'It all sailed rather close to the wind,' I said. 'A couple of near disasters. The party was the least of it. She's so angry all the time, and it's hard for me to stay kind in the face of constant rudeness.'

'I know,' said Mum. 'And yet you must.'

We walked on in silence for a while. The path was choked with autumn leaves, already beginning to turn to mush under our feet.

'Tell me about this Lara,' said Mum suddenly.

'Not much to tell. She's the mum of a girl in Miranda's class. Frances. And she has a little boy, Jonah. He's three or so. She's a restaurant manager.'

'She was very kind to invite you back to her house.'

'Yes. She's like that. . . Easy-going and generous. She was a professional dancer when she was younger, so Miranda naturally thinks she's the coolest thing ever.'

Mum nodded. I was conscious that there were several bits of relevant information I hadn't seen fit to impart – that Lara was single, that she was the woman who had taken the girls home the night Helen disappeared. I wasn't sure why not. Was it because I didn't want Mum to assume something was going to happen between Lara and me? Or because I didn't want her to tell me it shouldn't? There was no doubt that in Lara's darkened hallway, there'd been a moment when I'd felt a flash of attraction to her. Mum, as a psychologist, is altogether too perceptive. I wasn't lying to her. I just wasn't ready to have her cast her razor-sharp gaze on my life right then.

When we left Mum and Dad's, at about six, Tim said he'd come back to ours and help me get the girls to bed. He was no help at all, of course – without the excitement of Uncle Tim, baths, schoolbag packing and bedtime would have been a much smoother, less boisterous affair. But in the end we got them both to bed, just twenty-five minutes later than the appointed Sunday-night bedtime.

'Hungry?' I asked Tim.

'Nah, still stuffed from lunch,' he said.

'Me too.' I was itching for a drink. I'd only had one at Mum and Dad's as I was driving, and I'd been fantasizing about a cold beer all afternoon and evening.

I went into the kitchen and got us each one. We clinked our bottles together and drank – Tim slowly, me greedily. Tim was still savouring his first few sips and my bottle was empty. I went back to the kitchen and fetched another.

He ambled through to the living room and settled down on the sofa, his long legs stretched out in front of him. I had a few quick gulps from my second beer in the kitchen and went through to join him. He was scrolling through his phone, smiling at something he was reading. I flopped into an armchair. I felt bone-weary and bruised. The thought of starting a full week's work in just over twelve hours filled me with quiet dread. Much though I loved my brother, I just wanted a light, easy evening. No heavy chat. As I watched him, his smile faded, and I saw him look more serious, a small frown line appearing between his dark brows.

'Problem?' I asked.

'Not as such.'

'Potential problem?'

'Just a. . .' He hesitated, then looked up and gave me his roguish grin. 'Lady issue.'

'Is it. . . whatshername?' I trawled my memory for the last name he'd told me. 'Shannon?'

He looked genuinely blank for a second. 'Oh God, no. Ancient history, that.'

'So who is it now?'

'Someone I met a while ago.'

'Someone a little more age-appropriate?'

'You could say so.'

'Glad to hear it. You don't want to be that guy.'

'What guy?'

'The guy who finds himself at the precise tipping point where being slightly older and more sophisticated morphs into creepy old man.'

'I am not that guy.'

'Yet.'

'Fuck you!' He smiled.

'So is the age-appropriate one giving you grief?'

'Nah. All good,' he said, sitting up straighter. I could see he wasn't in the mood to expand on this, but I couldn't resist teasing him. He was my little brother, after all.

'So. . . are we looking at wedding bells? Am I going to be dusting off my top hat?'

He didn't even crack a smile. 'Oh no.'

'No?'

'This is something much. . . much more complicated. I don't want to go into it. . .'

'Come on, Tim.' I laughed. 'You think you have a sex life that's complicated? I've got a doctorate in complex sex lives.'

'This isn't sex!' he burst out sharply, and I stopped, surprised.

'What do you mean?'

'It's not sex. It's something. . . else.'

'Else?'

'Like. . . friendship,' he said, but his tone was unconvincing, as if this wasn't the word he would have chosen.

'Like a meeting of minds?'

'No. I mean, I don't understand her any better than I understand any women, but. . .'

'You want to?'

'I want to help her. And that's new for me. Wanting to help someone without getting anything in return.'

'Well, dear brother, that sounds suspiciously like love. When do we get to meet this amazing woman?'

He laughed. 'Oh, never. You know me. I'll fuck it up and it'll all be over before you know it.' He moved swiftly to change the subject. 'Never mind me though. I wasn't going to put you on the spot at Mum and Dad's, but am I right in thinking that the Lara that rescued Miranda's birthday party is the sexy redhead from the Bell and Anchor?'

'The same,' I said reluctantly.

'The hot single mother who totally blanked me and gazed at you like you were an adorable puppy?'

'On the night after we found out Helen had disappeared on

purpose? I think, if she felt anything for me, it was pity.'

'Pity can work.'

'You see? That was it.'

'That was what?'

'The tipping point. You just turned into the creepy old guy.'

Tim let out a bellow of laughter. 'So. You and Lara? Something going to happen there?'

'I don't fucking know, do I?' I said, checking my beer bottle, which was mysteriously empty. 'I mean, why should she come anywhere near me? I'm a fuck-up, an emotional wreck, living at the bottom of my overdraft with two traumatized children, a budding drink problem and a ten-year-old Ford.'

'And the beginnings of a dad bod,' Tim said, pointing at my soft belly. 'Letting yourself go there, bro.'

'Yeah, well,' I said self-consciously, heaving myself out of the armchair and heading for the kitchen to get another beer. I brought one back for Tim too, even though his first bottle was still a third full.

We sat drinking in comfortable silence for a while, and then he said gently, 'It might not be a bad thing, Samster. Even if it isn't a serious relationship. Just some companionship. Sex. Getting back on the horse, if you like.'

'That's all fine and well for me, but what about her?'

'She's a grown-up girl. Let her make her own mind up.'

'Not fair to tie her to a basket-case though.' I wondered how much I could tell him – about my anger, my late-night despair, the fact that only booze stopped me from exploding with fury. In the end I said, 'I'm still having the occasional meltdown. I am so, so not over this Helen thing.'

'It's not surprising though, is it?' Tim said. 'It was a fucking awful shock. And it's not like you get to confront her and yell at her, or even ask her why she did it. She's just gone.'

'Exactly.' I was surprised at how much he understood. Tim, who had never had a long-term relationship in his life. 'I fantasize about terrible things. I dream constantly about her. About screaming at her, hurting her even. . .'

'I don't think that's surprising. I don't think even Mum would be shocked by that. What does your therapist say?'

'My therapist? Oh. . . I only go for the family sessions. . . And I'm scarcely going to talk about wanting to strangle Helen in front of the girls, am I?'

'Shouldn't you be seeing someone separately? Just for you, I mean?'

'Maybe. But I can't afford it. Not the time or the money.'

'But. . .'

'I have to get on with my life,' I said, drinking deeply from my bottle. 'When Leonora died, I got the full works – grief counselling, help from Mum and Dad, help from you, and then Helen came along and was the answer to all my prayers. She swooped in, all clean and strong and organized and stable, and saved me from my grief. And look how that turned out. She disappeared. No warning. Nothing. Just gone.'

I was horrified at the bitterness of my tone. I'd accused Tim of being 'that guy', but there was another kind of 'that guy' too, and I didn't want to be him. I didn't want to be the guy who was twisted with hatred and resentment, who distrusted everyone. I think I horrified Tim too, because he was silent for the longest time. We listened to the distant hum of traffic and a faint hooting sound, which might have been an owl, or a faraway car alarm.

Eventually Tim said quietly, 'And you have no idea why? None at all?'

'What do you mean?'

'As far as you were concerned, you were happy?'

'Yeah, sure. I mean, we weren't in the first flush of love or anything. When you have a house and kids and work, things can get a bit. . .' I looked for the right words. 'Pedestrian. Business-like.'

Tim raised an eyebrow. That was exactly why he'd always avoided long-term commitment, I knew.

'I go over and over it in my head,' I continued. 'And yes, maybe she was feeling. . . neglected. I travelled for work a lot. I worked long hours. Maybe I wasn't always. . .' I trailed off.

'Always what?'

'I don't know. Present. Helen was so in control of the whole home thing – looking after the girls, running the house. I guess I left her to it. Took her for granted.' I thought of saying more, but I'd never spoken explicitly to Tim about the fact that I slept with other women. I wasn't about to say something now. Even though Tim had some pretty low standards for himself, I had a feeling he held me to higher ones.

'You're not the first guy to have been a bit unromantic,' he said. 'But let's face it, it was a hell of a thing she took on,' he continued carefully, 'treating your kids as her own, giving up her career. . .'

'I know,' I said, and my tone was harsh. 'I bloody know. And I was grateful to her every day. I know she knew that.'

'She was very career-minded when you first met, wasn't she?'

'I suppose so. We both were. For the first year or so we juggled the family and work thing between us, but then, as you know, we had a major round of redundancies and Helen lost her job. I kept mine, and got a promotion. It was the right thing for her to stay home with the girls. And for a good few years it all worked out fine.'

Tim nodded, satisfied, but the words sounded hollow in my own ears. 'The right thing.' 'All worked out fine.' It had been a little more complicated than that. It hadn't been as simple as Helen losing her job and me keeping mine.

The atmosphere in the company had been tense. Redundancies make people very jumpy, and when Chris had called me into the boardroom, I'd expected the worst. But what he said was that, with the restructure, there was a senior account manager position opening up.

'It's going to mean long hours,' he said, 'and quite a lot of travel. But I know with your circumstances. . .' I nodded. He pressed on. 'Tell me how to make this work, Sam. I want to give this to you. You're highly qualified, and the clients love you. I reckon you could turn things around, and with the commission structure, you could double your salary.'

There was a long, difficult silence. He was going to make me say it. 'I know you're going to be making some cuts in the marketing department,' I said hesitantly. 'Totally off the record, what are your plans for Helen?'

'I could get sued for having this conversation,' Chris said. He was sweating. He went on, haltingly. 'Hypothetically, and totally off the record, I have to lose two of the four people on the marketing team. Helen's our best performer. . .'

'But the most expensive.'

'Yes, the most expensive,' he admitted.

'Hypothetically though, if Helen wasn't working and was able to help me with the girls at home. . .'

'You'd bring in more revenue for the company, and you'd earn enough to compensate for what she's earning now.'

'So. . .' I nudged Chris, curious to see where he was going with this.

He shifted in his chair. He'd initiated the exchange, but it was making him very uncomfortable indeed. 'Well, she's been with us for slightly less than two years. I could offer her the two-year redundancy package to sweeten the deal. Do you think she'd go for it?'

'And have the chance to support me in my promotion?' I mused. 'I think so. She loves me. She wants me to succeed.'

There was a long, long pause.

'This conversation can never leave this room, Sam. I'm serious,' said Chris, mopping his brow.

'What conversation?' I asked innocently.

CHAPTER NINE

Lara

Inevitably, a few hours before we were due to go for dinner, Jonah got ill. He'd been a little off colour in the early part of the week, and by Thursday he was lying on his tummy on the sofa, listless and hot, his cheeks red and his nose streaming. It wasn't anything serious – a nasty virus – but he definitely wasn't up to going out in the cold. I'd have to cancel, or postpone. I was surprised how disappointed I felt.

I texted Sam on Friday morning: 'So gutted to have to cancel – Jonah has a bad cold.'

He replied immediately: 'Oh no! Was so looking forward to it.'

I was touched and surprised. 'Me too,' I replied before I lost my nerve.

'Who are you texting so furiously?' asked Mum.

'Sam,' I said. 'Just letting him know we can't make dinner tonight.'

'Why not?' said Mum, looking up from her newspaper.

'Jonah. He's much too sick to go out.'

'Hmm.' Mum's attitude to sick children is somewhat harsher than mine. 'You're probably right. He'll be a misery guts. Well, don't worry. You go. Take Frances. I'll stay home with Junior Snotbucket.'

'What? No. I can't leave him.'

'Course you can,' said Mum practically. 'I'll dose him up with ibuprofen. He'll be asleep half an hour after you leave. I can ring you if he gets bad. But he won't. He'll be fine.'

'I've already cancelled,' I said weakly.

'So uncancel. Go and have fun. You and Frances never get a girls' night out.'

It wouldn't strictly be a girls' night, though, would it? Sam would be there. Still, Mum was being so generous. And I had been looking forward to it, as, I think, had Frances. After the party, Miranda had been a little nicer to her and they had been hanging out together at playtime.

'Okay, Mum, thanks,' I said, and I picked up my phone and rang Sam. 'Hi,' I said quickly when he answered, sounding surprised. 'Does the invitation still hold? Mum's said she'll stay home with Jonah so Frances and I can come.'

'That'd be fabulous!' He sounded genuinely happy. 'Sad your mum won't be with us though, she's such fun.'

At six o'clock Frances and I walked down the road and caught the bus towards the high street. Sam had chosen a local Chinese restaurant. We'd never eaten there, but Frances had heard from friends that there was a gigantic fish tank in the restaurant with actual piranhas. She'd chosen a sunshine-yellow dress and a neat cardigan. She looked tall and slender and grown-up. I could see she'd made an effort to look nice, and I felt a tiny pang in my heart. I was glad I was able to give her this evening out after all.

My darling Frances is a careful, shy girl. She's not one for forming close, passionate friendship bonds, as so many little girls do. She tends to hang back. She has friends, and she's kind and quietly confident, so she's generally popular. But she doesn't let any of them get too close. I know, deep down, that this is the fault of her feckless father, and it is another on a long, long list of reasons why I want to punch him.

In the old days, she would never have made friends with a girl like Miranda, who was undoubtedly the Alpha Girl in their class, centre of the most popular group. Frances sometimes hung around on the periphery of that set, but I think she knew instinctively that the stakes were high for the girls in those exalted social circles, and that someone who was your best friend one day might cut you stone-dead the next, in the interests of social climbing.

But since Helen's disappearance, it seems Miranda hasn't been quite the star she once was. Her status has fallen due to their changed circumstances. Without Helen as the centre of the mums' social circle, without the endless round of social events that sprung from Helen's community work, Miranda's weekly whirl of play dates and extra-curricular events has largely fallen away. She goes to netball and dance at school, but I know that with Sam at work, many of her out-of-school classes like ballet and flute have had to stop. And secondly, the girls don't know how to talk to her. What are they supposed to say? Most adults don't know what to say. How are nine-year-old girls supposed to have the answer?

Frances has said in passing that Miranda is angry a lot of the time. At playtime and in class she shouts at people if they don't do things the way she wants them done. She's always been a perfectionist, but it seems to have got worse. It's made her less likely to be included in group activities, which has naturally made her even angrier. I know Sam kept Miranda's birthday party small for logistical and financial reasons, but I think he might also have struggled to persuade more than those six girls to risk the sharp edge of Miranda's tongue.

But after the slightly odd success of the party, things have improved for her. Those six girls have been kinder to her, and she's been, according to Frances, a bit happier and nicer to be around.

'I'm looking forward to seeing Miranda tonight,' she said suddenly, as the bus went over the crest of the hill. 'She's reading those Dragon Rainbowfire books too, and she said she'd lend me the next one.'

'That sounds good, love,' I said.

We'd managed to bag the front seats on the top deck of the bus. It was a lovely evening, crisp and autumnal and the sky was clear. I was with my girl and we were going for dinner with friends. I took the smallest guilty pleasure in the fact that Jonah wasn't with us – the girls were all old enough to sit politely at the table and talk, and I wouldn't be spending my evening chasing a boisterous three-year-old between the tables. It was going to be a civilized, almost grown-up evening. I felt a little bubble of happiness.

When we got off the bus, I smoothed the front of my blouse and Frances glanced up at me.

'You look good, Mum,' she said, eyeing me appraisingly.

'Thanks, honey.' I smiled.

'No, you do,' she insisted. 'You've normally only got two ways of dressing – posh for work or scruffy for home. And this is something in between. It's nice.'

Her scrutiny made me self-conscious, and I pulled my cardigan tightly around myself as we walked into the restaurant. Sam, Miranda and Marguerite were sitting at a big round table towards the back of the room. Sam stood when he saw us, and his grin was warm and welcoming. We went over to the table and Frances slipped in next to Miranda. Immediately, their heads came together and they began to whisper urgently. Sam put a hand on my arm and I saw him hesitate, and then he leaned in to kiss my cheek. He was clean-shaven, with a hint of lemony aftershave, but I also caught the bready note of beer from his skin. We all sat down. He and the girls had drinks already, and he hailed a waiter to get something for Frances and me. I briefly wondered if I should stick to water but then felt momentarily reckless and ordered a glass of Pinot Grigio. Live on the edge, I say.

Frances and Miranda were oblivious to us, talking in low, intense tones about whatever issue was utterly pressing right that minute. Sam had brought a notebook for Marguerite, who was happy to sit quietly beside him and draw, as long as every now and then he took the time for her to describe her picture to him. That left Sam and me in a position where we could actually have a grown-up conversation. It should have been great, but somehow I couldn't think of a single thing to say. I had hardly spoken to Sam one to one – why would I? We'd passed the time at the school gates on the rare occasions he'd been there to drop the girls off or pick them up. I'd seen him socially with Helen a few times. But a long, continuous conversation? We'd never had that. I was also conscious of the great swathes of things we couldn't talk about. I don't think I'd have talked to him about Helen anyway, even if we'd been alone, but talking to him about her in front of the girls would have been unnecessarily cruel, and potentially awkward.

I had little idea about what he did at work – something in advertising, I thought? I knew nothing about that, and I was sure he had no interest in the world of pub management. I didn't have a clue if he had any hobbies, or what they might be. Could I try talking about music? Sport? Politics? It was a long time since I'd been out for the evening with a man. I was desperately out of practice.

Sam was ill at ease too. When he did have a go at making halting conversation, he struggled to meet my eye, glancing at me briefly and then focusing over my shoulder, looking at the people in the restaurant and the street outside the window. It made me feel even more awkward. I was boring him to tears. Despite Frances' kind words, I was conscious of my faded blouse and jeans, my hair being in need of a trim and my lack of sparkling chatter. Helen would have had a million easy conversation openers. She'd have been perfectly, elegantly dressed, and she'd also have managed to bring brilliant educational but fun activities for the kids too. I slumped a little in my chair, overwhelmed by my un-Helen-ness. Poor Sam, I thought. I bet he's regretting this dinner invitation now.

We'd covered the weather and what we'd done that week, and the conversation dwindled to another awkward silence. I cast about for something to say. 'What are you drawing, Marguerite?' I began brightly, just as Sam said something too.

'Sorry,' I said quickly.

'Don't be sorry,' said Sam, his smile tight. 'You were saying?'

'No, no, you first. Sorry.' Why was I saying sorry again? Bugger. Now I was awkward, dull, scruffy and needlessly apologetic. What a winner.

'I was saying. . . that you were a dancer?'

He phrased it somewhere between a question and a statement.

'Yes,' I said. 'When I was younger.'

Despite the intensity of her conversation with Frances, Miranda's ears must have been attuned to the sound of the word 'dance', because she broke off and turned to us.

'When did you start dancing, Lara?' she asked. I remembered that she had always had that calmly self-confident way of addressing adults by their Christian names. Another Helen trait, I assumed.

'When I was three or four.'

'Me too!' she breathed. 'And did you do ballet? Or modern? Or jazz?'

'I did them all. It seems like I did nothing but dance after school and on Saturdays. I must have had days off, but all I remember is rushing from school to various studios. I got shoulder problems from lugging bags of dance gear around for years.'

'I used to do ballet and jazz and tap,' said Miranda, 'but I had to stop my Tuesday ballet and Friday tap because Daddy's at work. I only go on Saturdays now.'

The corners of her mouth went tight, and I could see she wasn't being sulky, just trying not to cry. I understood. Oh God, I understood. I remembered all too well the hierarchy of the dance studios. The girls who only danced on Saturdays were considered lightweights – not doing nearly enough to be taken seriously by the teachers or the three-or-four-times-a-week girls.

'I'm sorry about that,' I said. 'That must have been hard.' She nodded, and I suddenly found myself saying, 'Did you dance up at St Augustine's?' Miranda nodded. 'Frances goes to a ballet class there on a Tuesday too. I could take you as well, if you like. You could come home with Frances after school and I'll take you up together.'

Miranda's eyes widened, and she looked over at Sam, her face contorted with pleading.

'Oh no, I couldn't possibly expect you to. . .' he began. He didn't want to be beholden to me. I understood. When you're a single, working parent, it can feel like you're always begging favours that you'll have no way to repay.

'It's genuinely no bother at all,' I said, and, leaning close to him, I added quietly, 'Miranda's influence might help Frances. She's been asking me to let her give up because the class is too hard and she doesn't have any friends there. If Miranda goes. . .' I let my words hang for a while, and then a brainwave struck. 'If I do Tuesday, could you drop Frances back at mine after the Saturday jazz class? I want to start taking Jonah to swimming lessons and I just can't get the times to work.'

'Of course!' he said quickly. 'Listen, are you sure about the ballet? I mean. . .'

'Please, Dad,' said Miranda fervently.

'Of course I'm sure,' I said. 'What about Marguerite?'

'She'll be at after-school club,' said Sam.

'Will she be okay without Miranda there?'

Simultaneously, Miranda said, 'Yes,' and Marguerite said, 'No, I won't.'

Miranda shot a venomous look at her sister. 'You little. . .' she began.

'I can take Marguerite too!' I said quickly. 'If she doesn't mind sitting with me during the class.'

'I don't mind,' said Marguerite, looking back at her drawing. 'I went there before – loads. I play with my friend Isla. Mummy brings us both snacks.'

Sam shot me a look at this casual, present-tense mention of Helen. I glanced away. If someone was going to correct Marguerite, it wasn't going to be me.

'I'm sure we can make it work,' I said. 'I know Miranda's a talented dancer. If there's a way to make sure she gets to her classes, I'm happy to help.'

'Okay,' said Sam, but I could see his assent was reluctant. I could have pressed the issue, but the waiter came to take our order. Was he reticent about my offer because he found it hard to accept help? Or because he didn't want to entangle his family's life with mine?

Miranda cheered up immeasurably once we'd agreed about the dancing. She did her best 'making conversation', asking me all sorts of polite questions and being the picture of the perfectly behaved girl. I could see Sam watching her in wonderment. I guessed that maybe she hadn't been easy at home lately. Nevertheless, it eased the stilted awkwardness of the interaction between Sam and me.

When the food came, we all relaxed a little, and chat flowed more readily. Sam was on his third beer (or was it more? I was pretty sure he'd had at least one before we arrived. I hoped he wasn't driving). He did seem to be less distracted. He laughed with the girls and made walrus tusks by putting his chopsticks inside his upper lip. Miranda groaned and rolled her eyes; clearly this was an old dad joke. But even the eye roll lacked conviction. She was clearly so happy at the prospect of dancing again that nothing could dampen her spirits.

Sam tucked into his dinner with evident relish. I glanced at him and noticed how deftly he wielded his chopsticks.

'You've had some practice at that,' I said.

'Hmm?' He effortlessly scooped some rice into his mouth, then swallowed. 'Yeah, I lived in Japan for a few months. If it's the only way to eat, you gain some dexterity.'

'You lived in Japan? When was that?'

'Oh, years ago now.'

Miranda, who was listening in, said, 'Dad and Mummy used to travel all over the world.'

I was momentarily confused, partly at hearing Miranda say 'Mummy'. I'd never heard her say it before. And when had Sam and Helen found time to travel and live abroad for months at a time?

But Sam was smiling at Miranda. 'You're right. We did.'

'And when you came back from Japan, Mum was pregnant with me,' said Miranda.

'Indeed. And then along came you.'

They shared a little secret smile. It was obviously a family catchphrase, often repeated. The penny dropped. Miranda wasn't talking about Helen. She was talking about her real mother. Sam's first wife, the one who died. It occurred to me I didn't even know her name.

The enormity of the losses that little family had suffered struck me so hard I put down my chopsticks and sat quietly for a second. Those poor little girls. To lose their mother before they were old enough to know her, and then to lose the only maternal figure they'd ever known. . . It didn't even bear thinking about. Not to mention poor Sam. No wonder he was knocking back the beers. Someone else in his position might well be face down in a bucket of whisky. The fact that he kept going, kept working and functioning, was a miracle.

After dinner, Sam insisted on ordering a taxi for Frances and me. He had had quite a lot to drink, so I was relieved he wasn't driving the girls home – we were a five-minute walk from their house. As we stepped out of the restaurant, the taxi pulled up on the yellow line in front of us. The driver put on his hazard lights and was clearly impatient to get going.

'Thanks for a lovely evening,' I said, and I meant it. It had been strained at times, but I felt like we'd all managed to have a reasonable time in the end.

'No, thank *you*,' Sam said, and he took my arm and leaned in to kiss me goodbye. His lips, warm and firm, landed close to the corner of my mouth. He looked properly into my eyes for one brief, intense second and then stepped back. Frances and I climbed into the taxi and were whisked away down the high street.

Sam

I was actually quite drunk. No, scratch that, very drunk. I'd had a few beers at home before we went to the restaurant, and then quite a few more during the course of dinner. After so many years in the media industry, I'm used to drinking heavily and maintaining a facade of reasonably acceptable behaviour. I was competent, I remained upright and didn't slur my words, but I was actually very drunk.

I hardly remember getting the girls home. Marguerite was sleepy, so I carried her the last block or so and then upstairs. I let them skip their baths and got them to brush their teeth, pull on their pyjamas and fall into bed. Then I fetched another beer from the fridge and went through to the living room. I settled on the sofa without bothering to turn on the light.

I drank the beer down in one long swallow. I should have brought through more than one, I thought idly. Now I'd have to get up and get another. But I didn't move. I sat staring at the orange glow of the London night sky through the window. I hadn't bothered to close the curtains either. I could see the silhouette of a tree outside. We were heading towards December and it had lost all its leaves. Its bare, jagged branches looked like clawed hands flung up in surprise outside the window. Marguerite had named winter trees 'spike trees' when she was two or three.

Hark at me, a cynical voice said inside my head. Hark at me, going out for a polite suburban dinner with a hot woman and our various kids. I almost managed to make it look normal. Chatting about lifts to and from dance classes and passing the spring rolls, when all the time the rage was roiling inside me like great, black, oily waves. Because it was all so wrong. The whole bizarre, stilted situation. Because the woman sitting opposite me wasn't Helen.

Because my current account was so low, I had to put the dinner on my credit card, and I wouldn't be able to pay off the balance this month because the girls needed new school shoes and I'd just had confirmation that there'd be no bonus from work this month. I took them out for a dinner I couldn't afford to say thank you for one favour, and now she'd offered to do another one. I genuinely didn't have the energy to get to know Lara, even though I was sure she was a perfectly lovely woman.

And anyway, I found myself thinking, what's the point? Our lives are going to become intertwined because we're two single parents, so why wouldn't we help each other out? But what's the point of getting to know her, starting to sleep with her, which I'm sure will inevitably happen? What's the point of our 'falling in love', dating, moving in together? It was all so pointless, along with everything else in my life right now. No wonder I'd got drunk.

The night before had been a bad one. I'd had more than a few beers, and had stayed up too late, so I'd barely made it getting the girls to school. I felt so sick after I'd dropped them off that I actually had to go home and throw up. I cleaned myself up, but I felt so dreadful, I went into the kitchen to get something to eat before going to work. When I opened the fridge, there was only a tiny splash of milk left in the bottle. I knew I'd given the last of the cereal to the girls and the bread was mouldy. There was, however, one beautiful ice-cold bottle of beer lying on its side in the middle of the middle shelf. Like a gift. Before I could even think about it, I took it out, opened it and necked it. Yes, it was just past nine in the morning, but needs must. Instantly my head cleared. I went to the sink and rinsed my mouth out with water to get rid of the beery smell, and headed for the station. I'd be late for work, but at least I was feeling better.

When I got in to work, there was a Post-it on my desk asking me to pop in and see Chris as soon as I arrived. I'd have liked time to get a coffee, sit down, get my bearings, but whoever had written the note had underlined 'as soon' in a firm, passive-aggressive way. I sighed. I suppose I had come in late, even for me. I got up and headed for Chris's office, checking my reflection in the glass wall of the boardroom as I passed.

Chris glanced up as I walked in, and his eyes took in my untucked, unironed shirt and unshaven chin.

'Sorry,' I said. 'Didn't have any meetings today. I know I'm a bit scruffy.'

'Won't you shut the door, Sam?' he said. 'And have a seat.'

'Shut the door' should have been a clue. Chris has this cool, egalitarian, open-door policy. We're all supposed to be able to pop in and see him anytime. If the door is closed, something serious is going down.

I settled myself opposite him. 'What's up?'

'Not a lot, to be frank.' Chris is not one for small talk and he launched straight in. 'I've been looking at your figures for this month, and frankly. . .'

'They're shit,' I said. 'I know. I'm sorry.'

'They're not shit, Sam, they're non-existent. You've not brought in any new business this month at all. Not even a little leaflet campaign.'

'I've got a couple of big deals about to break. . .' I began.

'Is one of them with Bright Time?' he asked. 'They emailed me this morning to say they've been waiting three weeks for you to get them a competitor analysis they asked for. They can't wait any longer, so they've given the project to their other agency.'

Fuck, I thought. I knew something was falling between the cracks. I'd started the competitor analysis weeks ago but had got distracted.

'Jesus, Sam,' Chris said. 'Don't make me be the bastard here. We go back a long way. And you know how fond I was of Helen. . .'

His eyes slid away from mine then. He had the decency to look guilty. 'But you're putting me in a hell of a position. You keep dropping balls, not being here when you should be. . .'

'I'm looking after my kids alone,' I said. 'This isn't easy, Chris.'

'I know, Sam. I know. Fuck, I really know. I feel awful doing this. But we're struggling here. Times are lean and we are falling well short of our forecast for this quarter.'

Dear God, I thought. Was he about to let me go?

But he carried on. 'I have to give you a warning, because of the Bright Time thing. The board will have my nuts if I don't. Just. . . pull yourself together, okay? I need you to do that.'

I almost laughed. Chris had always been emotionally stunted, but that was blunt, even for him. I think he realized how heartless he sounded because he rose to reach across his desk and pat my shoulder in an awkward gesture of kindness. As he got closer, I saw his nose wrinkle and when he sat back down his expression was quizzical and suddenly cold. Obviously my drink of water hadn't entirely rinsed the booze smell off me.

So here I was, on the bones of my arse financially, contemplating starting a relationship with a woman I liked only slightly, and very possibly about to lose my job. What a fuck-up. Without thinking, I leaned forward, held the beer bottle by its neck and smacked it hard against the edge of the coffee table. It broke with a muted, ringing crack. Not loud – not loud enough to wake the girls. I looked down and in the half-light I could see tiny, bright shards of glass glinting on the carpet. I was too drunk to clean it up. And as I stared down, I saw a dark drop fall from my hand and spread in the pale pile of the carpet. There was a jagged gash in the skin between my thumb and forefinger. I'm not good with blood. I felt a sudden surge of nausea. I stood up, a little unsteady on my feet. I wobbled but managed to lurch to the bathroom and slam the door before I vomited up a nasty mess of beer and Chinese food while my gashed hand steadily dripped blood on to the floor.

When the retching was over, I wiped the floor and toilet bowl clean, flushed, and then sat with my back resting against the bath, my hand swathed in toilet paper. My head throbbed painfully and for the first time I realized how sore my hand was. I gingerly unwrapped it. I didn't think it would need stitches. If it did, it was too bad; it wasn't as if I could go to A & E now anyway, not with the girls asleep and no one to look after them. I stood slowly and looked at myself in the mirror. I was a mess and no mistake. Face puffy and blotchy, hair plastered to my forehead with sweat. I washed my face and brushed my teeth. The only consolation was that I was at least sober now. I took the first-aid box down from the bathroom cabinet – Helen had put it together, so it was still well stocked with plasters, wound wipes and gauze. I clumsily dressed my hand and tided up the bathroom.

I went through to the living room, painstakingly cleaned up the broken glass and scrubbed the blood out of the carpet. I used the little handheld hoover but was terrified I might have missed some bits of glass, so I moved the rug to cover that part of the carpet. Marguerite liked to kneel there and watch TV while she ate her cereal. I thought about one of her plump little pale knees being pierced by a shard of glass I'd left there after drunkenly smashing a beer bottle.

The tears came unexpectedly and with great force. I made it to my bedroom, shut the door, lay down on the unmade bed and sobbed and sobbed, burying my face in the pillow to muffle the sound. This was rock bottom. It had to be. I was incapable of helping myself. I needed someone to help me and soon, or everything was going to come crashing down.

CHAPTER TEN

Miranda

Last Christmas, we put up our Christmas tree on the first Sunday in Advent. It was a real tree, and Helen decorated it with big tartan bows she made herself, and silver balls, with smaller ones at the top and larger ones at the bottom. There were six presents each for Marguerite and me, and they were all beautifully wrapped and under the tree weeks before. There were also loads of presents for everyone else – teachers, friends, even my ballet teacher and the dustmen and the librarians. They were all perfectly wrapped as well, put under the tree and then given out.

Last Christmas, we had Christmas dinner at our house. We always had Christmas dinner at our house, and Granny and Uncle Tim were each allowed to bring something for everyone to eat, but Helen was in charge. It was always the same. Helen would get up early – even earlier than Marguerite and me – to get the turkey in the oven and set the table. And once we were up, we'd open our presents and then go to church. We'd get back and Helen would go into the kitchen while we played with our new presents, and then Granny and Grandpa and Uncle Tim would come with more presents and Uncle Tim's famous gammon and Granny's Christmas pudding.

It isn't happening like that this year. This year, we nearly didn't get a tree at all. I think Dad forgot, and when I asked him, he said there was no point in getting a tree because we'd be at Granny's house for present opening anyway. But then Marguerite cried like the giant baby she is. I normally get irritated at that, but this time it worked because it made Dad feel bad, and when he picked us up from after-school club the next day, he had a plastic tree from Tesco and a bag of baubles and tinsel.

It was a sad excuse for a tree, or that's what Dad called it. But it was actually quite fun because Dad got some cheesy Christmas music to play on YouTube, and he let me and Marguerite decorate the tree any way we liked. Helen never let us near the tree. She said we would mess it up. We got to put all the tinsel and all the baubles on the tree this year by ourselves. Marguerite put them anywhere, but I made it tidy and arranged them nice and evenly.

There wasn't a star for the tree – Dad hadn't bought one. Helen had this super-fancy star she got from some expensive shop in London and which she kept in a box in the loft. I suppose it's still up there, but I didn't ask to get it out. It would have looked stupid on our tiny fake tree anyway. Still, I thought we needed one, so I drew a star shape on some cardboard and cut it out, and got the tinfoil down and covered it. It actually looked quite cool, and Dad made a wire holder for it and put it on the tree.

Decorating the tree made me feel happy for about ten minutes. But then I looked at it and I realized it was a horrible cheap Tesco tree in our horrible dirty house and that everything – *everything* – was different from last Christmas.

We are going to Granny's house this year for Christmas. Not long after we went back to school in the autumn, Granny fell down when she was doing some gardening and broke her leg. That's why she hasn't been able to help Dad too much with looking after us. She's much better now, but she still walks with a stick. So while Christmas is at her house, I think Uncle Tim is going to do the cooking, which is a good thing because he is a chef. Marguerite is worried because she says Uncle Tim puts too much garlic and burny spices in everything he makes, even scrambled eggs. But Dad made him promise not to mess with the turkey, although he didn't say mess. He said another ruder word which he didn't use to say in front of Marguerite and me, but now he says it every now and then, especially when he's on the phone to Uncle Tim and thinks we aren't listening.

Dad's a tiny bit better than he was. I was worried about him a lot before. He was drinking a lot of beer. And I mean A LOT. The recycling was always full of bottles and he smelled of beer all the time. But now it doesn't seem quite as bad. He still has beers in the evening, but he's hardly ever on the sofa when we wake up in the morning. I think maybe he's beginning to forget Helen, or maybe it's because he's having a better time at work. It has been bad for him at work, which is why we don't have so much money anymore. That's why we didn't get a summer holiday this year. It's the first time in my whole life we haven't had a summer holiday. We spent our summer at Granny and Grandpa's. They were nice, but it was boring and lonely and I hardly saw any of my friends.

I think another reason that Dad is better is Lara. She takes me to ballet on a Tuesday now and Dad takes me and Frances to dance school on Saturday. We all usually end up doing something together after dance school. We go for a milkshake or once we went to the cinema.

But then there was this one night last week when I woke up in the night because I was hot. I think the heating was still on, even though it was the middle of the night, and I was thirsty. The clock in my room said one in the morning. I got up to go and get some water in the bathroom, but I could hear voices talking downstairs. I walked quietly down the stairs and saw that light was showing under the living-room door, which was shut. I thought maybe Dad had fallen asleep on the sofa again and the TV was on. I thought I might go in and tell him to go to bed, but before I could open the door, the voices went quiet and the living-room door opened and Dad came out.

'Hey, poppet!' he said, and his voice sounded fake and cheerful. He pulled the door shut behind him. 'What are you doing up?'

'I was thirsty,' I said. 'Why are you still up?'

'Oh, you know. . .' and his voice trailed off. 'I'm going to bed soon.'

'You've got work tomorrow.'

'I know.' He smiled. I looked at him hard, but he didn't look too drunk, which was good.

'Were you watching TV?'

'No, why?'

'I heard talking. I thought you must be watching TV.'

'Oh,' he said, and then, 'I was watching something on my laptop. Sorry if it woke you.'

We stood and looked at each other, and then he said, 'Come on, let's get you some water,' and he came upstairs with me to the bathroom and got me a drink of water and then tucked me up in bed like I was about four years old. I lay there, and just before I went back to sleep, I remember thinking it was strange that he shut the living-room door when he came out to find me.

The next morning he was extra cheerful, even though he couldn't have had much sleep. He was in the kitchen giving

Marguerite her breakfast and I went into the living room to get my school bag. There were two empty wine glasses on the coffee table. Two glasses? So maybe the voices I heard hadn't come from the TV or Dad's laptop. Maybe someone was here. But who would be here at one o'clock in the morning?

I went through to the kitchen. 'Who was here last night?'

'Hmm?' said Dad, but I know that hmm. It's what he says when he doesn't want to answer your question, so he pretends he didn't hear you properly.

'There are two glasses in the living room. Who was here? They must have come after we went to bed.'

I could see Dad thinking hard. He was probably trying to come up with a fib like 'Uncle Tim', but he knew I wouldn't fall for that because Uncle Tim lives in Bristol and if he's been here, we wake up and find him sleeping on the sofa.

In the end, Dad said, 'Frances' mum. She stopped by when she finished work. She works in a restaurant, you know that.'

'One o'clock in the morning is very late to be stopping by,' I said.

'It is. But I was still awake and we fancied a chat.' Then Dad got madly busy and started bossing us around about teeth brushing and packing bags.

In the end we got to school earlier than usual, and while we were waiting by the gate, I saw Lara and Frances coming down the hill, with Jonah running in front of them. I looked at Lara carefully. She looked tired, but quite happy, and while I was watching she gave my dad one of those special, secret smiles adults give each other and she mouthed, 'Hi' and waggled her fingers in a half wave. She didn't come over to talk to us, and in a way that made me even more suspicious. If they were drinking wine at one a.m. in the morning, why wouldn't she come and say hi? Instead she went and stood with some of the other mums on the far side of the playground and made a big point of not looking at Dad or talking to him. It was so obvious. She may as well have worn a big sign on her head that said, 'I was kissing Miranda's dad in the middle of the night last night.'

Anyway, I thought about it and I don't really mind. I mean, Dad must be lonely, and she is nice. She's quite pretty – not like Helen, but still okay-looking, and she's still thin like a dancer even though she's had two children. I like her house, and her mum, and Frances is my best friend now. I suppose. Jonah's annoying, but then so is Marguerite, so I can't complain about that.

We all went to a carol concert together last night at the local football ground, where we all got candles and sang. Helen would have packed an amazing picnic, but Dad and Lara bought sausages in buns there, and then we had candyfloss after, and that was cool. We're not seeing them on Christmas Day, obviously, but we're going to go ice skating outside the Natural History Museum on Boxing Day.

If you had told me last Christmas that our lives would be so totally, totally different by this Christmas, I would never have believed it. But here we are. Helen has vanished like she was a ghost and we are quite poor now. It should be the worst thing in the world, and in a way it was, but slowly things are getting back to normal. It's a different normal, but some of it is quite good.

Sam

I stood outside Tottenham Court Road station, the seething river of people flowing around me, and rang Lara. Her voice sounded calm and quiet in contrast to the din around me.

'Hi there,' I said, yelling over the ambient noise. 'Listen, Chris just rang in a panic and he wants me to go and see a client in Tooting to take an urgent brief. Is there any way. . .?'

'I'll pick up the girls, don't worry,' she said. 'Just give the school a ring and get a message to their classes so they know to expect me.'

'Thanks,' I said, relieved. 'You're a lifesaver. I should be able to get back to yours about six. I'll stop off at a supermarket and get pizzas for us all so you don't need to worry about dinner.'

'I'm working, so I'll be gone by then, but I'm sure Mum would be thrilled to get pizzas,' she said.

'Oh, I'll be sad not to see you.' I was trying to sound tender and affectionate, but as I had to yell to hear myself, the effect was slightly lost.

'Me too,' she said.

I hung up. We were doing a good job of using all the right words and being kind and sweet to one another, but there was a slightly stilted feel to it, as if we were saying lines in a play. She was lovely of course, and always eager to help. Almost too eager. But who was I to complain? She made my life easier.

What I didn't tell her was that Chris hadn't really given me a choice about the meeting. He'd called me in again to look at my figures, which were still way down. I knew I was doing better (if not turning up to work drunk counted as 'better'), but my heart wasn't in it, and I'd missed out on signing a few crucial deals.

'This should be a walk in the park,' he said, about the Tooting client. 'They want a poster campaign. See if you can upsell something digital as well. I need you to pull something out of the bag here, Sam. Otherwise we're going to have to seriously reconsider our position.' By our position he meant my position, and I knew a threat when I heard one.

The brief-taking meeting went smoothly and quickly. I managed to persuade them that they needed an email campaign and some banner ads too. The guy said if I got costings to him that evening, he'd sign everything off because they were on their month end and he had the budget to spend.

It took me less time to get back to north London than I'd expected. As a result, I was walking around Waitrose with a basket by around 5.30. It was a novelty not to be in a desperate hurry, so I was rather enjoying pottering through the store. I thought that perhaps I should get some flowers for Lara and her mum. There were some lovely gerberas. We needed a couple of things for home too – toothpaste and bread – so I strolled around the shop, picking up what I needed.

As I turned into the toiletries section, however, I stopped dead. A woman was standing looking at the shampoos at the far end of the aisle, her back to me. She was wearing jeans and a pink fluffy jumper, with a floppy, knitted hat at a jaunty angle on the back of her head. The hat covered her hair, but the stance, the curve of her hip and waist, the way she rested one foot in the instep of the other while she contemplated the products on the shelf. . . It was Helen. I was sure of it.

After the last debacle, when I'd hooted at the woman in the traffic, I decided to be more circumspect. I backed out of the aisle I was in, went to the next one along and swiftly walked the length of it so I could come into the toiletries aisle from the other end to catch her face to face. But as I swung around the corner, she came from the opposite direction and hit me squarely with her trolley.

'Sorry!' gasped the woman who was clearly not Helen.

'No, no, my fault.' She'd caught me sharply across the shins, and the pain shocked me into reality. She was a twenty-something blonde, with slightly protruding front teeth, pretty in a round-faced, sweet way. Close up, I could see she was a good inch or two shorter than Helen, and nothing at all like her.

'Are you sure you're all right?' she said, her eyes wide with consternation.

'Absolutely fine,' I assured her. 'I should pay attention to where I'm headed.'

Never a truer word, I thought, as I backed away and went to the tills to pay.

Once I'd got the kids home and into bed, I drank my way through six beers and half a bottle of vodka. When I woke up at 5 a.m., on the floor of the bathroom, I remembered the quotation I was supposed to have got to the man in Tooting. I couldn't even stand, let alone sit at my computer and create a spreadsheet. What was I going to tell Chris? I thought I saw my vanished wife in the supermarket so I drank myself stupid and missed the deadline?

Lara

So what is this thing between Sam and me? I don't know. I won't allow myself to even think the L-word. I think about him a lot but not in a mooning, teenage way. I worry about him, and I try to think of ways to make his life easier, and I wonder what he thinks about me. I also find myself wondering what's going to happen, because if we keep seeing each other, there'll be some big logistical issues involved in uniting our two households, if that doesn't sound too Shakespearean. And if it doesn't work out, I'll still have to see him at school every day for at least the next five years, which could be fantastically awkward.

I like him very much, but it's hard to separate that from pity, for a start, because he has had a shitty time of it. And it's also hard to imagine how we might have an easy, normal romantic relationship. We'd have to get past the issues of our four children, my live-in mother and his missing-but-still-lawfully-married wife. Not to mention Marc, who, if he hears I'm seeing someone, is liable to appear out of nowhere and complicate things. Christ. It was a lot simpler when it was just snogging behind the bike sheds, wasn't it?

It started as you might expect – lots of long chats over dinners with the kids and walks in the park. Then text messages about who had Miranda's ballet shoes became daily 'How was your day?' exchanges, then late-night text marathons and long phone calls.

We were texting one night when I was at work and it was quiet. I said I thought I'd close up early – it was about 9.30 and the pub was all but deserted.

'I know this is impulsive, but why don't you come by mine?' he texted. 'Girls are asleep. I've got a nice bottle of wine.'

I know a proposition when I hear it. I knew if we didn't have sex that night we would certainly be moving into a different phase in our friendship. I didn't respond immediately. I walked away from my phone and left it for ten minutes while I went to tell the kitchen to pack up. When I came back, he'd texted again.

'Oh God. Did that come out wrong? I read it back and it sounded really sleazy. I'm so sorry. Forget I said it. How do you get texts to self-destruct?'

I laughed, despite myself, and typed a reply. 'It didn't sound sleazy, unless you plan to be reclining on your chaise longue wearing nothing but a cravat and a cheesy smile. I'll hop in a cab and be over in half an hour, if the invitation still stands.'

He replied instantly. 'It does. Yes please. I'll get dressed now and pack the cravat away for another time.'

We didn't have sex that night, although there was a palpable tension in the room. We sat in the dimly lit living room, with the door closed, and talked quietly. It felt secret and intimate. I stayed for an hour, and then thought it best to head home, so I called another cab. When I stood to go, he stood too and moved close to me. The kiss was tentative, sad and sweet, and long. He stepped back, holding me lightly by my upper arms and searched my face with his eyes.

'Yes? No? Bad idea?' he said. 'I mean, I know it's a terrible idea on all sorts of levels, but I've been wanting to do that for the longest time.'

'Me too,' I said and I meant it.

I leaned in and kissed him again and this time the kiss got heated and we pressed close together. I could feel the warmth of his body. He's a tall, broad man and I could feel the strength of his desire. On the inside of my eyelids, I could see flashes of what was to come – him unzipping my skirt, pushing me back on to the sofa. Our trying to keep quiet but gasping with the urgency of it all. It felt rushed, and slightly terrifying. For him too, I think, because we pulled back at the same moment, both breathing hard.

'Oh my,' he said, and in the darkened room his eyes glittered almost dangerously.

'I should go.'

'Let the record show I don't want you to go,' he said in a rough whisper. 'But you're right, for all sorts of sensible, grown-up reasons.'

I didn't move, and we stood looking at each other like a pair of cage fighters about to go in for another bout. At that moment my phone began to buzz – the taxi driver, waiting outside. When I looked over Sam's shoulder, I could see the glow of the headlights catching the upstretched branches of the tree outside the window.

I looked back at Sam. 'We'll talk,' I said, bending to pick up my bag without taking my eyes off him.

My knees actually shook as I walked to the taxi. But for what reason, I couldn't actually say.

That night was four weeks ago. We've had sex since then – a lot of sex – quick, urgent, silent, standing up with my back pressed against a closed bedroom door, on sofas in his house and mine. None of it has been leisurely, loving or kind. All of it has been hurried and furtive, but in its own way exciting. Once, things were just getting heated between us when we heard Miranda in the hallway outside. Sam pulled away, went out to her and took her back to bed. It was a close thing. She could easily have walked in on us.

We've talked very little. We haven't discussed what this all means, or how we feel, or what the future might hold. I'm terrified to have those discussions, but I know we have to. Every time I go to his place on my way home from work, or when he comes to mine when the girls are staying over at their grandparents', I promise myself that I will initiate the adult conversations we need to be having. But I know as soon as I do, I'll break the spell, and the rare magic of this secret connection will be lost. So much in our lives is ugly, or disappointing, or banal or caught up in the grinding passage of the day-to-day. I want to have this strange, dangerous, unnamed thing for a little while longer.

Sam

I am a terrible, terrible man. She's a nice woman, a lovely woman, gorgeous (dear God, she is gorgeous, all long legs and slender, flat muscles – a dancer's body still). And I am using her and fucking her as if she's a. . . I don't know what. I don't love Lara. I'm not sure I ever will, or that I will ever love anyone again. I'm using her for physical release, and to fetch and carry my daughters. And she's allowing me to do it.

I remember the night we found out Helen wasn't coming back, that extraordinarily weird night when Tim and I went out drinking and ended up in the pub where Lara works. Tim eyed her up and flirted and she shut him down and I thought then that she disliked flirtatious bad boys and had seen through Tim's charming shtick.

It made me like her – clearly a woman who wasn't easily fooled. And yet she's letting me behave appallingly. We've spent several evenings where we've got together for movies or pizza, and then let the kids all fall asleep in front of the TV. We've gone upstairs to her bedroom for quick, dirty sex, and before there's a chance for conversation, I say I have to go, load the sleeping girls into the car and get out of there. Why is she letting me do it? Is it because I'm a 'nice guy'? Or is it because I am so damned tragic – once widowed, once abandoned – that she can't ask anything of me? I think that's probably closer to the truth.

All this was playing on my mind when we met one Saturday afternoon a few weeks ago to take the kids for a walk along the brook by the golf course near her house. The girls and I had walked down, or Marguerite and I had walked, while Miranda rode round us in circles on her bicycle. She'd already declared that going for a family walk was 'lame', and had only agreed to it at all because we were meeting Frances. If she and Frances were on their bikes and could stay far enough ahead or behind the rest of us, they might be spared the near certain death-by-embarrassment that would occur if we bumped into anyone from school.

As we turned the corner at the top of Lara's road, I could see all the way to the bottom where the stream crossed under the footpath and the walk began. Lara, Frances and Jonah were already waiting on the bridge. It looked as though they were playing Pooh Sticks – Lara was helping Jonah hunt for a suitable twig, while Frances stood by impatiently, her own collection of sticks held loosely in her hand.

Miranda freewheeled down the pavement ahead of us, tinging her bicycle bell, and Frances looked up. She immediately peeled off from the game and she and Miranda went into one of their huddles, sharing some vital piece of news. Lara and Jonah were too intent on the game to notice our approach and were leaning over the rail, looking for their sticks. I watched Lara, her, thick red hair hanging down and shining in the winter sunshine, her legs long and slim in jeans.

'Hi there,' I called, and she straightened up, brushed off her jacket and gave me a wide, warm and unaffected smile. I found myself grinning back, and when I got to her, totally on impulse, I gathered her in my arms and gave her a big smacking kiss on the lips and a long hug. Marguerite and Jonah ignored us – they were hunting for sticks to continue the game – but over Lara's shoulder I saw Frances and Miranda look at us, startled and slightly horrified.

To my surprise, Lara pushed me away firmly, frowning and shaking her head. I raised an eyebrow at her, questioningly.

'Let's walk, it's freezing,' she said, and wrapped her arms tightly around herself, warding me off.

Frances and Miranda were still watching us warily.

'Get your bike, Frances,' said Lara, her voice high and brittle.

Frances ran and collected it from the far side of the bridge. She put on her helmet and with a last backward glance she and Miranda set off on the path ahead of us.

Jonah and Marguerite pottered along in front of us. Marguerite was telling Jonah a long story involving some flower fairies and a unicorn. He was barely listening. He'd found an enormous stick, taller than him, and was manfully dragging it along. I expected Lara to tell him to drop it, but she didn't seem to be paying attention. She still had her arms tightly crossed over her chest, and her face, bright and rosy-cheeked before, looked pale and pinched when I glanced sideways at her.

'I'm sorry,' I said quietly.

'You should be.'

'You looked so lovely, and I was happy to see you.'

'Thank you,' she said, and I checked to see if she was smiling. She wasn't, but she didn't look quite so angry. She was so pretty, and so desirable, with her fine, fragile bones and wild russet hair. I found my mouth beginning to speak, without my brain having engaged at all.

'Anyway, I thought maybe it was time we. . .'

'We what?'

'Brought things out into the open?'

'What things?'

'Things. . .' I said awkwardly, beginning to feel silly, 'between us.'

'And it didn't occur to you that maybe we should have a conversation about this? That you might like to canvass my opinion on what those "things" might be? Maybe discuss when and if I might like to tell my own children?'

'I'm sorry.'

There was a long silence.

'We are in a weird situation here, Sam.'

'I know.'

'I mean, I know thirty-something relationships can get complicated, what with children and baggage and whatnot, but you and me. . . it's *very* complicated.'

'I know.'

We came out into an open bit of parkland, and I could see that Miranda and Frances had stopped on the path ahead of us. They were leaning on their bikes, looking back at us and talking together. They didn't look happy.

'It's just. . .' Lara said haltingly. 'If we start something and it all goes horribly wrong, well. . . what happens then?'

'We kind of have started something.'

'We've started having sex. But that's just you and me. If we involve the kids, if people find out. . . there's a whole weight on the relationship. A pressure. It suddenly gets very serious.'

I glanced over at her. This wasn't at all what I had expected. It hadn't occurred to me that she too might be ambivalent. She looked up at me. Her eyes were spectacularly green in the grey January light. It was terribly important, right at that moment, that I persuade her.

'Why don't we give it a go and see what happens?' I said. It sounded lame, but it was the best I could come up with.

'It's like sky-diving,' she said. 'Right now, we're still in the plane. But if we give it a go, we jump. And we can't change our minds and get back in.'

'There's an analogy in there somewhere about being chopped up by the propellers.'

'I'm a restaurant manager.' She managed a weak smile. 'That's about as much metaphor as I can manage.' She walked on a few steps and then stopped to look at me.

'This is scary, Sam. And the hardest part is, of all the people involved, you and I probably have the least to lose.'

We looked out over the frozen park. All four kids had gathered under a tree and were looking up at its stark, leafless branches. Miranda was pointing something out to Jonah, holding his hand.

'So what do we do?' I asked. 'Do we stop hanging out? Stop having sex? Go back to being school-gate acquaintances? Or do we jump?'

She was quiet for the longest time. Then she turned and stood facing me squarely. She made herself uncross her arms, and took a deep breath.

'Jump,' she said.

That evening, after the kids had fallen asleep, we talked late into the night. We decided that the parameters had to be firmly agreed. We'd tell the kids that we were 'dating,' and we'd tell Lara's mum. No one else for now. We'd see each other three times a week. No sleepovers. Yet. No big, long-term plans.

So that was it. We were in a relationship, albeit one with some serious rules and regulations. Except all the rules and regulations went out of the window pretty much on day one. The next weekend after our Big Talk, we ended up back at Lara's and the kids dragged mattresses in front of the TV to watch a movie. Predictably, they fell asleep one by one. Lara's mum was out for the evening with friends, and Lara and I sat in the kitchen splitting a bottle of wine, holding hands and talking quietly. It felt good to be affectionate with her. It felt comfortable and natural.

I looked at my watch at about eleven and said, 'I should get the girls home.'

Lara glanced out of the window. 'Yuck,' she said. 'Look at that.'

Sleet was falling steadily outside, and the tops of the trees bent and swayed in a strong, icy wind.

'That looks rough,' I said. 'Maybe it'll have died down in half an hour or so.'

But it didn't. The wet stuff kept falling and the wind kept howling. I must say, I didn't fancy carrying the girls, heavy with sleep, out to the car one by one and then making poor Miranda wake up and walk through the wet to get into the house.

'Maybe. . .' I said hesitantly, looking out of the window.

'You should stay,' said Lara firmly.

'Are you sure?'

'You can't take the girls outside in this. Let's take the little ones for a wee and cover them up warmly. We'll get up before they do and tell them you slept in the study.'

It was warm and quiet in Lara's big, brass-framed bed. We had sex (or was it making love?) and were both completely naked together for the first time. Afterwards, she fell asleep quickly, and I watched her eyes move restlessly behind the fine, thin eyelids. In repose, her face was young and almost plain – fine-boned and freckled, but pale, with narrow, neatly formed lips and light brows and lashes. She looked like a sleeping angel drawn by Edward Burne-Jones.

I was wide awake and aware that if any of the children woke before we did and came into the bedroom, my being naked in Lara's bed was far from ideal. I got up and pulled on a T-shirt and underwear, and then tiptoed to the bathroom for a drink of water. The sleet had stopped and I stood on the landing, looking out of the window on to Lara's overgrown garden. I remembered the first time I had come to the house – the day Helen disappeared. And even though this wasn't the first time I'd had sex with Lara, I felt a deep, painful pang of guilt. This was different from the one-night stands I'd had. For the first time, I felt I had been unfaithful to my wife.

Since that first night, there's been little point in sticking to 'rules'. It's easy for Lara to pick up all four kids after school, so she's been doing that, and while the girls and I stay at home during the week, we tend to stay over at Lara's house on Friday and Saturday nights now.

I didn't say anything to anyone at school, and neither did Lara, but the word soon spread. Ella approached me before school one morning, clutching a sheaf of tickets for the International Quiz Evening.

'You're always such a star at the quiz, Sam,' she said, resting a hand on my arm. 'I hope you and Lara will come.'

I looked at her, and her gaze was deliberately innocent.

'Sure, why not?' I said, and handed over a twenty for two tickets.

Lara suspected the news had passed through the kids. I imagined there had been a little espionage on the part of the nosier mothers – they'd have noticed Lara collecting Miranda and Marguerite regularly and would have pressed their children to ask ours what was going on. Helen always used to joke about the intelligence-gathering abilities of the school-gate mums. 'It took the US years to find Bin Laden,' she said. 'If they'd asked the mums at our school, they'd have had him by afternoon playtime. Someone would have known someone who knew his mum and what she once said to his Auntie Fatima.'

So Lara and I are in a relationship. And because of the way our families are put together, we're in a six-person relationship, which is by its nature not a very romantic one. Yes, occasionally Lara's mum keeps an eye on all the kids so we can go out for a meal or catch a movie, but Lara works most nights and wants to spend her weekend evenings with her children if she can. Even when we do go out, we talk a lot about the children, and about domestic arrangements, and end up coming home early to check on them all. Then we make love and fall asleep. In a funny way, it feels as if we've gone from friendship to being a middle-aged, long-term couple in a matter of weeks, without any of the romance and drama that usually comes between.

I have no complaints of course. Lara's a lovely woman. She's kind and steady, and having her in my life makes everything easier and less painful. I'm drinking less and sleeping more. I'm on to a good thing, obviously.

CHAPTER ELEVEN

Sam

This time, it was definitely Helen. Not a shadow of a doubt. It was the way the chestnut ponytail swung as she walked, almost skipping, in that brisk, efficient way Helen had. She was moving swiftly away, half a block ahead of me on Oxford Street, disappearing through the thick throngs of people – busy business people on their phones, oblivious to those around them, and impassable wedges of tourists dawdling three abreast. I was going to lose her, so in a desperate, possibly suicidal move, I stepped into the road and ran up the bus lane, shouting, 'Helen! Helen!' A black cab headed straight for me and hooted wildly, so I leapt back on to the pavement, shouldering a woman in high heels who lurched sideways with a cry. I heard the roar of her angry boyfriend, but only faintly, because I was off and sprinting again.

Helen, now only twenty yards or so ahead of me, suddenly turned right into a side road, and I barged through the crowds on the pavement to follow her. She could move faster now she was out of the throng, and by the time I had rounded the corner, she was already half a block away. I was out of breath – I'd got overweight and out of shape. 'Helen!' I called helplessly, but she didn't turn and I started to run again. I didn't mean for my hand to fall quite so heavily on her shoulder, but I was off balance and tired. 'Helen!' I said, and she stumbled, then spun round to look at me.

'Fuck off!' she said sharply, wrenching herself free from my grip. And even through the haze of my tiredness, I could hear that her accent was Eastern European and see that, of course, once again she wasn't Helen. Her thin, sharply pencilled eyebrows were raised, and when she snarled another insult at me, I could see her teeth were yellowed and crooked.

'Sorry. Sorry,' I said, stepping backwards and colliding with someone who was walking behind me. 'I thought you were someone else.' I held my hands up to show her I meant no harm, apologized to the frumpy, aggrieved woman whose foot I had stepped on and fled back in the direction of Oxford Street and the anonymity of the crowds.

I walked around for an hour or so after that, stopping every now and then in a bar or pub. I didn't drink beer. I didn't want to go back to Lara's smelling like a brewery, so I drank shots of tequila.

It wasn't just the sighting of another not-Helen, it was the call I'd had from the bank before that. I'd missed a credit-card instalment. It wasn't carelessness. I hadn't had the cash to make even a minimum payment. It was one thing after another: a leak in the bathroom, I'd needed a new suit, a grocery bill which was extortionate (but then I have been buying a lot of ready meals and booze), and then the car went in for its MOT and failed. In the old days, my salary and commission bonuses would easily have covered those costs, but these days, I'm barely scraping my basic. It's about enough for the mortgage payment, but not much else. I'm going to have to do something radical, I thought. And soon.

Lara

Sam was preoccupied. That's not unusual – he's often lost in his thoughts and the girls will shout at him shrilly to 'Listen, Daddy!', and I'll have to repeat a question three times before he pays attention. But today was different. He arrived late for dinner and smelling slightly of booze – for the first time in a long time he'd obviously stopped for a drink on the way home from work. He looked rumpled and stressed, like the Sam of the bad old days before we started seeing each other. It wasn't till I saw him looking like that that I realized how much better he's got in the past few months. He came in and sat slumped in an armchair in the living room while the girls cavorted around him talking over one another to share news of their day. He couldn't even manage to grunt or nod to pretend he was listening. Marguerite particularly began to show off and whine and be bratty, desperate for any attention, even the negative kind. So I bundled them all off upstairs to read Jonah a bedtime story and get him ready for bed. The two older girls love any opportunity to 'mother' Jonah (translation, boss him to within an inch of his life), and Marguerite will go along with it as long as the others are all doing it.

I went into the kitchen to get Sam his dinner, which I was keeping warm in the oven. He followed me into the kitchen. 'Do you have any beer?' he asked.

'No, sorry,' I said.

'What about wine?'

'Nope. I can offer you juice or fizzy water, that's about it.'

I might pop out and get some,' he said vaguely, but he didn't move towards the door.

I handed him his plate. He didn't thank me, just stood holding it absent-mindedly, at a slight angle. I was worried he might drop it, or tip the food on to the floor.

'What's wrong with you?' I asked, taking the plate back from him and setting it down on the table. 'You look terrible.'

His attention flashed back to me. 'Why, thank you,' he said, giving me his sweet, crooked smile. 'You say the nicest things.'

'I don't mean that. You look distracted. Upset. Did something bad happen at work?'

'No, nothing like that.' I could see he was weighing up whether to explain. Eventually, he said, 'I. . . I thought I saw Helen today.'

'Wait. . . what? Where?'

'It wasn't her,' he said hastily. 'Just a woman who looked like her, who told me to fuck off after I chased her up Oxford Street.'

'Wow,' I said.

'It isn't the first time,' he continued. 'It keeps happening. I catch a glimpse of someone and I'm convinced it's Helen. It never is though. Just a ghost in my mind.'

I wasn't sure how to respond. It had become almost pathological how Helen's name was never mentioned between us. He certainly never said her name in front of the girls, and never talked to me about her either. I'd been taking my cues from him so hadn't brought her up either. And now here he was, admitting he'd been hallucinating Helen all over town. I took a deep breath.

'Why don't you pop to the shop and get a bottle of wine?' I said. 'We'll talk about this when all the kids are in bed.'

Later, we sat together on the sofa. I usually like to sit in the curve of his arm when we watch TV, but today I found myself curled up on the far end, my legs pulled up under me. I needed a little distance for this conversation. Sam sat in his usual spot, at the other end of the sofa, staring at the blank TV screen and taking large, regular gulps from his glass of wine.

'So can you tell me about these. . . sightings?' I prompted gently.

He related a few incidents when he'd seen someone who had resembled Helen.

'I know it's crazy,' he said. 'I know it can't be her. There's no reason at all to believe she's stayed in London. I mean, why would she? But every time it happens, I can't help myself. I go into full adrenaline mode and I want to chase her and stop her and. . .'

There was a long silence.

'And what?' I asked.

'I don't know. Keep hold of her until she tells me. . . until she tells me *why*.'

There was such pain in that 'why'. There were nights and nights of analysis, of self-flagellation, of questions for which there were no answers. And all I could think was, I'm not helping him at all. There's this pit of pain in him, and there's nothing I can do to make it go away.

Hesitantly, I scooted along the sofa so I could take his hand in mine. 'I'm so sorry. I wish I could help you. Is there anyone you could speak to?'

He glanced at me. 'Have you been speaking to Tim? He thinks I need therapy. Can't afford it, I'm afraid.'

'I didn't mean that. I meant isn't there anyone you could speak to who might help you understand why she went? Or even where she might be? She must have family. Friends.'

Sam explained to me that she didn't. She'd had one uncle in Canada, apparently, who was now gaga and in a nursing home. No siblings, both parents dead. And no friends, other than the school-gate ones we both knew about. I knew they didn't know any more than I did. There'd been enough gossip about it, and no one had been able to offer anything but the wildest conjecture. I agreed with Sam. There was no one in our social circle who was harbouring Helen's dark secrets.

'What about before she came to the UK? She must have had friends in Australia.'

Again, Sam said, his searches had turned up blanks. He picked up his phone and entered a search for 'Helen Knight Brisbane'. The speed and assurance with which he typed it suggested to me he'd done this often before. And indeed, every link on the first page showed up in that purple colour which tells you you've visited that page before. He showed me the one school and one university image he'd found.

'Nothing else? Really?'

'Nothing.'

'Isn't that weird and suspicious in itself? Who has absolutely no web presence? Everyone gets tagged in a Facebook pic by an old friend, or crops up in pictures at a company away-day. She worked before, didn't she?'

'Yes, in marketing. In a similar field to me. We met at work.'

'And I assume that since she went missing, she hasn't cropped up online again?'

'Not once. She deleted her Facebook profile. That's the only sign I've had that she's still out there – one day it was there, and the next she deleted it.'

I paused for a second to take in the news that Sam had obviously been watching Helen's Facebook profile. Of course he would have been. It was understandable. I shook my head.

'It makes no sense. How does she disappear off the Net for eight years, between the end of university and coming to the UK, and then disappear again?'

'I. Don't. Know,' said Sam, and I could see he was getting tense. He didn't want to go over all of this again. It was a hopeless, self-destructive spiral, and he never got any closer to an answer.

He took a long gulp from his wine glass and emptied it. Then he pulled me to him firmly and began unbuttoning my shirt. He clearly wanted to forget, and this was the way he was going to do it.

Sam

'We met at work.' It sounds so trite, so pedestrian. Something like 15 per cent of couples meet at work. It makes the beginning of our relationship seem like one of those terrible stock photographs where a handsome guy leans against the wall by a water cooler as a pretty girl (wearing glasses to show she's clever and serious) listens to him raptly, holding an armful of files. It was nothing like that. Neither Helen nor I were ever able to remember the first time we met – we used to laugh about that, that neither of us had been paying attention at that significant moment in our lives.

I remember the first time I noticed her though. We were in a big team meeting and she was being perky and bright and Australian, and I thought she was one of the most irritating girls I'd ever come across. I knew who she was, obviously, but this was my first professional encounter with her. She was super-organized, with all her coloured pens lined up neatly along the edge of her notebook, and she'd come to the meeting with screeds of useful data and research and lots of well-thought-out ideas. I'd rolled in ten minutes late, and it wasn't till I sat down and glimpsed my reflection in the glass wall of the meeting room that I realized I'd forgotten to brush my hair that morning. I was hung-over and fuzzy. Leonora had been dead for about ten months, and while I was kind of managing, I still had nights where I drank and listened to her old CDs and cried. It was partially grief and partially self-pity because I was a twenty-eight-year-old widower with two daughters under four and back living with my parents.

So when I got to the morning meeting and Little Miss Perky Antipodean was passing around her crisp, photocopied pie charts and graphs, it got right up my nose. Someone passed me a sheaf of her notes and I deliberately pushed them away without looking at them. It was bratty and unprofessional, but I couldn't face her shiny enthusiasm. I saw her glance at me, and her eyes narrowed a little. 'Here we go,' I thought. 'She's going to tell me off like a naughty schoolboy.' But she didn't say anything. She talked less for the rest of the meeting, and I wondered if her more subdued manner was caused by my snub. I felt a little guilty, but I forgot about it quickly enough.

Later that afternoon, I was starting to fall asleep at my desk, so I went to the kitchen to make a cup of coffee. While I was stirring in an extra spoonful of sugar, my phone rang. It was my mum, who had collected Miranda from nursery.

'How is she?' I asked.

'Not so good,' said Mum, and I could hear Miranda's pitiful sobs in the background.

'I wanna speak to Daddy!' she wailed.

'Can you have a word with her?' said Mum.

'Of course.' I could hear the rustle as Mum bent down to hold the phone to Miranda's ear.

'Hey, poppet,' I said, and at that moment Helen walked into the kitchen. She saw I was on the phone and indicated she didn't mean to interrupt. She went over to the tap to refill her water bottle.

'What's up?' I said to Miranda.

'Come home, Daddy!' she wailed. 'I need you to come home.'

'I can't come home right now, sweetie, I'm at work. I'll be home in a couple of—'

'I need you now! I've got a poorly finger and a sore tummy. I need you.' She let out another long wail.

'Baby girl, I've got a meeting to go to. I'll get home as soon as—'

My mum cut in. 'It's me again,' she said. Miranda had obviously pushed away the phone, distraught that I wasn't going to drop everything and come home.

'How is she really?' I asked.

'She's under the weather, coming down with a bug or something. It's to be expected with all the germs at nursery.'

'She's only just got over an ear infection though.' I rested my forehead on the cool, smooth surface of the kitchen cupboard.

'Well, that's as may be, but she's definitely warm, and you can hear she's upset. I'll get her back to the house and dose her up with paracetamol. We'll see you later.'

My mum doesn't do game-playing, so I knew she wasn't trying to guilt-trip me into coming home. I couldn't anyway.

'Okay,' I said, reluctantly. 'Well, give her a kiss from me.' I clicked off the phone, then turned and saw that Helen was still in the kitchen, holding her water bottle in both hands and watching me. I gave her a half-hearted, insincere smile. I didn't appreciate her hanging around listening to my personal conversations.

'Go,' she said suddenly.

'I beg your pardon?'

'Go home to your little girl. I'll tell Chris you had to go on an urgent client visit.'

'I can't. . .'

'You can. Someone needs to go and pick up a logo on a flash drive from that insurance client.'

'I know, but. . .'

She stuck her hand into the pocket of her skirt. 'It so happens I did it at lunchtime, but nobody knows yet. You can bring it in first thing tomorrow. It's your alibi. Now go home and curl up on the sofa with that little girl.'

I looked at her, uncomprehending. 'Go,' she said again, and pressed the flash drive into my hand. I muttered thanks, then went back past my desk to fetch my jacket.

'Just popping to the insurance client to get that logo,' I said to Dina, the copywriter who sat opposite me. She barely looked up, just kept typing.

I walked quickly out of the office. Helen, now back at her desk and typing away at top speed, glanced up and gave me a bright smile. As I passed through the doors and headed for the lifts, I found myself thinking how pretty she was.

The next morning, I stopped off at the bakery on the corner of the road and bought a warm, flaky, almond croissant. I left it on Helen's desk with a Post-it note on which I'd scrawled: 'Thanks. From Miranda and me.'

Fifteen minutes later, an email popped up: 'Delicious, thanks. You didn't need to. Hx'

That afternoon, I waited for my coffee break until I saw her pass by to go to the kitchen for her water. When I walked in, she grinned at me.

'How's your little girl?' she asked.

'She's fine. Nothing wrong with her that a long cuddle and a game of My Little Pony wouldn't fix.'

'My Little Pony? I used to play with those when I was small.'

'You can't keep a good pony down, you know. They're like the Stones. Eternal classics.'

'You were widowed, weren't you?' she asked. When I looked surprised, she said, 'Sorry. I haven't been here long enough. I still ask direct questions – very un-British, I know.'

'It's okay,' I said. 'Yes, my wife died about ten months ago.'

'How old is your daughter?'

'Daughters. Miranda is three, nearly four. Marguerite is eighteen months. We live with my mum and dad at the moment. I couldn't work without them.'

She nodded, then waited for me to continue; her gaze was direct and warm. I liked the fact that she didn't flinch, or look uncomfortable or offer any platitudes. I was young to be widowed, so most people my age had no idea what to say. They had no experience of death and they tended to shy away or get upset on my behalf, which was unhelpful, as I ended up comforting them as they wept about my poor tiny daughters. But Helen listened and asked sensible, calm questions. I got the feeling that she'd faced difficulties herself and was thus more grown-up than her contemporaries.

After that, I made a point of meeting up with her in the kitchen most afternoons, trying to make it look accidental. I found myself thinking about her smile more often than I would have thought possible. Then, one sunny Wednesday, I was engrossed in typing an email when I realized she was standing beside my desk.

'I'm heading out to get a sandwich for lunch,' she said. 'Fancy coming along?'

I actually had my lunch already, in a Tupperware box in my bag – I was trying to save money, so I tended to bring food in from home – but I didn't hesitate.

'Yeah, sure,' I said, trying to sound casual. 'Give me a minute to finish this and I'll meet you in reception.'

One lunch became lunch two or three times a week, an exchange of phone numbers, and a reasonable amount of light banter via text message. I couldn't quite sort out what was going on, or indeed what my feelings about it were. I liked her, but Leonora hadn't been dead a year, so every time I found myself looking at Helen romantically or sexually, I'd be swept away with a wave of guilt and longing for my wife. I also couldn't read

Helen's intentions at all. Was she my work buddy? Was this a pity friendship? Or did she have feelings for me too? I couldn't imagine it. After all, who would take me on? I was a mess. I lived with my parents, for God's sake. I had no leisure time for dating or romance, and no money. I couldn't expect anything more from her than I was already getting. But what I was getting – oh, it was a small ray of light in my dark life.

And then, one particularly bad day, I had been out to see a client, who hated the designs I'd done, and I'd just got a text message from Miranda's nursery to say they'd had an outbreak of head lice. I walked into the building feeling tired and downtrodden, only to find that the lifts were all up on the top floor. I started to trudge up the stairs and about halfway up I met Helen, who was skipping down, on her way to a meeting. As soon as she saw me, her face broke into the happiest, most infectious smile, and she dumped her satchel and sat down on the stairs to chat to me, as if she had all the time in the world. It was like the sun had come out in that dingy stairwell. I made some lame, half-hearted joke and she laughed, a bright, delightful peal, and I thought with absolute simplicity, 'I am in love with her.'

For a year, I'd been unable to imagine a future beyond the dreadful day-to-day grind of survival, but all of a sudden there was clarity. Helen. Helen was my future. Helen, filling my arms, my bed, shining that sunshiny smile on my poor sad little girls. In a nanosecond, a whole stream of possibilities occurred to me. With two salaries, we could get a place together. I wouldn't be living at my parents' like a loser anymore. It'd take the pressure off me if I could share childcare with someone. Maybe I could get ahead at work? We could get married. Have a baby of our own. Build a new life. Yes. A future. Yes, there were practical ways in which this could work, but more than anything, I loved her. I really, really loved her.

As these thoughts tumbled through my head, I must have stared at her in a particularly gormless, goggle-eyed way, because she stopped laughing and said, 'What?'

And I found myself saying, 'Would you like to come to the park with me and the girls this weekend?'

Six years later, I woke up in another woman's bed, feeling like shit. I was much too hot under Lara's heavy down duvet. I was dehydrated and hung-over, and Lara's side of the bed was empty. I could feel from the stuffy air that she'd got up and put the heating on, which wasn't helping my thirst and general misery. Downstairs I could hear all four kids yelling and thumping, and the siren wail of Marguerite beginning to throw an A-grade tantrum. More than anything, I wished I could hide in the bedroom for the next several hours, but I had a fierce need to pee and an even more urgent need to drink several pints of cold water and then several more pints of coffee.

Was it possible to get up, pee and get some water, and somehow signal to Lara to bring me coffee, while still hiding from all the kids in the bedroom? How I wished I could. But I was conscious of taking far too much advantage of Lara's goodwill where the kids were concerned, and also that Marguerite in particular needed some quality one-to-one time with me.

While Marguerite ostensibly likes being part of a larger, more boisterous household, all this hasn't been easy for her. Frances and Miranda are inseparable and aren't always kind in the way they force her out of their games. And sweet though Jonah is, he's more than three years younger than Marguerite and not a proper playmate for her. A tougher kid might have fought for attention, or made their own entertainment, but Marguerite isn't tough. She's passive and shy and quite babyish for her age.

She has taken Helen's departure the hardest of all of us, in some ways. She's not angry with Helen, like I am, or icily indifferent, like Miranda. She desperately misses the only mother she has ever known. And so she whines. She's always whined quite a lot anyway, but it's got massively worse in recent months, and it makes her – it's hard to admit this, but it's true – annoying and not terribly appealing.

Lara has been endlessly patient and kind to her, but she (very sensibly) has kept a careful distance between herself and my girls. They're not ready for another 'mother' figure in the same mould as Helen. As for me, all too often I'm tired and ratty with the girls, and we have such limited time to get the necessary things done – homework, baths, chores and so on – that I don't have the time for affection, laughs, cuddles and stories, which is what Marguerite is sorely lacking.

No matter how grim I felt, I knew that what I needed to do today was make time for my younger daughter. I'd be taking Miranda and Frances to the dance school in an hour or so, and they'd be there till past lunchtime. Normally I ended up dragging Marguerite around the supermarket with me in those few hours, or I'd make her sit quietly and watch a DVD while I got on with work. But today I'd take her for a treat – she loved to go to Claire's Accessories and spend hours looking at the bits of jewellery and hair ornaments. I'd grit my teeth and let her browse for as long as she wanted and choose something special. Miranda would no doubt sulk about it, but that was too bad. She could have a solo indulgence another day.

At that moment the bedroom door was flung back and Marguerite stood there, her face red with indignation and her upper lip slick with snot.

'Hey, baby,' I said warmly. 'I was just thinking about you.'

'Miranda's being horrible to me.' Her voice hit a particularly high-pitched whine and I felt a sharp needle of pain in my left eye socket.

'I'm sure she doesn't mean to be, poppet,' I said gently. 'Look, give me five minutes to get dressed and I'll come down and talk to her.'

Marguerite ignored my words and stomped over to climb on the bed. She launched into a garbled litany of tragic complaints about her sister. She flopped down on the pillow, and I noticed she had her shoes on, which were pressing into Lara's pale blue duvet cover, and that her upper lip was positively dripping. I reached over her to Lara's bedside table and grabbed a tissue, but when I tried to wipe her nose, she batted my hand away and kept talking. I lost it.

'Off the bed!' I roared. 'Your filthy shoes. . .' She jumped at the sound of my shout and instantly began to cry. I could hear it all go quiet downstairs and I could imagine Lara looking up at the ceiling, hearing me shout and Marguerite cry. What a bastard she must think me.

'I'm sorry, poppet, so sorry I yelled,' I said gruffly, and I put my arms around my sobbing little girl. 'Listen, Daddy's been a grumpy old bear. What do you say I take you to Claire's Accessories when Miranda and Frances are dancing?'

The tears switched off like a tap and she beamed at me widely. 'Really, Daddy? Yes, please!'

And she hopped off the bed and disappeared downstairs, no doubt to gloat at her sister.

I swung my legs out of the bed and stood up. My head pounded fiercely. I wasn't sure I could take the shopping mall and hundreds of screaming children. Maybe I could put off the trip to Claire's Accessories till tomorrow? But as soon as I thought it, I knew I couldn't. Not unless I wanted Force 10 whining from Marguerite for forty-eight hours. A pee, a big drink of water, whatever painkillers were in Lara's bathroom cabinet, and a scorching shower, followed by coffee and bacon and eggs. That'd do the trick.

When I came out of the bathroom twenty minutes later, I felt immeasurably better – almost human.

And bless Lara, a steaming cup of coffee was sitting on the bedside table. I sat on the edge of the bed to enjoy the first few life-giving sips and noticed that the light on my mobile was flashing. A message? No, a missed call, from a long, international number I didn't recognize. +61? Where was that? I did a quick web search. Australia? Brisbane? How odd. The person hadn't left a message though. Could it be one of those spam callers, where you ring back and they charge you hundreds of pounds? Australia seemed an unlikely country of origin for something like that. I was contemplating calling the number to see, when my phone lit up in my hand and began to ring again. The same number. I answered.

'Is that Sam Cooper?' said a woman's voice, her Aussie twang unmistakeable.

'Yes, who is this?'

'The Sam Cooper who posted the message on Facebook about his missing wife?'

I paused for a second. That bloody post. I'd taken my original version down the day after Helen was reported found, but there was nothing I could do about the thousands of times it had been shared. It still periodically cropped up – some people never check the dates on those things – but then someone would post 'She's been found' and it would disappear again. Obviously this fruitcake hadn't got the message.

'Yes, that's me,' I said wearily. 'Thank you for your concern, but Helen isn't missing anymore, she's. . .'

'Is she back with you?' said the woman, and I could hear the surprise in her voice.

'Well, no, but. . . Listen, who is this?'

'This is Judy,' said the voice, as if this should mean something to me. When I didn't reply or show any sign of recognition, she said, 'Judy Knight? Helen's sister?'

PART THREE

CHAPTER TWELVE

Helen

She checked and rechecked the contents of her big blue handbag. Once she walked out of the door, that was it. Anything she didn't have now, she would not be able to come back and retrieve. She checked the doors and windows, made sure everything was exactly in its place as usual, and took a deep breath. It was time.

She stood by the living-room window and waited until she saw Mrs Goode come out of her house, clearly on her way to Sainsbury's. She always went at around this time. Mrs Goode stood on her driveway, fiddling with her shopping bags. Helen stepped out of her own front door. She gave Mrs Goode a cheery wave and called hello, making sure Mrs Goode noticed her and got a good look at what she was wearing. She locked the door – she had had a copy made of the mortice-lock key for the front door, but her own complete bunch of keys was in the satchel wedged behind the desk. She dropped the key into her handbag and set off, walking briskly down the street. If Mrs Goode had been paying attention, she might have noticed that Helen wore her hair in a low plait down her back rather than in her trademark jaunty, high ponytail. But why would Mrs Goode notice? And even if she mentioned it, who would think it meant anything? Helen got to the end of the road and glanced back to see if Mrs Goode was paying attention. She wasn't. She had gone back into her house, presumably having forgotten something.

Helen looked both ways. There was no one in sight. She took a right turn and walked into the park. Half past nine was a good time – the early-morning runners and commuters were gone, along with the dog walkers. Most mums who brought their babies and toddlers out for a morning walk had already gone home for their naps and snacks. The park was largely deserted and, anyway, Helen had already pinpointed her spot – a patch of dense woodland. Even though it wasn't far from the path, once you were inside it, you weren't visible. She was sure there was no one around, but she double-checked to be certain. This was the real point of no return. She hesitated for only a second, then stepped off the path and bent almost double to get past the overhanging trees and grasping shrubs.

Once she had pushed her way into the little clearing, she paused again, making sure there was no noise – no curious dogs or hidden walkers. Satisfied she was alone, she began. She pulled the floral dress off over her head in a single motion. Under the dress, she was already wearing calf-length black leggings. She took a plain black T-shirt from her bag and put it on, slipping off her pumps and replacing them with trainers. All of the black clothes were brand new – Sam had never seen them and so would not be able to identify them as missing from her wardrobe. She rolled up the dress and put it with the pumps into her bag. Then she took out the pair of sharp hairdresser's scissors which she'd bought some weeks before, and after a moment's hesitation, cut off her plait. She wrapped it in the plastic bag she had ready and placed it with the scissors in her handbag. She put on a pair of heavy-rimmed spectacles and checked her reflection. The haircut was brutal, but it would do for the next half an hour. She checked around her carefully, to make sure she hadn't left any traces of her presence, and prepared to move on.

Three minutes earlier, a pretty woman with long hair and a blue floral dress had walked confidently into the park. Now, a shy, hunched, bespectacled woman with cropped hair and wearing a baggy-T-shirt and leggings re-emerged on to the path. She looked at her watch.

Her biggest fear had been running into someone she knew on this first part of the journey, and it was realized. She saw Sarah Westwood, one of the mothers from school, jogging along the path towards her. Helen dropped her head and kept walking. Sarah was red in the face and puffing, and obviously lost in the music playing in her earphones. She barely gave Helen a glance as she passed. Helen gave a ragged sigh of relief. It didn't mean she was safe, just that she had passed that particular test.

She'd planned the route to her next destination carefully, avoiding any main arterials or roads where someone she knew lived. It took some brisk walking to get there at the appointed time of eleven o'clock. The small, neighbourhood hair salon, narrow and nondescript, was called The Cut Above. She'd found it some weeks before and had made an appointment there by phone, in the name of Ellen.

The women in the salon were occupied with chatting to one another and their regular customers, a row of formidable old birds who were there for their weekly set appointments. They paid barely any attention to the frumpy younger woman who had come in for a trim and highlights.

'Terrible cut you have there,' commented the woman who was looking after her. 'Looks like someone hacked your hair with a pair of nail scissors.'

Helen didn't reply, just gave a nervous smile.

'Colour first, then I'll cut and sort this mess out,' said the woman. Together, she and Helen selected some bright honey highlights, then she applied the colour and wrapped strands of Helen's hair in foil.

Once the colour was done, the woman moved around her hair snipping and tidying until Helen had a short, attractive pixie cut. She blow-dried it efficiently, if a little more stiffly than Helen would have done herself. Helen put her glasses on and looked at her reflection in the mirror. To all but the most observant onlooker, she would be unrecognizable. She paid with cash, shouldered her bag and left.

Her route into town was carefully planned and winding, again avoiding any main roads, or roads with petrol stations, cashpoints, bus routes or stations. She walked as much as she could through the parks – first Hampstead Heath, then Primrose Hill and Regent's Park. It took her more than two hours to walk into central London. Now she was in town, it would be impossible to avoid being seen by CCTV cameras, but, she reasoned, it was unlikely they'd be looking for her this far from home, and with the grainy quality of all but the most sophisticated CCTV cameras, no one would know they were looking at her anyway. Helen Cooper, with her long auburn hair and girly dresses, had vanished from the face of the earth.

She got on the Tube at Baker Street, using the new, unregistered Oyster travelcard she had bought some weeks before. As she sat down on the Jubilee Line train, she glanced at her watch. It was 3.20. On any other day, she would have been at the school gate, ready to pick up Miranda and Marguerite. She felt a lurch of nausea and panic, and she half lifted herself from the seat, ready to bolt from the train and run up the stairs of the station. But at that moment the doors slid closed and the train gave the high-pitched whine that signalled it was about to move. She was on her way.

Sam

'What do you mean, Helen's sister?' I said stupidly. 'Helen doesn't have a sister.'

'Is that what she told you?' said the woman. What was the name she had given? Judy? She laughed sadly. 'She probably told you she didn't have parents either. Well, she does. They're my parents too. They live in Brisbane, as Helen did for most of her life. And they're desperate for news of her.'

She left a pause, as if expecting me to say something, but I had no words to respond. What fresh hell was this? Just when I was starting to put my life back together again, some fruitcake pretending to be Helen's long-lost sister rings me from Australia. If she *was* ringing me from Australia. Maybe you could get software that rerouted your call?

She realized I wasn't about to respond, so she carried on. 'They're both quite frail these days. My dad had a stroke a year or so ago, and my mum—'

I felt a wave of anger so strong, it was like hot nausea. 'Listen, I don't know who you are, but to ring someone up out of the blue with some scam—'

'I'm not. . .' she began.

'I lost my wife. Do you get that? My wife. My life partner. And you think you can call up out of the blue and try and extort. . . God knows what from me? I haven't got any money, if that's what you were hoping for. Or maybe you like to torture people. . .?' I was aware that I was yelling, and also not making a lot of sense, but I was incandescent with fury. Who was this woman to crawl out of the woodwork, eight months after Helen disappeared, pretending to be her family?

If I thought I had frightened her and that she would hang up, I was wrong. Judy, or whatever her real name was, was made of sterner stuff. 'I can understand that it must be strange to get a call out of the blue from someone you had no idea existed. And I'm sure there are people who want to extort money from grieving families, but that isn't what this is about.'

'I—' I said, but she wouldn't let me interrupt.

'I'm going to say goodbye now,' she said firmly. 'I'm going to send you something, and if you believe me, you can Skype me. That way you'll see me face to face, and you can decide if I'm a bad lot.' Again she paused. Again I didn't answer. 'Okay, Sam,' she said calmly, 'I'm signing off now.' And she cut off the call.

I sat staring at the blank screen of my phone. What the hell was that? I couldn't believe that there were people out there who would prey on people like us, and so blatantly. I could imagine how it would have played out if I had believed her. At first she'd have worked hard to win my trust, making up loads of stories about Helen as a child; it wouldn't be difficult to convince someone vulnerable, as she clearly assumed I was. It was like those fake psychics who exploited the weaknesses of the bereaved and persuaded them there were messages from the other side. What did she think she could send me that would persuade me? A 'message' she had been asked to pass on by Helen? Well, she'd picked the wrong guy.

The bedroom door opened and Lara cautiously stuck her head around. 'Everything okay?' she said. 'I heard you yelling.'

I considered telling her about the phone call, but I could imagine her reaction – surprise followed by a million questions.

I was sure Lara, in her naivety, would think it entirely possible that this Judy woman was genuine. I couldn't face the debate.

'Bloody cold-callers,' I said, standing up briskly. 'Trying to tell me I'd been in a car accident and I could claim compensation. It's the third time this week. I may have lost it a bit.'

Lara didn't look convinced and for a moment I wondered how much she had overheard, but she didn't press the point.

'There's bacon and eggs downstairs,' she said. 'Come down before it gets cold. And I made a pot of that rocket-fuel coffee you like.'

I admired Lara's slim form and pert behind in her jeans as she descended the stairs ahead of me. I was a lucky guy. And when I got to the kitchen and saw the plate heaped with scrambled eggs, and the bottle of Tabasco right beside my plate, I felt even more vindicated. I let all thoughts of the Australian scam artist on the phone fly out of my head.

But as I sat back in my chair, replete, and reached for my second cup of coffee, my phone buzzed with an email. I saw that the sender was 'Judy Knight'. I tapped to open it. 'Your email address is in the Facebook post. I've attached some photos of Helen and me as children and a few from more recently, along with some old papers of hers – certificates and so on.' She finished the message with a simple 'J', and her Skype name. There were eight attachments. She was persistent, I'd give her that. I checked, and all the attachments were jpegs. I have good antivirus software on my phone and I ran a scan, which came back clean.

Reluctantly, I clicked on the first image and opened it. It had the slightly grainy quality of a scanned snapshot, and it showed two girls on a beach. The older, taller girl looked to be around sixteen, the younger one about ten. They both had long, light-brown hair and were unmistakeably sisters. The older one I didn't recognize. The younger one did, I had to admit, have something of Helen about her, but then I had never seen a picture of Helen at that age.

I clicked on the next image, and this one made me pause. It had been taken in the same high-school athletics arena as the photo I'd found of Helen online in my own searches, but it wasn't from the same batch. The one I'd found on the school website was of a sports day, but this one showed Helen training, aged around thirteen, younger than in the other photo. It was, however, unmistakeably Helen. I had seen her finish enough races to know her running style – the look of sheer determination that overtook her face, her tall, braced posture and long stride. She had run the same way at thirteen as she ran at thirty-three.

I looked up. Lara was upstairs. All the kids were in the living room, squabbling but in a low-key way. My work bag was in the hallway and I got up and retrieved my iPad, opening Judy's email so I could look at the pictures in a larger format. I took the iPad back to the kitchen and opened the other pictures. Here was a past for Helen I had never known existed – Helen with her parents standing outside a long, low, brick house (Helen looked like her mum; her dad was tall, stooped and kind-looking). Helen at a school dance on the arm of a tall, broad-shouldered boy, whose hair was too long at the collar. He had a protective arm around her shoulders. Helen at university, again with the older sister I now assumed must be Judy. The other attachments were a copy of Helen's birth certificate and her degree certificate. I'd seen the birth certificate before – a certified copy had been neatly filed with all of our other papers at home.

I opened the final picture. Helen didn't feature in this one – it was a portrait photograph of a woman of about forty, with jaw-length, mousy-brown hair. She had lines around her eyes, whether from stress, smoking or sun damage it was hard to say. I stared at the picture and was so lost in thought, I didn't hear

Marguerite come into the kitchen behind me. She stood at my shoulder, looking at the picture.

'That lady looks like Mummy,' she said.

I waited for Lara to come back down, then took my iPad upstairs. I shut the bedroom door, opened the Skype app and hesitantly typed in Judy's user name. She answered instantly, and the same face, so utterly like Helen's, popped up on my screen.

'Sam,' she said, and for a long moment we looked at one another in silence.

Then we both spoke simultaneously. 'I didn't know. . .' we chorused. We both laughed; a sad, bitter laugh from me, embarrassed from her.

'You first,' I said.

'I didn't know Helen had got married,' she said. 'I'm sorry. I would have loved to have known. To have known you. And your. . . kids? To have come to the wedding.' She smiled sadly.

'I didn't know anything,' I said, surprised at the anger in my voice. 'Nothing at all, it seems. And I still know nothing. All I know is that I'm going to keep finding out how little I knew.'

'I'm sorry,' she said. 'This must be so difficult for you.'

'It's not your fault.'

'No, but I do know Helen, and I know how she. . . compartmentalizes her life.'

'By "compartmentalize", I assume you mean she lies. I was with her for five years. Married to her for four of those. And she lied to me, every single day.'

'I know that's how it must seem. But she does that. She. . . closes off parts of her life. Walks away from them. She wasn't lying. We really are dead to her.' She laughed at this. 'That sounds melodramatic, but it's true. I saw her do it when she was a little girl. A friend upset her and she came home and said, "Shelley isn't my friend anymore." I laughed, because you know what little girls are like. They're always saying stuff like that and then the next day everything is hunky-dory again, without a word being said. But not Helen. She never spoke to Shelley again. Through the rest of kindy, primary school and high school, she ignored her like she didn't exist.'

That had a real ring of truth. One of the mothers at school had told Helen she would help with a cake sale but then hadn't turned up, leaving them short of helpers and running around in a panic. Helen wasn't rude or angry. She sent a short email to the woman asking her why she'd let them down. The woman replied saying, 'Sorry, I forgot, lol.' That lol did it. Helen blanked her forever more. A couple of the mums had mentioned it to me – they were in awe of how Helen froze the woman out. It wasn't vindictive, or angry or bitchy, she just stopped *seeing* her. She rendered her invisible. Was that what she had done with Judy, and then with me and the girls?

Judy was waiting for me to respond. I didn't know what to say. But at the same time, I didn't want her to go. There, on my screen, was Helen's face. Older, less groomed and shiny, but Helen's face nevertheless. Her smile, and, I saw with a pang, the same way of tucking a strand of hair behind her ear. What I realized most poignantly from talking to Judy was how much I missed Helen. I hadn't allowed myself to think about that. I'd been too busy being hurt, betrayed and angry. But I missed her. I realized I had to say something.

'So you saw my Facebook post?' I said. 'And you contacted me to. . .?' I didn't know why she had contacted me. It was unlikely she would be able to tell me where Helen was.

'I hardly ever go on Facebook,' she said, 'but someone I know in the UK had shared the post and it came up when I logged on yesterday. As you can imagine, I got quite a shock when I saw Helen's face on my screen. I haven't seen or heard from her in years. I read the comments under the post and someone said she had been found, but then someone else said she'd disappeared on purpose and had run away from her husband.'

'Run away from her husband,' I repeated, and snorted.

'That's what they said,' Judy said calmly. 'But I know that with Helen, things can often be more complicated than they first appear to be. The post had all your contact details, so I thought I'd better get in touch. I thought that I might know things about her that you didn't know, and vice versa.'

I nodded. 'I'm sure you know a lot, Judy, and I want to know it all, I just. . .'

'Need some time? I get that. This must all have come as a shock, especially just as you were beginning to pick up the pieces.'

I smiled at her, glad that we could see each other's faces. She was kind, I could see that. In another life, or rather, in a version of my life that was never going to happen now, I would have enjoyed getting to know her. I think I'd rather have liked having her as my sister-in-law.

'Tell me something about yourself, Judy. What do you do? Where do you live?'

'Ah, not much to tell,' she said. 'I live about a kilometre from where we grew up. I work in a local bookstore. Well, I manage it these days. Never married, no kids. I keep an eye on the folks, now they're getting on. I like to garden and I love my dogs.' She grinned apologetically. 'See? I told you. Not much to tell. Helen always said I was born an old lady. I used to mind when she said that, but I don't any more. Grew into my age, I reckon. It was Helen who dreamed of an exotic, adventurous life.'

We were back to talking about Helen and I wasn't ready for that. It was too raw, and Judy's passing comment made me seethe with a thousand unasked questions. Exotic how? Adventurous how? And would this information help me understand why she'd chosen to vanish? I felt a rising wave of panic.

'I need to go, Judy,' I said abruptly. 'The girls. . .'

'I understand,' she said. 'Listen, I'm here. With the time difference, this is a good time for me – I'm home from work, and I've had my dinner. On a day when the girls are at school, when you've got some time, you can call me.'

'Thank you, Judy,' I said. 'Thank you.' I didn't know what else to say. We stared at each other in silence for a moment, then she gave me a quick grin and I saw her lean forward to cut off the connection.

Helen

The Jubilee Line was fast – much faster than she had been prepared for. She was rattling through central London at great speed. She'd hoped for some time to compose herself, calm her racing heart and prepare for this vast next step, but within a few minutes, it seemed, they were pulling into Canary Wharf. She gathered herself and got off the train, checking behind her and around her to make sure she hadn't been seen by anyone she knew. They would be starting to look for her within the next few hours, so she was keen to get off the streets as soon as possible.

She walked briskly, head down, and was on a Docklands Light Railway train within a few minutes. She chose a window seat and turned her face away from the other passengers, watching the unfamiliar landscape of east London slide past. No one she knew would be anywhere near here, she was sure of it, and she had taken sufficient precautions with her appearance that a casual passer-by couldn't possibly mistake her for the suburban housewife missing from north London. Except. . . As the thought occurred to her, her hand flew up to her right ear, the ear turned towards the rest of the train carriage. The scar where the earring had been ripped out was plainly visible on her earlobe; a raised, white ridge. It was. . . How did they describe such things on detective programmes? A distinguishing characteristic? She'd barely given it a thought when her hair was long – it was easy to cover up if she wanted to. But now she had cut her hair short, there was no way to hide it.

The train pulled into Greenwich station and she slipped off it, trying to be as unobtrusive as possible and keeping her head down as she passed beneath the CCTV cameras. She needed to make one stop before she was safe. Somewhere in Greenwich there would be a branch of Claire's Accessories, where she'd be able to find clip-on earrings. A few pairs would do the trick, to help her conceal the scar.

Before Sam, before the girls, she had never had cause to step into one of the overcrowded little shops, its racks crammed with feathers, sequins and silly bits of fancy dress. But it was Marguerite's favourite place in the world, and as Helen walked into the store, she could almost feel Marguerite's sweaty little hand tugging her and pointing, quivering with excitement, at whatever bit of shiny tat had caught her fancy. The pain of it bent Helen almost double, and she stood for a moment in the doorway of the shop, holding herself tightly, her breathing uneven. Someone tried to come into the shop behind her and huffed with annoyance because she was blocking the entrance. Helen saw the assistant look up enquiringly. The last thing she needed was to draw attention to herself. She'd buy earrings later. Right now, she needed to get out of this public place. She turned abruptly and walked quickly out of the shop and off up the street.

Her destination was five minutes away, in a quiet street away from the hubbub of the middle of Greenwich. As she approached, she slipped her hand into her bag and drew out the keys. She'd had them zipped into a compartment in her bag for the last week, alongside the other mobile phone. There was a small parade of shops – a newsagent's, a scruffy shoe-repair shop which didn't look as if it got many customers, and a small, dusty art gallery which was seldom, if ever, open for business. Between the art gallery and the shoe-repair shop there was a black-painted door with a row of three doorbells beside it. Helen slotted her key into the door and pushed it open, checking again to make sure no one had seen her go in. She drew the door closed behind her. The tiny hallway was littered with pizza leaflets and the window ledge by the front door held a long-dead spider plant. She climbed the stairs, passed the first floor, where two front doors faced one another across a small landing, and continued up a second flight. There was only one door at the top; it looked new and was freshly painted a pristine eggshell white. '14C' proclaimed the brass numbers on the door. Helen unlocked the mortice and then the Yale lock and gently pushed the door open.

The room beyond the door was empty, the walls snowy white and freshly painted; in fact the smell of paint still lingered faintly in the air. The flooring was immaculate blonde wood. There was a tiny open-plan kitchen off to one side, separated from the main room by a breakfast bar. The door to the little bathroom stood open, revealing the brand-new fittings.

Helen dropped her handbag by the front door and walked slowly around the airy, empty space. She was still trembling from the stress of her journey, but for the first time that day she felt she could breathe freely. In fact, for the first time in months and months, she felt she could relax.

But there was no time for sitting around. She had to get started. The space was so pure, she felt loath to change anything about it, but she saw that along the wall beside the front door there was a row of boxes. These were all things she had bought online and which her landlord, owner of the art gallery downstairs, had generously taken in and put in the flat ready for her arrival. She used her new keys to rip open the tape on each box, and carefully unpacked the contents.

The first box held a single-sized duvet and pillow, tightly wrapped in plastic, along with a set of bed linen in pure white cotton, and a couple of fluffy white towels. The second held kitchen equipment: two saucepans, one small, one slightly larger, a couple of good sharp knives, and a single bowl, plate, mug and set of cutlery. There was also one finely shaped wine glass. A further box held white, floor-length cotton curtains of the right size to fit the wide window, and a small venetian blind for the bathroom.

She was hooking the blind up when the buzzer sounded. She went through and glanced out of the window on to the street. There was an Ikea van below. The deliverymen carried the wooden frame and single futon she had ordered up the stairs and put them below the window, and set the barstool beside the kitchen breakfast bar. They were surly men, without much conversation, and Helen was happy to see them go. If she had her way, they would be the last two people to enter her space.

She made up her bed and then opened the large box from an online clothing retailer. She unpacked her new clothes into the fitted wardrobe – leggings and jeans, big T-shirts and loose tops, a denim jacket and some Converse sneakers. The clothes were good quality but plain and not at all feminine. Not one item would have looked right in her wardrobe in north London.

Helen Cooper wore pretty sundresses in summer that showed off her slim, tanned legs, and neat miniskirts, bright, jewel-coloured jumpers, and expensive boots in winter. Any jeans she owned were crisp and tailored, teamed with smart blouses and well-cut jackets.

Helen Day's jeans were a loose, 'boyfriend' cut, already rumpled and faded. The oversized tops would conceal her figure, and the Converse and denim jacket, combined with the boyish haircut, would give her an androgynous air.

Helen Day. For it was, of course, Helen Day who had rented this flat, and Helen Day was in possession of deed-poll documents registering her legal change of name.

Helen glanced at her watch. It was past six o'clock. Where were the girls? Had they waited for her at the dance school or headed home? Had Sam worked out there was food in the fridge and freezer? Was he giving the girls dinner?

She sat on her barstool, cradling her left hand in her right. She stared at her watch. It was a slim, girlish watch with an expensive brown leather strap, a gift from Sam for her last birthday. She unbuckled it and laid it on the counter in front of her. Then, slowly, she drew off her engagement and wedding rings. She looked around the room and her eyes lighted on the small box from which she had unpacked her new coffee mug. She put the watch and rings in the box and, standing on her tiptoes, pushed the box to the back of the top shelf in the wardrobe. Then she picked up her keys and went out to buy food for her first night in her new home.

CHAPTER THIRTEEN

Sam

'Helen's got a *sister*? Fucking hell.' Tim was sitting opposite me in the crowded bar in Soho, leaning in to hear me over the braying bankers in the early Thursday evening crowd.

'A sister and parents. All still in Brisbane, very much alive.'

'And they had no idea about you?'

'None at all. Apparently Helen left Australia suddenly six years ago, and they haven't heard from her since.'

'So she's got previous.'

'Previous?'

'She's absconded before. Sorry, that probably sounded insensitive.'

'Absconded sounds like she escaped custody.'

'Well, did she?'

'What, you think I was holding her against her will?'

'Not you, numbnuts. When she left Australia. Was she in trouble with the law?'

'What? No.'

'So why did she leave?'

'I don't know yet. It was a shock, seeing Judy for the first time. She looks like Helen, but older. I haven't been up to asking too many probing questions.'

'But this. . . Judy. . . definitely doesn't know where Helen is now?'

'Not a clue.'

'Wow,' said Tim, taking a thoughtful sip of his drink. 'A whole family left behind.'

I raised an eyebrow at him, and he looked sheepish.

'I should stop talking, shouldn't I?'

'No, it's fine,' I said, taking a substantial gulp of my own drink. 'It's all fucked up. There's no point in pussyfooting around it. It raises a lot of questions.'

'Like what?'

'Like, how much do I ask Judy? How much do I really want to know? How many lies can I bear to hear unravelled? And what do I tell the girls, if anything?'

'What do you mean?'

'Well, if Helen and I were still together, they'd be so excited to discover they have Australian step-grandparents and an auntie. But what are these people to them now? There's no blood link, and soon there'll be no legal link.'

'Soon? Are you thinking about getting divorced?'

'Not thinking – I've started the process. If I can prove that Helen has disappeared and I've made efforts to find her, there are forms I can fill in. . .'

'Whoa,' said Tim. 'So soon? She hasn't even been gone a year.'

'And she's not coming back. I told you the night we found out she'd chosen to go that she wouldn't be back. I can't keep my life on hold indefinitely.'

'Why? What have you got in mind? Are you planning to marry Lara?'

'Oh God, no,' I said, too quickly and vehemently. 'I mean, not that Lara's not lovely. . . She is. It's just. . . I can't put myself and the girls through all that again.'

Tim nodded. And then he spoke, quietly. 'When she went, Sam, was there really no warning?'

'What do you mean?'

'You genuinely had no idea? You thought everything was fine?'

I shook my head.

'Do you remember when I arrived at your place when Helen was first missing?' Tim said gently. 'We had a late-night talk and you told me you and Helen had disagreed about having a baby?'

I'd forgotten I'd told him that. I'd been delirious with worry and exhaustion. What had I said? I felt a trickle of cold dread in my stomach.

'Yeah,' I said, my tone neutral and noncommittal. I didn't elaborate.

'You said you'd stopped having sex.'

'Not stopped,' I said. 'That sounds melodramatic. We were a long-term couple. It had been a dry patch, that's all. It happens.'

'You said six months.'

'Did I? I don't remember.'

'You said you tried to get her to go for counselling.'

'This is one of those wisdom-of-hindsight things,' I said impatiently. 'It all sounds much worse when you put it like that. We talked about it and she was adamant she didn't want a baby. I wanted to make sure she was sure. For herself. I mean, I have Miranda and Marguerite. . .' My voice sounded bluff and false, even to my own ears.

'Did something happen?' said Tim, looking at me intently.

I glanced up, and then refused to meet his gaze. I stared at the neck of my beer bottle and the ragged edge of my own thumbnail.

Finally I said, 'I've thought over every moment of the last year or so of our relationship, to try to work out if something did happen. If there were any clues. And. . .' I stopped. I didn't want to say it out loud. Tim sat there and waited. Eventually, I continued. 'There was this one day.' He nodded but didn't interrupt or prompt me. 'With the. . . the baby thing. Every time I brought it up, she'd get evasive. She'd change the subject, bring up something else that we needed to be doing – repairs to the house, a holiday coming up, what the girls were busy with at school. I felt like she was shutting me out. She got so busy with all the stuff she did with the school, and with studying – she was forever doing courses. And I was working really hard too. I felt like we never had a proper conversation. As if we kept missing each other. So I planned this weekend away.'

As I haltingly described what had happened, the weekend flooded back to me, and with the recollection, a nasty, acid surge of shame.

Mum and Dad had agreed to take the girls, and I'd secretly booked Helen and me into this beautiful country-house hotel near Cambridge. I rang her out of the blue on Friday at midday and told her that I had asked Mum to get the girls from school and that I was coming to pick her up for lunch. She was put out – she was busy, as usual – but I insisted.

She got in the car, and we started to drive. I headed towards the motorway.

'Where are we going for lunch?' she said, annoyed, and then I told her we were going for a surprise weekend away. I'd packed her a bag – clothes, toiletries, sexy nightie. I could see she wanted to say it was a bad idea, that she had plans, but I had checked her diary, and I knew that she had nothing crucial on that weekend. She knew it would be bad form to kick up a fuss when I'd gone to so much trouble, so she took a deep breath, gave me her brightest smile and leaned over to kiss my cheek and rest her hand on my leg.

We got to the hotel, which was gorgeous, and went up to our room. There was a big decadent four-poster bed, and as soon as we closed the door, I grabbed her and kissed her, and we had sex. It was fabulous, and after that she began to relax, and it looked like we were going to have a really good weekend. We dozed for a while, then got up and went for a leisurely walk in the grounds before settling down in the hotel lounge for cocktails. Then we went in for dinner, cooked by the Michelin-starred chef. She looked so pretty and relaxed, the place was luxurious and we had two whole days all to ourselves.

After dinner, we went back to the room and had sex again. Helen glowed – she looked happy and calm and beautiful. It was amazing. Afterwards, she lay with me for a while, then got up and went into the bathroom. I was sprawled on the bed, congratulating myself on the brilliant execution of my plan. Helen came out of the bathroom, holding her toiletry bag.

'Where are my pills?' she said. Her voice was sweet, but there was tension in it.

I said, 'Hmmm?' like you do when you're half asleep and you can see there's the possibility of a fight.

She kept her voice honeyed and said, 'You did a great job in packing for me, sweetie. You even put tampons in. I thought you'd be bound to forget something, so it wasn't a big deal that you didn't pack my contraceptive pills, because I always have a spare box in the side pocket of this bag. But they're gone.'

'Gone?' I said innocently. 'Are you sure? Maybe you took them out last time we went away and forgot.'

She stood looking at me, the bag in her hand. She didn't need to answer. We both knew Helen didn't forget things. I could see her thinking about confronting me. She was clearly upset, and it was quite possible we would end up having a row, and that would ruin the weekend.

'It's no big deal,' she said cheerfully. 'I'll pop to a chemist tomorrow and get the morning-after pill.'

Well, I was awake now. I struggled into a sitting position. 'Why?' I said, and my voice sounded louder and more aggressive than I meant it to.

'Because I'm bang in the middle of my cycle, and we don't want an accident!' Helen said, her tone becoming cheerier in response to my anger.

'An accident?' I swung my legs off the bed and stood up to face her. 'We're married. We're financially settled. We've talked about having kids. . .'

And for the first time, she let her gentle, smiling facade drop. 'No, Sam, *you*'ve talked about having children. I've told you I'm not ready. . .'

'But when will you be ready?' I exploded. 'Things are good for us now. I'm not sure what we're waiting for. Marguerite's in proper school now. . .'

'And so the minute things are a little easier, you want me to be tied down by a tiny baby? Or are you more concerned about neatly spacing your family?' She sounded properly bitter now. It wasn't a tone I had ever heard from her before.

Mostly, though, I was stung by her accusation. 'Do you think that's what it's about? Neat gaps between children? Do I look like someone who's got his family planning all in order?'

We stared at each other for a long moment and the air crackled with animosity. I tried to be conciliatory.

'I love you, Helen. You're my wife. I want to have a baby with you.'

I walked towards her, holding out my arms, trying to pacify her. She hesitated, then let me hold her gently. I could feel the toiletry bag between us, still tightly held in her fist. I took it out of her hand and dropped it on a nearby chair, then bent to kiss her. I was still naked, and I used one hand to untie the knot in her dressing-gown belt and try to shrug it off her shoulders. She twisted slightly out of my grasp, still kissing me, and knotted the belt again, tying a loose bow. I drew her closer and took a firm grip on the end of the silky belt, trying to undo it. She grasped it above my hand and held on to it tightly so I couldn't pull it free. I smiled against her mouth and pulled harder. She resisted, and I felt the tiniest flare of anger and frustration. I brusquely pushed her hand away, pulled hard on the belt and heard a small rip as one of the silky belt loops gave way. I pulled the gown open and tugged it free of her arms, so she was standing before me wearing a brief pair of panties. It was inexpressibly exciting. I was breathing hard, and I'm sure my intentions were all too clear to her.

She was pale, and I could see her shaking slightly, but she made no move towards me or away from me, and she didn't bend to pick up her dressing gown. In that moment, I genuinely couldn't tell if she was angry or aroused, only that she was in the grip of strong emotions that I had never seen in her before. I took half a step towards her, and she raised one trembling hand to ward me off. Her voice, when it came, was a growl.

'You steal my contraceptive pills and now you're going to rape me to impregnate me? What kind of animal are you, Sam?'

I stepped back sharply. 'What? I. . .'

'You took my pills, didn't you? Admit it. When you packed the toiletry bag, you took them out.'

I was too shocked to speak. Yes, as I'd put her toothbrush and moisturizer into the bag, I'd found the packet of pills and I'd removed them and left them in the bathroom cabinet. But it wasn't some kind of premeditated act; I wasn't trying to trick her. Of course not. This weekend had seemed like a great opportunity to move the whole baby thing along. I thought she wouldn't need them, that was all. I was about to start defending myself when she went on.

'Oh my God. It all makes sense now. You know where I am in my cycle. You knew this weekend would be optimum to. . .' She couldn't even bring herself to say the word 'conceive'. 'I can't believe I was such an idiot!' This time she did bend to pick up her dressing gown. She put it on, wrapping it tightly around herself and belting it with a double knot. 'Well, I'll take the car in the morning and drive into Cambridge and find a pharmacy.' Her voice was back to normal. Calm, organized, smooth Helen was back in the driving seat.

'No you won't.' The words were out of my mouth before I could stop them, and the rage followed swiftly behind.

'I'm sorry?' she said, and she gave me the look she gave Marguerite and Miranda whenever they committed a faux pas of manners, the look that said 'I'm giving you a second chance to retract and fix that'.

'You fucking won't. We will discuss this and thrash it out, but this is a decision we need to make together. You don't unilaterally—'

And that was when she made the mistake. 'Unilaterally?' she said scornfully. 'You're accusing *me* of making decisions unilaterally?' And then she laughed at me.

The rage broke, and in one stride I was across the room. I grabbed her by both shoulders and shook her once, hard. 'You little bitch!' I yelled. In the split second that I did it, I knew it was wrong. So wrong. I knew that I had overstepped a mark, that I had done what no decent man would ever, ever do. I was about to release her and beg her forgiveness, when I looked into her face. When I grabbed her, I had dug my fingers into her firm, slim upper arms. I wanted to release my grip, but she had gone limp in my hands and I could feel her legs were not supporting her. It was only my strength that prevented her from sliding to the floor. Her face had gone slack and expressionless and her eyes – to this day I don't have a word to describe what I saw. There was no anger, no fear or tears. Her eyes were dead flat and opaque, as if she wasn't in there. As if Helen herself had retreated from her body into another place, where I couldn't reach her.

And then, of course, I wept. I gathered her in my arms, carried her to the bed, covered her gently with a blanket and knelt on the floor beside her, begging her forgiveness.

After a while she returned to herself and gently touched my face. 'It's okay,' she said softly. 'It was a nasty row. It'll all be better in the morning.'

Eventually, I crawled on to the bed beside her. I slept as far away from her as I could, afraid to touch her body, but she let me lightly hold her hand in mine. When I woke up in the morning, she was gone. She returned half an hour later, and I knew she'd gone to find a chemist that opened early. We didn't discuss what had happened again. We spent a tentative morning together, walking around Cambridge, and then, by mutual agreement, went home that afternoon, a day earlier than planned. On the surface, everything went swiftly back to normal. Our relationship was smooth, warm and affectionate, and we got on well. But we didn't have sex again after that night.

When I finished telling Tim what had happened, he sat staring at me for a long time. I felt I had to say something more. 'I apologized and apologized on the night, but when I tried to talk to her about it after we got home, she basically said that it was in the past and we should forget it. Somehow, while we were forgetting the argument and my terrible behaviour, we also "forgot" the discussion about the baby. I felt I couldn't bring it up because I'd been such a pig, and she didn't mention it again. I somehow imagined that we might find a time when things were less pressured to discuss it. I had it in my head it might be on our summer holiday. But of course she was gone before the holiday could ever happen.'

'So you think that's why she went? Because she didn't want to have a baby?'

'It seems the only possible explanation.'

Tim let out a sigh. 'Wow.' He looked at me for a long moment, his eyes full of pity.

'Let's get another drink, shall we?' I said. I was itching for one, and the distraction would also stop Tim looking at me like I was a basket case.

'Another one? Really?' Tim glanced down at his own glass, which was still three-quarters full.

'Bloody hell, you drink slowly!' I tried to make a joke out of it.

'Not really, mate,' he said mildly. 'I'm known as a fairly heavyweight drinker usually, but these days you put me in the shade.'

I laughed, and glanced towards the bar. I didn't want to be having this conversation.

'Are you still drinking every night?' he persisted.

'What are you, my mother?' I said flippantly. He didn't dignify that with an answer. 'So I drink. I'm still functional. Still working. I can still get it up.'

'It's not great for the girls, though,' Tim said gently. 'Is it?'

'What? They're fine. I drink after they've gone to sleep.' I hoped neither of them had said anything to him about beer bottles or finding me on the sofa.

'What if something happened in the night and you had to rush one of them to A & E?' he said.

'That's what Uber's for,' I said and stood. I wasn't going to get into this with him now. 'I'm getting another. Do you want one or not?'

Helen

She barely slept that first night. She had never slept well in a new space, and every small, unfamiliar noise woke her. The futon was firm and comfortable but narrow after the king-size bed she had shared with Sam. And, of course, every time she woke, the thoughts crowded in. She was sure she had done the right thing – it was not a decision lightly taken, and it had been months in the planning. But the reality of it was that she felt crushed by a void, an aching emptiness at being away from Miranda and Marguerite. Had it been a mistake? Should she ring Sam and go home?

At three in the morning, she sat at the kitchen counter, cradling her phone in her hand, staring out through the open curtains at the night sky. She just needed to dial eleven digits and everything could go back to the way it was. There'd be rows, of course there would be, and fuss, but she could smooth it over like she always did, and within a week or so everything would be back to normal.

Normal.

It was the contemplation of that word that helped her to push the power button firmly, switching the phone off. She pushed it away from her until it lay in the middle of the spotless, empty kitchen counter. She had known this would be hard. But it was no harder than what she had done before. The first night was always the worst, and this time she didn't have Judy's shoulder to cry on. What had Judy said, that dreadful night all those years ago? 'You don't have to do one day at a time. Or even one hour at a time. Just do it one breath at a time. One in, one out. And gradually you'll get there.'

One breath at a time. Helen drew her jumper closer round her shoulders and concentrated on breathing in slowly, and out even more slowly. One breath at a time, until morning.

She slept, eventually, in the early hours. When she woke up, bright sunlight flooded her little flat. She sat up, bewildered, and looked around at its snowy emptiness, its sense of infinite possibility and expectation. And even though the crushing weight in her chest had not lifted one iota, she knew that she was not going back.

It was Thursday morning. She wondered what had happened the night before. Had Sam gone to the police? Had he contacted the press? Cautiously, she logged on to the BBC website on her phone, but there didn't seem to be anything there. She tried to tell herself that it didn't matter, anyway, what people were saying. It wouldn't change what she had planned, and she had sufficient confidence that she had taken the necessary precautions. No one had seen her on the move, and the changes to her appearance meant that she wasn't going to be spotted by chance by someone who had seen a picture of her. Equally, the distance from her home meant that it was unlikely she'd bump into someone who knew her well.

She showered and dressed. In her handbag she had the small tablet computer she had bought some months ago and kept hidden in the house in north London. It was with this computer, and using a new email address and identity, that she had made all the plans for her escape. She left the flat and found a coffee shop which advertised free Wi-Fi in its window. She bought a coffee and took a table in a back corner before logging on. She couldn't see anything on any of the mainstream news sites. She knew it was way too risky to log on to her social media accounts or open her email – if they were looking for her, they would be monitoring any electronic communications. After a moment's hesitation, she logged on to Facebook using Sam's details. There was something wrong with the site. There was a red number at the top of the screen, indicating that Sam had thousands of notifications. There was obviously some kind of bug. But as she clicked through to his profile page and saw the post he had written, with the picture of her, she realized what had happened. As she watched, the number of notifications clicked up and up as people commented and shared. She could feel her skin crawling as the picture of her in the blue dress (the dress which lay rolled up in the handbag at her feet) spread across the world. She felt as if her face was projected hundreds of feet high on the side of every building.

Somehow she hadn't imagined this. She'd thought that there might be the odd small news item, but not this social media eruption. As she watched, more iterations of the post popped up, and more people commented. She didn't dare click on any of them – if Sam was also online, he'd wonder why the notifications were disappearing before he'd even looked at them. Troubled, she closed Facebook and clicked back to the BBC site. And there, from the middle of the page, her own face stared back at her. With mounting unease, she went through the news sites again. Clearly in the last half an hour or so, a press release had gone out. When she opened the *Daily Mail* site, she saw that Ella Barker had managed to give an interview already – and had had time to get her hair done before the photographer took the pictures. Ella spoke as if she and Helen were inseparable, close confidantes, and Helen gave a wry smile. She'd listened to Ella talk incessantly about herself at various committee meetings for years. But Ella knew nothing, less than nothing, about Helen. As she was no doubt discovering.

She read through all the articles and was brought up short by a line which said: 'Mrs Cooper's children were looked after by a friend until their father was able to return from Manchester.' Manchester? What the hell had Sam been doing in Manchester when he was supposed to pick up the girls? She felt a flash of pure fury. No doubt he'd had some work 'emergency' and had texted her to collect the kids, without checking to see if it was convenient. Typical.

She felt wobbly with worry. So the girls had been left at school and had had to go home with a friend. Which friend? She wished she knew. It couldn't have been Ella, because she would have shoehorned that into her interview.

The waves of panic crashed over her again. Were they all right? What had she done? Once again, the thought intruded that she could give it all up and go back. Breathe, she told herself. Just breathe. She turned back to the drama unfolding on her tablet. In a strange way, this blanket press coverage made it easier to resist the urge. When she had been tempted to go back last night, she'd imagined a call to Sam, a quiet return, a private debate. But now? She'd return to the house in a hail of flashbulbs, requests for media interviews and speculation about what happened. Things had already progressed too far for her to go back. However impossible it seemed, the only way was forward.

She felt exposed, sitting in the coffee shop, so she gathered her things and left. There was a mobile phone shop nearby, and she went in to ask if there was a way to purchase internet access for her tablet. The assistant showed her how she could use her mobile phone as a Wi-Fi hotspot. She offered to pay for his time, but he waved away her thanks and blushed. The old Helen, perky and confident, would have taken his admiration as her due. But this new Helen, fearful, paranoid and hiding behind her long fringe, found it surprising and suspicious.

She returned to the flat, running up the stairs and double-locking the door once she was inside. She flopped down on the futon, shaking with relief. She was safe in there, for now at least. Once her breathing had returned to normal, she set up the tablet on the kitchen counter and went through the steps she had been shown to link it to her phone. The connection was slow, but adequate. She sat transfixed in front of the little screen for several hours, watching with trepidation as the story spread. She saw video of police teams with dogs searching the park and held her breath that they wouldn't find something in the spot where she had cut her hair and changed her clothes. She read the comments posted below the news stories with increasing horror and nausea. And every now and then she logged back on to Sam's Facebook and watched with horror as his post went viral all over the world. How the hell was she going to get out of this? She'd done her research, and she knew that what she had done wasn't illegal. It wasn't going to stop people hunting her down though. Unless she put a stop to it.

Several of the news stories had included a link to Missing People, a charity that helped those whose loved ones had gone missing. With shaking fingers, she logged on to their website. At the top of the page was a link titled 'I am an adult who is missing or thinking of going missing'. She clicked it and read it. She thought about ringing them, but she was sure they would try to persuade her to go home, or at least to speak to Sam, and she knew that if she did that, she'd be lost. That wasn't the answer, but somehow she needed to make the madness stop. Especially with what Monday held.

But within the site, she found the answer. All she had to do was go to a police station and identify herself. They'd ascertain she was safe and well, and that she had left voluntarily, and then the search would stop. After her painstaking escape, it was insane to think about walking into a police station, and the thought of it terrified her. It wasn't as if her interactions with the police in the past had brought her any joy. But there didn't seem to be any other way. She didn't feel up to it right then, however. She felt naked, as if someone had stripped off not just her clothes but her skin, and the thought of going out into a world which was plastered with images of her smiling face made her nauseous with fear. She disconnected the tablet from her phone, curled up on the futon, pulled the duvet up to her chin and fell abruptly into a deep, dreamless sleep.

She slept for fifteen hours and woke up stiff and aching, in the same position. She sat up and stretched. There was a faint glow outside the window, and when she checked the time on her phone, it was just after four in the morning. She was wide awake, and much calmer than she had been. She got herself a glass of water and walked over to the window. The street below was deserted, and the sky was beginning to lighten. There wasn't a soul about. Before she had fallen asleep, she had looked up the location of the local police station. It was a ten-minute walk away. The rest of Greenwich might be asleep, but the police station would be open for business. Now was as good a time as any. She went into the bathroom, showered and dressed, gathered her passport and keys, and went to declare herself safe and well. She didn't feel safe, and she definitely wasn't full of well-being, but she was sane and determined, and that would have to do.

CHAPTER FOURTEEN

Miranda

So we've had to move. It's awful, and I can't quite believe it. Dad sat us down and said that we needed to save some money and that the only way we could do it was by letting someone else live in our house. He said it was a 'discussion', but it wasn't, because even though we said we didn't want to, he'd already decided and gone to talk to an estate agent on the high street about it.

They found some people to rent the house really quickly. They are a family from Iran with two daughters who have come to London to go to university. The parents came to live in London too. They wanted to take the house with all our furniture in it and all the stuff in the kitchen and every cushion and every picture. I think that's really weird. I'd hate to live with someone else's stuff. Dad said they could, except for my room and Marguerite's room. He put new things in our bedrooms for the two students, and took our furniture and toys with us when we moved to this flat.

Dad keeps telling us that it isn't a bad flat – but it's so small. Really, really tiny. It's new, so at least it's clean and everything works. The building is down the hill from the school, but luckily not close enough that any of my friends might see me coming out of there.

I hate it. I hate the hallways we have to share with other people. Smelling other people's dinner cooking makes me feel sick. I hate having to carry my bike up the stairs into the entrance hall and then into the lift. I hate our tiny hallway, which is always a mess of shoes, bikes and coats. I hate that I have to share a room with Marguerite. Dad says I'm ungrateful, because it's bigger than the other bedroom. He can hardly fit his funny small bed in that one. He says it's called a three-quarter bed. I hate the minute, horrible bathroom, and the little kitchen, and the living room which is always a mess as soon as we play with anything. I hate it that there's no garden and I can't invite my friends over. Not that I would anyway – I'd be so embarrassed if they saw this place.

I hate Marguerite, who always has nightmares and moans in her sleep. She breathes so loudly with her rubbish tonsils and she still sometimes wets the bed. But, most of all, I hate my dad. I hate him so much. He's such a giant loser. I hate him because I've needed to get my hair trimmed for about three months and he doesn't even know where to take me. I hate him because he never knows where anything is. He never has money, and he drinks beer all the time. He drank a bit less when he first started being Lara's boyfriend, but now he's drinking loads again. I count the bottles in the recycling every morning, so he knows I know what a drunk loser he is. If I could run away and live somewhere else, I would. But the police would only bring me back. My life is a disaster.

To make us feel better, Dad took us to Bristol to visit Uncle Tim. Even though I still hate him, I was quite excited because I'd never been there before. Helen never liked Uncle Tim much, so if he ever invited us to go there to see his restaurant, she made an excuse that we were too busy and we didn't go.

We left early on Saturday morning and it felt like we were going on a proper holiday or adventure, even if we were only going for one day. We weren't going home though. We were going to stay at Granny and Grandpa's for the night, because Granny wanted to take us shopping on Sunday morning. Marguerite was so dozy when Dad put her in the car, she fell straight back to sleep, but I watched the sun come up properly. We stopped on the motorway and Dad got us McMuffins for breakfast. Then he said, 'You'd better make sure you still have space for lunch at Uncle Tim's restaurant,' and Marguerite and I said, 'We will!' and we both tried to pull our stomachs in to make them look hollow and flat, and Dad laughed.

When we got to Bristol, Dad drove straight to the restaurant. It was the kind of restaurant where you can see right into the kitchen over a counter, and Uncle Tim was in there doing something called 'prep.' We sat at the counter on tall stools and watched as he chopped things super-fast and shouted and yelled at the other people in the kitchen, who were all bashing and crashing pots and pans, and shouting, 'Yes, Chef!' to Uncle Tim like he was the captain and they were all soldiers. It was cool.

We stayed there until people started coming into the restaurant for lunch, then we got the best table and Uncle Tim and the waiters brought us loads of little dishes of food. Everyone was so impressed with Marguerite and me because we eat everything, or at least we'll try anything. That was something Helen taught us. The food was delicious, even though some things were a bit spicy.

After we'd finished eating, Marguerite started to get bored and whiny, and I didn't really blame her. We'd been in the restaurant for hours, it seemed like. Then Uncle Tim came out of the kitchen in his ordinary clothes, not his chef's whites, and said to Dad, 'Let's take the girls to Weston, to the beach.'

No one had told us that there was a beach, so we were very excited. It turns out Weston is a place called Weston-super-Mare. It took us about half an hour to drive there, and by the time we arrived it was quite late in the afternoon and the wind was blowing hard. It wasn't good beach weather, so we couldn't do any swimming or even paddling, and the tide was out miles and miles. But it was the biggest beach I'd ever seen, and there was all the space in the world to practise my handstands and cartwheels. After a while, Uncle Tim stopped talking to Dad and took out his phone to take pictures of me doing my cartwheels, and a few of Marguerite in the sand. He's not a soppy, kissing-and-cuddling kind of relative, but I think he likes us a lot, because he takes a lot of pictures of us whenever we see him.

I flopped down on the sand beside Marguerite, and we started building a castle together. The sand was perfect: wet enough to stick together, but not too wet, so using the bucket, we made lovely smooth towers. I sent Marguerite to look for shells and sticks for decoration while I carefully shaped walls between the towers. Using a stick, I drew lines so it looked like the walls were made of bricks. Dad and Uncle Tim were watching me and chatting at the same time.

'So how's it going with Lara?' Uncle Tim asked. I pretended I was concentrating hard on my wall. Adults seem to think if you're doing something else, you automatically become deaf, like they do.

'Okay,' said Dad. 'I mean, it's fine.' He didn't sound excited. I thought when people fell in love they got all gushy and kissy face. Maybe Dad and Lara are too old for that. Dad used to get gushy and kissy face for Helen though – he'd always say 'Love you' to her on the phone, or when he left for work in the morning. He'd often come up behind her in the kitchen and hold her from behind and kiss her neck. It was disgusting, but I suppose it was more the way things are supposed to be. Better than 'Okay. I mean, it's fine.'

'How's it going with your. . .?' Dad said. 'What are we calling her? Friend?'

'I shouldn't have said anything about it,' said Uncle Tim, and he sounded uncomfortable, which made me pay attention. Uncle Tim is never uncomfortable. He's always fun and easy-going. 'She's isn't. . . It's not. . .'

'Not what?' said Dad.

'Not what you think. There's nothing going on between us.'

'But you wish there was.'

'Well, what I wish doesn't come into it. It's not going to happen.'

'What are you saying, Tim? Unrequited love? Why? Is she blind? You're a catch!'

Uncle Tim laughed, but I could hear he wished Dad would stop asking. But Dad didn't.

'So, seriously, why not? Oh my God, is she married?' He whispered the last word, but I could still hear.

'It's. . . complicated,' said Uncle Tim.

I could see Marguerite coming back along the beach, holding her T-shirt out in front of her. She'd made it into a hammock and it was full of sticks and shells and things. When she came back, they'd stop talking, I was sure.

Uncle Tim saw her too, and he said in a rush, 'I don't want you to get the wrong idea about it. It's someone I care about. Have cared about, for a long time. She needs some help and support, and I'm happy to give it to her.'

'Without getting anything in return?' said Dad, and he sounded cynical.

Then Uncle Tim turned to Dad, and for the first time ever, I heard him sounding cross. 'Well, that's what love is, isn't it, Sam?

Giving without expecting in return. Wanting the best for the person. I'd have thought you of all people would. . .'

He stopped talking, and I couldn't help thinking it was only partly because Marguerite had reached us and tipped the big mess of stuff out of her shirt at Dad and Uncle Tim's feet. I thought that Uncle Tim had also stopped because he'd realized that maybe Dad didn't understand after all.

Sam

The morning after we got back from Bristol, my mum took the girls shopping for new clothes and I went back to the flat alone. It was a relief to get them out from under my feet. God knows, I never get any time to myself these days. And Miranda in particular has been a vicious little minx ever since we moved. Personally, I've found being in the new flat an enormous relief, and not just because I genuinely wasn't keeping up with the bills. It was the way the house seemed to accuse me. Every week, it looked grubbier and less cared for – the dust growing thick on surfaces, the carpet stained and trodden flat, the lawn choked with dandelions. It reproached me for Helen's absence and tortured me with memories. It gave me great pleasure to call in the deep cleaners (maxing out my last credit card) and hand over the keys.

I did consider pressuring Lara gently, to see if she wanted us to move in with them. I dropped the odd hint about us having to move, but she didn't leap to offer and, in hindsight, I'm glad. At least this way I still have some freedom and my own bolthole. The flat is small and plain, but it's a blank slate, and a lot easier to manage than that great big house. God knows what persuaded me to buy the house in the first place – I guess to show off. To flash the cash, show that I was the big shot now. The perfect, beautiful house was the ideal accessory for my perfect, sparkling wife. Goes to show how wrong you can be.

Lara was working all weekend, so I was all alone. I checked the time difference; it was midday in London, so 9 p.m. in Brisbane – a reasonable time to try and reach Judy. I opened Skype and saw that she was online. Hesitantly, I pressed the dial icon, and she answered almost immediately. The window showing the view from her web cam popped up, and I could see a wall with floor-to-ceiling bookshelves overflowing with volumes. Then Judy slipped into the chair, her smiling face filling the screen. She had a brightly coloured shawl around her shoulders, which she drew in with a shiver.

'Bit of an autumn chill this evening!' she said brightly, as if picking up a familiar conversation exactly where we'd left off.

I breathed out and relaxed. Like Helen, she had the knack of putting people at their ease. Unlike Helen, I hoped hers came from genuine kindness and interest. I checked myself. Bitterness came too easily to me these days.

'Hey, Judy,' I said, trying to imitate her easy, warm tone. 'How's it going?'

'All good, all good,' she said. 'Getting the garden ready for winter, such as it is here. It'll be mild, of course, nothing like yours.'

'Have you experienced an English winter?' I asked.

'Me? No, never.' She laughed. 'Never been out of Australia, me. Went to Perth once on a school trip, and been to Sydney a few times, but that's about it.'

'So it was Helen who was the adventurous one. That's what you said before.'

Judy frowned at this. 'Did I?'

'You said she dreamed of an exotic and adventurous life.'

'Dreamed of it. Never had it. Not with what happened with Lawrence.'

There was something about this name, a name I had never heard from Helen, that punched me right in the gut. The way Judy said 'Lawrence', I knew he was significant. Judy assumed I knew who he was, even though she was aware I knew next to nothing about Helen's past. I was certain I would regret asking the question, but I had to.

'Who's Lawrence?'

'Helen's first husband. You must have known. . .' she began, but then, seeing my face, she abruptly stopped. 'You didn't know.'

'No.'

There was a long, awkward pause. 'Well then,' said Judy. 'It looks like I have a lot to tell you.'

Helen

Once she had finished with the police, the relief she felt was immense. They'd gone through all the steps of the safe-and-well check and had been satisfied that she was neither mad, nor a criminal nor being coerced. The gentle-eyed police officer tried hard to get her to contact Sam herself, or at the least to tell him where she was, but Helen was adamant that this was her choice.

It was nearly 7 a.m. by the time she stepped outside, and the streets of Greenwich were filling with commuters, many of them grabbing an early coffee before they made their way into town for the last day of work before the weekend. Helen had things to do – she needed to be ready for the new week too. She'd only bought the most basic wardrobe online and would need to go shopping for more clothes. And there were all sorts of small things she needed for the flat – a drying rack for dishes, a spatula, some toiletries and some kind of hanging apparatus for laundry. There was a small, compact washing machine in the flat, but that was it. She thought about the spacious utility room in the house in north London, with its gigantic washing machine and tumble-drier, and sighed. This was another adjustment to her new life – knickers hanging on a radiator.

She knew, however, that the household errands would take no more than a few hours; beyond that, the weekend stretched like an infinite void. She thought about going back to the flat, but while its emptiness had seemed like a sanctuary, now it felt more like a prison. She couldn't imagine spending forty-eight hours within those four walls. She knew that if she did, all she would do was think about how weekends had been before – crammed with dance classes, birthday parties, barbecues and social events. Her weekends had been busier than her weeks, and she'd had to plan them to the minute, issuing pick-up and drop-off instructions to Sam so that both girls got to where they needed to be, on time and with the right equipment. She hadn't had an empty weekend for five years. What had she done before? Or on the odd days when the girls had stayed with their grandparents or had a sleepover? She couldn't remember. She supposed she might have gone running. Helen Cooper loved to run. Helen Knight had run too – run fiercely, competitively and well – until she was stopped. But now, standing in the street, looking at the line of weary, suited people stretching out of the door of the coffee shop, she made a decision. Helen Day would not run. Helen Day would do the leisurely cultural things that the other Helens had had no time for.

She joined the line outside the coffee shop. Once she got through the door, she scooped up a copy of the day's newspaper, which still featured her face on the front page. She folded it over, hiding the image. When she got to the counter, she ordered a large, full-fat latte with vanilla syrup, and a croissant. She took a table at the back of the coffee shop and sat sipping her coffee and slowly reading the paper from cover to cover. The picture and story on the front page no longer interested her. It was as if they were talking about some other person. Instead, she focused on international news, on reviews of theatre, books and art exhibitions. She read the round-up of films opening that day. She would go to the cinema, she decided, when she had finished shopping. She'd go to a big multiplex and watch two, or even three films back to back. And over the weekend, she'd go into town and see some exhibitions, or even a play, if she could get a cheap ticket. Instead of an infinite void, she would see the weekend as her first forty-eight hours of infinite possibility.

Sam

'Helen and Lawrence met at school,' said Judy. 'It was him in the picture I sent you. That was their official shot from the school formal.'

I remembered the picture. I recalled a big, beefy boy with the kind of unfortunate haircut we all had at one point, that unmistakeably ties us to the era in which we were teenagers. He had a wide, friendly face, and I remembered his arm, placed firmly round Helen's shoulders as if he couldn't quite believe his luck.

'So they were childhood sweethearts?' I prompted.

'Exactly. It was a bit like in the movies – he was the captain of the rugby team, she was a star athlete and top of the class.'

'And then?'

'Helen got a place at the University of Queensland. She wanted to do a business degree and then work in something related to sport.'

'And Lawrence?'

'Oh, he was never university material. He got a job working in the local gym, and did some construction work. Helen did well at university, as you can imagine. She was an academic star, and she was popular, involved in student activities and sport. She was always busy, and Lawrence found that difficult.'

'Not an unusual story, really – lots of high-school relationships struggle once you're out of the school environment.'

'Well, that was what we thought, Mum and Dad and me. We thought they'd drift apart and break up, and Helen would go on to date lots of guys at uni. But she was loyal to him.'

I didn't have anything to say in reply to that. A year ago, I'd have agreed – Helen did seem like a loyal person.

Judy continued. 'They stayed together right through her degree. He used to leave work early if she was training on the athletics track, and he'd go and sit and watch her. He went to every single social occasion. I think half the people Helen knew at university assumed he was also a student.'

'And the other half?'

'Thought he was a creep, actually. I did. He was so clingy. Helen got a chance to go to Sydney for a few weeks to do some work experience and he wouldn't let her go.'

'Wouldn't let her? How did he stop her?'

'Oh, the usual way blokes do. Sulked, raged, cried, threatened to go off with another girl. Acted like a child, basically. I told her to go anyway, and tell him to bugger off, but she didn't in the end. I tried to tell her that he was holding her back, but she wouldn't listen to a word of it. She said he was the love of her life, and that was that. She stopped speaking to me for a while even. I decided if I didn't want to lose her, I'd better back down. So I did my best to keep my mouth shut and make an effort with him.'

'And then?'

'She graduated, and at the graduation dinner with my parents and me, he got down on one knee and proposed. It was very public, in this big fancy restaurant and in front of her whole family. There was no way she could say no.'

'Do you think she wanted to say no?'

'Hell no. She was so happy, she burst into tears and said, "Yes, yes, yes!" I was the one willing her to say no. She was only twenty-two, for God's sake.'

'Wow.'

'Well, it all happened quite quickly after that. My parents forked out for this lavish wedding, and they gave Lawrence and Helen the deposit on their own tiny little apartment in Rocklea. Helen got her first job as a junior in a sports marketing company.' Judy suddenly broke off. She pressed her lips together, and with a shock, I realized she was fighting back tears.

'Once he had her in their own place, everything changed. He wanted to control her, you see. To own everything about her. She was so bright and sparky and beautiful, and I think he was terrified to let her out into the world, where other people would see it. And, of course, out in the world she was growing and succeeding and climbing the career ladder, and he was still just a brickie.'

'How did he control her?'

'He phoned her ten times a day, which got her into trouble with her bosses. He met her after work every day to walk her home. And then he got worse. He started pitching up at her office at odd times to check she was where she said she was. It all got rather embarrassing for her. He discouraged her from seeing me, and from seeing our parents. He cut her off from all her friends too. And once she had no support structure at all, the. . . the other stuff started.'

'He hit her,' I said dully.

'Such a well-worn story, isn't it? Almost a cliché. It started with a little slap because they had a row when she came home late from a run one day. Then he cried and cried and begged her forgiveness. And she forgave him. Until the time she was asked to work late, and when he tried to ring her she didn't answer because she was in a meeting room and didn't hear her phone. He was waiting for her outside the office when she came out and that time he punched her in the stomach. It escalated from there.'

Judy's face contorted, and she controlled her anger with an effort. 'Of course I didn't know at the time. I didn't have a clue. I must confess, to my eternal shame, that I didn't make much of an effort to see her, even. I was so disappointed in her for marrying him. Closing so many doors, restricting her choices. I knew she'd always wanted to travel, see the world, maybe work abroad, and marrying Lawrence seemed to guarantee that she'd be pregnant by the time she was twenty-five, and that'd be it. She'd end up being a dull Brisbane housewife. I didn't want to see that happen, and Lawrence was always so unpleasant when I rang the apartment or went to see her, so. . . I stopped trying, really. Got on with my own life. If I'd known. . .' Judy took a shuddering breath. 'If I'd known what she was going to go through, I'd have prayed for her just to be a Brisbane housewife.'

'So how did you find out?'

'It was inevitable that he'd end up hurting her enough that she had to go to hospital. He drove her there, but he was so out of control and disruptive, and I think the staff realized that what had happened wasn't an accident – not that Helen would have admitted to it. They called the cops and had him removed. She needed someone to take her home, and very reluctantly she gave them my name.'

'What had he done to her?'

'He smashed her face into a kitchen cabinet. She told the people in the hospital that she tripped and fell. But he'd been holding her by her hair, and he got a finger caught through her hoop earring. He'd ripped it right out—'

'Oh my God!' I almost shouted. 'The scar on her ear.'

'Yes.'

'She told me it happened at a music festival when she was a student.'

Judy laughed bitterly. 'As if Lawrence would have let her go to a music festival.'

I thought about Helen's odd aversion to having her hair touched. If I ever stroked it or tried to gather it up in my hands, she'd shy away. 'I don't like it,' she'd say, laughingly. 'I'm always scared you'll pull it.' And then I thought about the scar, the vertical line on her earlobe. Unconsciously, I reached up to touch my own ear. The thought of ripping right through the tender flesh of an earlobe – it made me shudder.

I looked back at the screen and Judy was watching me in silence.

'It's a lot to take in, I know,' she said.

'I never knew,' I said hesitantly. 'She never told me. . .'

'She never told anyone. I only know about that attack because she needed someone to get her out of the hospital. I know it's obvious to say that she's a private person, but she is. She keeps things to herself unless she has absolutely no other option. I can't tell you not to take this personally, but understand that this is who she is. It wasn't you that made her do this. It was her. All her.'

I knew she was doing her best to be comforting and I nodded my thanks. I wished that it was as simple as that, and that I could write off the whole thing to Helen's peculiar obsessive secrecy. I was about to say something when the doorbell went.

'I have to go, Judy,' I said. 'That's my mum bringing the girls back.'

'Sure,' she said. She seemed a little wistful, and we looked at each other in silence for a moment before we disconnected. I think we both imagined another life, where she might have known my daughters, if only by Skype, where she might have chatted to them over her sister's shoulder. But it was a life neither of us would ever have.

I went to buzz up Mum and the girls. They clattered up the stairs and rushed in, chattering excitedly and pulling garments out of bags. Mum followed, slightly more slowly, and when she came into the room I saw her watching me quizzically. I did my best to look happy and to focus on what the girls were saying and showing me, but the enormity of what Judy had told me kept crowding in. I wanted to sit by myself and look at the picture of Helen and Lawrence. I wanted to think about what she had endured, and why she had stayed. I wanted to talk to Judy and find out how she escaped. Clearly she had, and in doing so she'd left Australia and cut all ties with everyone. All of this sounded understandable, admirable even. But in a way, it made what had happened to the girls and me even worse. What had we done that was as bad as what Lawrence had done? Why had she vanished again?

Mum got the girls to go to their room and put away all their new clothes, then she made me a cup of tea and sat down opposite me in the living room.

'So how are you, my Sam?' she said, looking at me with her piercing eyes.

'Is that your therapist face?' I said warily.

'It's my mum face.' She looked around the room. 'The flat's looking nice. Better than it was. It must be easier to manage than that big house.'

'Is that parent code for "the house was beginning to fall apart from neglect"?'

'Goodness me,' she said mildly, 'you're looking for criticism under every comment, aren't you? No. I was just saying that this must be easier. What with working full time, and the girls. The house was a big responsibility. Practically and financially.'

Ah, so that was what she was getting at. What kind of a mess was I in financially? There was no point going there – Tim had told me that she and Dad were already concerned about their pensions. The last thing they needed was to worry about me and the state of my finances. Anyway, as long as I kept my nose clean and didn't lose my job, we'd be okay, more or less.

'It is,' I said eventually. 'I'm doing better.' This last was, of course, a blatant lie. I thought about telling her about Judy, and her revelations about Helen's past. But I needed time to think about what I'd learned. The girls were also in the next room, and all I needed was Miranda eavesdropping on the whole story.

Helen

Despite her optimistic intentions, the weekend was endless. She worked hard to fill it with films, meals, walks and gallery visits, but in the time between activities, and in the moments when she sat alone in a coffee shop or waiting for a train, thoughts of the girls rushed in, filling her with nausea, guilt and misery. She took to leaving her phone switched off and back at the flat, because the temptation to ring Sam came in almost overwhelming waves. Sunday night was the worst. She sat on the futon at the flat, watching episode after episode of *Friends*, the familiar lines washing over her, as she mechanically ate her way through a family-sized bag of caramel popcorn and then a gigantic bar of nutty chocolate. The stodgy food offered a dull comfort, and the canned laughter and bright colours of the TV show dispelled the black silence inside her head. She would have loved a drink, but she knew alcohol would lower her inhibitions and she'd end up making the fatal phone call. In the end she fell asleep half dressed, the futon still propped into a sitting position, her hands sticky with sugar.

She woke suddenly at five on Monday morning. For the first time since she'd left, a tiny sliver of optimism pierced the dread. Today, her new life was to begin. She went to the bathroom and showered and washed her hair. She had hours in which to dry it, apply her make-up and eat a small but healthy breakfast. She packed what she needed into her new black backpack, dressed in the navy trouser suit and white blouse she'd bought on the Friday, and by 7.30 she was ready to go. There was a full-length mirror on the back of the bathroom door. She examined her reflection. She looked elegant, business-like and slightly androgynous with her new short haircut and black-rimmed glasses. She'd chosen a style of suit that hid rather than accentuated her figure. It wasn't mannish or baggy, just professional. She looked nothing at all like Helen Cooper.

She washed her breakfast things, threw away the snack detritus of the night before and made her bed neatly. The flat looked as anonymous and featureless as it had the day she moved in. She picked up her bag, locked up and headed for the station.

She'd researched the journey of course, so she knew she had plenty of time, and, indeed, she'd left so early, she missed the worst of the commuter rush. By 8.15 she was sitting in a coffee shop in Stratford town centre, nursing a decaf cappuccino. She wasn't due in till 9.30. She felt desperate with jitters. Somehow, she hadn't anticipated the hours of waiting and introspection these past five days had allowed her. She'd imagined they would fly by. Now that she was in the last hour or so of this time alone, she was desperate for it to be over and for the next chapter to begin. In the end, she decided to be early. At nine she went to the bathroom in the coffee shop, brushed her teeth with the toothbrush she carried in her backpack, retouched the discreet make-up she'd chosen for her new persona, and set off on the short, five-minute walk.

The offices of Simon Stanley and Associates were in a new, modern building about ten minutes' walk from the station and the enormous shopping centre that now formed the hub of Stratford. The roads had the bleak, empty look of newly built areas – no trees or gardens lined them, and the streetlights started out from the wide, empty pavements like great, surprised insects. The buildings either side were still under construction, and while SSA occupied the top floor of the building, the offices on the floors below were still unfurnished and empty.

There was no one in the building reception downstairs, so Helen climbed the three flights of stairs. There was a toilet on the landing, so she stopped to check her reflection one last time. She brushed her neat, short hair behind her ears, straightened her shoulders, took a deep breath and walked briskly into the reception area of SSA. It was a wide, light room, with windows on both sides of the building. The rather startling bright red carpet was offset by the equally vibrant electric blue sofa. Huge posters of footballers, rugby players and athletes dominated every wall, and the glass coffee table was covered in a bright fan of sports magazines. A pretty woman of around twenty-five sat behind the shiny metallic reception desk, and two men were leaning on it, chatting to her. They all looked up when Helen walked in.

One of the men, the taller of the two, whose shaven head made him look older than his years, frowned in confusion as he looked at her. Then his face brightened and he smiled.

'Helen?' he said. 'You changed your hair.'

'Yes.' Helen smiled and touched her hair self-consciously, as if she had only just noticed the change herself. 'New job, new look!' she said brightly.

The bald man pushed himself away from the reception desk and came over to shake her hand. 'Welcome,' he said. 'It's great to have you here.'

'Thanks, Simon,' said Helen. 'I'm excited to get cracking.'

Simon turned to the other man. 'Tony, this is Helen Day, our new marketing executive. Helen, this is Tony Marinelli, head of sales. And this is Sophie Penn, our office manager.'

Helen shook hands. 'We're thrilled to have Helen on board,' said Simon. 'She's taken a few years out of work to travel and study, and she's ready and raring to go.'

It sounded to Helen like he'd written her profile on a dating app. She smiled at Simon, and at the other two. 'I'm thrilled to join SSA,' she said. 'I know this is an exciting time for you as a company, with the new energy gel account. . .'

'My baby,' said Tony, puffing out his chest.

'And I'm sure that together we can come up with some innovative tie-ins and marketing campaigns for them.' She gave them all her most brilliant smile.

Simon looked thrilled. 'Well,' he said, rubbing his hands together, 'let's show you your desk and get you settled in and then we'll see if you can hit the ground running!'

Helen followed him beyond the reception desk and into the open-plan office beyond. She wondered if he communicated exclusively in clichés. He showed her to a desk by the window. It had a new Mac, a phone and a view of the building site behind their offices. Helen put her backpack down beside the desk. Simon handed her a sheet of paper. 'Sophie's an IT whizz,' he said, 'so you should be all set up and good to go. User name and password are here,' he pointed to the paper in Helen's hand. 'All our working files are on the server. So have a good old dig around, and I'll come and chat to you in an hour or so.' He smiled at her again. 'I can't say how glad I am that we got you, Helen. Your background in sports is so perfect, and I know you'll bring something great to the company.'

Helen sat down at the desk. She took a notebook and pen out of her bag and placed them carefully on the empty surface. When she moved the mouse, the Mac gave a little growl and lit up, showing a log-in screen.

'Helen_Day@ssa.com', Helen typed, and then entered the password Sophie had chosen for her. As the icons popped up on the desktop before her, Helen allowed herself a slow breath out. She was here. She had fought her way free, and this was the first door opening, leading to the rest of her life.

CHAPTER FIFTEEN

Sam

Who the hell calls a meeting at Canary Wharf at 4.30 p.m. on a Thursday? A psychopath does, that's what I reckon. Either that, or a person who doesn't have kids. Or a partner. Or a life. I was fuming as I got on the Tube at Westminster. Luckily, Lara had agreed to take the girls home with her. Again. I felt a grinding guilt. I owe her so many favours that I have no chance of being able to repay them. I wish I was the kind of guy who could go round to her house at the weekend and do all those niggling DIY jobs, or make her garden beautiful, but I'm useless in both of those spheres. Helen was the gardener, and any DIY she couldn't do, we'd pay to have done by someone else. I could mow the lawn I suppose, or offer to kick a ball with Jonah in the garden, but that's scarcely repayment for countless pick-ups, meals and kindnesses to my girls and me.

To aggravate me further, there wasn't a seat. I found a segment of pole to hold on to as we moved through the City towards the east end of town. I kept an eye out, in case someone got up. My back ached, and I was hoping to have five minutes to check my emails before I went into the umpteenth client meeting of the week. I'd be working till eleven that night to catch up on messages otherwise. As I looked further down the carriage, I saw there was an elderly woman who had her bulky shopping bags on the seat beside her – a remarkably selfish act on a crammed, almost-rush-hour train. I seethed inwardly at the lack of consideration. I thought I might make eye contact with the person sitting next to her, to get them to ask her to move the bags. The seat was too far away for me to claim it, but someone else might like it.

There was a woman sitting in the next seat, engrossed in a book. It'd be difficult to catch her eye; she didn't look as if she would be likely to look up or look my way. She had the typical Londoner's pose – closed-off body language, eyes firmly down, neatly tucked into her seat with her elbows drawn in and her bag flat on her lap. Taking up the minimum room, attracting no attention. Funnily enough, I thought idly, she had something of Helen about her. Not in any overt way – she was plumper than Helen, with short blonde hair and a rather severe tailored business suit with trousers. Still, there was something. The curve of her cheek, the way she kept her fingers fanned along the top edge of the book, ready to turn the page quickly so as not to interrupt the flow of her reading.

We pulled into Waterloo and a great mass of people wedged their way into the carriage. Someone pressed the sharp corner of a briefcase against my calf, and I had to strain to keep hold of the pole and stop myself being knocked over. There was someone close to me who had had a lot of garlic for lunch, and someone else who was clearly a shower dodger. I silently cursed the inefficient product manager who was making me travel across town for this unnecessary meeting.

The torture continued for a few more stops until London Bridge, where most of the people on the train piled off. I breathed in deeply, relishing the sweat- and garlic-free air. There was a seat a little way down the carriage, and as I made my way towards it, I glanced idly towards the woman I had noticed earlier. She was still in her seat, still reading, and as I looked at her, she reached up and stroked her finger over the top of her ear, as if she was tucking her hair behind it, although her hair was too short to tuck. It was an utterly familiar gesture. Helen's gesture. Judy's gesture. I shook my head. I was being ridiculous. Women everywhere did that. I was back to seeing shadows of Helen everywhere I went. It was talking to Judy that had done it – put her front-of-mind again.

I sat down with relief and pulled my phone out of my pocket. I should be able to type at least one reply before we got to Canary Wharf, I thought. But somehow I couldn't concentrate on the email from my manager about revenue forecasts. I glanced over to the woman again. I was much closer to her now, but she was oblivious to everyone around her. In profile, her face was very like Helen's – the straight nose and the neat round chin. Her body was nothing like Helen's though; where Helen had been lean and firm, this woman was soft, with a roundness to her hips and a little rise of soft tummy under her smart jacket. And obviously one of Helen's most striking features had been her beautiful bright russet hair, whereas this woman was blonde. Not that it was inconceivable for Helen to be blonde. I mean, hair can be dyed. The woman had a neat, short crop, well cut, with a sweep of straight hair that fell over her forehead. As I watched, she reached up again to tuck her hair behind her ears and in that instant I felt as if someone had punched me in the stomach. There was a scar on her earlobe. A clearly visible vertical line, white against the honeyed tones of her skin.

Helen

It took her three months to create her first solo marketing campaign. It was a social media competition, with some online advertising support, for their energy gel client. The day it went live, she sat late in the office, watching the statistics, checking for click-throughs, responses, retweets. She knew it was far too early to see if the work was a success, but she couldn't look away. She'd spent hundreds of hours working with design agencies and creatives, tweaking, reporting back to the client, assessing, testing, reworking. Eventually, on that first night, the building security guard came up and gave her a stern look, so she reluctantly turned off her computer and headed home.

The next day she was in at eight, watching the stats again. Simon eventually dragged her out of the office for a celebratory lunch to stop her obsessing. She looked at him across the table at Wagamama. She'd become fond of him over the months they had worked together, in a distant, slightly maternal way. He was a sweetheart, full of enthusiasm and verve, but no great shakes as a businessman. If SSA ever got a half-decent client, they'd be bought out by a bigger agency in a heartbeat. He wasn't ruthless enough to make it with the big boys. From her own perspective, she knew SSA was a stepping stone to better things. She needed everything she did there to be outstanding, so she could take a gigantic step up on her next career move. She'd lost years. She had to move fast.

The energy gel campaign vastly outperformed its targets, and the sports nutrition company paid SSA a bonus, some of which went to Helen. Simon was delighted and immediately gave her another, bigger project to work on for a new brand of running shoe. If there was anything Helen knew a lot about, it was running, and she threw all her knowledge and experience at the project. She worked twelve-hour days, and spent her evenings researching and writing notes. Perversely, the more she thought about running for work, the further she moved from wanting to run herself.

She had stayed off alcohol completely, ever since she had begun her new life, but she comfort ate all the time, indulging in fast food, snacks and chocolate almost every night. She had a constant ache in her centre, which she knew came from missing Miranda and Marguerite, more than she had ever imagined possible. She worried constantly about how they were, what they were doing, how Sam was managing to care for them. Somehow, eating the sugary snacks made the ache abate slightly. She knew that eating her way out of emotional pain wasn't the answer, but even though the months were passing, she didn't miss the girls less or think of them less often. She needed a more practical, long-term solution to deal with the ache, and she set about finding one. It was dangerous, she knew that, and meant taking a gigantic risk, but she decided it was worth the gamble.

She had gained almost two stone, and her lean, muscular tautness had softened into pillowy curves. She rather liked her new body with its pale plumpness and the unaccustomed voluptuousness of her larger breasts. She liked to stand naked in front of the bathroom mirror and stroke the curve of her belly and admire the roundness of her thighs. She had also changed her hair. Every time she had a success at work, she took herself off to the little hairdresser's she had found in Stratford, and cut her hair a little shorter and went another shade blonder.

The running-shoe campaign was another storming hit, and Simon called her into his office – or at least his corner of their open-plan office – and told her he was giving her a 20 per cent raise. She knew he was trying to buy her loyalty and was desperate to keep her. She smiled and accepted the raise, but of course her CV was already out there on the desks of the biggest recruitment consultants in the field. She was almost ready for her next move and she would walk away from SSA without a backward glance when the time came.

She'd been offered a few interviews, but, as yet, nothing had been good enough to tempt her to leave SSA. Simon kept pushing good, exciting work her way, so for the moment she was prepared to bide her time. The latest project was a kinetic sports tape campaign, linked to a big international football tournament. It would mean liaising with agencies in Europe and South America if it came off. Less than a year into her new life and her first goal – building an international network – was within her reach.

'Go and see Gareth at the design agency this week,' said Simon. 'Get him to start scamping some ideas. It's early days, but I want to be ahead of the game when the brief comes in.'

She had agreed and had spent the morning and half the afternoon with Gareth. She would normally have gone back to the office afterwards, but she wanted some quiet time alone to work on the final feedback report for the running-shoe campaign, so she decided to head home and work there instead. The agency was in Green Park and she got on the Tube and managed to find a seat, even though it was almost rush-hour.

She'd probably spend three or four hours on the report when she got home, so she decided to indulge herself and read a book on the Tube. She was reading something about the future of virtual reality in marketing. Now she had a seat, she should have an uninterrupted twenty minutes or so before she had to change trains at Canary Wharf to go home.

Sam

I had to get a grip. All those times I'd been convinced I had 'seen' Helen, only to discover I was hallucinating. It was happening again, and before I embarrassed myself, I had to look away. This was just a woman who bore a passing resemblance. I must be imagining the scar. The train halted at Canada Water, where a lot of passengers got off and comparatively few got on. There was hardly anyone at all sitting between us now. I knew I shouldn't, but I used the commotion of people getting on and off to move a few seats closer. She didn't notice me. She was utterly engrossed in her book. I could see it was non-fiction, about virtual reality or something. Was that something Helen would read? How would I know? How would I know anything about what Helen might or might not do?

I stared at her hands. Were they Helen's hands? They were smooth and pale, with neat, short nails. Shorter than Helen wore hers, but then nails could be cut. No wedding rings. I looked again at her ear. There was definitely a scar there. But that in itself proved nothing. Anyone might have a scar on their ear. It could all just be a coincidence. There was more about this woman that was unlike Helen than like her.

I was suddenly aware of someone watching me. I looked up, and a woman in her early fifties with fierce, dark, arched eyebrows was staring at me. 'I can see what you're up to,' her eyes broadcast to me. 'Stop ogling her, you perv.' I stared back at her defiantly, and after a few seconds she looked away.

In that brief moment, the train pulled into Canary Wharf. I glanced over. If the almost-Helen was staying on the train, so was I, no matter how bonkers that seemed. I'd be late for my meeting, but that was too bad. But she wasn't. Her seat was empty, and as I looked around wildly, I saw her stepping off the train at the door furthest from me in the carriage. I leapt up and ran after her, stumbling over legs and bags. I half fell out of the door of the train, and to my immense relief, she was right there. She hadn't begun to move off along the platform, so great was the crush of people.

'Helen!' I shouted, above the hubbub, and she turned instantly, looking up at me, her face within inches of mine.

It was her. My wife. I was staring into Helen's face. Her eyes were wide and shocked, and her mouth opened. She tried to step away, but I caught her hand.

'Helen,' I said again, and for a moment that stretched endlessly, we stood in the impossible mass of people, utterly alone, just the two of us.

'Come on, mate!' yelled an aggressive voice behind me, and someone jostled me and shoved me firmly between my shoulder blades.

There was a fraction of a second where I was distracted. But it was enough. Helen snatched her hand free from my grasp and dived back through the doors of the train as they slid shut. The train whined and began to move slowly as I hammered helplessly on the closed doors. I watched Helen's bright blue eyes slide away from me and she disappeared into the dark tunnel.

CHAPTER SIXTEEN

Miranda

Dad wasn't back to pick us up. Again. For the third time in two weeks, Lara came to get Marguerite and me from the after-school club and took us back to her house. She said that Dad had a meeting. Dad always has meetings. It didn't bother me before, when we had Helen, because picking up was always her job. But now Dad pretends it's his job, except it seems like it's a job he can skip doing when he feels like it. It's not Lara's job either, and she always does her best to look like she doesn't mind, but I know she does. She looked tired when she came today. Jonah was hanging on to her hand and screaming. Frances looked cross too – she told me later she was in the middle of watching a programme on TV and she had to turn it off to come and get us.

Lara let us all go into the living room to watch TV, but I was thirsty so I followed her into the kitchen to get a drink of water.

She was standing staring into the open freezer. She turned when I came in.

'Oh, hi, Miranda,' she said, and did her best 'none of this is your fault' pity smile.

'Is everything okay?' I said.

'Hmm? Oh yes, all fine. Just trying to work out what to give you all for dinner.' I knew what she meant was that she was trying to work out how to make dinner go far enough for Marguerite and me, and possibly Dad too, when she hadn't expected to have to do that.

'Are we staying for dinner?' I asked. 'When's Dad coming?'

'He wasn't sure,' she said, and I noticed that she wasn't as good at keeping that tight bit of irritation out of her voice as Helen had been.

'Look!' she suddenly said brightly. 'Pizza bases!' I've got lots of cheese and pepperoni and ham and stuff. Homemade pizzas it is!'

I don't really like pizza, but it didn't really seem like the right time to say so.

'I can help you, if you like,' I said.

'No, don't worry,' she said, and lightly touched my arm. She's careful about touching me. No mumsy hugs or kisses. I'm glad about that. Marguerite will go and sit on her lap sometimes, when Jonah's not looking (he screams the place down if he sees her doing it).

The pizzas were okay. Well, not okay. They were doughy and horrid with cheddar cheese and plasticky ham, but the little kids and Frances liked them. Lara let us eat them in front of the TV. I thought about Helen's grown-up meals, with homemade pasta and beautiful salads with lots of colours in them. Sometimes she even put flowers in the salad.

It got to seven o'clock and Dad still wasn't there and hadn't phoned. Lara started to look stressed. She didn't have work tonight, but I know she was thinking about us and school tomorrow.

'Marguerite, Miranda, you've got pyjamas and things here, haven't you?' she said in that fake, bright, grown-up way. 'It's probably best for you to sleep over. When you go up to bath, give me your school uniforms and I'll give them a quick wash and iron.'

'I need my PE kit for tomorrow,' I said. 'And my geography book. They're all at the flat.'

Lara looked even more stressed. 'Well, when your dad gets here. . .' I could hear her silently thinking, 'if he ever gets here'. '. . . he can go and pick up everything you need.'

I wanted to argue, because it wasn't fair, but I also knew it wasn't Lara's fault. I went upstairs and took off my uniform. I had a drawer of weekend things in Frances' room, and I put on shorts and a T-shirt and made sure Marguerite did the same. I knew Marguerite's reading book was at our flat too. She was supposed to do reading every evening and now she would miss another night. She wasn't all that good at reading. She needed more practice. And then I thought, what if Dad doesn't come? Or what if there isn't time in the morning to get my PE kit and books?

I thought about this boy who used to be in our class called Mickey. No one wanted to sit next to him because he often smelled bad. His uniform was always dirty, even on the first day of term. He never had the right books or PE kit, and he was always late. The teacher used to get cross with him if he didn't bring in his homework, but then he'd say, 'I'm sorry, miss, but I slept on the sofa at my auntie's house yesterday. I haven't been home.'

I didn't like Mickey, and I would never have been his friend, but even I could see it wasn't his fault. Would everyone know it wasn't my fault either?

I went next door to Jonah's room and fetched Marguerite's uniform and took the bundle of clothes down to Lara in the kitchen. She was standing at the sink, staring out of the kitchen window, and she looked tired and cross. She tried to smile at me when she took the school things and put them in the washing machine. I couldn't help noticing that the other things in the machine were dirty dish towels, and I hoped my school uniform wouldn't come out smelling like greasy old pizza.

I said thank you to Lara and went back upstairs. We're poor and badly dressed and going to school without the right books and stuff. We've gone from being the best family in the school to being the almost Mickeys. It's all Helen's fault. Helen and Dad. I hate them both so much.

Lara

'So sorry. Something's come up. Running late.'

What kind of text message is that? What's 'come up'? As I loaded the machine with the girls' school uniforms, I wondered, not for the first time, if I was being taken for a total mug. I wasn't keeping score, but this was the third time in the last fortnight Sam had dumped his kids on me with scant warning. Dumped sounds harsh, but that's how it felt. This was one of my rare Thursday evenings off, and Mum was out at a film with friends. Sam and I hadn't arranged to get together and I'd been looking forward to some quiet time alone with Frances and Jonah, and once they were in bed, I'd planned to watch a soppy chick-flick and then get to bed early myself. Now I'd be doing a Cinderella, waiting up for the washing machine to finish so I could iron the school uniforms and hang them up to dry for the morning. I'd also somehow have to magic an extra two packed lunches for school tomorrow out of thin air. It was petty to worry about these details, but someone had to – and it sure as hell wasn't Sam. I understood that his job was unpredictable, but it struck me that as a single parent, he might do better to push back a little harder when people made unreasonable demands. He worked in advertising, for God's sake. It wasn't exactly life or death if he said he couldn't make a short-notice, after-hours meeting.

And anyway, hadn't his meeting been at about half past four? It was almost nine now, and all the kids were in bed. How long could it possibly have gone on for? I was being the domestic drudge while he was probably whooping it up in some classy bar in central London, which he would justify as 'client relations'. I caught sight of my reflection in the kitchen window: hair frizzy and coming free from my scruffy ponytail, stained old T-shirt, no make-up, and a face like sulky thunder, quite justifiably. What an appealing sight to come home to. Not to mention my irresistible conversation about laundry and PE kit. So he'd come swanning in from his exciting life in the city and I'd be the resentful, boring 'her indoors' who was no fun to be with. I felt like I was being totally set up to fail. I shook my head. This was Marc all over again.

When I'd thought about getting involved with Sam, I'd had misgivings – he was still grieving and there were so many practical considerations. But what tipped the balance for me was the fact that Sam was such a nice man. I thought I knew about bastards. After Marc, I thought my bastard radar was finely tuned. But it looks like Sam might be a bastard by stealth.

I looked at the clock. The school uniforms would come out of the machine in just over an hour. It wasn't worth starting a film just to have to interrupt it. I was considering watching whatever mindlessness I could find on TV when I heard a soft rapping on the front door. I took a deep breath and tried to wipe the sulks off my face. Sam and I needed to have a proper conversation about our situation, but answering the door with a dropped lip like a petulant teenager wasn't going to advance my cause.

I opened the door and the shock must have registered on my face, because Tim laughed.

'I'm guessing you weren't expecting me,' he said.

'Hi,' I said. 'Um, sorry. Good to see you. I thought you were Sam.'

'Is he not here?' Tim looked puzzled. 'I went past his place and it was in darkness. I reckoned he and the girls must be with you.'

'The girls, yes. Sam, no. He had a work meeting.'

Tim glanced at his watch and raised his eyebrows. 'Some meeting.'

I was irritated by his casual tone. 'Look, do you want to come in? You're welcome to, but I don't know when Sam. . .'

'Yeah, thanks, that'd be nice,' he said. He reached into the shopping bag he was carrying. 'I have a bottle of very nice red wine that I was planning on sharing with my big brother. He's a philistine when it comes to wine though, so it'd be good to share it with someone who might appreciate it.'

I wanted to disapprove of Tim. I'd had him pinned as a player the first time I'd seen him – a charmer with a taste for young, disposable women and an incorrigible flirt. But he'd been nothing but kind to me (and not at all flirtatious) since Sam and I had started seeing each other, and he was here on my doorstep with what looked like a very good bottle of wine indeed.

I fetched glasses and we went through into the living room. Tim was right. It was a smooth and velvety red, but probably too heavy for Sam. He'd have called it a 'headache in a glass' or wanted a big rare steak to have with it.

'So how are things?' I asked as casually as I could. I had never chatted to Tim without Sam before, and I realized I didn't know enough about him to ask any specific questions about his life.

'Busy. My commis chef walked out on me earlier this week. Decided the kitchen life wasn't for him. Too stressful, he said.'

'Couldn't take the heat, I reckon.'

Tim smiled. 'I think he was surprised that it impacted so badly on his social life, to be honest.'

'It's kind of the point of the hospitality industries,' I said. 'You're working when everyone else is having fun.'

'You're not working tonight?'

'No, rare night off.'

'And I bet you had plans that involved a bag of crisps and an early night, not skivvying for four children.'

'Chick-flick and chocolate, but the principle is the same.' I paused. 'It's not skivvying, though. They're lovely girls and I'm always happy to have them.'

'I guess Sam helps you with your kids too,' said Tim, and I noticed he was watching me closely.

I was disconcerted by his gaze and waited a fraction too long before I said, 'Of course.'

'Don't let him take the piss, Lara. He does that.'

'Does what?'

'Does that sweet, helpless, crooked smile and gets people to do stuff for him. My mum and dad fell for it for years when he was growing up. Leonora didn't take any shit from him, but Helen. . .'

He looked guilty for mentioning Helen.

'Helen what?' I prompted.

He paused for a moment and then said, 'I always thought they were a terrible combination. A person who needs loads of help, and a control-freak perfectionist.' He took a sip of his wine. 'I adore my brother, but he's a taker, and she was. . . not so much a giver as a doer. Now you. . . you're a giver. And you need to be careful.'

'Thanks for the warning,' I said coolly. 'It's not terribly loyal to your brother though.'

'I'd say it to his face,' said Tim. 'I have, on more than one occasion.'

I thought I should try to steer the conversation back on to safer ground, so I asked him what he was doing about finding a new commis chef.

'I've got the agency sending me someone new tomorrow,' he said. 'It's frustrating though. I put a lot of energy into training Kevin, and we were working on a new menu. . .'

'New menu?' I said. This sounded like something uncontroversial we could talk about. I'm not into cooking myself, but I've spent most of my working life around chefs, so I can talk foodie stuff with the best of them. Tim had been doing research into Middle Eastern cuisines and was trying to put his own spin on some recipes. We talked about harissa paste, and what you could get away with doing with cinnamon, and whether quinoa was hopelessly last year or not. The wine was going down easily, and I found Tim equally easy to talk to. I hadn't warmed to him at first, and I think he knew that. But chatting to him now I could see he was ambitious about his career, and driven. Just like the commis chef, his working hours would have cost him his social life. It would take an extraordinary woman to fit in around the lifestyle of a serious chef. Maybe his track record of brief, unserious relationships was born of practicality.

The washing machine beeped in the kitchen and I stood up rather unsteadily.

'Whoops,' I said. 'Nice wine, but it's more potent than I'm used to.'

'Where are you going?' asked Tim.

'The washing machine.' I waved in the direction of the kitchen. 'I need to iron the girls' uniforms and hang them out to dry for tomorrow.'

'I'll do it,' he said, hopping to his feet, looking much more sober than I felt.

'No, no, no. . .' I began.

'Yes,' he said firmly. 'They're my nieces. And besides, I'm a ninja ironer. Crispest chef's whites in the West.'

'Ninja ironer?' I followed him into the kitchen. 'Really?'

'It makes it sound cool, doesn't it?' he said, efficiently setting up the ironing board. 'Like I'm an ironing superhero.'

He pulled Marguerite's little gingham pinafore out of the washing machine and held it up to look at it.

'Yes,' I said. 'Exactly like an ironing superhero.'

He was a ninja ironer. I watched him as he expertly spun the pinafores and pressed each surface, flattening the collars and aligning the buttons. He got them looking much neater than I would have done. He doesn't look anything like Sam, I mused. He's compact and wiry where Sam is big and broad; dark-haired and olive-skinned where Sam is fair-haired with a light, English complexion. It's hard to believe they're brothers. Then he looked up and caught me watching him and smiled, and I saw the resemblance. They have the same heart-tugging charm. I would bet that the young women he's had his flings with wanted to do stuff for him too. He finished with the dresses and I got him a couple of hangers and he put them in the conservatory to dry.

The bottle of wine he had brought was mysteriously empty. I didn't have anything as classy, but I managed to root out a decent bottle of Merlot. As we sat back down on the sofa, I checked my phone.

'Nothing from Sam?' said Tim, noticing.

'Nope. It's probably client drinks or something.'

'Or something.' I wasn't sure what Tim meant and I didn't want to think about it too much, so I took another long sip of my wine. I was going to feel shocking when I woke up after all this red wine, but I'd deal with that in the morning.

Tim said suddenly, 'So tell me about you.'

'What do you mean?'

'I don't know anything about you,' he said. 'I know you've got two kids and you're a restaurant manager, but that's it.'

'Not sure there's all that much more to tell,' I said. 'I was a dancer once.'

'Ah yes. I knew that. Miranda told me all about it. So was that the big dream? Is it still the dream?'

'The dream?' I said stupidly, as if he had used a phrase I wasn't familiar with.

'The dream. Your ultimate goal. Raison d'être and all that.'

'Does everyone have to have one of those?'

'Doesn't everyone?'

'What, like a calling? A vocation? A burning ambition? I don't.'

'Don't you?'

'Unless being happy and having happy kids and a secure roof over my head is a burning ambition.'

He thought about it for a second. 'Yeah, that'll do.'

I laughed suddenly. 'Wow, imagine if I still had a burning ambition to dance. The pirouetting school-gate mum. There's a dance movie in that – like a modern-day *Flashdance*.'

Tim grinned. 'Sorry, that did sound trite, didn't it? A neat Hollywood answer.'

'So do you think everyone should have a singular goal?'

'No, of course not. I guess I always did. I knew what I wanted to do for as long as I can remember. So it's not always easy for me to understand that not everyone is like that.'

'Sam isn't.'

'Sam's ambitious, but in different ways. He's always liked money, and prestige and status. And he wants people to like him. So he worked hard for those things. Not for love of the work itself. He likes it in other people, though. His first wife, Leonora, was a musician, and he loved her passion and dedication.'

The girls have a picture of Leonora in their bedroom at Sam's flat. She was beautiful – dark and striking – and even in the black-and-white portrait you can see her fire and verve. First her, then Helen, all smooth elegance and sparkly intelligence. What the hell was Sam doing with me?

As if reading my thoughts, Tim said, 'Helen. . .' and then he stopped again.

'You can talk to me about Helen,' I said. 'I knew her quite well, you know. Well, I thought I did. I think everyone thought they did.'

'I didn't,' said Tim. 'We never really got on. She didn't like me.'

'Did you like her?'

He was quiet for a long time. I got the sense he was planning his answer very carefully. 'I respected her, if that means anything.'

'Respected?'

'I could see her power.'

'What, like a superpower?'

'No.' He laughed. 'Well, maybe, yes, a bit. She was powerful. Ambitious. No, that's not quite the right word. She was. . . competitive. She had to be the best.'

I nodded. I could see some truth in that. I sort of bumble through life trying to get things done, trying not to be an embarrassment to myself or my family. But I don't care what people think, most of the time. Helen had seemed to care fiercely. It didn't matter if she was baking a cake, or on a table at a quiz, or dressing her kids for a non-uniform day, she had to do it perfectly. Or, if you subscribed to Tim's view on it, better than anyone else. And to be fair, she had disappeared completely and untraceably. She was the best at disappearing too.

Sam

She'd been getting off at Canary Wharf, I reasoned, and when she saw me, she'd got back on the train. That meant she would have to come back to Canary Wharf, surely? Or maybe she'd got off to change trains, and she'd taken a different route to her eventual destination. There was no way of knowing, but all I had was the fact that she'd got off at Canary Wharf. After standing in the milling crowd in a state of shock for some minutes, I went over to the westbound platform. If she'd gone one stop and changed trains to come back, she'd get off here. But the platform was long and the crowds poured out of trains every few minutes. It was hopeless. I would never spot her in this seething mass of people. After half an hour or so, I felt battered by the constant jostling of the crowds, and faint from shock. I needed to get above ground.

I made my way out of the station and stood in the wide concourse in front of the entrance. All around me, people were meeting and greeting, kissing each other or shaking hands, going off together to bars and restaurants. I was supposed to be at a meeting, I thought vaguely. I looked at my watch. Five o'clock. I was over half an hour late. I took out my phone and rang my office. The receptionist answered, and I told her a garbled story about being taken ill on the Tube and having stayed down on the platform until I felt better. I asked her to ring the client and make my apologies, saying that I was going home.

'Poor thing,' she said sympathetically. She's a sweet girl, our receptionist, and I always make sure I'm nice to her, even a little bit flirtatious. She's a useful person to have onside. 'Look after yourself,' she added.

I should go home, I thought. There's no point in hanging around here. But somehow I wasn't ready to. I'd been so close. And maybe

Helen was nearby, in a bar or restaurant, and if I left now, I'd miss her and never find her again. I sent a quick text to Lara, saying something had come up, and I decided to walk for a while and look around. Just for half an hour or so, to put my mind at rest.

The bars and restaurants of Canary Wharf were beginning to fill up with suited businesspeople. The dress was more formal than the trendy, casual attire in the West End, where the media people congregate. I wandered from glass-fronted bar to bar, gazing in at groups of pink-shirted, muscular men. There were lots of women in heels and skirts, swinging their straight, glossy, impeccably coloured hair and laughing. None of them resembled the version of Helen I'd seen, with her severe blonde crop and buttoned-up suit. It was a pointless exercise, I knew, but I wasn't ready to give up. After an hour or so, I started to feel dizzy and thirsty, and I saw a vacant table outside a bar and sat down. A waiter took my order and brought me a cold pint, which I swallowed down in one go. While I waited for the next one, I spotted two young women, standing uncertainly, looking up and down the crowded tables. They were clearly searching for somewhere to sit. One of them caught my eye and indicated the empty chairs at my table. I nodded assent, and they came over to sit down.

I took out my phone and stared at it, trying to let them know that I didn't want to engage in conversation, but I needn't have worried. They both angled their chairs away from me and turned to one another, chatting in that breathy, interrupting, overlapping way young women do, carrying on several threads of dialogue at once. My second beer arrived, and to save time I ordered another immediately. The two women got their drinks too and kept chatting without drawing breath.

I stared out at the passing parade of people. Where was Helen? Was she around the corner, or already far away and fleeing further? Why was she still in London? And why did she look so different? From what she'd been wearing, it was likely that she was working. At what? Where? None of my web searches had turned up her name in any context. But that assumed she still had the same name – I'd been looking for Helen Cooper or Helen Knight. Perhaps she'd changed her name altogether?

What are the odds of bumping into someone in London? One in several million? And yet it happens. Had happened. Helen had obviously decided that it was worth the risk of staying in London, that the odds were overwhelmingly in her favour. She might easily have lived another lifetime in the city without ever encountering me or anyone she knew. But she'd been unlucky. She'd caught the wrong Tube on the wrong day, and despite the enormous changes to her appearance, I'd seen her.

My stomach churned. The pain of her leaving had been bad, excruciating even, but over time, with nothing to feed it, it had lessened. It had had to. I could only agonize over the facts I knew. I couldn't add any new ones. Without knowing where she had gone, or why, I had eventually had to get on with my life. My conversations with Judy had been illuminating about Helen's past, but they hadn't brought me any nearer to where she might be in the present. But now this.

In that one long moment of eye contact on the Tube platform, the wound had been ripped right open. I felt desperate, and my anger flamed high. How could she? How could she be living a few miles from us, from me and my daughters, and never make contact? How could she get up every day and go wherever she went, and then return to a home where she ate and slept without us? Without giving us a thought? How could she?

One thing was for sure. Beer wasn't going to cut it. I hailed a waiter (they were reassuringly available and attentive) and ordered a double tequila and soda, with another one to come as soon as I finished the first.

The tequila was sharp and fragrant and oh so cold, and I felt its effect from the first sip. It spread through my veins in a flood of cooling calm, and the rage that had been pounding at my temples receded a fraction. Thank God. A few more of these and I'd have recovered enough to go home. Or at least to go to Lara's and pick up the girls. I glanced at my watch. It was close to eight o'clock. There was no way I'd make it back before they had to be in bed. I was a good hour from home. Lara would put the girls to bed at her place, and I could just arrive and stay over. It wasn't ideal, and I was sure to get major sulks from Miranda about something she needed back at the flat, but I'd deal with it in the morning. I drained my glass and swilled the ice around, taking small sips to get every last bit of taste from it. I signalled the waiter that I was ready for the next one, and he moved back into the bar with impressive speed.

While I waited for my drink, I noticed that one of the two women sharing my table had left – I assumed to go to the toilet. The other, a petite girl with a thick mane of rich dark hair and impressively curvy breasts under her thin summer top, gave me a shy smile.

'Nice evening,' she said. 'It's warmer than I expected.'

Weather small talk. I could do this. We chatted about whether summer was really here, and how this summer compared to last summer, and the festival she was going to at the weekend, and how she hoped it wouldn't rain because she and her mates were camping and there was nowhere to plug in hair straighteners.

Then her friend came back from the toilet and looked mildly annoyed that Curvy Brunette was talking to me. The friend was tall and blonde and looked as if she disapproved of quite a lot of things. It seemed important that I should win her over, so when my order arrived, I offered to buy them a drink. This was not a successful tactic, as the blonde one clearly suspected any man buying drinks of nefarious motives. She got even more thin-lipped, but the dark-haired girl accepted a small glass of rosé. She smiled her thanks when the drinks arrived, and then looked down at the table shyly. A lock of her thick hair fell forward, and I was irresistibly reminded of Helen – or the Helen I had known before she went.

Curvy Brunette's name was Kelly, or maybe it was Kiki. I wasn't sure. It certainly didn't matter what it was when, some hours later, I was grinding up against her, leaning on a railing by the river, kissing her with drunken, open-mouthed lust. She was short, even in her sky-high heels, so I had to bend right down. Her mouth was small and narrow-lipped, and sticky with lipstick, a not especially sensual combination. I didn't care though. I stroked and squeezed her splendid breasts and did my best to lose myself in the drunken haze of the moment, the streetlights flaring in my half-closed eyes and the noise of the crowd eddying around us. She kissed me back enthusiastically, pressing herself against me, then she pulled back, her eyes unfocused with lust and wine and said, 'Do you live nearby? Shall we go back to yours?'

I almost laughed out loud. I could imagine what her idea of 'mine' might be – a cool bachelor pad in Bermondsey, or maybe somewhere like Hoxton. A big black leather sofa, an amazing sound system, white Egyptian cotton bed sheets, lovingly ironed and smoothed on to my king-size bed by my cleaner. How disappointed she would be by the reality of going back to mine. Which 'mine' would I take her back to? The house I owned, now rented out to strangers? My poky, depressing flat, with its damp towels and dust-ball-covered carpet, every corner crammed with the detritus of my daughters? Or should I take her back to the house where my daughters were sleeping right now, in the care of the woman who probably assumed we were in an exclusive relationship? Perhaps my elusive legal wedded wife would have a view on where I could take curvy Kelly/Kiki for a meaningless drunken shag?

The nausea came then, fast and hot. It was almost indistinguishable from the anger of earlier, but now it roiled around in my gut with large quantities of alcohol and absolutely no food. I pushed Kiki away.

'I'm sorry,' I said. 'I've got to. . . I've got to go.'

Her eyes hardened, and she looked at me appraisingly. 'Married, right?' she said. 'I should have known.'

I could have said so many things, but in the end I said, 'Yes. Sorry,' and stumbled away.

I was violently sick around the corner, and again before I managed to make it to the Tube station. I could barely focus to see the time, but, astonishingly, it wasn't that late. Around ten or so. There was a blinding headache starting to pound behind my right eye, I was desperately thirsty and my mouth tasted foul. I had managed to vomit without getting any on my shoes or clothes, but I could still smell it on myself. What a mess I was.

The human survival instinct is a curious thing, because I got back to north London without incident, and with absolutely no memory of how I did it. I must have changed trains where I needed to and stayed awake long enough to get off at the correct stop. A fine, cool drizzle was falling, and I hoped it might wash off some of the vomit, booze and perfume smell that hovered around me.

I passed my own block of flats and glanced up at the darkened windows. I was desperate to turn in there, have a long hot shower and fall face forward on to my unmade bed. But I'd made no contact with Lara since my early evening text, and guilt overwhelmed me. I didn't want the girls to wake up in Lara's house and for me not to be there. I squared my shoulders and continued my unsteady progress. I got to the front door of Lara's house and I could see that there were lights on downstairs. My heart sank. I'd kind of hoped she would be in bed, asleep, and that I could sneak in, wash and get into bed without having to talk to her. Maybe, I thought hopefully, she'd just left a light on for her mum, who I knew was out and coming home later.

I usually knock when I arrive at Lara's, even though she's given me a key. It preserves a degree of distance, makes it clear that I know it isn't my house. But this was a good time to use the key, if only to keep my entrance as quiet as possible. I fumbled and found the right one. I even managed to insert it, turn it and ease the door open without making too much of a racket. I stepped in soundlessly. I could hear low voices in the living room. I'd have to brazen it out, apologize for my lateness and be extra helpful and charming tomorrow. I slipped off my shoes in the porch and padded down the corridor in my socks. I turned into the living room, and as I did, I saw a muscular, tanned, male arm resting along the back of the sofa. The hand was inches from the long, pale stem of Lara's neck. Her head was bowed, but I could see she was smiling, her face half turned towards the man on the sofa beside her. I laughed in shock, and they both turned, surprised, to see me standing in the doorway. Lara and my brother Tim, curled up on the sofa together.

CHAPTER SEVENTEEN

Sam

I woke up very early and rang Chris' voicemail, leaving a message to say that I was sick and wasn't coming in. A twenty-four-hour bug or food poisoning or something. I tried to keep it vague and sound faint and ill and confused.

I was sick – my stomach ached fiercely and my hangover was punishing. I was awake well before the girls, and as soon as they were up, I shoved them into their school uniforms and said we were going back to our place to make sure they had what they needed for school. Marguerite was fuzzy and half asleep, but she's biddable and still small enough for me to dress her myself for speed. Miranda was obviously relieved; I could see she'd been worrying about the books and equipment she didn't have, so she got herself ready in a few minutes and we let ourselves out into the chilly, rainy morning. Neither of them noticed that Lara wasn't up and about and we hadn't said goodbye to her. I'd also got them out of the house quickly enough that they hadn't registered the rumpled sofa cushions and the folded blanket on the arm of a chair, clues to where I had spent the night.

There'd been an argument the night before – nasty, whispered and vicious. When I walked into the living room and saw Tim about to make his move on Lara, I'd growled, 'What the fuck is going on here?'

Lara leapt up, looking simultaneously guilty and angry.

'Where have you been?' she said.

'Well, obviously not here, which seems to have given you a good opportunity to get your leg over my brother.'

'What? I. . .' She was speechless.

Tim got up, deliberately more slowly than Lara had, and turned to face me with a glint in his eye that I knew meant combat.

'What's this, Samster? Attack is the best form of defence? Look at the fucking state of you. Honestly.'

'I think you should go,' I said.

'Pardon?' Now his eyes narrowed, and I knew I'd pissed him off. 'Last I heard, this wasn't your house. It's Lara's.'

'Yes, it's Lara's. My girlfriend.' I bit off the word. It was the first time I'd called Lara that. I didn't dare to look at her to see what she thought. 'So I'm not terribly sure what the hell you're doing here.'

'Looking for you, you idiot,' said Tim, and his voice got louder. Out of the corner of my eye, I saw Lara shushing him and glancing up at the ceiling.

'Looking for you,' Tim repeated in a harsh whisper. 'And where the fuck were you? Out getting rat-arsed and leaving Lara to look after your kids? Don't you dare claim the fucking moral high ground.'

'Can you both stop talking about me like I'm some kind of mute maiden?' said Lara, and when I looked at her, I realized that it was the first time I had seen her properly angry. 'Tim, thanks for everything, but I think it's probably best if you go. I'm so sorry.'

Tim hesitated for a good long moment, watching her to see she was sure. She was. He also waited, I was certain, to piss me off and show he was his own boss. He'd been my kid brother for all his life. He definitely knew how to push my buttons. Then he picked up his jacket, nodded to Lara, ignored me and walked out. I heard his car roar into life seconds later in the street outside, and he was gone.

I turned to face Lara and opened my mouth to speak, but at that moment we heard a key in the door, and Lara's mum's voice came floating down the corridor to us. 'Lara? Is that you? Did I just see someone leave?'

'Yes, Mum,' called Lara, keeping her tone even and calm. 'Sam's brother Tim. He popped by. Sorry you missed him.'

She went out into the hallway and I heard them talking quietly. It was likely Lara was trying to stop her mum coming into the living room and seeing the state I was in. Somehow she succeeded, and I heard her mum heading off up the stairs to her room, calling a quiet 'Good night' as she went.

Lara came back into the living room. 'I'm going to bed,' she said. 'You're in no state to talk now. You'd better sleep down here.' She indicated the woolly throw that always lay on the back of the sofa. 'You should be warm enough. I'll get your toothbrush and things and you can use the downstairs loo.'

She walked out of the room before I had time to respond. She was right, of course. Any conversation we would have was certain to turn into a row, and with her mum and all the kids upstairs, the fallout would be hideous.

She came back down within a minute or so, and, her face expressionless, handed me my toothbrush and a towel, and a T-shirt and a pair of shorts. Then she went out of the room, pulling the door closed behind her.

It wasn't the best night's sleep, unsurprisingly. Nausea, misery, fury and Helen's face kept looming over me out of the darkness. I'd doze for a few minutes and then jerk awake, shaking and sweating. Eventually, a grey haze began to creep over the trees, and I could make out the outlines of the shed, climbing frame and washing line in Lara's garden. I got up and pulled on last night's trousers, which still reeked of booze and shame, and made ready to get the girls out of the house.

Once we were back at our place, I left the girls bickering over the cereal while I took a scalding shower and shaved. I couldn't imagine ever being hungry again, but I knew if I didn't eat, I'd vomit or faint. My body was running on last night's tequila and adrenaline. I dressed and went into the kitchen, where I forced down a piece of toast and honey and a cup of instant coffee. Then I went into hyper-efficient mode and got the girls ready for school, making sure they had everything they needed. We were at the gates as soon as they opened, and I prayed I'd be able to get both girls to class and be gone before Lara arrived with her own kids.

I was lucky. Both girls' teachers were ready to usher the kids into their classes, and with a swift hug goodbye to Marguerite and a coolly offered cheek from Miranda, I was off down the hill to the station.

I'd have liked to get to Canary Wharf by seven or so, but with the school run, it wasn't possible. In the end, I got there by a quarter to ten. I knew that it was probably hopeless. If Helen passed through the station on her way to work, she'd be long gone, hidden in one of the thousands of anonymous offices. I had no hope of finding her here. And yet, here I was, walking up and down the platforms, then leaving the station and waiting outside the ticket barriers, scanning every face in the crowd. It wasn't rational, it wasn't going to work, but I had no other plan.

This place was the only clue I had to Helen's location in London and I wasn't ready to give it up. I was ready, however, to find somewhere to sit down. I left the station and found a small coffee shop with tables tucked away at the back and free, fast Wi-Fi.

Canary Wharf was a vast and busy part of London, and both Jubilee Line trains and Docklands Light Railway trains ran through it. I'd seen Helen here at around 4.30 in the afternoon, which was early to be returning home from work, so it was more likely she was passing through on her way to or from a meeting. She'd been on a Jubilee Line train. As she'd got off here, either this was her ultimate destination or she'd been planning to change to the DLR. I called up a Tube map on my iPad. Where could she go from here on the DLR? The answer wasn't promising: she could have gone north, south, east or west. Or she could have been going to leave the station to catch a bus, which added dozens more travel options.

Worst of all, it was just as likely that she was only in Canary Wharf to attend a meeting, as I had been. My office was in Soho, five miles away. I had probably been to this station a handful of times in my life. And of course now she knew I had seen her here, she'd probably do everything in her power to avoid the area, knowing that I would come and look for her. I needed a better solution. The trouble was, with my addled, exhausted and hung-over brain, I wasn't going to find the answer anytime soon.

I went home. I didn't have another solution, and I reasoned that if I could get some sleep and get to a point where I felt halfway normal, I might be able to think more clearly. It was nearly lunchtime by the time I got there. The girls were going to the after-school club and I didn't need to pick them up until 5.30. I made myself eat – more toast because I didn't have the energy for anything else – and then crawled into bed and fell into a dead sleep.

Sleep is a miraculous healer, because I woke up without the edge of hysteria or the sense that I was going to die of alcohol poisoning. I felt calm and sad and determined but no longer mad. It was about 4 p.m. and I lay tangled in my rumpled duvet and, for the first time, thought about the mess of the situation with Lara.

I knew perfectly well that nothing had happened the night before between her and Tim. I'm not stupid. I knew that I had caused a scene merely to cover my own guilt at my disastrous behaviour and to set up a situation where I didn't have to explain where I had been or why. Nothing about my experiences of the night before would bear retelling – seeing Helen, my drunken absence, what happened with the girl whose name I had completely forgotten. I behaved abominably, and all I could do was grovel and beg Lara's forgiveness. She's a lovely woman, and I knew she would forgive me, this time at least.

But what had Lara and Tim been talking about? I had to assume it was me, and how I'd been doing since Helen left. It made me feel deeply uncomfortable. It's not like I'm a divide-and-rule kind of person, but the thought of them discussing me, my behaviour and probably my drinking made my skin crawl. Oddly enough, separately, I probably see them as the two people I trust most in the world. But together? I didn't like the idea of them getting together to compare notes.

I knew I couldn't tell Lara about seeing Helen. Well, maybe not couldn't – I wasn't going to. Her response would likely be emotionally charged and complicated, and I'm confused enough about it as it is. In my drunken haze of the night before, I imagined telling Tim. But now I was deeply unsure about that too. I'd always thought of Tim as being unequivocally on my team. But his reaction last night showed that that maybe isn't the case. Anyway, it's not like there's anything to tell. One glimpse and then she disappeared. In a city of eight and a half million people, the odds of my finding her again are infinitesimal.

Lara

I heard Sam rouse the girls and get them dressed and then I heard them sneak downstairs and leave the house. I thought about getting up to say goodbye and maybe trying to make things okay with a look or a touch on his arm, but I stayed in bed with my back turned to the door. I had a lot to think about.

I got Frances to school and Jonah to nursery, and then I went for a walk through the park. It was a blustery, slightly ominous day and I wrapped my cardigan tightly around myself. Things had got complicated, it seemed. Or maybe that wasn't it. Maybe what happened last night exposed the situation for what it is – I've somehow got myself drawn into a very unsatisfactory relationship.

I don't love Sam. I'm attracted to him, I like him (most of the time, not so much last night), and I feel dreadfully sorry for him and the girls for what they've gone through. But he doesn't make my heart sing. If circumstances were different and we were just two single people who were dating, I could see us gradually beginning to see less of each other and then drifting apart. But the situation we're in is so much more complex than that. There are four little lives entwined with ours, and I like to think that, if nothing else, I've at least offered some kindness and stability to Miranda and Marguerite when they've needed it. If Sam and I split up, where would that leave them? Not to mention my own kids, who have become fond of the girls. And even though Sam isn't around my children all that much, Jonah in particular is enthralled by him. He has no memory of his own dad, and he loves having a guy to climb on and roar at and run up and down the garden with. If I'm honest with myself, I've kind of liked how our lives have become busier and more fun. Our little household has sometimes seemed small and quiet, but with Sam and all the kids, weekends in particular are lively, in a nicely chaotic sort of way.

All of that's great, but I'm not sure that I'm ready to take on Sam's deeper problems. It has gradually become clear to me that he has issues with alcohol. He doesn't drink every day, but when he does, he drinks a lot, and he lies about it. He'll bring a bottle of spirits to my house but keep it in his bag so I won't notice how much and how often he refills his glass. He never misses an opportunity for a beer – any time after about eleven in the morning is fair game for a drink. I've always worked in bars and restaurants, and you learn to spot the drinkers – not just people who sometimes get rat-arsed but people for whom the need for alcohol never goes way. For those people, it's like a constant low hum in them that they can't ignore. Sam is one of those.

And then there's his anger. The years of pub work mean that I also know a lot about male anger in all its variations – slow-burning resentment, belligerent yelling, and the kind of anger that comes from nowhere and lashes out in sudden violence. Sam's anger is well-hidden, kept deep down and only emerges when he's had a lot to drink. It comes out in the odd bitter, hate-filled comment directed at a politician or a celebrity, or, if he's very unguarded, in the way he says Helen's name if she comes up in conversation. So far, he hasn't yelled at me, except for his drunken outburst when he came in last night and accused me and Tim of God only knows what. But I suspect it might just be a matter of time.

But most of all, I can't forget what Tim said, about Sam being a taker. He clearly needs so much help. He's charming, and always grateful, so everything I do for him hasn't felt like a chore. But when I think about it, there's no payback. I don't expect quid pro quos, just the occasional offer to look after all four kids and give me a break. Some help around the house. The odd basket of groceries. But Sam has manoeuvred me into a position where I'm willingly his dogsbody and, up until now, I haven't resented it. I'm not quite sure how that has happened.

As I see it, I have three options. I could break it off with Sam, with all the heartache and difficulty that would cause. It would put the kids in an awkward position, and I'd still have to see him every day at school. I could leave things the way they are, and weather whatever storms come my way. That's unbelievably risky, and a route that promises lots of heartache. Or the third option: I could roll up my sleeves, confront Sam and do my best to help him sort his life out. Everything he's been doing seems to me to be a cry for help, the waving arms of a man drowning and unable to help himself. I could stand by and watch him sink, or I could throw him a life preserver and try to pull him to shore.

Sam

Much later, long after I got the girls to bed, I sat on the sofa in the darkened living room and stared at the TV. A film was playing with the sound muted – I had no idea what it was, but Daniel Craig was snarling and sweaty and running around with a big gun, so I assumed it was a James Bond film. I don't think I'd have gained much more from the plot if I'd seen it from the beginning with the sound up. As it was, the bright colours, flashes of explosion and staccato editing made the perfect backdrop to my fractured train of thought.

I was no closer to knowing what I should do about my relationship with Lara. 'Wait and see' was about the best solution I could come up with. We needed to have a proper talk, that was for sure, and for the girls' sake, I'd rather things didn't get too acrimonious. I needed to apologize for my behaviour the night before. That I could do. I had behaved badly, and turning up at her house, late and drunk and raving, without having contacted her all night, was clearly unacceptable. The difficulty was that I could apologize, but I couldn't explain. I'd have to make up something about work stress and hope that she accepted that.

Because obviously, I couldn't tell her about looking for Helen. I couldn't tell anyone, because anyone sane, especially those who love me, would tell me not to do it. They'd say, quite rightly, that Helen went of her own accord and took great pains not to be found. When I found her by accident, she ran away. I should let her go.

It's not as if I need her to grant permission for the divorce, and the house (thank God) is in my name, not our joint names. I've read about couples whose financial affairs were tangled and one party went missing. Being missing isn't a legal status – the person isn't dead, they're just not there. So if you need their permission to access a bank account, or sign papers or something and you don't know where they are, you're screwed. Accounts get frozen, and people end up destitute. I might be poorer than I used to be, but at least I'm not absolutely screwed.

So why couldn't I let this go? I wished I could, but I know myself, and I know that when I begin to obsess about something, I need to see it through. I sighed, and thought again about ringing Tim. I needed to talk about this with someone who would understand, who really got the situation. But Tim was out of the question. Lara might be blameless where last night was concerned, but I had been Tim's brother for long enough to know that his motives for being on Lara's sofa late at night might not have been squeaky clean. He wasn't the right person to take this to.

And then it dawned on me. I glanced at my watch. It was 1 a.m., so ten in the morning on Saturday in Brisbane. She might be out shopping or something, but it was worth a try. I pulled my laptop towards me, opened Skype and hit 'Call'.

Judy answered after a few rings. She had her hair scraped back and a baseball cap on, and she gave me a broad smile.

'Good timing, Sam,' she said cheerfully. 'I was about to head off to the bottom of the garden to battle the jungle and I'd never have heard your call.'

'I don't want to keep you,' I said.

'Not at all! Lovely to chat to you. Although I can barely see you. Are you sitting there in the dark?'

'Yes,' I said. 'The girls are asleep, and I don't want to disturb them.'

She nodded. 'So how're things?'

There was no point in messing around with small talk. 'I saw Helen,' I said baldly. 'She was on the Tube. She's changed her appearance – cut her hair short and dyed it blonde, gained weight. . .'

'But you're sure it was her?' said Judy. 'Stupid question. She was your wife. Of course you're sure.'

'Is my wife,' I said, and I sounded angrier than I meant to. 'She still is my wife.'

Judy looked as if she was about to say something, but she just nodded.

'I watched her for a while and when I was sure it was her, I went to talk to her. She got off at Canary Wharf, and I caught her.'

'Caught her?'

'I called her name, and I grabbed her hand.' Judy winced. 'I didn't hurt her,' I said quickly. 'She looked at me, and then she broke away and jumped back on the train and disappeared.'

Judy sat back in her chair. 'Wow,' she said. 'Well, there's a turn-up. So she stayed in London.'

'So it would seem. But I don't know where she went. She was getting off at Canary Wharf when I caught her, so she could have been changing trains there, or she might work there. I went back to look for her but—'

'You went back?'

'This morning. But of course there are thousands of offices and thousands of routes that go from Canary Wharf. There's no way of knowing where she went. So I was wondering if you had any idea where she might have gone?'

'Me?' Judy looked flabbergasted. 'How would I know? I haven't seen her for years, Sam. She disappeared on me too.'

'I know, but you know her, and—'

'I think you know as well as I do that no one actually knows Helen. Not really.'

I was forced to concede she was right.

'I never finished telling you the story about Lawrence,' she said.

'I want to hear it,' I interrupted, but right now I need to find Helen and—'

'And what?' For the first time in all of our conversations, Judy sounded angry. 'Make her talk to you, make her come back?' She leaned on the word 'make', with a kind of bitter sarcasm. I was stung.

'I don't know who you think I am, Judy, but I'm not Lawrence. I don't want to force her to do anything. I just want to talk to her.'

'I'm only going to say this once, Sam. I don't know where she is, and even if I did, I wouldn't tell you. She knows where you are. And if she wants to talk to you, she'll contact you.'

We stared at each other in silence for a long moment. Then Judy spoke. 'You can hate me if you like, but let me tell you the end of the story about Lawrence, and then maybe you'll understand a little of where I'm coming from.'

I nodded but didn't say anything.

'After Helen came out of hospital, she went back to Lawrence. We all begged her not to, but she said he was so sorry for what he had done and he was prepared to consider therapy. I loved that – "prepared to consider". Not actually going to go. He never did, by the way.'

She shook her head. 'Anyway, she went home, and the first thing he did was make her give up her job. He didn't want her going back to work with scars and shaming him, he said. And after that, step by step, he isolated her completely. He told her that our parents and I hated him, so he didn't want her to see them. He cut her off from all her friends. Because she wasn't working, he had control of the money and he wouldn't let her have any – he did all the shopping and drove to work so she wouldn't have the car. And most of all, he told her she was shitty and worthless all the time, so she didn't have the strength or the pride to leave.'

I couldn't imagine it. Not Helen. Helen, who was proud and brave and confident. Who wasn't afraid of anything. Was it possible that Judy was exaggerating?

'What happened?' I said. 'How did she get out?'

'I didn't give up on her that time. The one thing she had was a phone. Lawrence wanted her to have it so he could text her and call her fifty times a day and keep tabs on her while he was at work. But it meant I could call her too. And I did. I also used to go round there in the day when he wasn't there. As fast as he was feeding her propaganda about how useless she was, I was feeding her words of strength, and making plans for her escape. But I knew I needed to wait till she was ready.'

Judy sat forward in her chair and bowed a little, so I was looking at the top of her head. She folded her arms tightly, as if she was hugging herself. 'One Monday afternoon, I was round at Helen's. I'd brought my laptop so I could show her a website about a women's sanctuary she could go to, where they would help her to get back on her feet. Lawrence must have parked down the road and walked so we wouldn't be alerted by the sound of the car. He was in the flat before we realized what was going on.

'He started out being charming but in a terrifyingly quiet way. He said it was nice to see me. But then he asked me why I was there, wasn't I supposed to be at work? Why hadn't I come round after work, when he would be home too? I made up something about passing by and popping in.

'"Interesting that you brought your computer, just to pop in," he said. And he casually went over to my laptop and looked at the screen. We hadn't had time to close down the web page we'd been looking at. He read it all, standing very still, and then he picked up the laptop and threw it against the wall. Then he walked up to me – I was leaning against the kitchen counter – and lifted me off my feet by my throat. He was big, and very strong. He said some things, ugly, threatening things, but I don't know what. I was mainly clawing at his fingers and trying to breathe. Helen threw herself at him and tried to pull him off me, but he batted her aside without even looking at her.

'She always said that lying on the floor, looking at him holding me up, my eyes starting to bug, listening to him snarl filth in my face, was the moment she woke up. "It was like I'd been asleep for years," she said. She crawled across the floor and grabbed her phone. She dialled 000 and I heard her say, "Police. My husband is trying to kill my sister." I was on the verge of blacking out, but I remember thinking that her voice sounded strong and clear, not anxious at all. Lawrence hesitated for a second before he let me fall to the floor and went for Helen, but that gave her enough time to blurt out the address. As he roared, she skimmed the phone away from her and it came to rest under the kitchen table. He kicked her everywhere he could reach. She curled up into a ball, using her hands to protect her face and I remember thinking that she'd done that before. She knew what to do.

'I screamed at him to stop, and tried pulling on his arm, but he was like a possessed. . . I don't know. Like an enraged bear. I ran to the front door and yanked it open and started yelling for help. It was a weekday afternoon, so I didn't expect the building to be full of burly men or anything. But I figured if there were witnesses, he would be less likely to kill Helen and me.

'We were lucky. The cops weren't busy, and Helen's trick of skimming the phone away meant the line was open and the operator could hear our screams and the thuds of Lawrence's kicks. A car pulled up outside within a few minutes, and two of the biggest bloody police officers you ever saw rushed into the building. I directed them to the apartment and they pulled Lawrence off Helen.'

Judy took a pause. She shook her head. It was an awful story and I could see the memory was as fresh as if it had been yesterday.

'They locked him up, but we knew he wouldn't be gone for long. Helen had to go to hospital for concussion, but while she was in, I fetched all her clothes and things from the flat, and we moved her to a women's refuge. Not the one we had been looking at – we thought Lawrence might come searching for her there. Another one.'

'And then?' I asked.

Judy smiled. 'She wasn't lying when she said she woke up. She started to help other women in the shelter as soon as she arrived – with job skills, writing their CVs, that sort of thing. She campaigned to raise money and awareness. She begged for her old job back, and she moved into a shared apartment on the far side of the city. She changed her name too.'

I fought the urge to ask 'To what?' Instead, I said, 'And Lawrence?'

'Helen was given a protection order, but he didn't go to jail. When the case was over, he disappeared. His family thought he'd gone to Perth or something, but they didn't know for sure. That kind of worked in Helen's favour, because once she proved she'd made a reasonable attempt to find him, she was able to initiate a divorce without his consent.'

I smiled grimly. It was the same process I'd been going through here to divorce Helen.

'So she was doing brilliantly. Mum and Dad and I were all so happy. We'd got our Hellie back. She was doing well at work too.'

Judy stopped suddenly, and her face darkened. 'This last bit... Sorry, Sam. It's hard.'

'Take your time,' I said.

'Lawrence discovered that Helen had divorced him. He couldn't find her...' she said haltingly. 'She took a lot of care to disappear and cover her tracks. But he found me.'

'He found you?'

'You'll forgive me if I spare you the details.' She tried to smile, but failed. 'He's in prison now – they couldn't get attempted murder to stick, so he got done for grievous bodily harm.'

'Jesus, Judy.'

'I survived,' she said briskly. 'I'm still here. I'll never be a concert pianist, but that's okay. I'm tone deaf anyway.'

My confusion must have shown on my face. 'Of course... We haven't actually met, so you don't know,' she said, and she held up her left hand, the palm facing the screen. Her index finger ended at the first knuckle joint.

'He told me I'd lose one finger an hour until I told him where Helen was. He used an axe. I don't think he counted on how much blood there'd be. I think he got scared I'd bleed to death. So he ran away, and I managed to get free and call for an ambulance.'

'I'm so, so sorry,' I said. 'So sorry.'

'As I say, I lived. But as for Helen... Well, the guilt was too much, I think. She stayed for the trial and testified against him. And then outside the court after he was sentenced, she kissed me and Mum and Dad and said she was going home to her flat for a few hours and would come round later for dinner.'

'And you never saw her again?'

'No. We got one email, saying she'd gone to Europe and wasn't coming back and that she was sorry. Then she shut down the email account, so all our messages bounced back. We were heartbroken, of course, but over time we've become – kind of – proud of her. Proud of her for seizing the chance to start again.'

'And you've had no news of her—'

'Until I saw the Facebook post.'

We sat staring at each other in silence for a long time.

'So maybe,' Judy said slowly, 'you can understand now why I have complicated feelings about you hunting her down. Not hunting, if you know what I mean, but looking for her when she's made it clear she doesn't want to be found.'

CHAPTER EIGHTEEN

Sam

Judy and I said goodbye, and I sat back in my seat, my laptop resting on my knees. What she had gone through, what her family had gone through, was beyond horrifying. It was almost impossible to imagine that those things had happened to my Helen. And it was totally impossible to believe we had lived together so closely, as husband and wife for five years, and she'd never told me a single thing. Not even that she had been married before. Well, one thing was for sure – if Judy had hoped that her story would put me off trying to find Helen, she was wrong. I needed to find her more than ever. I needed to tell her I knew what had happened to her. I needed to ask her, face to face, why she had left me. And maybe if I could find her, I could help her to fix the part of her that was broken and made her run away. I knew now I wouldn't rest until I found her. The question was – how?

I stared at Daniel Craig on the screen. He'd got cleaned up and was looking muscular and suave in a dinner suit, snapping his crisp cuffs and walking quickly into some banquet or other. He had it easy. He knew what was what. He just had to leap from carriage to carriage on top of a moving train and shag beautiful women. What did he know about the complexities of life? He was just a spy.

A spy. Something about the idea brought me up short. Espionage. Counter-intelligence. Those were the techniques Helen had called upon when she disappeared. She'd managed to evade CCTV cameras and electronic tracking. She'd clearly left with enough cash to re-establish herself somewhere else. She'd found a way to create a new identity. She had, in the parlance of novels and films, gone into deep cover. But if she had managed to do it, could I not follow the same thought processes and work out where she had gone?

I've always loved a good spy thriller, or even a bad one, and I began to think about some of the techniques spies use when they have to disappear. Clearly, they need a new set of documents. Easy to achieve in a film, difficult for Joe Public, who lacks the CIA's resources or access to a dodgy gangster in an East End bar.

Helen had found a way to create a new identity. At least I assumed she had, because I had found no sign of the right Helen Cooper or Helen Knight in all my web searches. And yet, from my sighting of her, it was almost certain that she was working in a respectable, white-collar job. In my experience, especially working in the fields of marketing and PR, which is her background, it's impossible to be in a job without there being some kind of internet footprint. You'd be mentioned on the company website, or there'd be a report about your appointment or a notable project in a trade magazine. You'd need a LinkedIn profile so colleagues and clients could find you. So, assuming

Helen was working in her old field, whatever her new name was, there'd be some trace of her online.

I thought about some of the thrillers I'd read and the identities which spies concoct for themselves. Apparently (or at least the novelists would have us believe), these identities or legends often have some elements of the agent's real life, so they can recall these details with clarity – the same date of birth, the same school attended, the same first name. The latter is often used. If you were on your guard, you'd remember to respond to your codename, but if you were caught unawares by someone calling you from across the room, for example, it would be hard to remember your name was now Geoff when it used to be Bob.

So what if Helen was still Helen but now Helen Someone Else? There was no point in putting 'Helen' into a search engine. I'd get billions of hits. But what if I went on to some of the marketing publications and websites and narrowed the search? What if I only looked for articles in the field of marketing, in London, which mentioned a Helen, and which had appeared in the last year? How many could there be?

I logged on to a well-known online marketing magazine. I typed 'Helen' into the search bar. I got seven hundred hits. I found the tools to refine the search and narrowed the dates down, from the date Helen disappeared to the present day. We were down to a hundred and fifty hits. That didn't seem an insane number to check.

I scrolled through and quickly ascertained that at least half of the results related to articles written by a journalist called Helen Brady. I'd met her at a few marketing award ceremonies – a tiny, rabbity woman with white-blonde hair and a look of pink-eyed surprise that suggested she was allergic to everything. She definitely wasn't my Helen, so I ruled out any results that carried her by-line.

Across the other articles, there were about ten different potential Helens. I copied their names on to a list and then ran a search on each of them. One by one, I found them on LinkedIn or their company websites. I looked at their CVs and in all cases found pictures of them. None of them was my Helen.

Maybe this was a road to nowhere, but it was the best, indeed the only possible lead I had. I chose another marketing website and repeated the process. Still nothing. On the off-chance that I had had the wrong idea where the first name was concerned, I repeated the process on both websites searching for 'Knight' but again came up with nothing.

Maybe I was looking in the wrong places. Maybe she hadn't gone into marketing after all. I tried PR Weekly, and a few big websites devoted to design and advertising. No hits on either, and a disquieting sense that I was getting colder rather than hotter in my search. I paused to think for a moment. What had Helen been doing when we met? What had she focused on? She'd worked on a number of campaigns, but her biggest success was on a razor campaign linked to a world-famous tennis star. Sport. She loved sport, knew a lot about it, and had once told me that she'd worked exclusively in sports marketing in Australia. Was there a website devoted to marketing in sport?

There was. I ran the search for 'Helen', restricting the search dates to the last year. There were only a few entries, and they all related to two Helens – a Helen Berry, who was based in Manchester at a charity which encouraged sport in schools, and another Helen, whose marketing campaign for a big sporting gel brand had had great results.

I didn't discount Helen Berry; Helen could easily have been in London for a business meeting, and in a way, fleeing to Manchester would make more sense than staying in London. She didn't have a LinkedIn profile and I couldn't find a picture of her online. I did find her on the 'Contact Us' page on the charity's website though. On impulse, even though it was 2 a.m., I dialled her office number, taking care to hide my mobile number before I did so.

'Hi, this is Helen,' said a perky recorded message. 'Leave a message and I'll get back to you.'

Helen Berry sounded in her early fifties at least, with a strong Mancunian accent. Another dead end.

Which left one last possibility – the one working for Simon Stanley and Associates, a new (as far as I could tell) sports consultancy based somewhere in the east of London. That chimed with having seen Helen in Canary Wharf, but it wasn't much to go on. But again, I could find no image on Google, no LinkedIn profile, and the name was common enough that Facebook and Twitter threw up hundreds of possibilities. Could this Helen Day be my Helen?

Helen Day.

Helen Day. The opposite of Helen Knight. What happens to night when the light comes? Day.

With trembling fingers, I ran a search for SSA and found their web page. There was no picture of Helen Day, but there was a biography. Born in Australia, marketing degree from the University of Queensland, moved to the UK six years ago. I had found her.

It was the longest weekend of my life. I fell asleep eventually, on the sofa again. The girls woke me at seven (why was it torture to get them out of bed for school in the week, but they were up at the crack on weekends?). Miranda looked at me with ill-disguised contempt, and to my shame, I saw her look around the room, scanning for beer bottles or cans. It was scant comfort that there weren't any. My hangover from the Canary Wharf binge had lasted long enough to stop me drinking in the evening. Marguerite climbed on top of me as if I were a slightly uncomfortable extension of the sofa and reached for the TV remote. A bright and jangly tune, much too loud, blared out of the TV and the neon colours assaulted my bleary, unready eyes.

I tipped a grumbling Marguerite off me and stumbled through to the bathroom, then climbed into my own bed, leaving the girls to bicker in the living room. My phone lay on the bedside table and I picked it up. Unsurprisingly, I had no messages. I lay looking at the screen for a long time. It was early, but not so early that Lara wouldn't be up. Jonah's an early riser. Tentatively, I typed: 'I owe you an apology. Can we meet up today so I can say sorry in person?'

I sent the message and then stared at the screen, hoping she'd reply immediately. She didn't. After ten minutes or so, I got out of bed and grabbed a quick shower. I went into the kitchen to put the kettle on, keeping my phone in my hand all the time. Still nothing.

I felt overcome by a kind of restless energy, and while I waited for my tea to brew, I looked around our dingy kitchen. Something needed to be done. The limescale on the draining board got it first. Then I polished the sink and taps to a gleaming shine. All the ketchup bottles and plastic cups that never quite made it back into the cupboards were packed away and I scrubbed the countertops. Then I noticed how grubby the shelves in the cupboard were, so everything had to come out so I could clean each shelf too. An hour later and I was on my hands and knees, scrubbing the linoleum, and my phone was still silent.

The Cif cream and I were on a roll by then, so I attacked the bathroom next. All the towels went into the washing machine and I started stripping the beds so bedclothes could be the next load. I burned through the flat, hoovering, dusting, tidying away, ruthlessly throwing away toys that were broken or incomplete. The girls regarded me with mute incomprehension, staying out of my way and only intervening to complain when I threw away something they considered precious. Through all of this, my phone didn't ring or beep. By midday, I was exhausted and the flat was unrecognizable.

'It's got to stay like this now,' I told the girls.

'It won't,' said Miranda.

I knew she was right, but it had made me feel slightly better to take control of our space. The flat might be small and cramped, but when it's clean and tidy, it's not too unpleasant. And anyway, came the thought unbidden into my head, if Helen returns, we can put things back to the way they were and move home to our house, ultimately.

Now that I know about Lawrence, I'm certain I can fix things between us. I understand so much more – it makes such sense that that night in the hotel freaked her out. But at least I know that what happened wasn't my fault. And we can work through it together and make it all better. I'm not delusional, so I know there are a lot of ifs and buts and qualifications that stand in the way of that, but I'm hopeful. I feel sure that if I can find her, we can talk, really talk, in a way we never did when we were together.

Lara

My phone burned a hole in my pocket. Sam's text had been, unsurprisingly, carefully and perfectly worded. No excuses, just a request to be given the chance to apologize. He was good, I'd give him that. A text apology would have been too trite. A phone one would be awkward. But this – this was good. I just wasn't quite ready for it yet.

Someone else might say that I was playing games in not responding to the text, but I wasn't. I needed to work out the right response. And to do that, I needed to be certain I was taking the right course in letting Sam stay in our lives.

It was easy to ignore the phone for the morning – I took Frances to her dance class (I was unsurprised to see that Sam and Miranda weren't there), and then dragged both kids through a nightmarish supermarket shop. It was such an awful experience for us all that I splurged on a cheap lunch at the local Italian and we didn't get back home till after three. Jonah fell asleep almost instantly, curled up on the sofa, and Frances disappeared up into her bedroom with a new book I'd bought her.

So there I was, sitting at the kitchen table, an hour of quiet to myself, trying to work out how to reply. I took my phone out and let it lie in front of me on the table. Eventually, I typed: 'I appreciate the thought, but not today. Just need some time.' And I hit send.

His reply was almost instantaneous. 'I respect that. Hope maybe tomorrow?'

Again, I had to smile. He'd got the balance between grovelling subservience and insistent keenness just right. I couldn't fault him for that.

'I'll get back to you,' I typed, and, hating myself, I added a smiley face. Sam and I had joked about how much we loathed emojis. With that one little in-joke he would know he was forgiven. I wished I had the fortitude to keep him hanging on, worrying, but I didn't.

I had to work in the evening, so I got myself moving and made a halfway decent dinner for the kids and Mum, then spent an hour snuggled with a dozy, post-nap Jonah, watching a film, before I went upstairs to shower and dress.

It was another quiet Saturday night at the pub – always a worry. Every quiet evening we have makes me wonder if I shouldn't be looking for another job. It's not as if there aren't restaurant manager jobs to be had, but I've got comfortable there. I know the job inside and out, the commute is easy and the work isn't stressful. Still, it would be better to find something new at my own pace, rather than finding out we're shutting down and losing my job overnight. Even thinking about it makes me feel disloyal. I've been there for years, on and off – it was where I met Marc – and they've always been good to me.

I looked down the list of bookings, two tables of two at 7 p.m., and a table of six at 8.30. Unless we got twenty or thirty walk-ins, I wasn't going to come close to covering the cost of the staff we had on for the evening. I frowned at the computer, trying to work out if I should send one or two of the waiters home.

'Don't frown, you'll get wrinkles,' said a voice.

I kept my eyes on the screen, but even as I did, I felt my stomach plummet to the floor and my hands, resting on the keyboard, began to shake. I gave myself time to take a deep, slow breath before I raised my eyes.

'Marc,' I said calmly. 'Well, there you are.'

There he was. Tall, slender, his hair longer again, the sharp, expensive suit replaced by his more usual jeans and denim shirt. I steeled myself, stepped around the reception desk and offered him my cheek to kiss. He ignored my gesture, slipped his arms around me and drew me to him in a hug. I put my hands against his chest and pushed him away. I took a step back, and then scuttled back behind the reception desk, using the chest-high counter as a shield.

'So is this a flying visit?' I said coolly. 'It would have been good if you'd let me know you were coming.'

'I didn't know till this morning,' he said, and I could hear he'd picked up the faintest hint of an American drawl. 'A business thing came up.'

'On a Saturday?'

He shrugged, in a 'No rest for the wicked – or the massively successful' gesture that irritated me profoundly.

'So what is it you're doing now?' I asked, trying not to drip sarcasm off every word.

'Have you seen stuff on the Net about these personal rocket packs?'

'I beg your pardon?'

'You know, jet packs. Strap them on your back and fly away.'

'What, like Ironman?'

'Ironman has rocket *boots*,' he said, slightly impatient with my stupidity.

'Uh-huh. So you're making rocket packs rather than boots.'

'Not making,' said Marc, ignoring my tone. 'Marketing and distributing.'

'Marketing and distributing rocket packs. That sounds like a sure-fire winner.'

'Wow,' said Marc, his expression hardening. 'Less than a minute and you're already being a bitch.'

'Less than a minute and you're being a flaky, unreliable bastard, involved in yet another hare-brained scheme,' I said, keeping my tone low and my smile sweet. I'd seen that there were a couple of drinkers ordering at the bar. I really didn't want there to be a scene.

Marc shrugged. I knew he was considering turning on his heel and walking out. But to my surprise, he steeled himself and spoke calmly.

'You don't have to like me, or approve of what I'm doing. But I would like the chance to see my kids. I flew in today, and I've got back-to-back meetings from Monday, but tomorrow. . .?'

'You expect us to drop everything at no notice because you happen to be in town?' I found myself saying.

Marc's shoulders sagged. 'No. Of course not. But even if it's half an hour. . .'

He was playing the pathetic, humble card. And, as he had correctly assessed, I was playing the hard-nosed bitch one but would eventually give in. How could I possibly stand between my kids and their dad? If Frances found out her dad had been in London and she hadn't got the chance to see him, she would be heartbroken. Marc might set my teeth on edge and make me permanently angry, but his daughter adored him.

'As it happens,' I said begrudgingly, 'we haven't got anything planned for tomorrow.'

His face brightened. 'Can I take them out? Dinner? Movies? Ice cream?'

I knew there was no chance he'd be able to manage both kids alone for a whole day. I thought of him taking his eyes off Jonah and letting him get lost, or being unkind to Frances because he was stressed about managing a boisterous three-year-old. I was tempted to say he should just take Frances, but that wasn't fair on Jonah, who barely knew his dad and deserved time with him too. I sighed. 'I think you might struggle to manage Jonah at the moment. He's full-on. Why don't we all do something together?'

I saw a parade of emotions cross his face – annoyance that I clearly thought he couldn't manage the kids on his own, relief that he wouldn't have to, and something sly, as if he could see advantages in spending a day with me.

'Come to the house at ten,' I said. 'We'll see what the weather's like and then we can decide what to do.'

He made it by quarter to eleven, which was better than I was expecting. I'd told Frances he was coming at lunchtime. She'd still been frenzied all morning and had changed her outfit about fifteen times, made me do and redo her hair in three different styles and had one hysterical crying jag when I said I wasn't sure Marc would be staying for dinner.

'You're so mean to him!' she screamed at me, and slammed her bedroom door.

I stood outside the door and patiently explained that as far as I was concerned, he was welcome to stay, but that I didn't know what his plans were. The crying paused for a brief second and then started up again with fresh fury. I had to let her sob herself out. I knew how she felt.

The doorbell rang, and Frances went thundering down the stairs at a hundred miles an hour. I heard her ecstatic 'Daddy!' even though I was still in the bathroom upstairs. I squared my shoulders and marched downstairs.

As the day progressed, it became clear to me that Marc hadn't changed at all. He was full of flighty rhetoric about his business successes, but he did admit that he had sold his house and was 'sharing with a friend'. That meant one of two things – he was bunking on a friend's couch and was penniless, or he had found a girlfriend who was footing the bills.

And yet the kids loved him. Jonah took a bit of time to warm up, but then he played with him with boisterous abandon. He took great joy in running off across the grass, turning to face us, shouting 'Daddy!' at the top of his voice and then hurtling back to throw himself into Marc's arms. Frances stared at Marc, every second. If I hadn't quieted her every now and again, she would have talked non-stop, telling him anything and everything about school, her friends and her dancing. Marc nodded and tried to keep up with the endless monologue. Every now and again he'd ask a careful question to show he was still interested. One of these was 'Who's Miranda?' Unsurprisingly, Miranda featured large in almost all of Frances' stories.

'She's my best friend in the whole world except for you, Daddy,' said Frances, as if stating the obvious. 'Her step-mum ran away and disappeared and now her dad Sam is Mum's boyfriend.'

Marc shot me a sharp look. 'Is he now?'

'Yes,' I said coolly. I didn't elaborate further. I could see Marc wanted to ask some more questions but didn't feel he could. He didn't need to worry, however. Frances was ready to spill the beans.

'Sam and his kids stay over at our house a lot. It's like we're a big family with four children.'

'Sounds cute,' said Marc, but the way he said it didn't sound cute at all. 'Gosh, I wonder when Mum would have told me about all of this?'

'Around the time it became any of your business,' I said crisply, and instantly cursed myself. I had sworn I wouldn't get bitchy around the kids.

'Yeah,' said Marc in a slow drawl, 'I can see how some guy living rent-free in the house I paid for wouldn't be any of my business.'

I felt suddenly cold. He had a point. The house was his, after all. We lived in it entirely at his mercy. I did my best to keep my tone calm and even, but a wobble in my voice betrayed me. 'It's not like that,' I said. 'We're just dating, it's not serious. Sam has his own place. Like Frances said, his wife disappeared, so I help him out with his kids.'

Luckily this titbit was enough to distract Marc. 'What do you mean his wife disappeared?'

I relaxed a fraction and filled him in on the story of Helen's vanishing trick and its aftermath.

He shook his head. 'Mad bitch,' he said. 'Why didn't she just tell him she was leaving him, sue him for a bundle and cut up his suits like a normal psycho woman?'

He had some fairly archaic and misogynist views on how women might behave, but he also kind of had a point. I'd never understood it. If Helen had wanted to leave, why didn't she just tell Sam? Why the cloak-and-dagger secret flight?

'I don't know,' I said. 'And Sam doesn't know either. She just went, and she disappeared completely. No one knows where she is.'

'Maybe she's chopped up in bits and buried under his patio.' Marc laughed. 'Come on. I'm starving. Let's go and get some food.'

Reading between the lines, I didn't think Marc was all that flush with cash. He certainly wasn't playing the beneficent millionaire of a few years ago who had swooped in, paid off the house and knocked me up with Jonah. So I thought we'd go for the burger place at the end of the high street. It was cheap and cheerful, and Jonah could happily throw chips on the floor without offending the management.

Sam

My great purge of the flat had revealed plenty of gaps in our store cupboard. I made an extensive shopping list and dragged the girls out to the supermarket to get all the things we needed. I could glimpse a golden future of well-planned, home-cooked meals served in our tidy apartment. Maybe I could get a slow-cooker or something. Make soups and stews and freeze them. Helen would be so thrilled when she saw how well we were doing. I left the supermarket glowing with self-righteous goodwill, and when Miranda asked if we could go to the milkshake bar for a treat, I agreed readily. The girls had had a dull day so far, with all the cleaning and shopping. We loaded the groceries into the boot, and, leaving the car in the supermarket car park, walked down the high street together. I was half listening to a long story Marguerite was telling me about a baby squirrel (she was currently obsessed with squirrels), and half watching Miranda, who was walking a carefully calculated three steps ahead of us, trying to pretend we weren't together. She's got so tall, and she's getting slender, with a slightly womanly curve to her hips. She looks so like Leonora. It struck me how much the girls have changed since Helen left. How much she's missed. Marguerite losing her first two teeth and learning to ride a bike. Miranda passing yet another ballet exam. How could she bear it? Unless, of course, she never really loved them at all. But I don't believe that. I'm not sure what I feel – is it anger, or sadness? If only I could talk to her about it.

I thought of the details I had found for the woman called Helen Day, working in the agency in Stratford. On Monday, I could try to call the agency. But was that the right way to proceed? What if that spooked her and she disappeared again? Maybe it would be best if I went there instead.

'Look, Dad, there's Frances!' Miranda's excited voice cut through my thoughts.

'Hmm?' I said, looking around. She pointed, and I saw Frances walking on the opposite side of the high street. She was holding the hand of a tall, blonde man, chattering animatedly. Frances is a quiet, reserved girl, but she looked like someone had lit her up from the inside, and she was bouncing and grinning. Lara was walking beside them carrying Jonah on her hip, and she too was smiling up at the tall man. Marc. That had to be Marc. Funny, Lara hadn't mentioned he was coming into town.

'Can we go over, Dad? And say hello?'

I looked at Lara, playing happy families with Marc and their two kids.

'Not right now, love. That's Frances' dad, I think. Let's give them a little bit of privacy, eh?'

I watched the group on the other side of the road. So that was how Lara was going to play it. Cozying up with the ex because we weren't speaking. Well, two could play at that game.

CHAPTER NINETEEN

Sam

On Monday morning, I dropped the kids at school and then rang the office, saying I was still sick and was on my way to the doctor's. I boarded the Tube and headed for the centre of town, then changed on to an eastbound train to Stratford. The train was fairly empty by the time I got there. It was a little late for commuters, and too early for shoppers heading for the gigantic shopping mall which stood between the station and the Olympic Park. I left the station and went into a nearby coffee shop.

I got an espresso and sat down to look at the map on my phone. I'd put in the postcode from the Simon Stanley and Associates website, and it looked to be around half a mile from where I was. I didn't know Stratford at all and I took some time to memorize the route, so I wouldn't wander around looking too lost and conspicuous. I finished my coffee and set off.

I hadn't counted on the area being so undeveloped. I'd imagined a busy high street where I could find a coffee shop, or at least a bus stop, where I could settle in and watch the door of the office block. But SSA was in the only inhabited building in an otherwise half-built street. I felt exposed walking up the road. What if Helen's office overlooked the street and she was watching me approach? I wished I had thought to wear a baseball cap or a hoodie or something. I was walking on the far side of the road so I could get a good look at the offices, but I ducked across the street and stayed close to the buildings, hoping that would make me harder to spot.

I got to the front doors and looked in through the glass. There was no one in the building's reception area. Cautiously, I pushed at the door, but it was locked. There was a panel of buzzers and a laminated card with the SSA logo beside the top button but no other names. The building was three storeys tall, so I reasoned this meant they were on the top floor. Did that mean that SSA was the only company in the building? That somewhat scuppered my plans. I'd imagined sweet-talking a building receptionist, or, at worst, getting someone from another company to buzz me in. Now I had no way to get into the block, and I was just a slightly dodgy bloke hanging around the pavement in a deserted street.

I was at a loss. I hadn't thought beyond getting there, and I'd imagined there'd be enough bustle and crowd cover that I could wait in the foyer for Helen to emerge from the building. I didn't want to try to force my way into SSA and confront her in her workplace – having heard about Lawrence, I could imagine how she would respond to that. I had to retreat.

I cursed my lack of forward planning, and I felt doubly vulnerable walking back down the deserted street. I broke into a clumsy jog.

I was horribly out of breath by the time I reached the coffee shop by the station. It brought home how much I've let things slip. I haven't run or gone to the gym since Helen left (cancelling the gym membership was one of the first cost-cutting measures I took). And of course my diet of fast food, booze and self-indulgent misery isn't conducive to a svelte silhouette. Panting and sweating, I ordered another coffee, grabbed a bottle of water and slumped into a chair in a corner.

The coffee shop was a Starbucks – one of the ones set up with long tables and free Wi-Fi to encourage people to stay there and work. There were several earnest women with Macs and trendy glasses, and some blokes with hipster beards and tablets, all, I was sure, developing the latest ground-breaking app or writing the seminal east London novel. I had my iPad with me too, so I felt confident that I could sit unnoticed in my corner for as long as I liked, if I bought an espresso every hour or so.

I opened up the SSA webpage. It was slick and overdesigned, and a pain to navigate. There wasn't much substance to it, but the few case studies they featured suggested they were on the up and up. There was a key personnel page (except they'd called it 'The Gang'). I'd visited this particular page repeatedly. There was a pic and biography for the CEO, Simon Stanley – bald and young, and ambitious, by the looks of him; and the head of sales was a swarthy guy called Tony. There was the biography for Helen, which was pure fiction, or at least elided time considerably. It called her a 'talented freelance marketer' who'd worked on some key accounts, and then talked about her work in Australia. There was no picture. The last bio on the page featured 'office manager and all-round guru Sophie Penn', a beautiful mixed-race girl. I know how these small agencies work – they're always trying to look bigger than they are. If they were featuring the office manager as key personnel on their website, then that was probably all the personnel they had. By the looks of it, there were just four people working at SSA. I had pictures of three of them, and I knew the fourth. My spot in the corner gave me a good view of the concourse outside that joined the station to the shopping centre. If Simon, Tony, Sophie or Helen left the office for lunch or to go to a meeting, unless they had a car, they would have to pass my window. I just had to sit tight and keep watching.

It was easier said than done. After an hour or so, I was jittery from three espressos and my mouth tasted foul. I was desperate for the loo, and my attention kept wandering away from the window. I glanced at my watch. It was 11.30 a.m. It struck me that the men would be more likely to go to a meeting, but also that they might find a strange man accosting them and asking about their co-worker suspicious. Sophie, the 'all-round guru', probably stayed in the office, emerging only at lunchtime. My instinct was that she might be a better bet for information.

Having reformulated my plan, I went to the loo and then visited the newsagent opposite to get some chewing gum to get rid of the stale coffee taste in my mouth. I also bought a copy of *NME*. I wandered around until 12.30, then found myself a spot outside the station to stand, casually reading, as if I were waiting for someone. She was likely to take her lunch sometime between 12.30 and two, I reasoned.

After a day of frustrations and dead ends, I was finally rewarded. Sophie walked briskly into the concourse at about ten past one. She was chatting on her phone and swinging an empty shopping bag. She was pretty – tall and slim with a mass of dark hair and wide, smiling, green eyes. I pushed away from the wall and followed her into the shopping centre. She walked around for a while, chatting on her phone the whole time, looking into the windows of shops. Every now and then she'd stroll into a store and I would wait outside. She didn't stay in any of them for more than a minute or so – she was clearly browsing, rather than shopping seriously. It was the twenty-fifth, possibly too late in the month for clothes shopping on a receptionist's salary.

After about ten minutes she finished her call and abruptly reversed her course, almost walking into me. I let her pass and then turned to follow her. She walked quickly towards the entrance, and I had to trot to keep up with her. Then she swerved and headed into Marks & Spencer. It was a huge store, and I was worried she might leave by another exit, so I followed her in. She was still moving quickly, as if she knew where she was going, and I found myself following her into the food hall. She went over to the fridges filled with sandwiches and salads, and started picking out items. She grabbed two sandwiches and a couple of tubs of salad, so I assumed she'd been sent to get a lunch order for the whole office. She stacked the items precariously on one arm and reached for a bag of crisps. The top sandwich toppled off the pile and as she lunged for it, the pile collapsed and she dropped everything. I rushed over and helped her to pick up the items.

'Thanks.' She smiled at me. 'Should have got a basket.'

'I'll grab you one,' I said, spotting a stack of them at the end of the aisle. I ran and got one for her, while she protested, but when I got back, she tipped her items into the basket and I handed it to her.

'Thanks,' she said. 'I always try to carry too much.'

I gave her my most disarming smile. 'That's a lot of lunch.'

'Everyone in our office is stuck in this massive brainstorm, working on a big proposal,' she said. 'I got sent out to get supplies.'

'Ah, I've been there,' I said, grabbing a sandwich and drink for myself, trying to look like another casual shopper. 'Will you be pulling an all-nighter?'

'It's probably going to be a late one. We've got this marketing executive who's a real firecracker. She's great, but she's such a perfectionist. She won't stop till every detail is exactly the way she wants it.'

'Sounds like a nightmare.'

'Nah, she's cool. She just works harder than anyone I've ever known.'

'Well, good luck,' I said, and forced myself to walk away. I wanted to press her for more details, and ask her more about the marketing executive, but I was scared I would make her suspicious. The last thing I wanted was for her to go back to the office and tell Helen about the bloke in the M&S who was asking after her. I paid for my lunch, keeping a discreet eye on Sophie, two tills further along. As soon as she'd loaded her purchases into bags, she strode out of the shop. She gave me a vague smile as she went, but she was already dialling on her phone and beginning another call. I knew she'd have completely forgotten me by the time she got out on to the pavement.

I had to collect the girls from after-school club at five, so there was no way I could wait around for the SSA lot to finish their brainstorming. It didn't sound like Helen would be emerging from the building for many hours to come. I was satisfied with my day's work though – I knew where the office was, and Sophie's description of the perfectionist marketing executive made me even more convinced that I had found the right Helen.

I got back to north London with plenty of time to spare, so I went to the flat and sat down to plan my next move. I wanted to be able to catch Helen outside of the office, but it would only be possible to do that first thing in the morning or at the end of her work day. As a single, working parent, I couldn't see how that was going to be possible. At the times Helen was going to work or coming home, I would be doing the same, and I also had to drop off and collect the girls. It might take a few days to catch her too; I couldn't be sure that I wouldn't miss her the first few times. I gave it some thought. Catching her going home seemed more likely than catching her on the way in. If I was even a minute too late in the mornings, she'd be in the office already and I wouldn't even know I'd missed her. But if I could get to Stratford by 4.30 or so – from Sophie's workaholic description, she'd be unlikely to have left before then – I'd have a good chance of spotting her as she left to go home. I could use the Starbucks as my observation post.

That would mean leaving my own office by four at the latest, and staking out Stratford for up to three hours. And if I spotted her, what then? Would I follow her? I didn't know yet. All I knew was that I needed time, and that was what I didn't have. I needed a way to get the girls cared for that would allow me to be absent without a real reason until around eight, for several consecutive nights.

It took a while to construct a plan, but I got there. I made a phone call, and within minutes I had bought myself the hours I needed. I felt a little guilty about lying to Mum and Dad, but it was for the greater good. Every step in this plan was one closer to having our family back together again. I knew Mum and Dad might not get that now, but they would in the long run.

I'd told them that I had to undertake an urgent training programme at work – I made up something about social media metrics, which I knew would flummox them – but that doing it would hopefully earn me a promotion and more money. They agreed to pick up the girls every day, take them back to the flat, supervise homework and give them dinner.

Then I took a deep breath and rang Chris at work. He's clearly sick to death of me. He didn't even bother to sound happy to hear my voice.

'Sam,' he said shortly. I could hear he was still typing at top speed while he talked to me. 'How are you feeling?'

'Pretty rough, if I'm honest. It was a nasty bug. I've only just shaken it.'

'Mm,' he said. He didn't sound like he believed me. I didn't blame him. 'Did the girls get sick?'

'No, thank God. They're. . . okay.' I left the smallest pause between my words. He stopped typing.

'Okay?'

'Well, they've had some trouble at school. Fighting, and. . . you know.' I kept the explanation deliberately vague.

'Man, that's tough,' said Chris, and I knew I'd won him over. 'Anything I can do?'

Chris really is a nice guy. I felt bad, but I kept thinking to myself that this was for a greater good.

'Well, if I could possibly work flexibly for a few days, a week maybe. . . You know, leave early, so I can be with the girls in the afternoon, give them support. . . and then do some hours in the evening from home to catch up—'

'Of course!' Chris cut in. 'Whatever you need. Just make things okay for your girls.' He and his girlfriend have a new baby, named Arthur. He's besotted, and as a result, big on the rights of children.

I thanked him profusely, promised I would be at work bright and early the next morning, and rang off. I sat back in my chair and checked my watch. Nearly time to collect the girls.

I did my best to look industrious all of the next day at work. I typed furiously, answering emails and writing up reports, and I ate my lunch at my desk. My mind was buzzing with plans for later. At 3.30, Chris came over and touched my shoulder.

'Hey, man, you're going to set that keyboard on fire. Shouldn't you get going for your girls?'

I glanced at my watch and faked surprise. 'You're right,' I said. 'Thanks. Look, I've still got to finish the report on the test campaign for Robert and Roberts. I'll get back on it as soon as the girls are in bed.'

'Of course,' said Chris.

I thanked him and packed up my things. As soon as I was out of the building, I set off at a jog for Waterloo station. It was a good fifteen minutes from my office, but it would get me on the Jubilee Line, and I could be in Stratford in fifteen minutes or so. I also reasoned that going to a station away from my office would make it less likely that I'd bump into a colleague who might wonder why I was heading in the opposite direction to where I lived. I was impatient on the journey, worried that I might somehow miss Helen, that she wasn't in the office anyway. I tried to relax by telling myself I had a few days to get this right, but the jitters prevailed.

When I got to Stratford, I went into the Starbucks and bought a bottle of water. I was definitely too tense for several hours of coffee. There was a long counter by the window which looked out on to the concourse and offered a clear view of the entrance that Helen would have to come through. I'd planned ahead this time and bought a baseball cap, which I put on and pulled down over my face. She wouldn't be looking out for me, but if by chance she looked through the window, the cap might stop her recognizing me. I glanced at my watch. Just after four. I'd probably erred on the side of caution by several hours. Still, there was nothing to do but sit and wait. I didn't want to read or work, risking missing her. She'd only be in view for a matter of seconds before she disappeared into the station.

We've come to expect constant entertainment in the twenty-first century. It's incredibly hard to sit and wait. All around me, people were on their phones, scrolling and texting. The few that weren't were typing on tablets or computers or reading books or newspapers. It felt odd indeed to sit, and I was worried that I was conspicuous through my lack of electronic activity. I grabbed a discarded paper from a nearby table and put it on the counter in front of me. After ten minutes or so, my phone buzzed with a text, and with great relief, I took it out. It was from Lara.

'Hey. How are you doing?' If it's possible for a text to sound tentative, this one did. I felt a twinge of guilt. She'd barely crossed my mind since I'd seen her in the street with her ex on Sunday. I had no idea what to say. I still owed her an apology, but the night I'd seen Helen felt like a lifetime ago. So much had happened in between.

'Hey,' I typed. 'A little better than last week. I'm so sorry about. . .'

I'll never know what made me look up at that second. A flash of blonde hair, maybe? I glanced up just in time to see Helen walking briskly into the station. Until that moment, there had been the possibility that I'd got it wrong, that Helen Day was someone else altogether. But here she was. I felt a flash of exhilaration so powerful I stood involuntarily.

She was dressed in another severe business suit. This one was red, a colour she had never worn when we were together. She was carrying a portfolio case of the type that artists use for artwork, and she had a black backpack on her back. Seeing her in motion, I couldn't believe I'd ever doubted my first sight of her. The hair and clothes might be different, and she may have gained weight, but that bouncy, positive walk, as if she was being propelled forward, was unmistakeable. I dropped my phone into my pocket, grabbed my bag and rushed out of the coffee shop, just in time to see her pass through the ticket gates and into the station. There was one heart-stopping moment when I couldn't get my own card out of my pocket to get through the gates, but I made it in time to see her head off down a long corridor towards the Jubilee Line platforms. I jogged along until I was about ten yards behind her and then fell into step, keeping her bright blonde hair in sight. A train pulled into the platform as we got to it, and I watched which carriage she got into. I ran down the platform (it was too early to be properly busy) and hopped into the next one. I walked to the end of the carriage so I could stand by the door and look through the small window to watch her. I knew it was unlikely she'd glance up and see me, but I kept my cap on and turned sideways to be less obvious.

She'd got a seat about halfway down the carriage, and I saw her put her backpack on her lap. She drew out a Filofax diary, like the one she'd always used when we were together. She read through some notes and made a couple of quick, decisive annotations. My heart ached with love. I missed her so much. I wanted to slip into the seat next to her and put my face in the curve of her neck to smell her skin. She checked her watch, and again the familiarity of the gesture made me sigh. I noticed she was wearing a different watch, not the elegant one with the brown strap I had bought for her. This one looked big and chunky, almost masculine. She'd chosen it to suit the new Helen.

The Tube sped into Canary Wharf and I braced myself, expecting her to get off, but she didn't even look up. She was focused on her notes. I watched her for a few more stops, drinking in the chance to study her face for an extended period of time. I think I was almost hypnotized, so that when we got to Green Park and she stood abruptly, I was caught off guard. I managed to throw myself off the train too, and to my enormous relief, her route towards the exit took her away from me, rather than towards me. If it had been the other way, she would have bumped straight into me, and it would have been Canary Wharf all over again. I followed her through the corridors and up out of the station.

She turned decisively as soon as she was outside, and walked briskly through the streets of Mayfair. It was clear that she was going to a client meeting. I followed, a discreet distance behind, and saw her turn into a Georgian townhouse in an expensive mews. When I was sure she'd gone inside and the door was shut, I approached and checked the nameplates beside the door. It was an exclusive area, so there were no brash logos, just company names engraved on small brass plaques, three of them beside three polished brass bell pushes. The names were all acronyms, and I had heard of none of them. I had no way of knowing which of the offices Helen had gone into. It was irrelevant – one of the companies was obviously a client of SSA's. She'd gone for a meeting and would emerge sooner or later. I checked the time: 5.15. Late to be starting a meeting, I thought. She probably wouldn't be too long, and I had a few hours before I needed to be back to see to the girls. There was a lovely old-fashioned pub at the end of the block. Helen would have to pass it on her way back to the station. I went inside and found myself a window table, ordering a beer.

Forty-five minutes later, she emerged from the building. She no longer had the portfolio bag. She stopped outside and took her mobile phone out of her rucksack. She checked her messages, and then I saw her dial and begin to talk as she walked. I shrank back from the window as she passed, then gulped the last mouthful of my drink and followed.

There was no risk of her turning back and seeing me. She was entirely immersed in her phone call. Who was she talking to? I wanted to believe she had rung her boss at SSA to report back on the meeting. But what if it wasn't him? What if she was ringing a boyfriend to say she was on her way over to his place? I felt a hot rush of jealousy. I wanted to rush up behind her and snatch the phone out of her hand.

She got to Green Park and marched through the barriers, cutting off the call as she went through. I found I had to run to keep up as she strode briskly down the escalator and turned confidently towards the eastbound Jubilee Line platform. There was no train at the platform when I reached it, so I hung back, out of sight in the main concourse, until I heard one pulling in, then again made my way on to the carriage adjoining Helen's. It was past six o'clock and I was running short of time if I was to be back home by eight, as I had promised my parents. She had to be on her way home now though. I didn't want to let her go.

I watched her through the window. On this journey, she left her Filofax in her bag and instead took out a set of headphones and connected them to her phone. I knew she wasn't listening to music – she'd never had any time for idle entertainment. She'd have some improving book or an informative podcast playing. She also seemed settled, and showed no sign of getting off. I'd expected her to change at Canary Wharf, or possibly one of the other stops, but she relaxed back in her seat and didn't seem ready to get off. My nerves became more and more frayed with every passing stop. The train rattled on, and it became clear that she was going all the way to Stratford. Was she going back to the office at this hour? Or did she live in the area too? I thought it unlikely but not impossible. Time was ticking and I was getting further and further from my own home.

She got off at Stratford, the end of the line, and I followed her only far enough to see that she was indeed going back to the office. At 6.30 p.m. That was some hard-core dedication to the job. There was no way I could wait for her to emerge, and no possible way of knowing what time that might happen. I was forced to admit defeat, return to the station and hope I could make it back to north London in time to put the girls to bed.

I was back in the Starbucks at 4.30 the following afternoon, but this time the wait was much longer. No late-afternoon meetings for Helen today. Time ticked, I drank juice, water and coffee, and developed such an urgent need to go for a pee that I had to abandon my post for three nerve-wracking minutes. I worried constantly that I might have missed her, or that she wasn't in the office at all, but just when I was considering giving up, at about 6.15, she came into the concourse wearing black jeans and boots, a tailored pink shirt and a cropped black jacket. It was more casual than the outfits I'd seen her wearing before, more what a woman might wear if she knew she had a day in the office with no client meetings. She looked sexy, in a slightly intimidating way – kind of biker-chick chic.

I followed her into the station again, but instead of heading for the Jubilee Line, she swerved off towards the Docklands Light Railway. My heart leapt. Did that mean she was actually on her way home? Would I be able to find out where she lived?

Again, she plugged in her headphones, which made me a little bolder. She'd be immersed in what she was listening to, not paying much attention to her environment. The DLR didn't have separate carriages, so I sat a few rows behind her, watching the nape of her neck as she looked out of the window. She changed trains at Canary Wharf and so did I, and it was soon clear that we were heading south-east. There was something about her more relaxed demeanour that made me sure she was on her way home. South-east? What was in the south-east? What had made her choose this corner of London? I thought I understood. London is so big, and people generally move only in the areas in which they live and work. The girls and I live in north-west London and I work in the West End. By choosing to live and work in the south-east, she may as well have moved to Timbuktu.

As the train was about to pull into Greenwich, she took off her headphones and put her things away in her bag. This was obviously her destination. I got up quickly and moved further down the carriage, so that if she turned back to walk to the door, she wouldn't see me sitting behind her.

She walked to the door in front of her seat, reaching into her pocket for her Oyster card. The train stopped and we stepped out. My heart pounded as she turned towards me, walking towards the exit. I dropped my wallet on the ground and bent to pick it up as she passed, keeping my head down and hoping the baseball cap concealed my face. She didn't appear to notice me, and when I dared to look up, she was a few yards further along the platform and I was free to stand up and follow her. We left the station, and I walked behind her as she meandered down the street, clearly not in a hurry. She went into a Sainsbury's, and I crossed to the opposite side of the road and waited until she emerged, carrying a bag of shopping. Then we continued down the street until she took a right turn and then another, into a small side street. She stopped outside a door between two neglected-looking shops. She put the shopping bag at her feet and reached into her backpack for her keys.

Now.

I stepped up beside her and said, 'Helen.'

PART FOUR

CHAPTER TWENTY

Helen

Simon was out of the office the afternoon she was due to go to QVA. It made things much easier. She liked Simon and didn't want to lie to him. She told Sophie something vague about going to check out a possible venue for an event they were planning for a client. The next day, she would just say the venue hadn't been right at all.

She'd calculated her journey time carefully – half an hour to get to Mayfair, and fifteen minutes to find QVA and get inside. She had her big artwork folder with her, which made sense if she was meeting a client at an event venue; they might well look at designs together when they were there. But instead of set designs, the case contained her portfolio – boards of the campaigns she had done for SSA, and some from her previous working life. She'd had them mounted at considerable expense, and the portfolio looked sleek and professional.

She hadn't been looking to move jobs, not quite yet, anyway. But while working on the kinetic tape campaign, she'd met the two brothers who ran QVA, Bruce and Jaego Chertsey. They were twins – burly, blonde men who looked like they'd rowed and played a lot of rugby in their teenage years and had the unmistakeable sheen and confidence of an expensive public school and lots of inherited money. When they'd launched the agency, they'd been a joke in the marketing industry; everyone had assumed they were a pair of dilettante posh boys with no real substance. But they were smart. They set up an elegant office in the best part of town, used their considerable contacts book (and that of their parents) to bring in initial business, and then went about hiring the best account managers, marketers and creative teams. In short, they delivered, and the business continued to roll in.

Bruce was the more charismatic of the two, the agency's front man and new-business-development whizz. He had extravagant waves of bright golden hair and the demeanour of a well-bred but boisterous golden retriever. People adored him. Jaego was quieter, slimmer and darker, and his eagle eye and ruthless efficiency kept the company's finances on track.

When Helen met them both at a big round table of agencies involved in the kinetic tape campaign, she felt immediately drawn to them. Their energy was infectious, and their confidence irresistible. She went home and spent some time looking at their website and the coverage they'd got in the marketing press. She looked up every employee of the company that she could find on LinkedIn and examined their CVs, matching them to current and past work on the company website. Then she set about writing Bruce and Jaego a letter, explaining why they should hire her as the new marketing manager they didn't yet know they needed.

They were surprised but arranged a telephone interview with her the following week. She'd gone to sit in the Starbucks in the station at Stratford and talked to them for half an hour. A few days later, they called and asked her to come and meet them. They thought they had a position for her. The job at QVA would be a big step up: another 50 per cent on her salary, a small team to manage, and the real possibility of winning some awards. They also talked about the likelihood of an international secondment. This was what swung it for her. Travel was a vital component in her medium-term plan.

It was clear from the moment she walked into their meeting room that they had already decided to hire her. She'd spent ages preparing a detailed presentation, but they were less interested in that than in her notice period. They wanted to get her in as soon as possible, she realized. When Jaego asked her about salary expectations, she added £5,000 to the figure they'd initially suggested, and they agreed without turning a hair. When she left, they told her she could expect an email with a formal offer letter to arrive before she got home, so she could get on with writing her resignation letter.

She left QVA and headed for the Tube. There was a message on her phone from Simon, asking her about some media figures on the kinetic tape campaign. She rang him back as she walked to the station and briefed him. She had all the information in her head, so that wasn't difficult.

'Where are you?' he asked. 'It's noisy.'

'Just popped down to the shopping centre to get something to eat,' she lied. 'I'm going to try and get the report off my desk tonight.'

'Jeez, Helen, there's loads to do. You'll be there half the night.'

'That's okay. I want to get you a draft tomorrow.'

'You're such a star,' he said gratefully. He might not feel that way tomorrow, she thought.

She finished her conversation with Simon as she got to Green Park. It was a lot to take in. Her plans had accelerated and she needed some time to regroup. She took out some headphones and chose some music – jazz, instrumental, soothing – and sat enjoying the music and feeling her own stillness and breathing as she travelled to Stratford. She loved the Tube and the sense that in this noisy, crowded space you could be utterly alone and unobserved.

She got back to the office just as Tony and Sophie were leaving for the evening. She worked, focused and uninterrupted, for three solid hours, until she had finished the report to her satisfaction. She did it not only because she felt loyalty and gratitude to Simon, but also because it was a comprehensive record of her work on her biggest project to date and she wanted it for her own portfolio. Her last task before she left for the evening was to type and print her letter of resignation and leave it on Simon's desk.

The next day unfolded as she had imagined it would. Simon called her into his office, looking pale and tense. She sat down and calmly explained that she had been headhunted by Jaego and Bruce, leaving out the fact that she had approached them. She told him what they had offered in terms of salary and prospects, and she saw him wince. She knew perfectly well he couldn't match their offer. She thanked him for all the opportunities he'd given her, and assured him that she would do her best to find ways for the two companies to work together in the future. She could see him struggling with himself; he clearly felt betrayed, but he also knew that this was the way things happened in the fast-moving world of business. It wasn't personal. Then his hard-nosed professional side kicked in, and he said, as pleasantly as he could, that she'd have to begin gardening leave immediately. She understood perfectly. She knew that as soon as she resigned and admitted who she was going to work for, he'd want her out of the office. She couldn't expect to keep working for SSA with access to their client files and records when she was going to work for the competition.

Sophie was gutted when she heard the news, and Tony was furious. He took her leaving personally. That was the problem with working for a small company, Helen thought. People thought they were your friends. She stayed for the whole day, making sure all her files were in order and easily accessible on the company hard drive, and filing and reorganizing all her emails so that Sophie could access them for any information she needed. She spent several hours that afternoon briefing Simon on all her current work, so that no loose ends would be left dangling.

She had little in the way of personal effects in the office – a few notebooks, a container of artificial sweeteners and a spare jumper. She packed these into her backpack at the end of the day and headed for the station. Simon said vaguely that they would all get together in a few days for farewell drinks, but she thought this was unlikely. Tony was too angry and Sophie looked like she'd been crying. And so with minimal fanfare, she walked away from SSA, likely never to return.

It was, as these things so often were, anti-climactic. She remembered on the train that she had finished the milk that morning and that she didn't have any vegetables for her dinner, so she stopped off at the Sainsbury's on her way home. She'd got to her door and was reaching into her backpack for her keys when she heard her name. 'Helen.'

Sam.

Her instinctive reaction was to turn and run. But in the same second, she knew there was nowhere to run to, and she stood her ground. She'd expected this moment, deep down, and here it was. They stood looking at each other in silence for the longest time. He looked rough, she thought. The time she'd seen him at Canary Wharf, she'd got such a fright that she hadn't really registered any details about his appearance. But now she had time to look at him, she could see he'd gained weight and stopped shaving every day; he was a pale, rather unhealthy-looking version of the man she'd married. He hadn't had a haircut for a while, and his hair, which was naturally curly, stood out from his head in a bushy cloud. When they'd been together, she'd trimmed it for him every few weeks. She knew every whorl of his hair, every curve and bump of his skull. He was staring at her too, but without the same sense of discovery. She knew she looked different, and yet he didn't seem surprised by the changes in her appearance. He was watching her warily, as if he was sure she would bolt again and he was ready to stop her this time. But she wasn't going to run. He was here. She had to face him.

'Is this your. . . place?' he said eventually. 'Can I come up?'

'I don't want you to come inside,' she said. 'But if you wait here while I put my things down, we can go for a walk in the park.'

She thought he might argue, might even try to force his way inside, but he paused and then nodded, hesitantly. Then he stepped back to show he wasn't going to be obstructive. She had her keys in her hand, and she opened the street door and stepped through, closing it quickly behind her.

She ran up the stairs to her flat and opened the door, locking it behind her. It was exactly as she had left it that morning. Maybe she could stay up there, wait for him to go away? But of course he wouldn't. And even if he did, he knew where she lived now, and he would be back. Better to face it now. She put her shopping away in the fridge, carefully folded her shopping bag and stowed it in a drawer and put her backpack in its accustomed spot on her dresser. Then she checked her reflection in the mirror. She looked pale and pinched. She shrugged off her jacket and replaced it with a soft black hoodie. Then she put her keys in her pocket and went back downstairs.

Sam looked astonished when she emerged. He clearly hadn't expected her to come back. She gestured with her head that they should walk, and they set off side by side, up her street. She led him through the side streets until they came to an entrance into the park. It was a cloudy evening, and there weren't many people about.

They still hadn't spoken, and they began to walk up the hill towards the Observatory. Neither of them was as fit as they had been, Helen observed. She remembered coming to the park in Greenwich with Sam and the girls, about two years ago, on a family outing. She and Miranda had run up the hill, laughing, and Sam had put Marguerite on his shoulders and jogged up after them. When they'd reached the crest of the hill, they'd collapsed on the grass, laughing, but neither of them had been out of breath or tired. Now she felt her legs ache, and she had to work hard not to pant. When she glanced at Sam, she could see beads of sweat along his hairline. Clearly his exercise routine had also gone by the wayside. About halfway up, she saw a bench and indicated that they should sit down. Sam flopped down beside her gratefully. He felt no need to pretend he wasn't knackered. He sat back, his hands on his knees, and wheezed unashamedly.

They stared out across the park for a long time, and eventually Sam said evenly, 'So, how have you been?'

'Okay. You?'

'Not great.'

The silence continued. Then he said, 'You work at SSA?'

She hesitated for an instant and then said, 'Yes. Is that how you found me?'

'Marketing press. I searched for people called Helen.'

She raised an eyebrow, impressed, but didn't respond. He let the silence grow and grow, so eventually she said, 'How are. . . the girls?'

'Up and down. Miranda is angry, understandably. Marguerite regressed for a while, but she's doing better now.'

She nodded. 'How's work?'

'Pretty shit. Chris has been understanding, but. . .'

'But what?'

'He's running out of patience with me. He gave one of my key accounts to Verity.'

'Oh, is Verity still there?'

'Yes, she's flying high. She brought in a big vodka account.'

'Really?'

'Well, not big, more like a niche brand. She thinks we can grow it big though.'

'With the right campaign, she might do it. She's good with those small brands.'

'She is, but she wants to play with the big kids,' said Sam, and he began to tell a story about Verity's presentation at a big conference. He was relieved to have something neutral to talk about and he rattled on while she listened. She couldn't quite believe that after nearly a year, this was the banal, emotionless conversation they were having. The big stuff was too big, she decided. Where did they begin? And as he had found her, it was his choice when he asked the questions. She'd just have to decide when and how to answer them.

Sam had got the bit between his teeth, and he talked more. He told her about his mum's accident, and that she was recovering well. He told her Marguerite had lost her first teeth and learned to swim, that they were living in a flat now. He didn't seem angry. He was giving her information, as if she was a friend he hadn't seen for a while and he was catching her up. She was astonished at how calm he was. How calm she was. After the time he had grabbed her hand on the Tube, she'd lived in a heightened state – she'd looked for him round every corner. Somehow, she had known he would find her again and he had. And here they were, sitting on a bench, engaged in small talk. Eventually, he said, 'And how have you. . . been?'

'Okay,' she said carefully. 'Working mainly. Just working.'

'What kind of thing have you been working on?'

She found herself talking about the energy gel campaign and what she'd done for the running-shoe company. He knew the marketing business, so he asked intelligent questions. When she shared some of her results, he raised an eyebrow.

'You were always good, but those are impressive results. Very impressive. Have you entered the campaign for any awards?'

'I think Simon has,' she said. She was about to add, 'But I won't be there to accept them if we win,' but she stopped herself. She wasn't going to tell him that she'd left her job. Not yet, anyway.

There was a long silence then. Evening was falling and the shadows had lengthened across the park. Although it had been a warm spring day, now that the sun had gone in, it was decidedly chilly. She drew her hoodie tighter around her and shivered a little.

'You're cold,' Sam said. In days gone by, he'd have put an arm around her to warm her, but he made no move to touch her.

'A little.'

'I need to get back for the girls.'

'Yes.'

They stood and walked back down the hill, side by side, in silence. When they left the gates of the park, he turned towards the station and then stopped, as if to say goodbye. He wasn't going to walk her to her door – he was clearly intending to head straight home. She didn't know what to say.

'Can I come and see you again?' he said.

Before she had time to think about it, she found herself saying, 'Yes.' And then, 'I'm off work for the next couple of weeks. If you're free in the day. . .'

'I'm free,' he said quickly. 'How about Friday?'

She nodded. And before she could say anything more, he

raised a hand in farewell and walked briskly away in the direction of the station, leaving her behind.

Sam

I fell asleep on the Tube – something I almost never do, unless I've been drinking. I think it was a kind of instinctive survival reaction. I wasn't ready to process what had happened, so my brain shut down. I woke up abruptly, just before my stop, and stumbled blearily off the train. The world had changed, but the station looked as it always did. I mounted the stairs and walked on auto-pilot towards the flat. There was my car, and Mum and Dad's Vauxhall parked directly behind it. There was the tree, the front door, here were my keys in my pocket. The world kept turning and everything was exactly as it had been, except. . . Except I'd found Helen.

How many times had I imagined that encounter? In my mind's eye, I ran over the scenarios I had envisaged. I'd thought that I would grab her and hold her, shake her, hit her, kill her even. I'd thought I would cry and yell and accuse, hurl abuse at her. Instead, we'd walked in the park and chatted about work like two distant acquaintances. She was a stranger.

I climbed the stairs to our flat rather than taking the lift, giving myself a few extra minutes to compose myself. When I let myself in, I could hear the girls laughing and chatting excitedly in the bathroom, and Mum's soothing tones as she got them ready for bed. Dad was in the kitchen, washing up, Radio 4 playing softly as he worked. I walked in behind him and touched his shoulder by way of greeting. He looked up and nodded at me.

'There's a bowl of spag bol in the fridge. Just gone in. You could pop it in the microwave.'

'Thanks, Dad,' I said. 'I'm not hungry right now. Maybe later.'

'Good course?' he asked.

I looked at him uncomprehendingly for a long moment then remembered my cover story. 'Yes,' I said. 'Although at the moment I'm getting more questions than answers.'

'Well, time will tell,' Dad said sagely, drying his hands on a dish towel.

'I'm going to go through and see the girls,' I said.

Both girls were tucked up in bed, and Mum was sitting on the end of Marguerite's, reading a chapter from *Mary Poppins*. My mum has a beautiful reading voice, deep and warm, and she gave subtle accents and different vocal tones to each character. I stood in the doorway and listened too. Miranda, of course, was far too old to be read to, but she was lying on her side, watching Mum, rapt and quiet. Marguerite waved to me vaguely, but I could see her eyelids were drooping and she was almost asleep. Mum noticed too. 'That's enough for tonight,' she said, closing the book.

'Noooo,' protested Marguerite weakly.

'Say night to your dad, girls. Tomorrow is another day,' said Mum, patting them each on the head. She squeezed my arm as she went out of the room.

I bent over the girls' beds and kissed them, inhaling the clean, bedtime smell of them. Miranda threw a long, skinny arm around my neck, surprising me. 'You smell nice,' she said.

'Do I? What do I smell of?'

'Outside. And not of beer. Night.' And she turned her back, drew the duvet up to her chin and closed her eyes.

I turned off the lamp and stood for a time, watching them in the dim light that spilled in from the hallway.

When I went through to the living room, Mum and Dad had their jackets on and were preparing to go.

'Don't you want to stay for a cup of tea?' I said. I wasn't sure I was ready to be alone quite yet.

'Thanks, my darling, but no,' said Mum. 'Your dad's tired.'

Dad actually seemed all right, but when I looked at her, she seemed strained. There were shadows under her eyes and she was leaning slightly to one side. Her recently mended leg must still be giving her pain. She's getting on a bit to be running after two boisterous girls for three or four hours at a time. I felt a lurch of guilt, and moved in to put my arms around her.

'Thanks for looking after the girls,' I said, hugging her. 'I appreciate it so much. What I'm doing this week will make such a difference to us all, and you've made it possible.'

She looked at me in that piercing, loving way she has. 'As long as you're sure you're doing the right thing,' she said, 'we'll support you all the way. You know that.'

I couldn't shake the feeling that she knew more than she possibly could. She's like that, my mum. Even if she doesn't know the facts of a situation, I always feel she can look into my soul and see things I wish she couldn't.

Once they'd gone, I looked around the flat. They'd left it tidy and ordered, so I couldn't distract myself with housework. I still wasn't hungry. I thought about getting a beer, but Miranda's comment stayed with me. I found myself sitting on the sofa, staring out of the window at the trees, now covered in the fresh green leaves of early summer, thinking about everything and nothing. I was nowhere near sorting out my feelings about Helen or our encounter, and I felt I had learned nothing about her reason for going or her current state of mind. She didn't seem to hate me, but then she didn't seem to like me either. The most important thing was that she hadn't run away, and she'd agreed to see me again.

A sensible man would go to bed, I thought, before the desire for booze got too strong and another night was lost to pointless agonizing, drinking and self-pity. Unfortunately, I'm not a sensible man. One beer, that was all. Just one. I'd watch the first hour of a loud, mindless shoot-'em-up movie on my iPad, and then I'd go to bed.

Three beers later, I was staring at a series of spectacular explosions on the screen when my phone buzzed. Helen, I thought, and my heart lurched. But it was Lara.

'I'm downstairs,' her text read. 'Can I come up?'

How could I say no? She knew I was home – my car was outside and the living room lights were on. And it would be good to see her. We needed to clear the air, resolve things and end them properly.

When I opened the door to her, I was momentarily surprised. She looked gorgeous. She'd come from work, so she was smartly dressed, but I'd somehow forgotten how tall, slender and elegant she was. She gave me a shy smile and brushed past me as she came into the flat. She was wearing a silky black skirt that ended just above her knees and a pair of high heels that I didn't remember seeing before. She's tall anyway, and the shoes made her as tall as me. Her blouse was white, a sheer thing that also looked unfamiliar. She went through to the living room and I stopped in the kitchen to get her a glass of wine and me another beer. When I came into the living room, she'd sat down on the armchair, back straight, knees together and hands resting in her lap, as if she was in the headmaster's office awaiting a reprimand.

I handed her her drink. 'How have you been?' I asked carefully.

Unlike Helen, she didn't seem particularly interested in small talk or banalities.

'Bit shit, actually. I'm not terribly sure what happened last week, but we somehow seem to have gone from quite a happy place to. . . I don't know what you'd call it? Broken up? Is that what happened? And I'm not quite sure why.'

She looked up at me, her green eyes wide. Her face was calm and her voice low and even, but there was a pinched look around her mouth that told me that coming out with that had cost her dearly, and that she was close to tears.

'I'm sorry,' I said.

'For what?'

'Hurting you. You don't deserve it. You've been nothing but kind and generous to me, and I have taken huge advantage.'

'Before last Thursday night, I wouldn't have said so.'

I behaved badly. I'm sorry.'

'Apology accepted. Now can you tell me why?'

'Things... get to me,' I said finally. 'Work... work is frustrating and it makes me angry pretty much all the time. And the girls... I feel like I'm not doing a good job at the office, and I'm not doing a good job at home. Just... failing everywhere. And now I'm failing you too.'

I dropped my head into my hands and rubbed my face. I felt like a monster, lying to this good, kind woman. I couldn't look at her.

Suddenly, I felt her hand between my shoulder blades. She'd crossed the room and sat beside me on the sofa. She gently rubbed my back, muttering in a low and soothing voice, as she might do for a sick child. 'I know, I know,' she said. 'But you're not failing anyone. You're doing as much – more – than anyone could be expected to do.'

I took a deep, shuddering breath and kept my face buried in my hands. She leaned in, resting her head on my shoulder, and continued to rub up and down my back rhythmically. I could feel the coolness of her slim hand through my shirt, making a trail on my hot skin. I leaned slightly into her touch. She sensed my response and pressed herself closer to my side, sliding her arm around my waist. She used her other hand to tug my fingers away from my face, her touch gentle but insistent, and she turned my face towards her. She was very close to me, and I couldn't focus on her at all, just sense the bright circles of her eyes and the sweet warmth of her breath. I kissed her.

I eased her back on to the sofa, pressing the length of my body against her. Then I rolled us so she was on top of me. She was hesitant at first, but then her soft hair fell over my face and her lips were warm. She could feel my body respond, and I sighed against her mouth. After a moment, she pulled away and stood in front of me. In a fluid motion, she unbuttoned her skirt and let it slither to the floor, then peeled off her shirt so she stood before me in her brief black pants and bra. She was breathtaking. I had to make it stop, I thought, as she slid back into my arms, her pale skin smooth and cool against me.

Afterwards, she lay with her head on my chest. We were silent for a long time. Eventually, she said, 'I'm not giving up on you, Sam. I know you tried to push me away, but it's not going to work. You and the girls need kindness and consistency right now, and I'm good at that. So you can be flaky and horrid if you must, but I plan to stick around.'

'You're very direct,' I said.

'Well, I think there's no point in games at this point,' she said, playing with the fingers of my left hand. I felt her fingertips brush lightly over my wedding ring. I drew my hand away and sat up.

'From a purely practical perspective,' she said, 'you need help. How have you managed this week? You must have had to leave work early every day.'

'My mum and dad. . .'

'You can't ask your mum and dad to look after the girls. They have to drive forty-five minutes to get here, and your poor mum's only just stopped using her walking stick.'

I remembered my mum's pale, tired face and I knew she was right.

'But. . .'

'Frances and Jonah have missed the girls like mad. Let me pick them up on Friday. I have to work on Thursday evening, but we could have dinner all together on Friday. A barbecue, maybe, if the weather holds?'

I could see what she was trying to do. She wanted to get us back to the place we had been as quickly as possible, get things back into a steady routine. She'd decided that was what I needed to help me get over my. . . How would she explain it to herself? My 'blip'? My 'fugue state'? I could see she'd thought it all through and decided that she was on my team, like it or not, and that somehow she was going to make it all okay.

I should have said no. I should have told her that we couldn't be together, that I was in no position to be in a relationship with her. But Friday was the day I was going to spend with Helen, and after that, I might have a better idea of where we were headed and what would happen between us. And on top of that, a terrible, evil, small and selfish part of me knew that if the girls were at Lara's, I wouldn't have to rush back as I would have had to do if they were with my mum and dad. 'Okay,' I said. 'Thank you. That's amazing of you. Only, I'm doing this course at work at the moment and it finishes late. I might not make it back for a barbecue on Friday. But at the weekend, for sure.'

She looked a little disappointed, but she smiled, kissed me and slipped off the sofa to get dressed. 'I'll see you on Friday then,' she said, smiling broadly at me as she stepped back into her skirt.

'Friday,' I said. 'Definitely.'

CHAPTER TWENTY-ONE

Sam

I rang her doorbell and she came down immediately, as if she had been waiting for me. She wore black leggings and a baggy T-shirt with a denim jacket, as the day was unseasonably overcast and blustery. We greeted each other without touching, and in silent agreement walked towards the park. We took it slower up the hill this time, but ended up sitting on the same bench, looking out over the city.

I let the silence grow for a long time, and then I said, 'So, Judy contacted me.'

I felt her stiffen beside me, as if she was suddenly alert.

'How?'

'The night you went missing, I posted an appeal on Facebook. It went viral, as these things do. Made it to Australia. She saw it and rang me.'

'How is she?' I couldn't read any emotion in her voice. I glanced over at her, and she was resolutely staring out at the horizon.

'She seems well. Loves her garden and her dogs, she says. Still lives close to your parents.'

I saw her swallow.

'They're fine too,' I added quickly. 'Getting older, Judy says, but okay.'

She allowed herself a nod.

'She's not angry with you. She misses you terribly, but she understands why you went.'

Again, she didn't reply.

'She told me. . . a lot of things, Hel. About Lawrence, and what he did to you. . . and her.'

She exploded. 'She shouldn't have done that.' She jumped up from the bench and walked away. She stood a few yards off, her back to me, her arms tightly folded. I could see the muscles in her calves flex and she tipped up on to her toes, ready for flight.

'She was trying to help me understand,' I said as calmly as I could, walking up behind her. 'She didn't do it to betray a confidence. She just. . . well, she reached out to someone who shared her experience.'

'The experience of being abandoned by me,' she said tonelessly.

'Yes.'

I took a careful step closer. I didn't want her to run away, although I was unsure what I would do if she tried. Grabbing her and wrestling her to the ground would be counterproductive.

After a long, long moment, I saw her relax, ever so slightly. She let her heels drop to the ground.

'I stayed here, you know. . . when I first came to London.'

'Stayed where?'

'Greenwich.'

'I thought you lived in that shared flat in Willesden Green.'

'I moved there after about a week – I found it on Gumtree. But I started out here. I came to London in such a hurry. . . I. . . left Australia suddenly. There wasn't time to plan in detail, or do much research.'

I smiled wryly. 'You? Doing something without planning? Unimaginable.'

There was a twitch at the corner of her mouth. Not a smile, but almost. 'Stupid, I know. I didn't know many areas in London, but I'd heard of Greenwich. Because of the. . . you know. . .' She gestured up the hill behind us, towards the Observatory. 'Meridian. And the Mean Time.'

'Of course.'

'So I googled "budget hotel in Greenwich", and I ended up here, on my first day in London.'

'Right here?'

'Right here,' she said, gesturing to the bench behind us. 'It was the second night I'd ever spent on my own. The first was on the flight over. The second night was in this funny little hotel down the hill from here.'

'Second ever night on your own?'

'I moved straight from my parents' house to a place with Lawrence. Then. . . the refuge, then the flat I shared. Never alone. Always someone else there. So the freedom of that little room in the hotel. . .' She paused. 'I'd have stayed longer if I could have afforded it, but I needed a proper place to live and a job.'

It felt like it was significant, so I prompted her. 'And you came up to the park, that first evening?'

'I couldn't sleep. I was all screwed up from the jet lag. It was still light, so I put on my running things and I ran into the park. And when I got to the top of this hill and saw this view. . .' She gestured out at the city. 'It was all there. Everything. Infinite possibility. And all of it was mine. It felt like I was being reborn. I was so scared, but. . .'

'But what?'

'Excited. So excited.' She drew in an unsteady breath. I stepped alongside her so I could see her face. She was looking out, her eyes restlessly combing the skyline, as if she'd gone back six years, to that day when she could have had anything, done anything, been anything. And, like a blow to the gut, I realized that she had gone back. She'd retraced her steps to the place where anything had been possible. Before me.

Then, to my surprise, she turned to me. 'I wrote to you.'

'Did you?'

'I've been working on a letter to you. For months. Ever since I left. I don't know if I would ever have posted it. . .'

'A letter saying what?'

'You can read it, and then you'll know.'

'When? When can I read it?'

'It's in my flat,' she said and then she stepped closer to me and looked directly into my eyes. 'Do you want to come back to my flat?'

As soon as she closed the street door, we grabbed each other. It was less kissing, more wrestling – aggressive, rough and urgent. We stumbled up the stairs, unwilling to let go of each other, and she fumbled with the keys to unlock the door. We fell into the room and I half registered that it was empty and flooded with clean light. Then I guided her backwards and pushed her on to the single futon, pulled off her Converse sneakers and her leggings, and unzipped my own jeans.

At around three in the afternoon, Helen stood unsteadily and walked over to the little open-plan kitchen. I rolled on to my back and stretched. The little futon was narrow and we'd been entwined on it for several hours. I watched her as she sliced bread and made us cheese and salad sandwiches – a scraping of butter for her, a thick layer for me, no cucumber for her, extra tomato and a little sprinkling of chopped onion for me. She was still naked, and I could see the imprint of my fingers on the back of her thigh. Her body was different and yet the same. She had gained weight, but it sat beautifully on her, and her trim, athletic figure was now a bounteous hourglass. She was softer and curvier, but the smooth, firm texture of her skin was the same, the sound she made when she came was the same, and the delectable, sweet scent of her was as it had always been.

She put the sandwiches on a single plate, swept up the crumbs, tidied all the ingredients away, and then brought the plate and a bottle of water she'd fetched from the fridge back over to the futon. She pushed my leg aside and sat down, putting the plate between us.

'I only have one plate. Sorry. We'll have to share,' she said, biting into her sandwich.

'I don't mind sharing.' I propped myself up on one elbow and took a gigantic bite of my sandwich. 'Oh my God,' I said thickly, through the mouthful, 'that may be the best thing I have ever tasted.'

She grinned at me, and took another huge bite herself. I liked this version of Helen – she was earthy and sensual in a way that was new to me. Impeccably controlled Helen would never have walked around naked, made sandwiches and eaten them on the bed. If the sandwich hadn't been so utterly perfect, I'd have thought this was a completely different woman. She finished her sandwich, carelessly swept crumbs from the edge of the futon on to the floor and lay down, pulling me on top of her again.

After that time, I think I must have passed out from sheer exhaustion. I woke up a little while later. Helen had tidied away the plate (and swept up the crumbs on the floor, I noted). She was dressed again, in her leggings and T-shirt, sitting at her kitchen counter on a high barstool, writing something. I struggled into a sitting position.

'Everything okay?' I asked. I blinked around blearily, looking for my phone to check the time. She nodded but didn't say anything, just kept writing. I saw that she had picked up my clothes, discarded in a trail across the floor some hours before, and folded them into a neat pile beside the futon. My phone and keys rested on top. I grabbed my phone. 5.30. I saw there was a text message from Lara and I felt a pang of something. I knew it should have been guilt, but it felt more like irritation.

'Weathers good so we are having the barbecue,' she'd written. 'Not sure what time you'll be back but be great 2 see you.'

I knew I was being petty, but the missing apostrophe in 'weathers' and the '2' instead of 'to' got on my nerves. I must have frowned, because Helen said, 'Problem?'

'No,' I said, clicking out of my messages. 'Just something I have to sort out.' I reached for my clothes and began to dress. It seemed like the right thing to do. 'What are you writing?' I asked, pulling on my socks.

'Nothing,' she said. 'Just something I have to sort out.' She smiled at me teasingly as she echoed my words, and slipped the pages between the covers of her Filofax. She hopped off the barstool and came over to me. 'You'll need to get back,' she observed.

'Not immediately,' I said. 'We could have dinner.'

'What about the girls?' she asked. 'Who's looking after them?'

'A friend,' I said shortly. I expected her to ask which friend it was, and I knew I wouldn't be able to keep my temper if she did. She had no right to ask who was caring for the children she'd walked out on. She didn't ask.

Once I was dressed, I realized there was little point in staying in the flat. It was spartan in its appointments, to say the least.

Other than the futon and the barstool, there was almost no furniture. Helen wasn't lying when she said she had only one plate – she had only one of everything. I had a strong feeling that I was the first person other than her to have entered the space since she'd moved in.

'Shall we go out and get a bite to eat?' I said, going over and slipping an arm around her waist.

'Sure,' she said, leaning into me momentarily. That moment of closeness, the softness of her against my side, the tickle of her hair against my neck – it was more intimate than the sex we'd had that afternoon, more loving, and, if I dared to think it, more hopeful. I kissed the top of her head and went to the bathroom to use the loo and splash my face with water. I wished I had a smart shirt to put on, and some aftershave. I was taking my wife out to dinner, after all.

I opened the bathroom cabinet and with a pang saw the products Helen used, lined up neatly on the shelf. There was her usual moisturizer, body lotion, face-wash and brand of deodorant. She had a new make-up bag, with shades I assumed were better suited to her blonde colouring, and a couple of bottles of perfume. I sniffed them cautiously. I recognized neither of them. She'd clearly decided that Helen Day would smell different from Helen Cooper. But as I'd just experienced, the essence of her came through. She was still my Helen. There was little else in the cabinet – a packet of contraceptive pills (this didn't surprise me), and a single gold hoop earring, resting on the bottom shelf. She must have mislaid the other one. I closed the cabinet softly, careful not to make a sound, and went out into the main room.

We left the flat hand-in-hand and strolled down the road.

'What do you fancy eating?' I asked.

'Don't know,' she said. 'Up to you.'

'Well, what's good around here?'

'No idea. I haven't eaten out much around here. I can tell you what's likely to be on special at the Sainsbury's Local if you like.'

I imagined her coming home every night from SSA, making herself a meal for one, sitting alone in that empty flat. It made no sense. To have given up what she had, what we had. . . for this? I walked a little quicker, grasping her hand firmly.

'There was that sushi place we came to,' I said. 'That time we came down here with the girls. Do you remember?'

She nodded. We'd had a lovely family day out in Greenwich a couple of years before. At the time, the kids were obsessed with sushi and wanted to eat it whenever we went out. Helen had found a sushi bar, where we were given huge platters of beautifully made maki and nigiri, and the chef had taught Miranda and Marguerite to make their own hand rolls.

It was shameless, choosing somewhere we'd gone as a family. I wanted to remind her of what she'd lost. I recalled how the girls had scoffed their hand rolls, and I talked about how they still loved sushi, how we'd gone and done a sushi-making class together and Marguerite had eaten more than anyone else. Helen laughed easily and asked lots of questions about the girls.

'Is Marguerite cycling yet?'

'She sort of was, but we've gone backwards a bit lately,' I said ruefully. 'It was all going quite well, but now we're in the flat. . .'

'I guess it can't be easy, lugging bicycles up and down three flights of stairs,' she said, helping herself to another California roll.

'No,' I said, and took a deep drink of my beer.

It was the strangest evening. For long periods of time we chatted and laughed as we always had – finishing each other's sentences, communicating in the peculiar shorthand of a married couple.

'You know. . .' I began at one point, describing a mutual acquaintance.

'Oh God, yes,' Helen replied. 'Does he still have the. . .?'

'It's even bigger now!' I said, and we laughed.

It simultaneously filled me with joy and hope, and flooded me with black dread and anger.

On the one hand, we seemed to be back pretty much where we'd left off. On the other, there were the vast acres of damage done between us. How would we find our way back to each other? Every now and then the conversation would falter as these realizations hit us in waves, and after a while the waves got closer and closer together. It became clear that we were going to have to face the big issues. We couldn't continue to respond to the enormity of our situation with either small talk or sex. And along with that, I recognized that beer alone probably wasn't going to get me through the evening.

I offered to get a bottle of wine, but she declined. 'I've kind of given up drinking,' she said.

'Kind of?'

'Well, not kind of. I have given up. Completely.'

'Ah, well, I've clearly been having your share,' I said, defiantly waving to the waiter to get another beer. Helen looked at me steadily. She was never one to nag or sulk. If she didn't like something I was doing, she'd steadfastly ignore it, while setting a higher standard for herself. That was clearly the tactic she was adopting here, but this time I was having none of it.

'Life is, as you can imagine, a little bit crap,' I said, leaning back in my chair. 'The girls and I crammed into a tiny flat, no disposable income, a shit job. . .'

'I know that some of that is my fault,' she said calmly, looking me in the eye. 'Your responding to it by drinking yourself insensible every night is not my fault.'

'No,' I said. 'But you broke me, Hels. You broke me. I have spent every minute of the last few months trying to understand what

I did wrong. Why you did what you did. How you could just. . . walk out and leave. And sometimes drink is the only thing that can dull the pain.'

She nodded. 'I'm in no position to judge, and for what it's worth, I'm sorry. I never wanted to cause so much pain.'

'So why did you?'

'Why did I what?'

'Why did you go? Why did you go the way you did?'

'Because I had to,' she said simply. 'I wrote it all down. I wrote it in the letter.'

'Where is this letter? When can I read it?'

'I'll let you have it when you leave tonight,' she said, and I saw her glance down at her bag. She clearly had it with her. 'I don't want to be with you when you read it.'

'And after I've read it? Where does that leave us?'

'Where do you want it to leave us?' she asked, but she didn't raise her eyes from the tablecloth.

'Back where we were. In our home. Together. A family.'

She nodded but didn't say anything. I knew it wasn't a yes, but at least she didn't say no.

I wasn't hungry any more. I didn't even want my beer. I reached across the table and took her hand, her dear, smooth hand which fitted mine so well, and I rubbed the place on her third finger where her wedding rings used to rest. She squeezed my hand in return, clutching it hard, as if she needed me to hold her steady. I felt my eyes fill with tears.

'I love you so much, Helen.'

'I love you too.'

We sat like that for a long time, and then she spoke suddenly.

'What's your address?'

'What?'

'The flat. What's your new address?'

I told her. She nodded. Hope leapt in my heart. Why did she need the address? Was she thinking of coming to see us, to begin the process of coming back to the family? I smiled at her. She smiled back and then said gently, 'You should get back to the girls.'

'I know. I don't want to leave you.'

'Me neither. But we have to. Tomorrow is another day.'

She gave me her brightest, most heart-breaking smile, and I remembered the day she'd met me on the stairs at work and sat down to talk to me and smiled like that and I'd fallen in love with her.

I went to the counter to pay the bill. When I came back to the table, I saw Helen slip something into her bag.

'What was that?'

'Your letter.'

'Can I have it?'

'In a bit,' she said, standing. 'I'll walk you to the station,'

We walked to the station entwined like a pair of teenagers, our arms round each other's waists, stopping every now and then to kiss. I felt like my heart would burst. Just before we got to the station, she stopped and drew the envelope out of her bag. 'Can you promise to wait until you get home to read this?' she said.

I thought about having to go to Lara's and the conversation we needed to have. Could I wait until after all of that? 'No,' I said truthfully.

'I thought not,' said Helen, and in one swift motion she turned and dropped the envelope into a post box. I hadn't even noticed that we were standing beside one.

'What? What the fuck?'

'It's got a first class stamp on it, and your address,' she said calmly. 'You'll get it on Monday.'

I shook my head. 'You're mad.'

She silenced me with a kiss. It was the longest, sweetest, sexiest kiss I had ever experienced. It turned my bones to jelly and my brain to mush.

'Go home,' she said. 'I love you, Sam.' Then she turned, waved, and disappeared around the corner.

I went down into the station and caught the train in a haze of joy. What a day. What a day. It had been beyond my wildest dreams. We'd made love and talked, she'd told me she loved me. The time I had spent with her had dispelled my crushing anger, but I was under no illusions – we had a long way to go. I would feel angry again, and so would the girls. We'd also have to address the issues that had made Helen leave in the first place. I felt much better equipped to face them now I knew about her previous life with Lawrence. We could work as a team and she could seek professional help.

I could see that working had become vital to her, so we would have to factor that into our plans too. She wouldn't be able to stay at SSA – the commute to Stratford from north London would be punishing. But there was no reason why she shouldn't find a good role at a company closer to home, as long as the hours were flexible. And my hopes for another child would have to be shelved, for now at least. It would all be about compromise. And I wanted to compromise. I was happy to. Helen hadn't even given me the chance to enter the negotiations before.

I changed trains at Bank and rattled towards home, day-dreaming about our future, a future reframed in sunlight. With Helen earning as well, we'd definitely be able to get the house back. Our tenants' lease was up in a couple of months, and I could opt not to renew it. I thought of us all back around the table together, our beautiful home made clean and new again, and my eyes filled with tears.

Before any of that could happen, though, I needed to sort out my personal life, which had got a little complicated, to say the least. I should have gone with my instinct and broken up with Lara as soon as I first saw Helen. I'd been dishonest. And what had happened between us the other night on my sofa had been. . . unfortunate. When Helen came back, I'd have to come clean about Lara. And I'd do my best to avoid any out-of-town sexual mishaps. It was too risky. It wouldn't do to start our marriage again with any secrets between us.

I got off the Tube and checked my watch. It wasn't all that late – 10 p.m. The kids would definitely be asleep. A good time to talk to Lara. I set off to walk to her house, my pace fast and determined. Clear, unequivocal, polite. That's how it needed to be.

CHAPTER TWENTY-TWO

Lara

Getting four kids into bed was no mean feat, not least because Marguerite and Miranda regarded me with wary suspicion. They hadn't seen me at all for a week, and Miranda at least is quite grown-up enough to know that that wasn't accidental. They'd just been told that I would be picking them up from school and they were coming back to mine to stay. Sam had said he didn't know what time he would be back, so I half expected that he'd take a moment to ring and say goodnight to the girls, or at least text, but there was nothing. That put me on edge, and Marguerite's incessant whining before bedtime made me even tenser. Miranda was good and did what she was told, but at one point, as I brushed Jonah's teeth and yelled at Frances and Marguerite to get their pyjamas on, I caught Miranda looking at me with such resentment it stopped me in my tracks.

'It's not my fault your dad is such a flake,' I wanted to say. 'I'm not the bad guy here.'

Eventually, though, they were all in bed and asleep – in Miranda's case, restlessly so. She'd kicked off her covers within half an hour of going to bed, and every now and then let out a small moan, obviously in the grip of disturbing dreams. I went downstairs and slumped on the sofa. Mum was sitting doing the crossword, with the telly burbling on in the background. I was exhausted, and happy to sit in companionable silence. Mum had other plans, however.

'So Sam's kids are back here, are they?'

'Mmm,' I said. I thought that by keeping my answers monosyllabic, she might get the hint that I wasn't too keen to pursue this conversation.

'Where is he this evening? I forget,' she said innocently. She hadn't forgotten. I hadn't said.

'A work thing.'

'At nine o'clock on a Friday night?'

'He's been on a course. They went for drinks and dinner.'

She nodded, and I saw her write something into her crossword.

'I offered to have the kids,' I burst out. 'We're all going to have a nice weekend together.'

She looked up at me over her specs and said calmly, 'I'm not the person you have to persuade, Lara.'

That did it. I jumped off the sofa and stropped off to the kitchen like a sulky teenager. I sat at the table and fumed. I lived with my mum and we were arguing about my boyfriend. I was hiding in another room rather than having an adult conversation about things I knew to be true. I may as well have been sixteen. Only I was bloody thirty-five years old.

I knew what I should have said to her. I should have said that I had made my choice. That however badly he behaved sometimes,

Sam was a good man. He'd had a shocking time of it, and he and his daughters were in need of help and support. I could give that to them. It was a gamble that I believed would pay off for me and my children, in the long run. So this was my choice and could she please respect it. That's what I should have said. That's what I would say. I resolved to go back into the living room and say it. Just as soon as I could get the words out with some real conviction. In the meantime, I continued to sit at the kitchen table and stare at my hands, which looked thin, bony and surprisingly old on the wrinkled tablecloth.

I was saved from having to lay out my manifesto by a knock on the door. Sam, home at last, I thought, and I jumped up with relief to let him in. Maybe he'd swoop in with flowers and apologies, win over my mum and convince me that I'd made the right decision to stick with him.

As soon as I opened the door, I could see that this wasn't going to happen. He wasn't holding flowers. His clothes were crumpled and his hair was all over the place. He looked flushed and agitated. Not drunk – well, probably a bit drunk, but that wasn't what was firing him up. There was something else. Something big and cataclysmic. I was tempted to shut the door in his face and never hear what blow he'd come to deliver. But then what? What would I do? Keep his kids forever?

'Lara,' he said, and took a breath. Whatever he had come to say, he clearly intended to blurt it out on the doorstep, where the rest of the street could listen in.

'You'd better come inside,' I said quickly, and then remembered my mum in the living room, and all the children upstairs. 'Come into the kitchen,' I said. We can go through into the back garden.'

As we passed the living room door, I sang out, 'Sam's here, Mum!' so he would know she was there.

'Hi,' Sam called to her, and I was surprised at how calm and normal he sounded.

I opened the kitchen door so that the light would spill out on to the patio beyond. It's nothing like the beautiful, wide patio at Sam and Helen's old house, just a few square feet of cracked paving, with weeds poking up between the stones, and a set of grubby white plastic patio furniture. It's just a place to be outside, for those few short months of the year when we can actually use our garden. The lawn is long, but it was littered with Jonah's toys, and Frances' bike lay tipped on its side. It wasn't the most glamorous of spots, but it was as much privacy as we were going to get.

The delay had somewhat taken the wind out of Sam's sails, and he stood awkwardly, as if he couldn't decide how best to proceed. I chose a chair and sat down, then looked up at him expectantly. Eventually, he too drew up a chair and sat, resting his elbows on his knees and leaning forward. I don't know what I expected him to say. That he wanted to end it? That he'd lost his job? I didn't anticipate what he came out with though.

'I've spent the day with Helen.'

'What?' I said stupidly.

'Helen. I found her.'

'When?'

'A week or so ago.'

'A week?' I said incredulously. 'And you didn't tell me?'

'I didn't tell anyone. The girls don't know, or my parents.'

'Where. . .? What. . .? How?' Somehow, I was only capable of blurting out single words. I had so many questions, I didn't know where to begin. He'd said he'd found her. Did that mean he'd been looking for her? When?

I didn't need to interrogate him. The words began to spill out of him.

'I saw her on the Tube, you see, at Canary Wharf, and then I searched online and found where she worked. Then I followed her home. Then we talked, and we agreed to spend today together, and—'

'Hang on,' I interrupted. 'You agreed when?'

'What?'

'When did you agree to spend the day together?'

'I don't know. . .' he said evasively. But I knew I had him.

'You do know. When was it? When did you agree to meet up?'

'Wednesday, maybe?' he said cautiously.

'So before Wednesday evening, when I came to your flat and we had sex on the sofa?'

'I. . .'

'You fucked me, knowing you were planning to see Helen thirty-six hours later?'

He raised his hand. At first I thought he was trying to placate me, but then I realized he was shushing me. My voice had started to get loud. As more pieces began to fall into place, it became clear that I wasn't going to get any quieter.

'So you fucked me on the sofa and then palmed your kids off on me today so you could go off and see Helen in secret? Did you fuck her too?'

He didn't answer, but he didn't even have the grace to deny it.

'Jesus Christ,' I said, and I stalked off down the garden. I couldn't even bring myself to look at him.

'Lara, I'm sorry,' he said pleadingly. 'This isn't how I wanted things to be. But Helen is my wife. . .'

'She was your wife on Wednesday too,' I spat. 'Didn't stop you then, or at any time in the last few months. . .'

'Lara, you came on to me, to be fair. . . And anyway, I bet you put out for Marc the other day, didn't you? I saw you together. You didn't bother to tell me he was in town, did you?'

'Fucking hell!' I exploded. I was way past caring if the neighbours could hear. 'I didn't tell you about Marc because I didn't want to upset you, or upset Frances any more. She was in bits after he left. And anyway, absolutely nothing happened between us!' This was true, but my own protestations sounded hollow. I couldn't believe he was throwing this back on me. I was ready to scream.

I heard a sharp intake of breath and a small, unnatural cry. Miranda was standing in the kitchen doorway. She looked slight, clad in pink pyjamas which had got too short for her, and her long feet and ankles stuck out, skinny, pale and vulnerable. She was looking at her dad, her eyes big in her pale face. Sam followed the direction of my gaze and turned, seeing Miranda.

'Sweetie, it's fine,' he began. 'We were having a discussion. . .' He took a step towards her. She cried out, a mixture of disgust and misery, burst into tears and fled away from him. We heard her bare feet thumping up the stairs, then the door to Frances' room opened and banged shut with a thud.

Through the open kitchen door, I could see my mum silhouetted. She had come tentatively into the room, and she was hovering, obviously trying to decide if she should intervene. What a mess.

'Go and call a cab,' I said to him coldly. 'I'll pack up the girls' stuff. Take them home, and don't come back here. Ever.'

Miranda

Our lives are disgusting. Everything about the way we live is disgusting. We used to be the best family in the school, and now we're the family where people have screaming fights in the garden for everyone to hear, like in *EastEnders*, and my dad is always drunk and we live in squalor. People pity us and I can't bear it. I hate my dad so much. I hate him. I want to go back in time to before Helen ran away. I want my life back.

Lara kicked us out. She actually kicked us out on to the street in the middle of the night. After I came downstairs and heard the screaming, I ran back upstairs and hid in Frances' bottom bunk. I prayed they'd leave me alone. But then Lara came upstairs. I thought she was coming to check I was all right, but she put on the hallway light and opened Frances' door, then she picked up my bag and started packing my things into it. She did the same with Marguerite's stuff. She was about to carry the bags downstairs, and she turned around and said, 'I know you're awake, Miranda. Your dad's calling a taxi. Go downstairs and wait with him. I'll bring Marguerite down.' I could hear she was trying to be kind and gentle with me, but she was obviously furious.

I crept out of the bed and carefully smoothed the duvet into place and straightened the pillow. I stood on tiptoe to look at Frances in the top bunk. She was lying still, with her eyes closed. But I think she was pretending to be asleep. No one could have slept through the racket the adults had made.

Except Marguerite, it turned out. I went downstairs and stood in the hallway. Dad was in the living room, talking to the taxi company on the phone. Lara came downstairs carrying Marguerite in her arms like a baby. Marguerite's head was lolling back and her eyes were tight shut. Lara went into the living room, and I saw her put Marguerite on the sofa, then she went into the kitchen and slammed the door behind her. I stood in the doorway and looked at my dad. He'd finished his phone call and was standing looking down at his phone. The weirdest thing was, he didn't look upset. It looked like he and Lara had just broken up, but he looked absolutely fine – happy even.

The taxi took forever to come, and when it pulled up outside, Dad carried me out (I was still barefoot) and put me on the back seat, then ran in to get first our bags and then Marguerite. It was a minicab, an ordinary car, and Dad didn't even strap me in. He sat with Marguerite still asleep on his lap and gave the driver our address. Helen would never, ever have let us go in a car not strapped in, or not in car seats when we were little. It was like Dad didn't care about us at all. When the car started, Marguerite woke up. I don't know why, of all the things that had happened, that was what woke her, but she woke up then and started to cry. I didn't blame her. Dad kept patting her back and saying, 'Shhh, sweetie, it's okay. Everything's going to be okay.' And he was smiling. Smiling! I hate him.

I think he actually has gone mad, because he spent the whole weekend cleaning the flat again. He went to the supermarket and hired one of those carpet-cleaning machines, and he tidied and scrubbed everything in sight. He kept checking his phone and looking out of the window into the street. I don't know why. I saw what Lara was like. I'm 100 per cent certain she isn't going to forgive him for whatever he's done. He didn't seem sad or upset though. In fact, the opposite. He had this mad, happy energy and he kept grabbing Marguerite and kissing her and hugging her. He tried it once or twice with me, but I pushed him away hard. He had our uniforms all clean and ironed by Sunday afternoon, which was a first, and he even polished our school shoes.

He got us to school super-early on Monday morning, and that was a relief, because there was no chance of us bumping into Lara. Frances ignored me in class. Not rudely, she just pretended she couldn't see me. She can be cold when she wants to. I remember when she wanted to be my friend, because everyone did, and I thought she was too boring. Now she thinks she's too good for me. It kind of helped me to get through the day, because I stayed furious with her, and it meant I didn't worry about Dad.

He came to pick us up at after-school club super-early, and Marguerite was annoyed because she'd been playing with one of her lame little friends and she didn't want to go, but he practically dragged us out of there and hurried us home. He ran up the stairs and flung the door open. The post was all on the floor, where it had been pushed through the letterbox, and he grabbed it and went through the letters like a mad man. He found the one he was looking for – a big fat white envelope that looked like it had lots of pages in it. He dropped all the others on the floor and went into his bedroom and shut the door, leaving Marguerite and me in the hallway, with the front door wide open. I shut the door and tidied away our bags and shoes and the rest of the post, and took Marguerite into the kitchen to give her some juice and a biscuit. We went into the living room, and I'd just turned on the TV when Dad came bursting out of the bedroom. He looked terrible. I thought – he's sick. He's going to have a heart attack.

'Come on, girls!' he shouted. 'We have to go now. NOW!'

He was so scary that Marguerite and I ran to the hallway and put on our shoes. I thought – he has to get to the hospital or he's going to die. He rushed us out of the flat and down the stairs and bundled us into the car. As he pulled out of the parking place, he was dialling on his phone.

'Daddy, you shouldn't use your phone when you're driving!' said Marguerite, alarmed, but he ignored her. Whoever he phoned answered.

'Mrs Goode?' asked Dad. 'Mrs Goode, it's Sam Cooper, who used to live next door. Yes, I'm fine. Listen, Mrs Goode, I have an emergency. I can't explain, but I need to ask you a huge favour. Can you look after my girls for a few hours? Please, Mrs Goode, I haven't got anyone else to ask.'

I don't know what she said, but I assume it was yes, because Dad drove too fast down the road and then turned into our old road, the road where our house is. He pulled up, not even properly close to the pavement, and hurried me and Marguerite out of the back of the car. He dragged us up the path of the house next door to ours, where the old lady lives. She opened the door as he got there.

'Thank you,' he said. 'I don't have time to explain, but this is life or death.' And then he shoved us through the door. He didn't even say goodbye.

Mrs Goode put a hand on each of our shoulders, and we saw Dad go back towards the car, hesitate for a second and then run off down the road towards the station. And, surprise, surprise, Marguerite began to cry.

Helen

Luckily, Bruce Chertsey was the kind of person who had his work email on his phone and kept a constant eye on it, so when Helen sent him a message first thing on Saturday morning, he got back to her within the hour. They corresponded back and forth over the weekend, and she presented herself at the offices of QVA at nine on Monday morning. She waited anxiously in the reception area, and at a quarter past, Bruce strolled in, carrying two Caffè Nero takeaway cups and with his sunglasses nestled in the abundant curls on the top of his head. He gestured with his head for Helen to follow him, and went through to the boardroom. As she came into the room, he handed her one of the cups. 'Cappuccino okay?' he said by way of greeting. She nodded and they sat down.

'We're taking a gamble on you, that's for sure,' he said, without preamble.

'I appreciate that, and I won't let you down,' said Helen.

'And you're available immediately?'

'I am, but officially I'm on gardening leave from SSA. . .'

There was a telephone on the conference table and Bruce pulled it towards himself, without taking his eyes off Helen.

He picked it up, hit 0 and said, 'Gaynor, get me Simon Stanley at SSA.'

A few seconds later, the phone rang once and Bruce picked it up. 'Simon,' he said, with easy camaraderie, 'how are you, you bald bastard?' He listened for the reply, which Helen assumed included a few choice but friendly insults because Bruce had poached her from him. Then Bruce said, 'Listen, you've put our lovely Helen on gardening leave, is that right?'

Simon replied in the affirmative.

'What if we pay you the equivalent of her notice pay right now, and you promise not to sue her for breach of contract? I need her for something, and I need her now. Nothing in your field, so it's not a direct competition thing.'

Simon, to his credit, did his best to haggle and negotiate, but Bruce's bluff, charming manner hid a core of steel. Simon managed to argue for a slightly higher compensation payment, but in the end agreed to release Helen from her contract immediately. Bruce signed off with a few more posh-boy insults, and hung up.

'Jaego's in his office. He's got the contract all drawn up. Sign now, and we're good to go.'

Helen nodded. 'Thank you,' she said.

'Don't disappoint me, Helen. I'm going to need you to hit the ground running and make this thing work. I'll make sure you have all the briefing notes you need, and we'll set you up with a company credit card that you can take with you before you go.'

They shook hands, and Helen went to see Jaego in his office next door. Forty-five minutes later, she stepped out on to the pavement. There was a light, cold breeze, which ruffled her hair and made her draw in a sharp breath. She had an enormous amount to achieve today, and very little time.

CHAPTER TWENTY-THREE

Helen

My darling Sam,

Do you remember at our wedding, when you made your speech, you told the story of when you fell in love with me? You began to speak, with all the usual raucous 'how the hell can we believe you' chanting from Tim and your mates, but as you talked about meeting me on the stairs and how I smiled at you, everyone went quiet and then erupted in a collective 'Awwww'. It was beautiful.

It was my job on that day to sit beside you and look demure and mute, and blush when you complimented me, and laugh when you said 'my wife and I' for the first time, and I did all of that. Nobody, including you, has ever asked to hear the story of when I first fell in love with you. So I thought I would begin this letter by telling you.

A few months after we started dating, I was offered a training course in Edinburgh. You probably don't remember it, because it wasn't a huge deal. Just a week in Edinburgh, staying in a hotel and doing intensive work on the new phenomenon that was social media. Except to me it was a huge deal, and not only because I'd only ever been to two cities in my life – Brisbane and London.

You see, I was married before, and the relationship was. . . not good. His name was Lawrence. We got together when we were still at school, and he proposed at my graduation dinner. I thought he was the love of my life, and it wasn't until I was much older that I realized I believed that because he had always told me it was true.

He was always jealous and possessive; when I was sixteen, that was flattering and exciting, but as we got older, he became more obsessive. He wouldn't let me do anything without him – he used to follow me around and phone me ten times a day when we were apart.

Then, when I was at university, I was offered the chance to go away and do some work experience in Sydney. It was a great opportunity – they only gave it to the top students on the course, and it almost always led to improved prospects and a job after graduation, or at the very least a great addition to your CV. I was so excited. I had such ambitious plans for my career. I'd made a wish-list of all the things I wanted to do: work in Sydney, win an award, work in at least two other countries and then launch my own agency. It looked like my first step was there for the taking.

But Lawrence couldn't let it happen. I think he knew that if I went, I wouldn't come back, or at least I would ultimately outgrow him and move away. So he bullied and begged and threatened me. He told me that the only reason I'd been offered it was because my lecturer wanted to sleep with me, that I wasn't all that talented, that I'd fall apart if I went to stay nine hundred kilometres away from him. He browbeat me until I was exhausted, and in the end I didn't fill in the application forms and the opportunity went away. And at that moment a door closed, and my world got a little bit darker.

That may seem like a strange analogy, but let me explain. When I was a little girl, my mum and dad were the most positive and encouraging people in the world. They used to tell my sister Judy and me that we could do anything and be anything we wanted. My dad used to say, 'Life is like a long, light corridor. When you're born, all the doors are open, and there's lots of light flooding the corridor, in all different colours. As you go down the corridor, if you're not careful, things can happen that close the doors one by one. The corridor gets dark, and you have fewer and fewer doors that you can go through. Those doors are all doors of opportunity. So keep them all open, and if a chance comes to go through one, say yes.

Go through it. You might choose to come straight back out again, but go.'

Lawrence was a door shutter. He shut doors, locked them and then kept all the keys. He kept doing it until I was all alone, in a pitch-dark corridor. Then something terrible happened, and he went to jail, and I was granted the tiniest chink of light.

I fled to London, and I came to live in Willesden Green and worked at Superhero Inc., where I met you.

You probably don't know this, but I was terrified, all the time. I did my best to work hard and be nice to everyone, but I was totally faking it. It was the first time I had lived way from home, and the first time I had left Brisbane, let alone Australia. I didn't know what to do or how to act. So I fell back on being the 'good girl.' My parents taught me obedience as a child, and I learned the lesson well. I learned to be biddable and helpful and nice, because then people would like me. I was always polite, well behaved, neatly dressed, with beautiful handwriting and nice manners. A girl who got all As and was praised for her excellent cross-country running times and her citizenship and her lovely sponge cake and her smooth hair.

So I was good when I moved to London, and that helped me get by. People liked me and I did well at work, and my housemates enjoyed the fact that I cleaned and cooked nice meals for them all.

I was back in a corridor of light – there were quite a lot of doors open that hadn't been opened before – and

I was beginning to move along it, tentatively but happily.

And then along you came, and you made my heart ache, with your grief and your sweet little girls and your handsome, handsome face. I liked you so much, but I remember the exact moment I knew I loved you.

Wow. . . I've written a great big loop, and I'm back to the point I was making at the beginning of this letter. The training course in Edinburgh. It was perfect for me – just the qualification I needed to take me a notch up the career ladder. But when the email from my manager, Sinead, landed in my inbox, my heart sank, and I felt a door slam and the light dim a little. How could I go? It fell in a week when we'd planned to go and see a play, and have dinner with your mum and dad for the first time. There was no way you'd let me go. I'd have to tell my manager I couldn't do it, make an excuse and swallow the disappointment. I put off sending the email and made myself busy with another task.

And then, an hour or so later, you came and perched on the edge of my desk and folded your arms.

'I like shortbread,' you said.

'Pardon?'

'I like shortbread, but don't buy me a tartan anything. So tacky.'

'What?'

'Sinead told me she's sending you on the social media course. It sounds brilliant. Just don't bring me a

teddy bear in a kilt, okay? Although Marguerite might like one.'

'But I can't go. . .' I stuttered. 'Your mum and dad, and the tickets for the play. . .'

'Don't be crazy!' You laughed. 'We can go and see my mum and dad the following week, and I haven't booked yet for the play. It's the most brilliant opportunity, and I'm so proud of you for getting this chance.'

And you leaned forward and kissed me lightly on the lips, which was a shock, because we hadn't told anyone at work that we were seeing each other yet. Then you winked at me, and winked at Emma Jane, who sat next to me (remember her, the one we used to call the Dementor?), and you went back to your desk.

I sat there, dazed. Blinded by the light. And all of a sudden, I realized that there was another kind of relationship – the kind where the person you are with doesn't close doors, they open them. They open them and push you through, or they take your hand and go through the doors with you. And I thought, Sam is that opener of doors. And I love him.

And of course I didn't just fall in love with you. I was already in love with Miranda and Marguerite. Miranda, with her straight back and serious air, at three, already such a perfectionist. I saw so much of myself in her. And Marguerite, who would toddle up to me and curl up in my arms like a soft little animal, utterly trusting. I'd had very little experience of children before – none of my own, and no nieces or nephews. Lawrence wouldn't allow me to have friends, so I never got to know the children of friends either. I wasn't maternal, by which I mean I had never wanted any of my own, but I fell in love with your daughters in a way I never believed possible.

And so now I was in love with all three of you, and I wanted our lives together to be perfect. I know it'll come as no surprise to you, Sam, but I'm a perfectionist. When I came into your lives, you were messy with grief, living with your parents and struggling to get by financially, and there were so many opportunities for me to help, to bring order to your lives.

I could help financially first; with my income, we were able to get our own place. But then you got the promotion, and I lost my job. I was devastated. I wanted to look for another, but you managed to persuade me it was best for all of us if I stayed home as you'd be away so much. It wouldn't have been my choice at all, but that was how the chips had fallen, so I made the best of it. I really did. I did my absolute best, looking after the girls. I had this picture in my head of how families should be, and I went all out to make it happen – a beautiful home, lovely meals and the same person waiting at the school gate every day.

But I couldn't shake the feeling that, somehow, my redundancy hadn't been fair. I'd thought I was doing so well, and I couldn't understand why, of everyone in our department, it was me who got the push. It wasn't until two or three years later, at the Christmas party, that Chris's PA, Millie, got pissed and told me I was the best marketing manager they'd ever had. 'Off the charts!' she slurred. 'Best ideas, best results. The best!'

'So why did they let me go?' I asked.

She winked and said, 'Old boys' club. Chris and Sam did a deal, didn't they?'

I got her another glass of wine, and she told me you'd persuaded Chris to let me go so I could look after the girls and you could have your promotion. She threw up after that, and I held her hair back in the ladies'. Deep down, I'd probably always known you'd done something like that.

I knew then that I needed some kind of self-protection plan. But it was so difficult, and I got increasingly worried. I tried to stay employable. I kept going on those courses, tried to keep up to date with marketing trends and innovations. But every course I did, the other people got younger, and I felt more and more out of touch. I turned thirty, then thirty-one, but the people I studied with were still so young and ambitious. Assuming I didn't go back into full-time work while the girls were still at school, I'd be forty-five when I finally got back into the workplace. And in our field, full of hardworking young things, I might as well be a hundred. I'd be useless.

Then you started piling on the pressure to have a baby of our own. I knew I didn't want to, but my instinct was to please you. I nearly gave in. So nearly. But I knew that if I did, I'd be slamming the last door shut forever.

I knew what you'd say – what most people would say. That I wouldn't be closing the doors of opportunity; that I'd be going through a door and entering a whole other world of possibility, of family and child-rearing, and what a noble and worthwhile pursuit that was. But the point was, it wasn't my possibility. I had never, ever wanted to have a baby of my own. It wasn't my door to go through. It was yours. In my eagerness to please you and the world, to be the good girl, I'd almost lost sight of myself.

I think that's what happens to the good girls. They devote their lifetime to pleasing others, and they never stop to think about what pleases them. What they want. They create a persona that perfectly fulfils a role, and they never pause to say, 'What do I want? Who do I want to be? How do I want to look? What work do I want to do? How do I want to have sex? What lights the fire in MY heart?' I was staring down a long, dark corridor, which led towards a future I would never have chosen for myself.

I tried to talk to you about it, but you probably don't remember. I tentatively mentioned that I was worried about my career possibilities passing me by. I said that it concerned me that I'd never really travelled.

You said that I didn't need to work, that we were doing brilliantly financially. You said we could travel together when the girls were grown up; you joked and said, 'We'll be too old for backpacking. We'll have to be those old farts who go on cruises.' I was a good girl, of course, so I didn't argue or push the point. But the sense that I was trapped began to overwhelm me.

And then, of course, I became aware of your extra-curricular love life. I suppose you thought you were so cautious, but you left all the obvious clues – receipts in your pockets, the stench of perfume on your shirts, even a naked photo on your phone. All so obvious. So tacky. So careless. I knew if I confronted you, you'd cry and turn your beautiful blue eyes on me and tell me it meant nothing, and you'd be telling the truth. And in fact it was the sheer meaninglessness of it that made it so insulting. That you'd risk everything for a shag.

Then, one day, I dropped the girls at school and went for a long run. I ended up far from home, in Highgate. I paused to catch my breath and buy a bottle of water, and I happened to glance in the window of an estate agent's office. Alongside the ads for million-pound houses, there were pictures of apartments – white walls, blonde-wood floors. Empty. Clean. Flooded with light from their big picture windows. They were the most beautiful places I'd ever seen. I imagined getting my keys for a place like that, walking through the door with just a bag. Flinging all the doors of possibility open and starting again.

It was a game at first, making my plans to disappear. I fantasized about how I might do it. I thought about how we leave an electronic trail wherever we go, so I started to think about how I could avoid doing that. I'd need cash, as I wouldn't be able to use a card. I'd need a new passport and a new identity. I'd need separate bank accounts and a new electronic profile.

It was purely theoretical until that night in the hotel. That was the first time I realized how serious you were about us having a baby and how much pressure you were willing to exert to make it happen. It wasn't up for negotiation at all, was it? I knew if I stayed, sooner or later you would make me do it. And that was the point where my plans got real.

I started saving cash, bit by bit, until I had enough to buy a small tablet computer and a pay-as-you go mobile with an unregistered SIM. I started a new email account in the name of Helen Day. I got a post-office box at that mailbox rental place on the high street. I applied to change my name to Helen Day by deed poll, and once I had those documents, I was able to open a bank account in my new name. I set up a LinkedIn page and started applying for jobs. It took a while, but eventually I got the job with SSA. I told them I needed a month before I could start. I went down to Greenwich, and I found my flat. I told the landlord I was getting divorced. With my existing credit profile as Helen Cooper, I passed all the checks, but he was happy to give me the lease in my new name. I ordered everything I would need online, and on that day in May, I walked away from our life and into my new one.

I moved into the flat of my dreams, an empty white box. It was deliberately like that, and it still is. Because this is my third go at starting my life, and I can't get it wrong again. Every choice I make needs to be deliberate. Every career move, every item I buy, every opportunity I accept needs to be because it's what I truly want, not because someone else tells me it's the right thing. Not because I'm doing it for the greater good, or to please someone.

I've gone back to the dreams I had as a teenager – carefully planned career moves, then my own company, and lots and lots of travel. At the moment they're all I have, but I'm refining those goals all the time.

I am so sorry, Sam. It may not seem like it, but I do love you. I love you and I see you for who you are. You are not an opener of doors. You're as much a closer as Lawrence was. You're just stealthier, and you're selfish. You close other people's doors to open your own, and I couldn't let that happen to me anymore.

So I left to save my own life. It hasn't been easy. I have missed you and the girls every minute of every day. I still get twitchy at six o'clock every evening, worrying about whether the girls are getting a proper dinner. I worry about who does Miranda's hair for dance, and whether Marguerite has stopped saying 'wabbit'. I miss them so much, and I wish I could have seen Miranda's birthday disco and the Harry Potter cake.

I know you will never be able to forgive me, but over time, I hope you might be able to understand.

You know what I am, Sam, I'm all or nothing. And I can't be all, so I have to be nothing.

All my love,

Helen

Lara

I was mostly okay. I had moments of pure fury where I wanted to throw things (and I did – I threw all of Sam's clothes and bits and pieces into a bin bag and chucked them away). I shed some tears, in the privacy of my room; not for Sam, but for the fool I'd been. I'd always kept my guard up after Marc, but Sam had completely taken me in. I'd even done my best to fight for him, like the gullible idiot I was. I apologized to Mum and Frances for the trauma of Friday night, and I was sorry that Miranda and Marguerite were upset, but mostly I felt a sense of relief. I knew where I stood, and we could pick ourselves up and get on with our lives again.

I didn't see him at school on Monday morning, which was a relief, and I knew the girls would be at after-school club so there was no risk of seeing him in the afternoon either. I would see him at some point, obviously, but I'd cross that bridge when I came to it. On the whole, though, I was definitely okay. It could have been so much worse.

On Monday evening at about six, after I'd given the kids their tea and while I was getting ready to go to work, the doorbell rang. My heart sank, which must be a sign that I was really okay. 'Please don't be Sam, coming to grovel,' I thought. And it wasn't.

It was Tim, standing on the doorstep, grinning nervously. 'Sorry,' he said, 'I know it didn't work out too well the last time I tried this, but I'm looking for Sam. He's not at home.'

'Well, he's not here,' I said. 'Try Helen's place.'

'What?' Tim's eyes widened with shock.

'Helen. Sam found her, and it's apparently all going to be okay and they'll be playing happy families in no time.' I tried not to sound too bitter.

'What?' Tim repeated, and I swear I saw him sway on his feet.

'That's all I know. Sorry. He found her and they're getting back together. Sorry. I know it must come as a shock—'

'I have to go,' he blurted, and he turned towards his car.

'Tim. . . wait!' I said. 'You look freaked out. Don't you want to sit down for a moment?'

'No,' he said, and when he looked back at me, his eyes were wild with panic. 'I have to go now. Sorry.' And he sprinted down the path, jumped into his car and roared off down the road.

Sam

When I started reading, I thought it was a love letter – a promise of her return. When I reached the end, I knew it was a goodbye. I sat on the edge of my bed, staring at the closely printed pages. But I know where she is, I thought. I can go and see her and persuade her that she's wrong. That she's got me wrong. That she can have her dreams and still be with me. I can—

And then I remembered that she'd posted the letter, instead of giving it to me. Why had she done that? To buy herself time. She'd given herself three days. It was possible I was already too late. But I had to try. I stuffed the letter in my pocket and went and grabbed the girls. Taking them to Mrs Goode's was an act of sheer desperation. There wasn't anyone else I could leave them with. Not Lara, obviously, and it would have taken too long to take them to my mum and dad's place.

Initially I thought I would drive, but once I'd dropped the girls off I realized that trying to cross London from the north-west to the south-east in rush hour could take hours. Coming back from Helen's on the train on Friday evening had taken just under an hour. It was interminable, but the safest option. I left my car where it was and ran to the station.

As we rattled along from stop to stop, my skin crawled with irritation. The inaction was killing me. I took out the letter and began to go through it again. In my first feverish reading, I had missed so much. As I went through it more slowly, something leapt out at me and made me pause.

It was right at the end, where she talked about missing us. She mentioned the disco and the Harry Potter cake. I'd never told her about that – mainly, I suppose, because of the link to Lara. So how had she known about it? And then I remembered something she'd said on Friday night, at dinner, about my carrying bicycles up three flights of stairs. It had niggled at me, but I couldn't work out why. Now I understood. I'd given her our address after we'd had that conversation. I had told her we had a flat, but not where. How had she known we lived on the third floor?

As I changed trains at Bank and started on the long journey to Greenwich, a last, heart-crushing thought occurred to me. The earring in her bathroom cabinet. Helen's ears weren't pierced. How arrogant I'd been to imagine that I was the only person who had been inside her flat.

I paced up and down the train carriage like a demented person for the last few stops, and practically wrenched the doors open at Greenwich. I hit the platform running, and I didn't stop till I got to Helen's door. I pounded my fist on the buzzer, even though I was almost certain it was hopeless.

'Helen!' I shouted. 'Helen!'

The door to the shop next door opened, and a man stepped out. He had long grey hair and little round glasses.

'I'm sorry for the noise,' I said. 'I'm looking for my wife.'

'Are you Sam?' he said, and I stared at him, open-mouthed. 'I'm Brian, Helen's landlord.'

'Where is she?'

'She's gone, I'm afraid. But she asked me to let you upstairs. She said she left some things there for you.'

He reached past me and unlocked the street door, then handed me the bunch of keys. 'Just drop them in on your way down,' he said. 'I was sorry to see her go. She's been a lovely tenant.'

I took the stairs two at a time, and let myself in to Helen's flat. It was hard at first to see whether she was gone or not. There'd been so little in the flat to start off with. The futon was still there, although the bedclothes had been stripped. And then I saw that there was a row of cardboard boxes in the kitchenette, neatly labelled 'Charity shop' in Helen's handwriting. I lifted the lid on one; it had all of Helen's kitchen equipment in it. The wardrobe was empty of her clothes.

She had left a small selection of objects on the kitchen counter, with a Post-it affixed in front of them. 'Sam.' There was a box, which contained her wedding rings and the watch with the brown leather strap that I'd given her for her last birthday. And there was her little tablet computer and mobile phone. I tapped the power button and the tablet lit up. It had very little on it – she'd wiped her email account, her web history and any documents – other than one folder of photos on the desktop. I opened it.

There was a picture of Miranda at my parents' house, on her birthday weekend. Another of Marguerite, wobbling along on her bike. One of me, on the sofa in my flat, a beer in my hand. Miranda turning cartwheels on a beach, hair flying around her head like a halo. So many pictures.

The door opened, and the landlord put his head around it.

I looked up. 'Where did she go?' I said brokenly.

'Canada. For work. That's all I know. I'm sorry.' He hesitated. 'There's, er. . . someone else here.'

I nodded. 'I know. Let him in.'

Brian stepped aside, and Tim walked into the room. Brian withdrew, closing the door behind him. Tim looked pale and out of breath.

'When?' I said.

'A few months after she left. She contacted me by email first. She begged me not to tell you. She was so desperate for news of the girls, and of you. She needed to know you were okay.'

'And you listened to her?'

'She told me she was definitely never coming back, and that if you knew, it would torture you. And then you started seeing Lara. . .'

I shook my head and looked down at the pictures on the screen.

'Why? You didn't even like her. She didn't like you.' But even as I said that, I knew it wasn't strictly true. It was quite possible that Tim keeping his distance from Helen may have had another cause.

'I'm sorry, Sam.'

'It was Helen. The unrequited love you talked about. Giving love without expecting anything in return. It was Helen. But you did expect something. Did you get it?' I reached into the box where Helen's rings and watch lay and lifted out the single gold earring. 'You did, didn't you?'

'No,' said Tim. 'Maybe you would have done something like that, but I wouldn't, and neither would Helen. The last thing she needed in her life was another man.'

'Well, she's gone now. For good. I hope you're happy,' I said viciously.

Tim didn't say anything. He stood and watched me, his face full of an inexpressible sadness. Behind him, through the window, I saw the sun sink below the rooftops, staining the clouds a deep red.

Miranda

Mrs Goode made us a tea of fish fingers and salad. Marguerite loves fish fingers, so she didn't cry or whine, even though Dad had just dumped us on some strange woman we hardly remembered. Mrs Goode wasn't too fussed about table manners. She didn't even seem to mind when Marguerite picked up her fish finger in her hand and dipped it in a great puddle of ketchup. After we'd eaten, Mrs Goode said we could go outside while she tidied up, and then we'd watch something on the telly.

We both wandered out into the back garden. Marguerite started picking daisies out of the lawn. I went over to the fence. There was a pile of bricks and a few old ceramic plant pots. I stacked up the bricks and put a few of the plant pots upside down on top.

'Come here,' I called to Marguerite, and together we climbed up to peer over the fence into our old garden.

The grass was long and shaggy, and there were quite a few dandelions in it. There was no one outside and the patio doors were closed. It looked different. There were new cushions on the chairs, and a brightly coloured cloth on the table. From where I was balanced, I could reach out a hand to touch a branch of the tree we used to climb in our garden, so we could look into Mrs Goode's house. But I couldn't go in. It was like looking into an enchanted garden, but I didn't know the words of the spell that would allow me to enter.

CHAPTER TWENTY-FOUR

SIX MONTHS LATER

Sam

'What do you reckon? Salad or vegetables?' I asked.

'Salad,' said Miranda 'I've got lots of cress in the greenhouse, and we've got nice tomatoes. Granny likes those.'

'What about potatoes?'

'Potato salad!' suggested Marguerite.

'Good call,' I said, and went to put on a saucepan of water to boil.

'Did you light the barbecue yet, Dad?' Miranda asked, looking at the clock.

'I have, just waiting for it to cool down. We want to start cooking around the time they arrive.'

'Will they be able to find our house?' asked Marguerite.

'I talked Grandpa through the directions and stayed on the phone with him while he put the postcode into his satnav. They'll be fine.'

This was to be their first visit to our cottage, and the girls were understandably nervous. So was I, but I was sure they would love it. It's a sprawling, single-storey building in a tiny village in Warwickshire, and although it looks like nothing from the front, the back is all glass and opens on to a rolling lawn that leads down to the banks of the Avon.

I sold the London house; the Iranian family decided they liked the city and wanted to stay where they were. We managed to do a deal without involving an estate agent, which gave me sufficient equity to put down a deposit on this place and leave myself with much smaller mortgage payments. There's a lovely school in the village, and a dance academy for Miranda, as well as stables where Marguerite has started riding lessons, which she loves.

In a final act of generosity (aimed at the girls, not me), Chris made me redundant rather than firing me, so I got a bit of a payout when I left Superhero Inc. It was more than I deserved. I've since found a job as an account manager for a small local events company. It's not glamorous. It's not London. But it's steady, and as much as I can manage, with the girls. My boss, Erica, is understanding and flexible about family commitments, as well as my AA meetings. She's happy for me to work from home quite a lot of the time too.

I stirred the marinade I had made, and began to pour it over the chicken we'd be barbecuing. While I did, I looked out over the garden and watched my daughters, now both so tall, walking back towards the house carrying handfuls of herbs and tomatoes. They were laughing together about something, and I was awestruck at their beauty. It's not that they've changed dramatically, but they're both beginning to lose that pinched, anxious look, and the fury that used to radiate from Miranda has abated, most of the time. We aren't entirely out of the woods, but she is infinitely better.

Six weeks ago, I had an email from Helen. She asked, tentatively, if she could write to the girls. I immediately rang my mum and we discussed it at length. In the end we agreed that I should ask Miranda and Marguerite. They both said they would like it. Helen has been sending them an email every week, to Miranda's account. I haven't asked to read them, but Marguerite tells me she is very happy in Canada, that work is going well, and that she has plans to travel to India later in the year.

I heard the crunch of tyres on gravel and turned my attention to the window on the street side of the house. My dad was parking his Astra, carefully parallel to our car. I watched him unplug the satnav and pack it away in the glove compartment, and then go round the car to open Mum's door and help her out. She's stopped being stoic and has agreed to keep using a walking stick. It frustrates her, but it makes us all feel better. They moved towards the house, but I kept watching the car.

The back door of the car opened, and Tim stepped out. Our eyes met through the kitchen window. We looked at each other for a long moment. Then I gave him a nod and went to open the door.

EPILOGUE

The laptop sat in the middle of the table. Inactivity had darkened the screen, and the machine had gone into sleep mode. Suddenly, the screen lit up and the computer whirred into life as the Skype window opened and began its melodic ringtone. It seemed no one would be near enough to hear it, but, just in time, she rushed in from the garden and clicked on the mousepad to answer the call. It took a moment for the video window to open and the pixelated resolution to clear. She found herself looking into bright blue eyes framed by a sweep of honey-blonde hair.

'Judy?' said the face on the screen. 'Is that you? It's Helen.'

The End